CW00487218

THE MAN WHO MADE PENGUINS

The Life of Sir William Emrys Williams

SANDER MEREDEEN

Sir William Emrys Williams, c.1965.

THE MAN WHO MADE PENGUINS

The Life of Sir William Emrys Williams

Editor-in-Chief, Penguin Books 1936-1965

SANDER MEREDEEN

THE MAN WHO MADE **PENGUINS**
The Life of Sir William Emrys Williams

By Sander Meredeen

Published by Darien-Jones Publishing.

This Collector's Limited Edition was published in Great Britain in 2008 on behalf of Bruce and Clive Meredeen in memory of their father Sander Meredeen (1928-2007) by Darien-Jones Publishing, Hillside House, Pitchcombe, Stroud, Gloucestershire GL6 6LN, United Kingdom.

Designed and produced by Nicholas J Jones Graphics
Book design copyright © Nicholas J Jones Graphics 2007

A CIP catalogue record for this book is available from the British Library.

ISBN 978-1-902487-03-8

The author and publisher have made all reasonable efforts to contact copyright holders for permission, and apologise for any omissions or errors in the text matter, quotations, extracts, photographs and captions reproduced in this book. Corrections may be made to further printings.

Printed in Great Britain using papers made from trees that have been legally sourced from well-managed and credibly certified forests.

Jacket photo: William Emrys Williams – Lotte Meitner-Graf studio portrait, 1965.

Telephone: (01452) 812550 Fax: (01452) 812690
E-mail: djp@nicholasjjonesgraphics.co.uk

Contents

For my grandchildren:
Rachel, Jessica, Ben and Elena.

Sander Meredeen – 2007

One of the jobs of biography is to bring back the lost or the forgotten, or people to whom justice has not been done.

Richard Holmes: Sidetracks *(2000)*

Preface

I cannot conceive the slightest reason why anyone, even 30 years from now, should want to write my biography.

W E Williams to Dr Thomas Jones,
13 December 1946

When he died in 1977, William Emrys Williams was acknowledged as 'one of the most powerful cultural mandarins in the country'.[1] For thirty years, from 1936 to 1965, as chief editorial adviser at Penguin Books, he shaped the reading habits and filled the bookshelves of a generation. For twelve years, from 1951 to 1963, he was arguably the most successful and innovative Secretary-General of the Arts Council. A pioneer adult educator in the 1920s, he served as Secretary of the British Institute of Adult Education (BIAE) through the 1930s, emerging as a leading advocate of lifelong learning for all. During the Second World War he created and directed the Army Bureau of Current Affairs (ABCA) for the War Office – but still found time and energy to write his weekly column of radio criticism in *The Listener* as *Critic on the Hearth*. Author or co-author of more than twenty books, he was described in *The Times* at his death as 'one of the greatest and most effective mass educators of his time'.[2] Yet the one hundredth anniversary of his birth in 1996 passed virtually unnoticed.

To his family and early friends, Williams was always known as Billy. He was Billy when he met Gertrude Rosenblum at university, and he remained her Billy through their sixty years of married life. His long-term mistress, Estrid Bannister, marked the difference: she called him Bill. More widely known as 'ABCA Bill' or sometimes as 'Pelican Bill', he was generally addressed as W E Williams, and in later life as Sir William. In his schooldays, he sometimes signed himself simply as Emrys. But few people, if any, seem to have called him Emrys. Once, during a 1965 House of Commons debate, an opposition spokesman referred disrespectfully to Regional Arts Councils as 'little Emryses'.[3]

Bill Williams led a complicated life – or rather a series of parallel, interconnected lives. When setting out to research this biography, my task was made no easier by Williams' habit of covering his tracks, for reasons that soon became apparent. Thanks to the discovery of revealing letters hidden in dusty archives, and fresh information buried in official documents, I have nevertheless been able to reconstruct the plural lives and loves of a remarkably energetic and productive man.

From 1918, when he graduated from Manchester University, until his death in

1977, Williams devoted six decades of his life to one clear mission: the promotion of cultural democracy – through lifelong learning; through open, guided discussion of the widest range of social and political issues; and through providing ordinary people with easier access to the arts – paintings and sculpture, novels and poetry, music and drama, opera and dance, radio and television. He fervently believed that an appetite for the arts amongst ordinary people grows by what it feeds on – hence his missionary zeal.

This biography of Bill Williams fits no conventional pattern. Apart from the first chapters – which describe his early life and explore the youthful influences that helped shape his character in later life – the book is closely modelled on Williams' own lifetime practice of what we shall call 'thematic segmentation' – each segment focussed on one self-contained strand yet inextricably linked to other strands. It revisits his life in a series of chapters, each devoted to one thematic strand in his complex career. The final chapter brings those strands together, with an overall assessment of the man and his work, his failures as well as his achievements, his immediate impact as well as his longer-term influence. To help readers disentangle those strands, *Appendix A* provides a list of W E Williams' publications, *Appendix B* provides a chronology of key events, and *Appendix C* summarises his career profile.

Was Bill Williams' life a purposeful crusade or a mere 'chapter of accidents'? Was he a prodigious manipulator, with his finger in too many cultural pies? How else did he contrive to be at the right place at the right time to fill so many influential and prestigious positions? Or was he simply born under a lucky star, which allowed him to exploit the many twists of fate that seemed to mark his whole life? The new evidence brought forward in this biography should help readers to decide for themselves.

Many people have sustained me in my quest for William Emrys Williams. I owe them all my immense gratitude. Special thanks are due to Sylvia and Peter Bradford, generous friends and constructive critics who provided the inspirational spark and without whom this book would never have been finished let alone published; to Dr Malcolm Ballin for brilliant notes and comments on an earlier draft; to Jocelyn Hartland-Swann for his masterly editing of the final text from my tatterdemalion manuscript; to the late Dr John Crammer, Tom Chamberlain, P W Gathercole, Margaret Heald, Stephen Hobbs, Peter Mann, Peter Preston and Dr Dugald Stewart for generous encouragement and stimulating suggestions. The errors, omissions and infelicities that remain to haunt me are my own.

Sander Meredeen, Stow-on-the-Wold – January 2007

Acknowledgements

Throughout my ten-year quest for W E Williams I have been helped by many people who talked to me about the man, his life and his work, who contributed memories and anecdotes, directed my attention to material I might otherwise have overlooked, and who gave technical and helpful personal advice.

I gratefully acknowledge my indebtedness to the following individuals and institutions and apologise to those whose names have been omitted through oversight.

Rev Graham Adams, Congregational Federation, Nottingham
Dr Malcolm Ballin, Cardiff University
Richard Bond, Local Studies Unit, Central Library, Manchester
R A Butler Archive, Trinity College, Cambridge
Tom Chamberlain
Lord Clark Archive, Tate Gallery
Professor Clyde Binfield, University of Sheffield
Christine Coates, WEA National Archive, University of North London
Peter Cox, Dartington Trust, Devon
Croft and Grigg Papers, Churchill College Cambridge Archive, University of Cambridge
Professor Cyril Ehrlich
Tony Field, formerly Finance Director, Arts Council of Great Britain
Peter Gathercole, Darwin College, Cambridge
Robin and Susie Goodliffe
Professor Brian Groombridge
BB Hanley
Steve Hare, Penguin Collectors' Society
Jocelyn and Sarah Hartland-Swann
Margaret Heald
Professor Robert Hewison, University of Oxford
David Holbrook, Downing College, University of Cambridge
Enid and Robin Huws Jones
Stephen and Lesley Hyde
Lord Gowrie, former Chairman, Arts Council of Great Britain
Graham Jones, National Library of Wales, Aberystwyth
Institute of Directors

Dr Elaine Kaye, Mansfield College, University of Oxford
Keynes Archive, King's College, Cambridge
Helen Kitchen
Lawrence Mackintosh, Arts Council of Great Britain
Peter Mann
Harold Marks
Professor John Morgan, University of Nottingham
Ann Morton, Public Records Office
Hannah Lowery, Penguin Archive, University of Bristol
Professor K O Morgan, University of Oxford
National Art-Collections Fund
Dr Peter Nockles, John Rylands Library, Manchester
Professor Philip Olleson, University of Nottingham
Carol Peaker, University of Cambridge
Professor Peter Preston, University of Nottingham
Douglas Rust
Sir Roy Shaw, former Secretary-General, Arts Council of Great Britain
Tanya Schmoller, President Emeritus, Penguin Collectors' Society
Professor Alan Sell, University of Aberystwyth
Professor Peter Stead, University of Wales
Brian and Kathleen Thompson
Alan Tuckett, Director, NIACE
Jeff Walden, BBC Written Archives, Caversham
Professor John Worthen, University of Nottingham

Bruce and Clive Meredeen wish to thank and particularly to acknowledge the vital contributions of Nick Darien-Jones (Designer) and Dr Malcolm Ballin (Editor), since Sander Meredeen's death in September 2007. Without the generosity of their advice, time and spirit, this book would probably not have been published. They believe the high quality of the publication makes it a fitting tribute to their late father's work. Thanks also to Caroline Sheldrick for proof reading and editorial comment.

Prologue: Brandy in paradise

> I am terribly lucky to feel as fulfilled as I do in all the work I have done. I accept the inevitable twilight, and I feel nothing but thankfulness for all the exciting opportunities I've enjoyed. It's been a wonderful and amusing ride.
>
> *W E Williams to Allen Lane, 20 April 1965*

> It is terrible to reflect on how few of us are left... I miss him [Allen Lane] greatly as I am sure many do, but so many of his pals have now joined him that they should be having a pretty convivial time together.
>
> *W E Williams to Eunice Frost, 15 February 1973*

We are in the last days of March 1977. In the intensive care unit of Stoke Mandeville hospital, a distinguished man of letters lies dying. A lifetime's heavy smoking and drinking have punished his liver, riddled his lungs, and congested his coronary arteries. But he has no regrets: 'It's been a wonderful and amusing ride'. His closest friend and working partner, Allen Lane – King Penguin – is already seven years dead. William Emrys Williams, Prince of Penguin Editors – his staunch drinking companion through thirty years of critical and commercial triumph – will shortly join him for brandy in paradise.

In his final hours, his mind slips into the river of memory, retrieving images from a long and richly rewarded life. A carefree boy runs free in Wales. A student dances with his future wife at a university party. A young teacher guides a class of schoolboys through a Wordsworth sonnet. A WEA tutor discusses Virginia Woolf's latest novel with his adult students. He makes his first broadcast, stammering into a large BBC microphone. He lingers over brandy with Allen Lane, after an editorial conference in Soho. He makes his way home – not to his wife but to his mistress, Estrid Bannister. He dodges bombs down the Euston Road during the Second World War. He tours the country, directing the Army Bureau of Current Affairs for the War Office. He is appointed Secretary-General of the Arts Council. He kneels to be dubbed Knight of the Realm by Queen Elizabeth II. He has achieved more in one lifetime than most other men. Some impossible dreams have been realised; some ambitious plans are still incomplete.

His wife, Gertrude, a distinguished academic, now sits at his bedside, comforting him as best she can. Undergraduate sweethearts in the First World War, they have been married for almost sixty years. She has encouraged him from his obscure beginnings to become one of the most influential figures in British cultural life. They have been together through two world wars, sharing the most dangerous days and nights of the century. She has stood by him through his trials and tribulations, tolerating his infidelities and colluding, through twenty years of their married life, in his long relationship with Estrid Bannister. He has survived throat cancer and several minor heart attacks. She can do no more for him now than wipe his brow, smooth his pillow, and hold his hand, recalling the good times they have shared.

Until a few days ago he was still at home, dictating his 'invented biography', his memoirs of fifty years in public life – 'a kind of history of culture in my time'.[1] Determined to see the book completed and in print, he often asked his secretary, Joy Lyon, to stay overnight and make an early morning start. But he tired quickly and the autobiography progressed slowly. At eighty, his brain was still sharp but his familiar physical and mental stamina were greatly diminished.

His time in hospital is thankfully brief. On Wednesday 30 March, Sir William Emrys Williams BA, CBE, DLitt, holder of the American Medal of Freedom, dies of bronchopneumonia, with congestive cardiac failure and coronary heart disease, aged eighty. His grief-stricken widow phones his secretary to break the news. Both women are engulfed in tears. Whilst Gertrude keeps vigil over the body of her dead husband, his secretary gathers up the typescript of the unfinished memoirs, stuffs it into her briefcase, and returns to London. Back in her flat, near Marble Arch, she pours herself a large whisky, empties her briefcase into the domestic grate, puts a match to the stolen typescript, takes the whisky bottle and her sleeping tablets, and retires to her bedroom.

The body is found on Friday 1 April 1977. The Westminster Coroner, Professor Keith Simpson, tells the Inner West London Coroner's Court on Wednesday 13 April that Joy Maudie Lyon killed herself, her death being due to an overdose of alcohol and barbiturate, self-administered whilst suffering from depression. She has drunk the equivalent of 14 tots of spirit, and taken 30 grains of barbiturate. A close woman friend confirms that Joy was a heavy drinker and had taken an overdose seven or eight years earlier. She was just forty-eight years old.

Gertrude Williams is angry, bewildered, distraught. She cannot bring herself to accept what has happened. Coming so soon after her husband's death, Joy's suicide is intolerable. How dare 'that woman' do such a thing? Gertrude is over eighty, but she is nobody's fool. There is only one plausible explanation for Joy's actions. By taking her own life, she has proclaimed to the whole world how much she loved Bill Williams, and that she cannot live without him. She has not only stolen and destroyed the only copy of his autobiography: she has deliberately set out to displace Gertrude as principal mourner.

In accordance with his wishes, Sir Williams' funeral is private. Following the cremation, Gertrude scatters his ashes in the garden of their home, in a quiet Buckinghamshire village where they spent their final years. She survives him for another six years; but her friends report that 'she was never the same woman after he died'.[2] Devastated by her loss, she increasingly withdraws from public life, spending much of her time alone, drinking more heavily, comforted by her beloved black poodle, Tempo.

On 1 April 1977, *The Times* obituary describes Sir William as 'one of the greatest and most effective mass educators of his time'.[3] Gertrude keeps that obituary notice close to hand, as a reminder of her husband's many outstanding achievements. To occupy herself in her widowhood, she sets herself one final task: to write her own memoir of her Billy, her Educator Extraordinary. It is not intended, she tells us, as a conventional biography but as an historical record of 'the many important contributions' her late husband has made 'to the life of this country'.[4] She begins the story with his early years, as 'a youth in Wales'.

Billy and Gertrude on a river trip with Prof. Samuel Alexander, philosopher and writer, 1920s.

Thomas Owen Williams, father of William Emrys Williams.

One:
A youth in Wales

> Much of a Welshman's talk is like the play of a kitten with a ball of wool, a tossing and twisting of ideas into a tangle of shapes by under- and over-statement, for the sheer fun of provoking slow and stolid listeners… The Welsh are artists, deviously honest, and they give a finish and colour to their statements beyond what the occasion demands in the eyes of plain people.
>
> *Thomas Jones: 'Welsh Character',* The Listener, *31 January 1934*

'Lay bare the facts of any life', wrote Williams in 1935, 'and you will find they take you only part of the way. The rest is a no-man's land of surmise and assumption'.[1] Before setting out to explore that no-man's land, we must begin with such facts as we have. But which of the many relevant facts should we select in our quest for William Emrys Williams? For biographers are not merely fact-gatherers or fact-analysts. The questions we ask, the particular facts we choose to gather, and the way we approach their analysis, all reflect our existing ideas of what is significant. Everything depends on what we know – and don't know.

In a brilliant and provocative essay on biographical method, John Worthen, biographer of D H Lawrence, speaks of the 'necessary ignorance' that bedevils every biographer:

> We must remind ourselves that the biographer is ignorant: not just accidentally ignorant but ignorant by the very nature of the biographer's trade; necessarily ignorant, hamstrung by the accidental survival of materials, obliged to make and impose a pattern where none exists, forced to construct a narrative where the only materials he or she possesses have also to be the only significant events within it, pressured by his or her publisher not to keep on putting in sentences describing his or her ignorance.[2]

Professor Worthen suggests that a notice should be affixed to every literary biography: 'Some or all of this may be wrong'. Every aspiring biographer should heed the message behind that mischievous suggestion. For if we are not always sure of the motives that govern our own behaviour, if we cannot always explain our lives to ourselves, how can we be certain of anything we say about the lives of others? For that reason, this biography has made extensive use of quotations to corroborate a factual point or support an inference. Where the factual evidence is missing, circumstantial or weak, the text has adopted more cautious language. Sometimes we can only speculate; more often, we simply do not know – and should say so. As John Worthen concludes: 'Ignorance is implicit in the nature of our business; and we should embrace its necessities'.

In setting out to research and write this biography, more than ten years ago, I had no systematic theory. Instead I tried to establish the essential facts about Bill Williams' life – his birth, his family background, his education, his marriage, his career and finally his death – and to follow wherever those facts led me. At both ends of his life, I was confronted with a brutal conflict of 'facts'.

That Bill Williams was born on 5 October 1896 is undisputed. But where exactly was he born and into what condition of life? *The Times* obituary of 1 April 1977 told me that 'He was born at Capel Isaac, a village in Carmarthenshire. His father, Thomas Owen Williams, was a carpenter; his mother a farmer's daughter from nearby Llandilo [sic]'.[3] That unequivocal statement was confirmed by Williams' entry in the *Dictionary of National Biography*. But Gertrude's memoir of her late husband informed me, with equal clarity and conviction, that 'He was born in 1896 in a small farm in Morfa Bychen [Bychan], a neighbouring village to Cricceth [Criccieth], the village in which Lloyd George was born, a few miles inland from Portmadoc [sic]'.[4]

Amongst the documents available to Gertrude when she wrote her memoir was the formal address by Professor Gwyn Jones, when presenting Bill Williams to the Congregation of the University of Wales on 11 July 1963, on the occasion of his being awarded the Honorary Degree of Doctor of Letters. In that address, Professor Jones stated unequivocally that: 'William Emrys Williams was born in a Carmarthenshire village, and is Welsh of the Welsh'.[5]

Why did Gertrude set aside such authoritative evidence? What persuaded her to invent a totally different birthplace and to contradict the 'facts' supplied by Professor Jones and confirmed by *The Times*, and the DNB? The most plausible explanation is that she genuinely believed that Billy had been born at Morfa Bychan in North Wales – and that the person who had convinced her of that 'fact' was probably Billy himself. In which case, the 'facts' as given in both *The Times* obituary and in the *Dictionary of National Biography* were clearly wrong.

All four sources cited above proved to be incorrect. At the Family History Centre in London I obtained a copy of Bill Williams' birth certificate. It reveals that his mother, Annie Williams, registered his birth on 6 November 1896 at 'the Hulme sub-district of the Chorlton Registration District in the Counties of Manchester and Lancaster'. The birth took place neither at Capel Isaac in Carmarthenshire nor at Morfa Bychan in North Wales, but at an altogether more prosaic address: '16 Raglan Street, South Manchester'.

I spent some time reflecting on that revelation. Was Bill Williams 'Welsh of the Welsh', as Professor Jones declared? Was he, in the strict sense, a Welshman at all? Was he even conceived in Wales – let alone brought up there 'speaking nothing but Welsh for his first eight years of life'? If the reported 'facts' about Williams' birth were so unreliable, what hope was there of establishing reliable information about other incidents in his long and eventful life?

I then read a revealing interview with the late Humphrey Carpenter, biographer of W H Auden, Benjamin Britten, Archbishop Runcie, and playwright Dennis Potter, describing how he set about the task of explaining the course of his subject's life:

> I always feel in each life I tackle that there is some hidden story or fact, some clue, which when you get hold of it begins to unravel the whole thing. You still won't get the complete truth about that person; but you'll get a kind of truth, which works within its own terms.[6]

Shortly after reading that interview, I consulted Sylvia Bradford, Gertrude Williams' niece, about some unexplained aspects of Bill Williams' character. She told me that, after Gertrude's death, she had found a passionate love-letter from Billy to Gertrude, tucked inside one of Gertrude's bedside books. Sylvia had kept that letter for some years and then destroyed it to respect its privacy. A considerable but self-effacing poet herself, Sylvia said she wondered whether Billy had ever written poetry for Gertrude. When I asked what had given her that idea, she immediately replied: 'Oh, Gertrude once told me: "You know, he always wanted to be a poet".'[7]

Might that unexpected revelation provide the clue – the single thread – to unravel and explain the rest of Bill Williams' life? If he was a frustrated poet, did he continue to write poetry in later life – to Gertrude perhaps, to Estrid, or to Joy Lyon? Had any of his poetry survived his death? Another visit to the British Library failed to produce a single line of Williams' poetry in his twenty or more books.

In the John Rylands Library in Manchester, I eventually unearthed Williams' undergraduate poetry, quoted in Chapter 3. But there is no trace of any later poetry. Having reflected long and hard on the frustrated poet theory, I concluded that it did not provide the one explanatory thread I was vainly seeking. If there is one single clue to the life of William Emrys Williams, it has eluded this persistent researcher. It is surely expecting too much for any single thread to unravel the whole complex texture of a person's life. Three strands in Williams' life nevertheless do stand out as more significant than others. First, as his full, rich and resounding name implies, William Emrys Williams was a Welshman – 'Welsh of the Welsh', as Professor Jones called him, despite his English birth. His *Times* obituary tells us that 'Williams lived in Wales until his eighth year, was then Welsh speaking, and retained strong

Welsh characteristics throughout his life'.[8] Cultured and articulate, his mature personality combined many of the passionate characteristics of the traditional Celt – even though he spent most of his life in England.

J E Morpurgo, who worked alongside him at Penguin Books, confirms that:

> William Emrys Williams was a Welshman to every letter of his unmistakably Welsh name... The rich rhythm of his Welsh voice, cunningly modulated by a controlled stammer, freed him from the suspicion that hung over so many of the Oxonian and metropolitan popular educators of that era.[9]

At school, Williams wrote an essay, quoted in Chapter 3, which reflects his strong emotional attachment to his Welsh cultural heritage. In early adult life, he was befriended by Dr Thomas Jones, arguably the most influential Welshman of his generation. Williams regularly turned to TJ for advice and help throughout his career. TJ's hand may be detected behind Williams' first significant appointment, as Secretary of the BIAE, and in his later selection as Director of ABCA. TJ also made sure that Williams was present at the inaugural meeting of CEMA.

Throughout his work at CEMA and later at the Arts Council, Williams was surrounded by fellow Welshmen: Walford Davies, Wyn Griffith, Gwyn Jones, Ifor Evans, Huw Weldon and others. In his five years of *Listener* reviews, Williams frequently explored Welsh themes and nominated several Welshmen, including Sir Walford Davies, Emlyn Williams and Wynford Vaughan Thomas, amongst his favourite broadcasters. At Penguin Books, he collaborated for over thirty years with his namesake and fellow Welshman, Allen Lane, born Allen Lane-Williams. As Editor-in-Chief, he helped to select for publication many books by Welsh authors; yet his five anthologies of Penguin Poets do not include a single Welsh poet – not even Dylan Thomas, the most illustrious and popular of modern Welsh poets. That may explain why, in his mature years, he acknowledged to Dr Thomas Jones that he had perhaps neglected his Welsh heritage: 'Latterly I have felt a need to be a Welshman in more than blood and association; I'd like to help in the cultural movements in Wales'.[10]

The second significant thread in Williams' life also derives from his early years: the profound influence of his father. Thomas Williams, a practising craftsman, made sure that his son absorbed the craft ethos, taught him to value true craftsmanship, and helped him develop his skills in analysing and solving practical problems with economy of time and materials. Bill Williams did not follow his father into the wood-working trade but he was always a superb craftsman. As a writer and jobbing journalist, he turned his hand, like any good craftsman, to whatever task confronted him: an editorial, a review, a report, an anthology, or a full-length original book. In his first book, significantly entitled *The Craft of Literature*, he made explicitly clear that the writer's craftsmanship always reflects the person behind the writer: 'Whatever subject he chooses to write upon, or whatever branch of his craft he practises, the man will reveal himself in all he writes'.[11] That was certainly true of Bill Williams.

The third, profoundly important and long-lasting influence on the young Bill Williams was his Congregational upbringing – a highly significant factor in shaping his fundamental beliefs and his system of values. Congregationalism was a major contributory source of his independence of mind, and of his emphasis on communitarian rather than individualistic values. The fact that Williams abandoned his attachment to the Congregational Church in early manhood does not detract from its pervasive influence on his habits of thought, his metaphorical language, and his preferred modes of action. In more than a dozen books, in scores of articles and in hundreds of letters, his language is permeated with biblical allusions and Judæo-Christian ideals and values.

Amongst the dominant Congregational influences on Bill Williams' life, the most potent was his commitment to free and open discussion as the royal road to enlightenment. Having experienced the intensity of chapel discussion in his childhood, he never abandoned the idea that well-informed, well-directed discussion represents the best means of promoting clear thinking and rational decision-making on issues of public concern. In adult education, in *Art for the People*, in his work with wartime ABCA and its peacetime successor, the Bureau of Current Affairs, and especially in his broadcast criticism, Williams insists that 'ordinary people' achieve personal growth and transformation through the vigorous exchanges of well-led, group discussion. That passion for open debate sprang directly from his early exposure to the animated discussion of wide-ranging subjects, far beyond the bounds of religion, at meetings of his local Congregational community.

Given those early and enduring influences on Bill Williams' life, it is impossible to view his working life as a sequence of unrelated episodes – as 'chapters of accidents' – threaded together by chance. The convenient fact that he happened to be in the appropriate place at the right time for certain key events cannot be entirely coincidental. More than one cultural commentator has noted that Williams had his fingers in many pies. So many fingers in so many pies was the result of something more than mere accident.

In this biographer's view, Williams' life is more intelligibly construed as a coherent and consistent crusade for cultural democracy. Throughout his adult life, he pursued two key objectives: lifelong learning and easier access to the arts for all. Those objectives derived from his conviction that broad-ranging, liberal, continuing education – including frequent, intelligent exposure to the arts of literature, theatre, music and painting – gives new meaning to life, liberating individual potential, bringing aesthetic pleasure, political enlightenment and democratic participation to ordinary people in an increasingly materialistic and alienated society. But before getting too far ahead of ourselves, we must return to the first traces of the Williams family.

The surname Williams is virtually synonymous with Wales. It recurs with greater frequency amongst those of Welsh descent than any other surname, with the possible exception of Jones. Professor Kenneth Morgan, leading historian of modern Wales, identifies more than forty men named Williams who played distinguished roles in Welsh public life over the past hundred years.[12] William Emrys Williams, alas, is not amongst them. The form of his name follows one classic pattern of Welsh name-giving: William, son of William – hence the suffix *s* – is distinguished from other William Williamses by the addition of that distinctive middle name – *Emrys*, cognate with Ambrose: one who prepares, serves or tastes ambrosia: the elixir of life; the food of the gods.

The Wales into which William Emrys Williams was born on 5 October 1896 may seem at first sight an unlikely cultural cradle for a future Secretary-General of the Arts Council or the distinguished Editor-in-Chief of Penguin Books. An ancient kingdom, largely enclosed by magnificent mountains, Wales had remained for centuries steeped in its own history and culture, locked within its distinctive systems of thought, clinging to its traditional religious beliefs, speaking its own language, singing its own songs, reciting its own poetry, revering its own bards. Nowhere was that traditional Welsh culture more cherished or better preserved than in the towns and villages of North Wales, a distinctive sub-culture that persists to the present day.

The industrial revolution, which transformed large parts of England and Central Scotland in the late 18th and early 19th centuries, hardly touched Wales, except for some parts of its southern coastline and a few miles of its upper river valleys. Until well into the second half of the 19th century, Wales remained predominantly agricultural, with small, isolated hill farms, with mining and quarrying, as the principal sources of employment. For more than a century – from Benjamin Disraeli's first Conservative Government of 1868 to Tony Blair's first New Labour Government of 1997 – coal, iron and steel were amongst Wales's leading industrial exports. Welsh slate roofed English homes; Welsh water slaked English thirsts; Welsh wool clothed English backs; Welsh lamb appeared regularly on English dinner-tables.

Most Welsh production was small-scale handicraft for local consumption, with craftsmen fashioning local materials into traditional Welsh products for local markets. Since lowland Wales was covered with native forest, wood was the most abundant natural material. As a result, Welsh craftsmanship in all forms of wood-working became highly developed.

Wood-working skills were in the Williams family blood. Bill Williams' paternal grandfather, William Williams, born in Beddgelert in 1815, the year of Waterloo, was a ship's carpenter who worked all his life on the construction or repair of the great Welsh sailing ships of his time. He married Sarah in 1838, producing three children, two daughters and one son, Thomas Owen, born in 1862. The Williams family lived at Morfa Bychan, a hamlet, tucked into the coastline of Tremadoc Bay, midway between Criccieth and Porthmadog, at the south-east corner of the Lleyn Peninsula, in North Wales. Garreg Wen Bach (Little White Rock) was a tiny, isolated farmstead, the diminutive suffix *Bach* distinguishing it from Garreg Wen proper. This was the larger adjoining farm, renowned in Welsh history and literature as the birthplace of Dafydd y Garreg Wen (David of the White Rock), famous Welsh harpist and song-writer, who flourished in the 18th century, producing a stream of poetry and melody which continues to feed the artistic hunger of the Welsh people.

In the early years of the 20th century, Porthmadog was a bustling port, crowded with great sailing ships, plying their trade in Welsh cargoes around the world. There is said to have been a harbour on the Afon Glaslyn estuary from earliest times. Porthmadog developed rapidly in the 18th century as the leading export centre for Welsh slates, transported by road or tramway from the great slate quarries of North Wales to Porthmadog, for trans-shipment to destinations across the oceans of the world. It was from Porthmadog that many of Bill Williams' uncles set sail as the masters of three-masted schooners, whalers, or those less glamorous vessels which carried Welsh slates, for example, to Hamburg or Athens. In the posthumous memoir of her late husband, Gertrude Williams tells us that:

> Several of [those uncles] were drowned at sea and his grandparents were so anxious to save their ewe lamb from this fate that they decided that Billy's father should not go to sea but should train as a shipwright – the nearest thing to a sailor.[13]

The 1881 census for Morfa Bychan shows William Williams, aged 66, a Ship Carpenter, and his wife Sarah, presiding over a household comprising their only son, Thomas Owen Williams, Billy's father, aged 19 and single, pursuing the trade of Joiner, and two unmarried older sisters: Jane, aged 33, employed as a waitress, probably in one of Porthmadog's hotels or seamen's hostels, and Elizabeth, aged 25, employed as a dressmaker.

At the 1891 census, the Williams family was still living at the same address. But Sarah Williams, aged 77, had been widowed for some years. The census return shows her as Head of the Family, comprising a married daughter, Catherine Jones and her husband, Evan, and their children. By 1891, Sarah's only son, Thomas Owen, aged 29, had left home to seek more regular employment in Manchester. That is confirmed by the Lancashire electoral registers for 1900 to 1905, which show him living at 16 Raglan Street, a small terrace house in the Hulme district of South Manchester. It is likely that whilst working in Manchester Thomas Owen first met Annie Jones, daughter of a farmer from Llandeilo, Carmarthenshire, who may also have gone to Manchester in search of regular employment. How else would he have chanced to meet an attractive young woman from one of the most distant and inaccessible parts of West Wales?

Thomas Owen Williams is shown on his son's Birth Certificate as being employed in 1896 as a 'journeyman joiner' – a skilled craftsman working in wood. After completing five or perhaps seven years apprenticeship to the trade, he was a self-employed craftsman, hiring himself out by the hour or the day to anyone needing his skills. The status of joiner was always superior to that of carpenter but somewhat below that of cabinet-maker, the aristocrat of the wood-working trades. A typical village carpenter was capable of doing most of the rougher jobs in wood, requiring only modest levels of accuracy or finish, like erecting and maintaining the timber framework of houses, barns and out-buildings. Decorative or ornamental wood finishes called for the services of a joiner, capable of working in a wider range of more expensive materials to much closer dimensions. More complex and expensive items – such as the veneers found in fine domestic furniture – had to be ordered and custom-made in a cabinet-maker's workshop to the most exacting standards, requiring the highest levels of skill.

The fact that Bill Williams' father was employed as a joiner, rather than a carpenter, is more significant than might at first sight appear. It means that he was amongst the most skilled artisans in his own village, and probably for miles around. That level of skill not only conferred higher status but also meant that Thomas Owen could command a higher rate of pay for his services, when employed. Therein lay the problem, for there was little work for a joiner in an isolated Welsh village at the turn of the 19th century. Bill Williams' father was therefore obliged to work away from home, undertaking skilled work wherever he could find it, but securing a premium price for his services. There was nearly always work for a capable and reliable joiner in any large town or city. Since North Wales lacked many large towns, the prospect of finding work in Liverpool or Manchester was always appealing, even if it meant transporting the family there for extended periods, or months of self-imposed isolation from the family, which brought its own special problems.

We know little of the personal relationship between Billy Williams and his father. The one certain influence his father exerted was that of working to exacting deadlines and to the highest standards of craftsmanship. As Gertrude Williams tells us:

> [His father] was a very fine craftsman as is shown by the fact that he was chosen to work on the restoration of the stalls of Manchester Cathedral.[14]

In later years, Thomas Owen may well have taken his young son to Manchester Cathedral, pointing with pride at the results of his skilled handiwork. The fact that this was the Anglican Cathedral appears not to have raised any ethical problems for Thomas Owen, despite the fact that he was a devout Congregationalist.

The influence of his mother on the young Billy Williams is more difficult to determine. Annie Jones was a Welsh country girl. Like most young women of her age and background, she seems to have developed into an extremely practical, hard-working character. Her choice of Thomas Owen Williams as a suitable husband was certainly inspired. They evidently enjoyed a happy and fulfilled married life, and went on to have four children – one son, Billy, and three daughters, two of whom died in infancy.

In late Victorian Wales, the rate of infant mortality was falling but still high, as it was throughout the rest of Britain. The death of not one but two young daughters must have been harrowing for their parents, and for young Billy. Such tragic deaths were a frequent occurrence in village life, their effects no less traumatic for the surviving siblings than they would be today. There is no evidence, however, to show that Bill Williams looked back on his childhood as anything but happy and carefree. He grew up in a close and loving family to which he remained loyally devoted through most of his life. He and his surviving younger sister, Edith, were close in their early years but were later sadly estranged.

Billy attended the all-age, bilingual, village school near Morfa Bychan where he proved a quick and attentive pupil, keen to read everything that fell into his hands, whether in Welsh or English. No school records survive to show whether he was much above average as a primary school pupil. But his parents recognised signs of unusual intellectual gifts in both their surviving children and this may well have proved an important factor in their decision to move the family from Wales to Manchester in 1904. That move would have provided more reliable employment for Thomas Owen and much better opportunities of secondary education for his children. Gertrude Williams tells us that:

> Thomas Owen Williams, the father, was not only deeply religious but very determined that his remaining children should have as good an education as his earnings as an artisan made possible.[15]

The Congregational Church in Wales, of which both Billy's parents were devout adherents, was the second formative influence on their young son, as on many others of his generation. In the case of Billy, it seems to have played a determining role in his young life and throughout his teenage years. For just as his own parents had not allowed him to go to sea, so Thomas Owen was very much opposed to his son following him into the wood-working trade, like his father and grandfather before him. Instead, he developed an early ambition for his son to make a career in the ministry of the Congregational Church. Young Billy Williams seems to have been happy to go along with his father's plans.

There was nothing in the least protective or sentimental in Thomas Owen's ambition for his son, for the beliefs and teachings of the Congregational faith were anything but emollient. Amongst other virtues, it taught strict adherence to the biblical code of ethical behaviour, the importance of independent thought, the primacy of personal responsibility and concern for community, coupled with a healthy scepticism of bureaucratic authority.

It is not always easy for contemporary students of social history to appreciate the crucial role played by the Welsh religious revival of the 19th century, and of the non-conformist church in particular, in sustaining and developing Welsh culture – its language, poetry and music – as well as its religious fervour and political radicalism. A respected Welsh writer offers this explanation:

> In Wales, radicalism is the child of Nonconformity. The structure and organization of Dissent, its particularism, its methods of government, its lack of hierarchy and its reliance upon co-operation rather than command, its climate of controversy and its emphasis upon individual opinion, all fostered independence of outlook. With the Bible for textbook and supreme authority upon the conduct of daily life, everything depended upon personal interpretation of the code. Authority was subject to question, and a vigorous and sturdy form of democracy spread throughout the country.[16]

That quotation provides an intelligible account of Welsh radical non-conformity. But what were the specific forces that kept the country distinctively Welsh?

> The answer lies in the chapel, as a social as well as a religious force in the life of the whole country... Social life centred in the chapel: it was truly a meeting place. It was not only the young people, the children, who went to Sunday School: the bulk of the adult congregation was there, arguing theology in small classes. ...young and old attended the Literary Meetings, as they were called: the name is misleading, for they were competitive festivals for authors, musicians, poets, craftsmen and reciters of verse. All this was, of

> course, the natural prolongation into the present century of the pattern of life laid down, in its essential features, in the two preceding centuries, and it all happened in Welsh. And if a Welshman looks back on it all and has to admit, if he is honest, that standards of achievement were not very high, that real quality was rare, the fact remains that it was unique in these islands, this concern of the common man in the arts, the labourer, after his day's work, struggling with things of the mind in consort with his neighbours. That must never be forgotten in any assessment of the Welsh people.[17]

We know that the Williams family were regular chapel-goers. It therefore seems highly likely that 'this concern of the common man in the arts', together with 'this struggling with things of the mind in consort with his neighbours', played a significant part in the intellectual development of the young William Emrys Williams.

In a book on Dr Thomas Jones, founder of Coleg Harlech, best known and best loved Welsh college of adult education, Peter Stead has written that TJ was greatly influenced by the discussion groups which characterised Welsh Sunday schools.[18] Professor Stead insists that Welsh Sunday schools operated 'at a very high intellectual level' – quite distinct from the English tradition. In his judgement they were 'at least as important as schools' in inculcating the Welsh devotion to matters intellectual:

> Welsh youngsters would continue to attend chapel long after normal leaving age, taking part in adult classes which served as a training ground for debate and argument on the widest range of issues, both theological and secular.[19]

The potency of the chapel as a primary source of Bill Williams' social and intellectual formation can be explained in more sociological terms:

> Chapel-going was a habit. What else would one do on Sunday? Where else could one spend a week-day evening, where else could one meet one's friends, male and female? There was no Village Institute, no Church Hall, and the schools had no seating accommodation for adults. For many, of course, chapel-going was something more than a habit – it was a vocation. Suddenly, this spiritual hurricane, the Revival, swept over the land, quickening the pulse of life in Wales into a fever. Crowded chapels, fire upon the lips of men, singing so intense in its emotional powers as to be almost compelling, suborning thought and speaking direct to something older. No one who has not heard a body of Welsh men and women singing in this state can form any idea of the effect of the repetition, in harmony, of a couplet or a verse of a hymn; it can bring about what can only be called an incandescence of the spirit.[20]

In later life, Bill Williams clearly remembered his early exposure to Welsh Sunday sermons. Writing in 1950 about various influences on the work of D H Lawrence, he recalled the rapturous effect produced by some of the Congregational preachers he had encountered 'as a youth in Wales'. The memory of their sermons evidently still haunted his imagination in later years:

> Those who follow this passionate and volcanic writer [D H Lawrence] through his poems or stories or essays will find no difficulty in discovering his 'message' – except, perhaps, on those not infrequent occasions when, carried away by fervour, he is inclined to lapse into the incoherence of a revivalist preacher. This parallel comes particularly to my mind because I remember, as a youth in Wales, listening so often to some celebrated preacher who became rapt to such an extent that he temporarily abandoned his discourse in favour of passages of sheer incantation.[21]

The young Billy Williams seems to have been unusually impressionable and responsive to the power of language – more specifically of Welsh language – to move both listeners and readers. In the beginning was the word; and the word was *hwyll* – that peculiar Welsh gift for fervent oratory and the ability to sway others through impassioned and poetic language, in religion, politics and the arts. In his account of the making of modern Wales, Professor Kenneth Morgan analyses this national love of language, poetry and rhetoric amongst his fellow countrymen and women, and in particular, of their skilful use of its power to persuade:

> One of the most important features of the Welsh in the past hundred years, after all, is that they have been intensely political people, born orators, skilled committee men, 'fluid people' like Thomas Jones, 'able to charm the birds off the bough', like Lloyd George.[22]

It was the magical power of language to charm – more especially perhaps the hypnotic power of Welsh prosody – the musical sound of the spoken language and the incantatory quality of Welsh poetry – which filled the head and excited the imagination of the young William Emrys Williams:

> For it must be stressed that this Welsh prosody is not a pattern on paper to please the eye of the reader: it is a pattern of sound in the air, and it must be sounded. No Welshman reads this poetry with the eye alone, whether it be 500 years or 5 days old. The necessity for 'sounding' does not arise from rhythm or cadence or vocal inflexion alone – all poetry can call upon the same reasons in its aid – but from a strict consonantal pattern which is its very essence and is imposed upon rhyme.[23]

By his eighth year, Billy Williams had absorbed all the major influences that were to shape his later life: from his mother, the importance of family life; from his father, the virtues of hard work and skilled craftsmanship; from his school teachers, the love of learning, language and poetry; and from the Congregational Church, the critical importance of communitarian values, and of working to improve the lives of others. Those cultural influences combined with an unusually energetic nature to produce a young man with a highly-developed social conscience, determined to do some good in the wider world – perhaps as a teacher, missionary or minister. Billy Williams was now ready to take his first steps into that wider world.

Two:
Manchester – the intellectual seedbed

> The period we call Edwardian [occupies] an odd pivotal position between the nineteenth century and the twentieth: it was not quite Victorian, though conservatives tried to make it so, nor was it altogether modern, though it contained the beginnings of many ideas that we recognise as our own…[which makes] the Edwardian period both interesting and important, for out of the turmoil contemporary England was born.
>
> *Samuel Hynes:* The Edwardian Turn of Mind, *1968*

In the fifteen years between 1904, when young Billy Williams and his family arrived in Manchester, and 1919, when William Emrys Williams BA left Manchester for London, the world was turned upside down and inside out. In 1904, the nation was still mourning the death of Queen Victoria, three years earlier. By 1919, King George V was on the throne. The Edwardian era had come and gone. War, revolution and turmoil had changed the face and the character of Europe. From Berlin to Birmingham, and from Moscow to Manchester, the pre-war world had disappeared and life would never be the same again.

From the Great Exhibition of 1851 to the First World War, Britain dominated world economy, becoming principal creditor nation by virtue of its leadership in manufactured goods, in commerce, shipping, banking, insurance and financial credit. For Britain, the decade preceding the First World War saw remarkable industrial progress and general prosperity, despite some serious labour disputes. Between 1900 and 1913, the monetary value of British exports more than doubled. For design, quality and value, British goods were best. Imperial Preference reigned supreme throughout the world's biggest trading block – the British Empire – which still appeared to stand proud and strong.

While London was the seat of monarchy, government, and the arts, the basis of Britain's prosperity lay in its northern manufacturing areas. Clydeside and Tyneside built and maintained the world's largest merchant fleet. Birmingham and Newcastle supplied the world's heavy engineering goods. Liverpool and Manchester handled more cargo than all other British ports taken together.

Edwardian economic enterprise benefited the whole economy but was nowhere so impressive as in Britain's textile industry. In 1900, cotton was king. In Lancashire alone, the number of cotton looms rose by nearly a quarter between 1900 and 1914. Thanks to cotton, Manchester soon became the third city of the Empire.

William Emrys Williams – graduation, 1918.

As its inhabitants were fond of reminding themselves: 'What Manchester thinks today, the rest of the world thinks tomorrow'. Three examples illustrate the basis of that bold claim: first, the dominance of the Lancashire textile industry, centred on Manchester's renowned Cotton Exchange; second, the vigorous growth of local government, with its emphasis on the provision of cost-controlled, municipal services; third, the development of a thriving metropolitan culture, exemplified by the growing reputation of Manchester University, the campaigning journalism of the *Manchester Guardian*, and the exceptional popularity and success of Manchester's Hallé Orchestra.

Manchester's booming economy, the prospects it offered of regular employment, and its lively culture, combined to attract large numbers of economic migrants and political refugees to the city. In the final decade of the 19th and the first decade of the 20th century, immigrants streamed into Manchester in tens of thousands – from Ireland and Wales, from the rest of the UK, and from further afield. These newcomers brought with them to the city a hunger to succeed and a thirst for a better quality of life. The skills and ambitions of immigrants added lustre to Manchester's prosperity. For reasons of mutual support and protection, most new immigrants sought to preserve their distinctive identities by living in virtually closed ethnic communities. The most colourful and vibrant were established by Irish, Welsh and Jewish immigrants, each community clustered around its respective place of worship – church, chapel or synagogue.

It was to the Hulme district of Manchester – and the expatriate Welsh community gathered together around the Booth Street Congregational Chapel – that Thomas and Annie Williams brought their young family in 1904. Hulme was a respectable, working-class district, comprising narrow rows of terraced houses, on the south side of the city. Having settled his children in the local primary school, Thomas earned his living as a joiner in and around the city. His income was modest but it was regular. Members of the Williams family were better housed, clothed and nourished than those of the city's many unskilled and unemployed workers. Above all, the children of skilled workers enjoyed better educational opportunities – and developed higher career aspirations – than their counterparts in less favoured circumstances.

Billy made his way to the Central High School for Boys in Whitworth Street where he proved an industrious and promising pupil, more interested in poetry and literature than games or out-of-school activities. After Manchester Grammar School, the Central High School was the best known and most prestigious of the city's secondary schools. Its students followed a wide-ranging syllabus and were expected to produce work of an academic standard that would qualify many to go on to university. Whether their parents could afford to let them do so was another matter.

Billy Williams was evidently keen to demonstrate his early writing skills. His account of 'An Open-Air Geography Lesson', based on a school visit to Prestwich, appeared in the Central High School magazine for 1912, offering the earliest known example of his keen observation, poetic imagination and adolescent writing style:

> Leaving the rustic path, we saw a water-logged depression, on which, in parts, actual pools of water had collected, and from the lower end of this depression a tiny rivulet flowed, drawing its supplies from the subterranean channels of water in the hollow. We followed this little stream along the first part of its course – the torrent course – observing the furious rushing of the water, and its effect on the banks, one of which had been worn quite steep, while at the base of the opposite one deposits of mud and stones were seen. Now and again a sturdy little waterfall bounded recklessly over a ledge of rock, a foot or two in height, and once a tiny tributary brought its contribution to the "main" stream... As we left Nature behind us and approached the busy town, the silvery, mystic voice of the rippling stream was borne to us faintly on the breeze saying: "Boys may come and boys may go, But I go on for ever."[1]

In a more extended piece, published in 1913, his last year at school, Billy provided his English readers with an insight into those powerful Welsh myths and legends which fed his youthful imagination and which helped form his own self-image:

> Far, far away amid the black mountains and gentle valleys of wild Wales there still burn the fires of a powerful mythology. Welshmen are naturally superstitious, and, in spite of their deeply religious emotions, many of them have a profound belief in the supernatural and mystical. When the thunder crashes over the mountain-tops, and when the lightning flashes fiercely across the deep valleys, you may be sure that in the tiny cottages on the mountain-side the grandfathers are telling the children to listen to the voice of God, and to remember that His angels are riding abroad in their fiery chariots...
>
> Wales abounds in such traditions...which are to be found not only in manuscripts and libraries, but in the hearts of its people. Far removed from the noise and bustle of England, the Cymry have clung tenaciously to all their traditional lore and legend, and have handed the quaint tales on and on, from generation to generation in the language which their fathers spoke a thousand years ago. They have fulfilled Taliesin's prophecy to the letter:
>
> "Their Lord they will praise,
> Their speech they will keep,
> Their land they will lose,
> Except Wild Wallia."[2]

That final quatrain was taken from the title page of George Borrow's *Wild Wales*. The poetic transformation of 'Wales' into 'Wallia' was not Billy's schoolboy gloss on the name of his native land but, as Borrow himself explains in his *Introduction*:

> The inhabitants, who speak an ancient and peculiar language, do not call this region Wales, nor themselves Welsh. They call themselves Cymry or Cumry, and their country Cymru, or the land of the Cumry. Wales or Wallia, however, is the true, proper, and without doubt original name, as it relates not to any particular race, which at present inhabits it, but to the country itself.[3]

Wild Wales, the fourth of Borrow's books, was first published in 1862. Less well-known than *The Bible in Spain* (1843), *Lavengro* (1851) or *The Romany Rye* (1857), *Wild Wales* was highly popular with the English-reading public in Wales. It was already in its seventh edition when Billy Williams quoted from it in his 1913 schoolboy essay. That confirms he knew the book from his Manchester schooldays, and possibly earlier – captivated no doubt by George Borrow's 'fiction of vagabondage'. Fourteen years later, in 1927, Williams chose a selection from Borrow's works, when compiling the first in a series of anthologies from the English classics that he edited over the next fifty years, mainly but not exclusively for Penguin Books.

One notable feature of the two schoolboy pieces is that Billy signed them quite simply 'Emrys' – the only recorded occasion when he chose to use his second Christian name, unadorned. If the first piece is poetic reportage, the second reveals the feelings of a maturing young man, uprooted from his Welsh homestead, looking back with pride and nostalgia to his early years as 'a youth in Wales'. His own grandfather, William Williams, may well have urged him, during a thunderstorm, to 'listen to the voice of God and to remember that His angels are riding abroad in their fiery chariots'.

As Billy progressed through secondary school, taking home glowing reports of his academic progress and promise, his father was confirmed in the belief that his son was destined for life in the Congregational ministry. In this he had the full backing of his wife, Annie, the hard-headed housekeeper, very much aware of the risks and frustrations, the long working hours and modest earnings of a skilled craftsman. Perhaps it was the Minister of the Booth Street Welsh Chapel who first suggested that, if Billy maintained his academic success, he might be awarded a Congregational scholarship to help send him to theological training college. Whether Billy fully shared his father's enthusiasm that he should become a Congregational Minister is not clear. But he certainly wanted to go to Manchester University and was committed to English Language and Literature as the main subject of his first degree.

In 1901, the university announced that Charles Harold Herford, Professor of English at University College, Aberystwyth, had accepted an invitation to become the first occupant of the university's new Chair of English Literature. Herford was a fine, discriminating critic and an industrious author, described in the *Dictionary of National Biography* as 'the most accomplished English scholar of his age [who] concentrated on the ideas and the characters of the men behind the books'.[4] In 1895 he had published a model edition of Spenser's *The Shepherd's Calendar*, followed two years later by *The Age of Wordsworth*, a widely acclaimed study of the romantic movement in literature. In 1899 he published the first ten volumes in the Eversley Edition of Shakespeare and later went on to make outstanding contributions to the Oxford Edition of Ben Jonson. Above all, Herford was an inspirational and much-loved teacher of English literature who fired the imagination of his students by his enthusiasm for his subject, and his gift for communicating complicated ideas in clear, vivid language.

Shortly after his eighteenth birthday, on 5 October 1914, Billy Williams entered the University of Manchester and began attending Herford's first lectures in the Faculty of Arts. Two months earlier, on 4 August, following Germany's unprovoked invasion of Belgium, Britain had declared war, shattering the customary peace of the academic community. The war would rob the university of many of the most promising young scholars of their generation. Vice-Chancellor Weiss welcomed the 1914 intake of students by telling them that the university was living through 'unusually difficult times'. Some young men had already abandoned their studies and volunteered for active service, without waiting for Kitchener's call. Those who had been members of their School or University Cadet Corps soon gained a commission and departed for the Western Front, where they were amongst the first casualties of the conflict. The University of Manchester, like every other university throughout Europe, began publishing lists of the first men killed on active service. As the war dragged on, the lists grew longer and longer.

By 1916, the horrifying increase in casualties on the Western Front led Williams' fellow countryman, David Lloyd George, now Secretary of State for War, to introduce compulsory military service. Williams had never been a member of the Cadet Corps and was certainly not a volunteer. He arrived at university with a Central School scholarship, perhaps supplemented by his local Congregational church, with every intention of training for the ministry. As a potential minister of religion, he was not exempt from military service but could count on deferment until the completion of his postgraduate course. So he settled down to study the great classics of English Literature, acutely aware of the likely fate of many of his contemporaries. He was an avowed Christian – very likely a pacifist – who could see no moral justification in killing young Germans in the cause of international peace. We do not know whether he professed any left-wing views before arriving at university. But the war may well have driven him, like others of his generation, to a much deeper probing of his ethical and political position, and to a radicalisation of his views.

In her account of this crucial period, Gertrude Williams is tactfully silent about the war. She says nothing of Billy's liability for military service and simply records that 'Billy went on to the Central School for Boys, from which he won a classical scholarship to Manchester University'.[5] There is, however, no evidence that Billy ever studied either Latin or Greek at university, or that he ever wished to do so. With a classical scholarship, he would surely have studied Classics. In fact, he spent his three undergraduate years studying English Literature, the subject to which he returned repeatedly and passionately throughout his life. Had Gertrude got the facts wrong? Was she simply confused in her later years? Or had Billy persuaded her that he had once been a 'classical scholar'? There is evidence that he was not averse to adding a colourful gloss to objective fact.

Charles Harold Herford seems to have exerted a long-lasting and wholly salutary influence on Williams. Herford not only directed and supervised his reading: he sharpened his critical faculties and was surely influential in forming his literary taste and judgement. He also served as an outstanding role model of the best kind of teacher, communicating to his students a passionate commitment to his subject, shaping their immediate ideas and values, and so indirectly influencing their career plans. If Williams' parents were responsible for their son's persevering character, Herford must be given the major credit for his intellectual development and his maturing literary sensibility.

Herford's 1902 essay on 'The Permanent Power of English Poetry' discussed the potency of English language and literature in the lives of 'ordinary people'. The impressionable Williams almost certainly read Herford's essay, which may help to explain his lifelong love of poetry with its permanent power to elevate human thought and feeling, to illuminate everyday experience, and to provide inspiration and pleasure. He was already working hard to deepen his knowledge and understanding of English literature, using every opportunity to cultivate his undergraduate writing skills and to get himself into print. The most immediate outlet for such writing was *The Serpent*, the official organ of the Manchester University Unions.

The Serpent for March 1917 included two contrasted contributions over the initials WEW. The first, described as 'A Fragment' from 'An All-Owens Revue', was a satirical sketch, heavily laced with contemporary student jargon – an example of fashionably bright and irreverent undergraduate humour; the second, a poem characterised by mawkish Edwardian sentimentality. Similar light verses by WEW appeared in succeeding issues of *The Serpent*. Only one merits serious consideration. It appeared in *The Serpent* for December 1918, some time after Billy had met and fallen in love with his fellow undergraduate, Gertrude Rosenblum. Here at last there is genuine emotion and the true expression of tender feeling:

For G

They did not sing of you in Babylon:
They garnered gold and ivory and lace;
And fought; and loved a little – and were gone;
O they have died who never saw your face!

They never saw you walk the Trojan walls,
(And what they killed there for I have forgot);
They dreamed of Holy Grails in Arthur's Halls,
Who never heard your name in Camelot!

Therefore the earth is full of ghostly kings,
Who will not sleep till they have kissed your eyes;
And I have heard the beat of angels' wings,
At night against the Gates of Paradise.[6]

This may not be great poetry, but is important for what it tells us about Williams' poetic sensibility in his late teens, and his thinking about his possible future career. Many years later, in the Introduction to his anthology of *Selected Poems by D H Lawrence*, he was to write:

> The fame of D H Lawrence rests mainly on his novels, yet the first of his works to be published was a number of poems which appeared in The English Review in 1910. He was then a young schoolmaster of twenty-four, and for many years had been writing poems of modest distinction but much promise. Most of them were acutely autobiographical, for to Lawrence his poetry was, in a sense, a log-book of his own emotional experiences. To some extent that is true, of course, of all poetry, but there is a difference in the degree to which poets talk to themselves, and the early Lawrence was intensely pre-occupied with personal relationships and problems which he tried to resolve into poetic utterance.[7]

The mature Bill Williams – writing in his sixties and recalling his own early attempts to resolve his 'personal relationships and problems' in 'poetic utterance' – seems to find parallels between his own life and that of a literary hero. Like Lawrence, Williams had been 'a young schoolmaster of twenty-four' whose early poems were certainly autobiographical and 'of modest distinction'. Regrettably they show little promise of a career as a professional poet. With the exception of that one poem 'For G', his undergraduate verses should probably be read as 'a log-book of his own emotional experiences'.

When Billy met Gertrude, at a meeting of the University Labour Party, few of their friends expected them to forge a long-lasting relationship. Their family backgrounds, religious upbringing and economic circumstances were very different. They were enrolled in different faculties, and had very different ideas about their future careers. The fact that they met at all is one of those extraordinary 'chapters of accidents' that recur throughout Williams' life. Gertrude Rosenblum was the youngest of five daughters of orthodox Jewish parents, who had arrived in Manchester as immigrants in the 1890s. Before the Great War, Gertrude's father – Israel Rosenblum, a cotton shipper – had built up a family business and begun to enjoy a moderately prosperous lifestyle in Higher Broughton, one of the city's leafier suburbs. Gertrude was a highly intelligent, bookish girl, spoiled by her parents and her four older sisters. If, as reported by members of her extended family, she was her father's favourite daughter, that was due more to her intelligence and personality than her appearance. She was dark, dumpy and bespectacled. Had she been her father's son, rather than his daughter, Gertrude might well have become a rabbi. But her father was not the conventional Victorian *pater familias*. Recognising her intellectual gifts, he and his wife strongly supported her plans to go to university and to have a career of her own, rather than stay at home and await the arrival of an eligible – that is, an orthodox Jewish – husband.

Gertrude chose to read economics and politics at university, became a committed member of the Labour Party, and was already deeply immersed in the policy issues of urban poverty and social deprivation. She soon set her mind on pursuing an academic career. Billy for his part was a poor, Welsh, scholarship boy, engrossed in the languor of lilies and the rapture of roses of English poetry, with little or no interest in politics. His father, who exercised a decisive influence on his son's thinking, earnestly hoped and prayed that his son would successfully complete his university studies and then dedicate his life to the Congregational Church. Despite those obvious differences in their backgrounds and personal lives, Gertrude and Billy nevertheless had some things in common: both their families were 'incomers' to the city of Manchester; both had known relative poverty but had remained in the city and both had prospered, each in its own way. Their respective children, Billy and Gertrude, were both native Lancastrians, born within three months of each other, and had grown up within a short tram-ride of each other's homes. But there the similarities ended.

Manchester's Jewish community was one of the oldest, largest and most thriving in Britain. *Sephardi* Jews, of Spanish and Portuguese descent, had settled in Manchester from as early as the 17th century. In the late 19th century they were followed by much larger numbers of *Ashkenazi* Jews, from Central and Eastern Europe, fleeing religious persecution and economic discrimination. Each wave of new immigrants was supported with charitable benevolence by more established Jewish families and soon absorbed into the religious, cultural and working life of the community. Israel Rosenblum was very much the product of his background and generation. He personifies one familiar stereotype of the late-Victorian middle-class Jew – combining the qualities of the shrewd, self-made business-man with those of the devout Talmudic scholar. It was a matter of justifiable pride to Israel Rosenblum that his father-in-law, Jakob Abeles, was descended from thirteen generations of rabbis and scholars. Jakob's fourth daughter, Louise, was intensely conscious of that scholarly tradition, as evidenced by the care and attention she and her husband devoted to maintaining an orthodox Jewish home in Manchester.

Louise herself seems to personify another familiar Victorian figure – the formidable Jewish matriarch, somewhat arrogant and sometimes over-bearing, who lavished motherly love on her daughters whilst imposing a strict, conformist regime. Everyone who met her felt Louise's dominant personality. By all accounts, she was a vigorous, self-centred woman who knew exactly what she wanted and generally got her own way. When she married Israel Rosenblum in her home town of Berlad in Romania, she was just twenty. Over the following seven years, she produced five daughters, the youngest of whom was born in 1897 and named Gertrude – *Gitel* in Hebrew – after her maternal grandmother, Gertrud Abeles. Having made a new life for themselves in the Jewish quarter of Manchester, Israel and Louise Rosenblum were determined that their daughters should benefit from the progressive secular education provided by the Manchester school system.

The home life of the Rosenblums of Higher Broughton contrasted sharply with that of the Williams family of Hulme. Gertrude's mother presided over a moderately prosperous, strictly observant, Jewish home, where the orthodox Jewish dietary laws of *kashrut* were strictly observed. Candles were kindled every Friday evening, with the traditional blessing over the plaited *cholah* loaf, to welcome the Jewish Sabbath. There were traditional Jewish dishes on the table and a large, boisterous family, augmented by other members of the community, joyfully celebrated Jewish festivals. At that time orthodox Jews rarely invited non-Jewish guests to share family meals.

Billy's mother managed a much smaller and less affluent household at 16 Raglan Street in Hulme, paying no less attention to domestic economy, cleanliness and efficiency. Thomas Owen and Annie Williams raised their family – Billy and his older sister, Edith – on a skilled craftsman's pay, in one of Manchester's respectable if less salubrious districts. There were no dietary rules – except perhaps a strong preference for Welsh lamb and scofa bread – but the traditional Edwardian non-conformist Sunday was rigorously observed with regular attendance at Congregational chapel and a strong family commitment to communitarian values and projects.

The domestic lives of the Rosenblums and the Williams were otherwise worlds apart. It seems unlikely there would have been any contact between the two families had their children not been students at the same university. They met by chance, fell in love, and decided to marry. When destiny brought them together, the sharp differences in their family backgrounds and value systems were all too obvious. Those differences were soon to have a profound and potentially devastating impact on the young couple's relationship and their chance of future happiness.

William Emrys Williams (centre, back row) at Lancaster Independent College, 1918.

Gertrude Rosenblum (first left, front row), Manchester Women's Fencing Club, 1916.

Gertrude Rosenblum and William Emrys Williams (third and fourth from left, back row), Economic and Social Science Society, Manchester University, May 1917.

Three:
Billy and Gertrude

It was at the University that I first met Billy. He was a few months older...so I was one undergraduate year behind him. As soon as we met we fell in love and remained so for the rest of his life until his death.

Gertrude Williams: W E Williams: Educator Extraordinary, *2000*

Even her closest friends would not have described Gertrude Rosenblum as demure. From her earliest years, she displayed a self-assured, assertive personality, which combined something of her mother's dominant character with much of her father's rabbinical turn of mind – that ingrained habit of intense scholarly enquiry, passionate argument and a total conviction of the rightness of her cause. Her intellectual gifts, coupled with her determination to succeed on her own merits, made her a formidable, independent-minded young woman, with a strong sense of direction and a touch of arrogance. It was not just her mind that was rapier-sharp: as a member of the University's Women's Fencing Club, Gertrude represented Manchester with distinction at inter-varsity matches. Nobody was surprised, therefore, when she was awarded First Class Honours in her final degree examinations and announced her intention of pursuing postgraduate studies at the London School of Economics. What astonished her friends – and mortified her parents – was her announcement that she and Billy Williams were engaged to be married.

If the son or daughter of an orthodox Jewish family wishes to marry out of the faith, they invariably come under enormous pressure – from their parents, their extended family, the local rabbi and senior members of the community – to end the relationship immediately. Those brave or foolish enough to resist such pressure are made to understand clearly that their refusal to conform to traditional community values is likely to result in implacable hostility and social ostracism for the rest of their natural lives. Even today, in ultra-orthodox families, a year's ritual mourning is still observed for a son or daughter who abandons the Jewish faith by intermarriage: they are regarded as dead.

When Gertrude took Billy home to meet her parents in the summer of 1918, she was fully aware of the risks involved. With rabbinical thoroughness, she would have rehearsed her argument, making her position unequivocally clear. If her parents refused to recognise Billy as her husband-to-be – it was too much to expect their blessing – she would marry him despite their objections. She and Billy loved

Billy and Gertrude Williams 'Wedding Bliss', 1919.

each other. They were old enough, intelligent enough, liberated enough to know their own minds. They were no longer living in some 19th century Polish ghetto but were about to enter the third decade of a century of scientific progress and emancipation. Gertrude and Billy saw themselves as fully-fledged members of that enlightened, modern generation. They refused to be thwarted by tradition, shackled by convention, or deterred by the superstitious prejudices of an older generation.

The Rosenblums pleaded in vain. Gertrude was determined to marry 'her Billy' even if that meant forfeiting the love, affection and support of her entire family. The consequences were unpalatable but inevitable. Gertrude and Billy both intended to pursue postgraduate studies, so there was no realistic prospect of early marriage. And they certainly could not afford to set up home together. Gertrude had no money of her own in her early twenties, other than what might have come to her by way of an academic scholarship. If the Rosenblums refused to fund Gertrude's studies in London, the young couple's immediate prospects were miserable.

Billy, for his part, seems to have taken the Rosenblums' objections more seriously – apparently much more so than Gertrude herself. He respected their religious convictions, however much he might resent their social implications. He, too, came from a close and loving family. But where Gertrude's family refused to acknowledge Billy, his own parents welcomed Gertrude into their home and blessed their intended union. The fact that Gertrude was Jewish was irrelevant and unimportant. Billy loved Gertrude and was equally determined to marry her. But his moral and social sense – as well as his economic self-interest – made it imperative to avoid a rift in the Rosenblum family, if at all possible. He soon demonstrated how far he was prepared to go to avoid such a rift.

If the Rosenblums insisted that Gertrude must marry a man of the Jewish faith, Billy was willing to undertake the necessary instruction and prepare himself for conversion to Judaism. Whether he intended to abandon his commitment to Congregational Christianity is unclear. Perhaps he envisaged some kind of compromise or convergence between Judaism and Christianity. He would become a Jew – but a 'Christian Jew'. Such an idea may seem ludicrous today, but it was very much in keeping with the more adventurous spirit of the immediate post-war period. Some elements in the Christian Church had always sought to 'bring salvation to the Jewish people' by persuading them to embrace the divinity of Jesus Christ. Here was an opportunity to try out that idea in practice. Perhaps Billy was arrogant enough to think he might convert the Rosenblums, however unlikely that might seem.

Not only was he prepared to contemplate conversion: he was willing to face the intellectual, psychological and practical consequences. He began his instruction in

Judaism with his future sister-in-law's husband, Ralph Woolf Crammer, married to Gertrude's sister, Margaret. Somewhat older than Billy, Crammer was a London schoolmaster who had been a conscientious objector during the war and been professionally penalised for his pacifist convictions. According to his son, Dr John Crammer, his father

> ...was himself an atheist at the time. Then or later they got on badly. Bill couldn't stand my father's pedantic obsessionalism and he thought Bill unscrupulous and immoral.[1]

Whether Ralph Crammer seriously believed in Billy's wished-for conversion is not clear. By John Crammer's account, he detected some ambivalence in Billy's motivation. The left-leaning, socially responsible schoolteacher seems nevertheless to have exerted significant influence on Billy's thinking about his future life and career at a crucial stage in his personal and intellectual development.

Within a few months, Billy not only gave up his instruction with Ralph Crammer but abandoned any kind of religious observance. According to Robin Huws Jones, a normally reliable source, Billy made sufficient progress towards conversion to have contemplated – and perhaps to have undergone – adult circumcision.[2] Such an heroic symbolic gesture was totally misconceived. Despite Billy's plans for conversion, there was little prospect of his being accepted by the orthodox Jewish community, which strenuously discouraged converts, even in exceptional circumstances. If Gertrude had become pregnant with Billy's child, those exceptional circumstances might have been found. But she had not. At that point, fate took a decisive hand in determining the lovers' future.

When Williams began his undergraduate studies at the University of Manchester in 1914, he had a scholarship from the Central High School, which paid his university tuition fees. But what was he to live on? He had declared his intention of preparing for a career in the ministry by registering at the Lancashire Independent College (LIC), a Congregational training establishment at Whalley Range, close to the centre of Manchester. The LIC had at its disposal sixteen scholarships and bursaries, seven of which were open to students entering theological training. The College Annual Report for the academic year 1914 shows that, on entering his junior year, Williams was awarded a Raffles Scholarship, worth £30 per annum for each of two years. In 1916 he was awarded a Sharrock Fellowship, again worth £30 per annum, over three years. He was thus able to live as a residential student at the College throughout his time as an undergraduate.

In the summer of 1918, Billy and Gertrude both successfully completed their degree courses. But where Gertrude graduated with First Class Honours in economics and social science, Billy achieved no more than a General Pass Degree in the Faculty of Arts – a result that gave no indication of intellectual distinction, and no promise of exceptional achievements ahead. Fortified by her academic success, Gertrude soon made plans to move to London to begin her postgraduate studies at the London School of Economics. Billy remained in Manchester where he embarked on the first year of his Bachelor of Divinity degree at LIC.

In the early twentieth century, LIC was to the non-conformist ministry what the LSE was to the labour movement – a powerhouse of ideas and professional training for committed young enthusiasts. Headed by William Henry Bennett (1855-1920), an Old Testament scholar of genuine distinction, and a former Fellow of St John's College, Cambridge, LIC had by 1918 probably passed the peak of its influence as the leading non-conformist theological college of the day. Its teaching staff included the remarkable Robert Mackintosh (1858-1933), a Scot of formidable intellect, a charismatic teacher-scholar, and a major influence at the college. The impressionable Williams could not fail to come under the influence of both Bennett and Mackintosh in his theological views, his values and his ideas for his future career.

The war had taken its toll on candidates for the ministry. Some had volunteered to join the army and been killed on active service; others had abandoned their studies and were an irreplaceable loss to the ministry. Many developed serious misgivings about the war and the killing of fellow Christians. As the war dragged on, year after year, with no end in sight, a powerful strain of pacifist thinking spread amongst students at LIC. Why should they devote years of their life to the gospels, immerse themselves in the ideas and values of the Christian Church, and be ordained, simply to minister to the dying, the bereaved, and the disfigured casualties of the bloodiest war in history? There are no surviving letters or diaries to tell us what Williams felt about the war and its psychological effects on a sensitive young man. At the outbreak of war, in August 1914, a million British men volunteered to fight for King and Country. Many of Williams' friends and fellow students gave up their studies to join the ranks. Billy was not amongst them. As his later career and writings would show, he was a genuine patriot who loved his country, and he wanted to serve the wider community. For years he had been preparing himself mentally and psychologically for the life of an ordained Congregational Minister. Why should he give that up for the violence of war? We do not know whether he shared the pacifist views of Bertrand Russell and others, who opposed the Great War on ethical or religious grounds.

Towards the end of 1918, the war was suddenly and unexpectedly over. Equally suddenly, in the spring or early summer of 1919, in his first year at LIC, Williams abandoned his studies and moved to London. What led him to that momentous decision? In the Annual Report for 1918, the College authorities included this cryptic notice: 'William Emrys Williams was granted leave of absence to work for the YMCA in London'.[3] There was nothing very remarkable in that simple announcement. Hundreds of young men volunteered their services to the YMCA during and immediately after the war. There were no fewer than 10,000 YMCA centres providing welfare and social services to Allied forces during the Great War. It is an historical irony that the YMCA was never more flourishing than during the two world wars. But the LIC's Annual Report for 1919 included another brief but more dramatic announcement: 'William Emrys Williams has resigned his place as a student at the college'.[4] There were no further details. So why had Billy resigned? The results that flowed from his resignation proved critical for the rest of Billy's life and work – and for Gertrude's life, too. It is therefore important to probe Billy's motives for what appears, at first sight, to have been an impetuous and irrational decision. The evidence, such as it is, comes from three sources: first, from the College archives; second, from Gertrude Williams' account of what happened; and third, from Bill Williams himself.

At first sight, there seem no good reasons for questioning the College's innocent explanation that Billy initially took leave of absence to work for the YMCA in London and later resigned, implicitly to continue that honourable work. Having spent three years as an undergraduate, he may well have been reluctant to contemplate a further three years of postgraduate study in Manchester, especially after Gertrude had left for London. He needed to earn his living; he had found useful work with a Christian community, which needed his enthusiastic services; and he wanted to be with Gertrude. Why should he not resign?

Writing of those events many years later, Gertrude Williams reports a remarkable incident at college which, if true, throws a very different light on Billy's resignation:

> [In 1919] the authorities of his college discussed the situation with him and said they were perfectly willing for him to continue with his BD degree but they felt they should warn him that it might prove very difficult for him to be called to a Congregational church with a Jewish wife. He therefore gave up his course and came to live in London with me as his wife and that meant he had to find some way of earning a living.[5]

Is it likely or even credible that the College authorities would have taken the drastic step of warning him of the likely difficulties he could expect to encounter in his future career with a Jewish wife? Was it in their interest to take such action in the immediate post-war world, when they needed every graduate minister they could produce? Or was Gertrude offering a convenient rationalisation of the crucial events of 1919? Did she want Billy out of college and with her in London, where she knew there was greater scope for his talents? Did she want him to abandon his ministerial vocation and become more directly involved in education, which she considered more important and worthwhile? Did she 'invent' her explanation for his decision to abandon his studies? Or was she recounting something that Billy himself had once told her, perhaps in confidence?

We know that Gertrude herself had no religious beliefs. Despite – or perhaps because of – her orthodox Jewish upbringing, she was certainly agnostic and probably an atheist by the time she got to university. Billy, for his part, had already demonstrated his pragmatic attitude by his willingness to convert to Judaism for the sake of Gertrude's family. If her story is true, she had the perfect reason, or excuse, for persuading him to abandon his divinity studies, especially since his plans for conversion to Judaism had come to nothing. However mixed his motives, the fact is that Billy gave up his postgraduate studies in 1919 and made his way to London. But why did the College allow him to resign so easily, and without apparently requiring him to repay any part of his scholarship?

Graham Adams, General-Secretary of the Congregational Federation, has offered his own view of this reported incident:

> I hardly think that Bill Williams would have been told of any difficulties in obtaining a Church with a Jewish wife. Congregationalists have tended to be fairly open-hearted toward other believers. I would, however, have thought the college authorities might have in the records the reason for his leaving. Certainly it would not happen today![6]

Unfortunately, the College records no longer exist. But there is no convincing evidence of religious bigotry amongst the Christian non-conformists of Manchester in 1919. So were there other, more hidden, reasons for his resignation? Billy's own explanation came many years later. In 1973, at the age of seventy-six, writing more than fifty years after the event, he explained how and why he abandoned his studies in favour of his 'evangelistic' mission in education:

> I had been trained to be a Minister in the Congregational Church, and was on the brink of being ordained, at a tender age, when I found myself doubting the doctrines I was required to accept, despite the fact that they were more liberal than those of any other Christian denomination. I defected to education, I suppose, because in that field I could find scope for my deep social concern and idealistic beliefs.[7]

Once again, at first sight, that seems a perfectly plausible explanation. But should we trust Billy's self-exculpation after the passage of so many years? Is this simply another example of Billy's gift for romancing his early life? His parenthetic phrase 'I suppose' is also worth noting. Looking back in 1973, after an interval of more than fifty years, he writes as if he could no longer recall exactly why he 'defected to education' but that he supposed it was because he could find more scope for his 'evangelical fervour'. His reference to 'doctrinal doubts' seems much more plausible – until one sees through the surface veneer. For when he resigned in 1919, he was certainly not 'on the brink of being ordained'. In fact, he had not completed the first year of his arduous divinity studies.

Dr Clyde Binfield of Sheffield University, a leading historian of Welsh non-conformity, offers his own view:

> Williams' piece of autobiography is both plausible and disingenuous (or at least, affected by the passage of time). No doubt Congregationalism was more liberal than any other Christian denomination with an ordained ministry, at least in Britain, though does that mean he had not considered the Unitarian ministry? And that phrase "the doctrine I was required to accept": that, in the context of 1918-20, is disingenuous: his ordination would really depend on the local church that called him to its pastorate...
>
> If Williams found a church and the personal chemistry clicked, and a call was issued and accepted, then he was well away. My hunch is that he did indeed have doubts; that these were recognised by his tutor, and that his "intermediate" step to YMCA work was mooted as providing a breathing space experience of activist Christian work, while he took stock.[8]

That seems to provide a satisfying explanation of Billy's decision to resign, which honours the complexities and ambiguities of human motivation. Aged 22, Billy was at a turning point in his life. He had graduated in the year the Great War ended. He had seen his friends join up and leave for France, where many were killed or maimed. He had fallen in love with Gertrude Rosenblum and inevitably come under the influence of her strong personality. To gratify his father, however, he felt he must complete his studies and then serve the Congregational Church. How then could he afford to throw away his vocational training and his career prospects?

Dr Elaine Kaye of Mansfield College, Oxford, another leading authority on non-conformist church history, offers her own views:

> I take a rather different view from that of Graham Adams. I think it is quite possible that at that date Congregational churches might have been reluctant to call a minister with a Jewish wife; not so much because they were anti-semitic, but because at that time a minister's wife was expected to take a particular role in a church. However open-minded the staff may have been, every student was dependent on a 'call' from a particular congregation. But it is likely that Bill Williams' own doubts about doctrine also played a part in his decision.[9]

Whichever explanation we choose to accept, the next steps for Billy were irrevocable. He not only turned his back on his long-standing aim of becoming a Congregational Minister: he abandoned any kind of religious belief or practice. Throughout the rest of his long life, in his work, his letters, or his voluminous writings, there is not a single indication of his interest in religious observance or affiliation. That chapter of his life had abruptly closed. The next chapter – with Gertrude – was about to begin.

William Emrys Williams – schoolmaster with pupils (left) and at back garden door, 1920s.

Gertrude Williams.

William Emrys Williams in his late twenties.

Four:
London – 20 years of adult education

> He is in adult education because he believes in it. He believes in it not because he wants to make people pundits or Marxists... Williams is too knowing an observer of human life, too good-humoured a partisan to want or expect more of adult education than enabling people to grow up and enjoy life.
>
> *H L Beales on W E Williams,* Miscellany 12, *Penguin Collectors' Society, 1997*

In November 1918, the guns fell silent and the Great War was over. Like millions of others around the world, Billy and Gertrude rejoiced and gave thanks for peace. Having cheered the troops home and celebrated the Allied victory, they turned their thoughts to the work of building the peace. Billy had not served in the army or contributed in any way to the war effort. Perhaps his conscience was relieved by the thought that now, at last, he might work in some practical way for his country's recovery. A million British men were killed in the war – which meant half a million fatherless children. Fathers are irreplaceable. Who would supply the masculine role models for the next generation of young men?

In the autumn of 1918, Gertrude began her postgraduate studies at the LSE. By the middle of 1919, Billy abandoned his training for the ministry and joined Gertrude in London. Having confirmed her intention to marry Billy, Gertrude clearly understood that she must make her way without the emotional or financial support of her family. But she was not without guidance. Her sister Natalie had created a precedent by marrying George Smith, who was not Jewish. As a result she, too, had experienced total rejection by her family. Although the Rosenblums adamantly refused to meet Natalie or her husband after their marriage, Gertrude never lost touch with her sister. On the contrary, her marriage to Billy brought the sisters closer together. The rift in the family was hard to bear for all concerned. But it was inevitable. When Gertrude made up her mind, she was not easily deflected: a hallmark of her character. To their credit, the Rosenblums later relented and did have some social contact with both Gertrude and Billy.

Armed with her First Class Honours degree, Gertrude had no difficulty in securing a place at the London School of Economics, Britain's centre of excellence for postgraduate studies in the social sciences. Her career plans ran in parallel with her personal plans to marry Billy. She had her studies as well as marriage to look forward to. But Billy urgently needed employment. In what appears to have been one of those flashes of insight that recurrently illuminated his life, Billy recognised the conjunction of a need and an opportunity. The need to start earning his living in London, close to Gertrude, was paramount. But he was professionally unqualified to do any significant or well-paid job. He was personable and enthusiastic; he spoke and wrote well; but he had few other assets – financial, academic or social. He was not a well-groomed public schoolboy; he had not attended Manchester's prestigious Grammar School; and he had obtained only a modest degree. He had no family connections and no powerful backers to launch him into London society, or help him establish a career. He relied instead on his native wit and creative energy – plus Gertrude's moral and, perhaps, financial support.

We surmise that, sitting one day in his college library, reading the *Manchester Guardian*, he discovered that the Young Men's Christian Association (YMCA) was calling for young men to work with fatherless boys in London. Here was an inherently worthwhile job that allowed Billy to salve his social conscience whilst earning his living from the moment he arrived in London. It was some combination of those motives that led to Billy's appointment in 1918 as Boys' Club Leader at the YMCA in King's Cross, one of the poorest and most deprived districts of London. He threw himself energetically into his work and seems to have made an immediate impact. For the first time in his life, Billy had established himself entirely by his own efforts. The job was poorly paid, but it was satisfying work, with accommodation provided. And he was no longer financially dependent on Gertrude's scholarship money.

Gertrude's postgraduate studies at the LSE deepened her undergraduate interest in household expenditures and poverty in Britain, subjects which would absorb her for the next twenty years. By chance, her field of research was closely related to the very social group in which Billy had found employment. Gertrude was young, ambitious and impatient. There were relatively few job opportunities for young academics but she was well qualified and her research got off to a good start. With the prospect of a new husband and a new professional career, Gertrude embraced the opportunities she craved: to make her way by her own efforts and talents, and to be judged by her own character and personal achievements, not by her gender, her marital status or her family background.

Gertrude had lost the support of her family, but she had Billy's love, his respect and his unqualified encouragement. They were undoubtedly happy and fulfilled for the first time in their lives. Despite having little money, they were now able to enjoy some of the many attractions that post-war London offered: its great libraries, museums, art collections, parks, concerts and other modest entertainments. They both enjoyed eating out at affordable restaurants and threw themselves into the post-war passion for dancing. Above all, they wanted to marry and settle down to a shared life as soon as either of them secured some employment that paid enough for them to live on.

In the autumn of 1919, Gertrude was appointed Tutor in Economics at the oldest women's college in Britain – Bedford College in Regent's Park, London – and her academic career was launched. Despite disappointments along the way, she never looked back. Gertrude and Billy were now able to fulfil their long-cherished ambition to marry. The civil ceremony took place quietly at the Hampstead Register Office on 29 November 1919, witnessed by two of Gertrude's closest friends, Muriel Moyes, a promising young sculptor – who later tragically took her own life – and her partner, George Bryant. Neither Billy's nor Gertrude's parents attended; but Gertrude's older sister, Natalie, and her husband, George Smith, were present to demonstrate their solidarity. On his marriage certificate, Billy described himself as 'Superintendent of YMCA Club' – an unfamiliar title, which Billy may well have conferred on himself – giving his address as 'The Hampden Club, Phoenix Street, St Pancras' which sounded impressive but was, in fact, the YMCA hostel. Gertrude gave her 'rank or profession' as 'Tutor at Bedford College' and an address in West Hampstead. The newly united Mr and Mrs W E Williams settled down to married life in Gertrude's West Hampstead flat.

Billy's work at the YMCA Boys' Club seems to have been largely administrative with few opportunities to share his love of literature with the young men of King's Cross. He enjoyed his work but, as Gertrude points out, he soon recognised

> ...this could not be a satisfactory life's work. He got on very well with the members and always felt that he had learned an enormous amount from his contact with them but he could not contemplate devoting his life to them nor did the work give full scope to his university education.[1]

If there is a hint of false pride in Gertrude's reference to Billy's university education, she may well have encouraged him to fulfil his potential in more promising directions. In Gertrude's account, Billy then had another of his 'bright ideas' – or perhaps another bout of inspired opportunism:

> Almost by chance, he determined to write to the Director of Education for Essex. He had no previous connection with this county and one might say he picked it out with a pin, but that day he received a telegram to apply to the Leytonstone High School for Boys and within a week he found himself as the Senior English master at that school. He proved to be a born teacher. He liked the Headmaster and his colleagues and the feeling was reciprocated.[2]

Leytonstone High School for Boys was a progressive East End grammar school, one of several such schools, endowed by wealthy London merchants 'for the benefit of poor Christian boys of this parish'. The school set high academic standards for its pupils, many of whom won a place at university, before going on to build successful careers. Once Billy was settled at the High School, the young couple rented a modest house in Leytonstone and set up their second married home together. The area was overcrowded and polluted so they soon moved further out to a house at Brow Hill, close to the open countryside of Epping Forest.

As a university teacher, Gertrude was a well placed, though hardly an impartial, judge of Billy's qualities. 'A born teacher' says Gertrude, his six years of school-teaching proving to be 'amongst the happiest of his life'.[3] An enthusiastic arts graduate, he was steeped in the English classics at a time when high culture, good taste and literary style were still considered worth cultivating and preserving. Passionately committed to literature – and to poetry in particular – Billy rapidly developed the skills needed to share his love of language and literature with others. For six years, from 1920 to 1926, as Senior English Master at Leytonstone High School, Billy encouraged successive intakes of Essex boys to appreciate the finer points of Shakespeare and Milton, Keats and Wordsworth. The challenge of introducing his young pupils to the delights of English poetry soon prompted him to seek a wider audience. Like his tutor, Charles Harold Herford, he found he possessed a gift for communicating complex and subtle ideas with great clarity. The results emerged in the form of Billy's first book, *The Craft of Literature*, published by Methuen in 1925. This was a bold venture for both author and publisher for the book had to compete with many long-established books of a similar kind, used by generations of school students but aimed in effect at their teachers, who were not always keen to replace a familiar textbook with something more up-to-date but untried and untested.

The Craft of Literature disclaimed any lofty aims. As a practising schoolmaster, Williams knew he must lead his young readers by the hand into the deeper waters of literary criticism:

> The subject-matter of literature, as of all the arts, is the stuff of life itself. In literature, life, "like a dome of many-splendoured glass," is seen from all angles. It covers the whole breadth, depth, and diversity of life, it voices the experience of men in all situations and at all times. Things seen, felt, thought, or imagined, worlds known, or lost, or hoped for. All this is the range of literature; to which our study in this book, concerning itself rather with forms of expression, must always be subsidiary.[4]

The book's emphasis was very much on the art or craft of writing – in the original

Greek sense of technique or developed skill. Williams dispenses with literary theory and concentrates instead on showing his readers, in practical terms, how a writer produces his literary effects. In short, this was a brief but appetising 'rough guide' to English literature, its distinctive forms and qualities, with numerous examples drawn from his favourite poets – Shakespeare, Wordsworth, Browning, and Hardy amongst others – and novelists, including Jane Austen, Bronte and Dickens. In a book of fewer than 200 pages, Billy encapsulates the spirit and forms of English literature.

The book is dedicated 'To G', with its echo of his earlier undergraduate poem. In his Preface, Billy acknowledged the constructive criticism that Gertrude had provided on the text:

> The deficiencies of this book would have been greater than they are but for the advice and criticism which my wife has given me during its composition.[5]

Encouraged by the favourable reception of his first book, Billy lost no time in tackling his second. Schoolteachers in the 1920s enjoyed relatively short working hours and long annual holidays, and Williams maintained a high level of creative output over the next three years, producing no fewer than six books of impressive quality between 1925 and 1928. The first two were favourably reviewed and sold well enough for Methuen, his publisher, to encourage him to continue with his writing plans. Some combination of the financial rewards plus the intrinsic satisfaction of becoming a published author motivated him to continue with his writing career.

Where his first book had offered a broad survey of English literary forms, his second, *First Steps to Parnassus*, published by London University Press in 1926, is closely focussed on poetic expression:

> If the reader of this book chances to be endowed with the poetic talent, an incomplete acquaintance with the technique of verse-making will certainly not prevent him from writing poetry. But the poetic endowment is exceedingly rare; and this book addresses itself to that very large class whose cradles the muse of poetry did not bless. In this class we recognise three categories. First, those who very properly feel that it is not necessary to be a poet in order to attempt verse-composition, those who, from time to time, feel impelled to record in verse some objective or subjective experience. Second, those trying to develop a decent prose style. Third, those who lack the inclination or the confidence to write at all but who yet find satisfaction in reading poetry.[6]

A Progressive Course of Precis and Paraphrase, published by Methuen in 1927, was Billy's third book. Although its title is somewhat forbidding, the text is written in a clear and refreshing style, with some memorable verbal images, as in the opening definitions:

> Precis is an exercise in compression which, like an Oxo cube, must contain the essence of the original. Paraphrase, by contrast, expands and clarifies the author's meaning by conveying the sense and feeling of the original text in the student's own words.[7]

The exercises in successive chapters become progressively harder, fully justifying the book's title, culminating in some severely taxing problems in the difficult arts of compression and exposition of meaning. Seventy years after publication, its tone seems a touch austere; but its advice is still relevant, sensible and pungently expressed; and its exercises still present the conscientious student with some tough intellectual challenges.

Williams' fourth book, also published in 1927, was quite different. Methuen was about to publish *Shakespeare to Hardy*, an anthology of poetry selected by Sir Algernon Methuen for use in schools. Williams now contributed *A Critical Commentary on 'Shakespeare to Hardy'*, a compendium of useful insights and illuminating comments on the poems and their authors. Although slight in scope, it is an excellent early example of Williams' lifelong concern with the needs of the uninitiated – here, students struggling to understand and get the best from English poetry.

In 1928, Williams turned back from poetry to his delight in English language. *Plain Prose: The elements of a serviceable style* built on the successful formula of his earlier books by providing a comprehensive guide to good English prose – essential to clear and vital communication. This is the work of a Welshman, with a degree in English, sharing his love of what by now had become his first language, whose musical cadences always stirred him. His own light-footed and highly serviceable style is well illustrated in this example of how to produce vivid description:

> Stevenson wisely counselled the novice to practise the substitution of adjective by characteristic verb: instead of writing yellow corn, write the field of corn rippled... Its colour is known; and the business of the writer should be to bring to life some characteristic which will bring it to the reader's eye... Mr D H Lawrence finds something new and significant to say of a cold bright sky: "There were big frosty stars snapping ferociously in heaven".[8]

His next book, *Selections from George Borrow: chosen and edited by W E Williams*, published by Methuen in 1927, was the first in a remarkable series of selections from the English classics that Williams produced over the years, alongside his own original texts. His *Borrow* anthology includes a lengthy introduction to the author's life and times, with detailed notes on the style and content of his work. Unfortunately, none of his later selections – from Wordsworth, Tennyson, Browning, Hardy, and D H Lawrence – contains comparable introductory material.

What aspects of Williams' personality are revealed by his decision to publish those particular selections from the English classics? First, he never did anything by half. Between 1925 and 1973, Williams produced no fewer than twenty books, of which he was sole author, joint author, major contributor or editor – an impressive literary output. Second, his devotion to the English classics remained undiminished over fifty years. Third, Williams worked throughout his life to encourage less privileged readers to sample and savour these classic texts, by offering them an appetising selection from the complete works. Williams emerges here as one of those natural-born killers of complacency in promoting greater access to great literature for the general reader. He is not simply a stimulating and original writer but a pioneering populariser of high culture, striving to make the English classics less intimidating and more accessible to the mass of 'ordinary people', and not just the favoured few.

Williams' choice of George Henry Borrow for his first selection was no accident. His enduring love of Borrow's work may be explained in part by their shared passion for well-constructed English prose:

> Borrow's style is emphatically a model for anyone who wants to develop a virile and decisive narrative style... His sentence-forms are well-varied; and at their longest they very seldom lose their unity. In the second place, he has an extensive and expressive vocabulary, although he makes no ostentatious display of new words; and he avoids the highly latinized polysyllabic affectation. His diction is for the most part simple, Saxon and concrete. Finally, he knew how to use the historic present tense; and he never risked the penalties which an abuse of that tense, only too common amongst unpractised writers, inevitably inflicts.[9]

Williams clearly admired Borrow's content as well as his style. Every true lover of English prose may take pleasure in the haunting quality of Borrow's incantatory lines from *Lavengro* (1851):

> There's night and day, brother, both sweet things; sun, moon, and stars, brother, all sweet things; there's likewise a wind on the heath. Life is very sweet, brother; who would wish to die?[10]

In the decade following the Great War, Billy and Gertrude Williams might well have found life very sweet. Painful war memories were beginning to recede. Wireless broadcasting was increasingly popular. New dance-music and jazz-bands were all the rage. Talkies were in their infancy with Al Jolson and Charlie Chaplin already 'smash hits' in London. Billy and Gertrude were relatively well-paid teachers, with good career prospects. They could now afford to indulge their taste for the better things in life: dining out, evenings at the theatre, weekends in the country. They both loved natural scenery and enjoyed walking in the English countryside. Hiking and other outdoor pursuits were very much in vogue. It comes as no surprise to discover that Billy and Gertrude kept a much-favoured gypsy caravan – in true George Barrow fashion – near Tring in Hertfordshire, for regular weekends out of town. Billy's formal contract required him to teach, to take his share in the school's administration, and to undertake some after-hours activities. Always the conscientious professional, he nevertheless found time and energy for extra-mural activities, especially when they were well paid. He was soon supplementing his schoolteacher's salary with a modest trickle of additional income from the sale of his first books.

Gertrude, for her part, travelled daily from Essex to teach and research at Bedford College in Regent's Park. Like Billy she, too, was dedicated to her professional work and spent most of her non-teaching time researching into various aspects of poverty and working-class life. Although her contract required her to research and publish in the social sciences, writing did not come easily or naturally to her. She was slower to mature as an author, more inhibited about letting go of her work, and somewhat less productive than Billy.

The Williamses could now afford to look for a more modern house, closer to Central London and its cultural attractions. In 1924 they moved into a newly-built, two-bedroom house at 93 Wentworth Road, Golders Green, close to the recently-opened Northern Line tube station. Their new house had the feel of a country cottage, with cosy, small rooms and plenty of open space all around. Dr John Crammer, Gertrude's nephew, recalled his first visit to the house, which had 'a brook at the bottom of the garden, and open fields beyond'.[11] Golders Green was never quite Hampstead, but it was within easy walking distance of the Heath. Later they moved into a more desirable house in Hampstead Garden Suburb.

In the spring of 1926, shortly after Williams' first book was published, Britain's schoolteachers, like everyone else, had their eyes fixed on less literary matters. In March 1926, the country's coal miners rejected the findings of the Samuel Commission Report, recommending the rationalisation of the mining industry into larger units, with some reduction in wages. On 1 May, the miners were faced with a lock-out by the mine owners. On 4 May, the Trades Union Congress set up a Strike Committee in support of the miners, and called one-and-a-half million workers out on strike in support of the miners. The General Strike, which lasted from 4-12 May 1926, threatened to paralyse the national economy, focussing the inherent conflict between workers and bosses in capitalist societies, and dividing families and friends in their loyalties to one side or the other in the conflict.

Billy and Gertrude were in no doubt where their sympathies lay. They were clearly on the side of the miners against the employers and the government, but they seem to have taken no active part in the dispute. The TUC had called out workers in transport, printing, iron and steel, and power, but not schoolteachers or university staff. Within nine days, Britain's first and only General Strike was over. But those tumultuous events proved a radicalising experience for both Billy and Gertrude, as it did for many others on the moderate Left.

Another, more personal, matter must have tinged their life with sadness. After seven years of marriage, Billy and Gertrude remained childless. Was that a matter of choice and conscious decision, or a biological inability to conceive? There is ample evidence to show that they both loved children and enjoyed their company in a family setting. Gertrude's niece, Sylvia Bradford, has recalled the fun and games she enjoyed as a young girl, when visiting her aunt and uncle. Billy was a natural extrovert who went out of his way to ensure that young visitors received their full share of his attention.

Having settled into their respective careers and graduated from comparative penury to moderate comfort, it might seem obvious that this loving couple would wish to start a family of their own. In January 1927, when Gertrude celebrated her thirtieth birthday, there was still time for her to conceive had she wished to do so, and if it were biologically possible. It has been suggested by Robin Huws Jones, who knew her well from those years, that Gertrude may have valued her academic career more highly than having a family of her own.[12] Gertrude was a sophisticated young woman of the 1920s, who understood that she was theoretically free to decide for herself whether or not to start a family. She evidently decided against. Enid Huws Jones, Robin's wife, reported that Gertrude was nonetheless openly envious of her women friends who managed to combine family life with a professional career.[13]

In the 1920s, contraception and infertility were nothing like so well understood as they are today. So the likelihood is that one or other of this loving couple was infertile. If Gertrude had wanted children, she was sufficiently well-informed and self-assured to seek specialist advice on the subject. Whatever advice she received, she seems to have reconciled herself to her situation and got on with her busy life. Outwardly she gave no indication of any special distress. There were, however, some episodes in her later life which suggest that she was never fully reconciled to having no children.

In 1926, after six years of schoolteaching, and the publication of his sixth book, Billy grew restless. Having passed his thirtieth birthday and taken stock of his life, he decided to make a major career move. But in which direction should he turn?

Although Gertrude does not record the fact, Billy had been supplementing his schoolmaster's pay since 1925 by working as an evening class tutor, offering a one-year course in English literature, organised by the Workers Education Association (WEA). In another of his periodic inspirations, he submitted an audacious proposal to the Workers Education Council:

> At that time, when the depression in trade had led to over three million unemployed, the main subject that most students wished to study was economics and its social connections. Billy had to persuade the authorities to allow him to make a very real break by offering three-year courses in English Literature. To the surprise of most people, these courses proved immensely popular. They appealed primarily to those who had been forced by economic circumstances to leave school at the age of fourteen (then the regular leaving age) but whose own predilections or, perhaps, their family background, had led them to become readers of books which they could get from the public library.[14]

Billy's proposal was immediately accepted. In 1928, he was appointed Staff Tutor in English Literature in the Extramural Department of the University of London. That courageous appointment – the first of its kind in Britain – was not merely a turning point in Billy's career. Apart from his marriage to Gertrude, it was probably the most momentous decision he ever made, with profound consequences for him, for adult education, and for popular access to the arts and culture in Britain. For it led to significant consequences unknown to Billy or to anyone else at the time. As one leading reference work perceptively notes: 'The record of his widening and developing influence continued from that date'.[15]

More immediately, Billy faced the task of providing attractive and effective evening classes for his adult students. Gertrude, who herself taught an evening class in economics to a group of adult students, came to the conclusion that 'the whole thing had been misconceived'. She found that her students could not keep up with their demanding reading schedule or attain the standard expected in their written assignments:

> How could it be otherwise? The students were tired from their day's work, the books were too difficult to understand and the students had never had experience in putting their thoughts on paper. My own personal experience was that one had to mark a student as having produced the necessary essay if he was able to offer a sheet containing a few disjointed sentences.[16]

Billy's English Literature classes were evidently much more successful. Students of literature may have been less ideological and less politically motivated than students of economics, many of whom were trade union activists. Billy's approach to his adult students was probably different from Gertrude's more traditional university teaching. She reports that his classes achieved remarkable results:

> I remember one particular class that Billy took whose members were so impressive that we decided to give them further opportunities. We arranged that about a dozen of the best should come to our house in Hampstead Garden Suburb every Tuesday evening for further discussion on a more friendly basis than is possible in a full class. I provided them with beer and sandwiches – as most of them came straight from work – and often a heated and very good discussion went on until the early hours of the morning, even though they knew that by that time they might have a long walk home because public transport had ceased and only a few had bicycles.[17]

The majority of students who attended those discussion groups were not middle-class intellectuals, bank clerks or schoolteachers, but mostly manual and lower-grade clerical workers. The one Gertrude remembered best was a 'tramway conductor'. These were the 'ordinary' people whose imagination was fired up by Billy's talks on the English classics and who soon found themselves caught up in passionate discussion of the latest novel by Virginia Woolf, D H Lawrence or J B Priestley.

In 1929, within a year of his appointment as Staff Tutor in English Literature, Billy was invited to become editor of *Highway*, the monthly journal of adult education, published by the WEA. Billy jumped at the chance to cut his journalistic teeth in the one specialist field of which he had direct experience. He clearly wanted to bring about radical, long overdue changes in the format, content and management of *Highway* itself. But Billy would never have undertaken such additional work without Gertrude's agreement – and without being paid for it.

On 24 October 1929, better known as Black Thursday, after months of extravagant speculation, the New York Stock Market crashed. There was wild selling on Wall Street, followed by economic slump and recession, with massive cut-backs in government education spending on both sides of the Atlantic: not the best time to become editor of a national adult education journal. The December 1929 issue of *Highway* nevertheless carried this important announcement:

> The next issue will appear under the direction of the new Editor, W E Williams. Mr Williams is a staff tutor in Literature in London and has been taking tutorial classes there for the past four years. That his interest in the movement has not been narrowly confined to class work is shown by the fact that Mr Williams is a member of the London WEA District Council and Executive, and of the Executive of the London Branch of the Tutors' Association. He has, moreover, been responsible for organising and helping WEA Dramatic groups in the London area, and the widespread fame of his Summer School revues testifies to his understanding of the lighter side of adult education.[18]

This unexpected pen-portrait of Bill Williams – the lively, versatile, dedicated, good-humoured WEA tutor – seldom emerges from his more serious writing: the ever-inventive Bill Williams who, at the end of an exhausting Summer School, summons the energy and enthusiasm to write and direct a light-hearted entertainment, including sketches which almost certainly had fun at the expense of the tutors, including Billy himself.

In his very first edition of *Highway* for January 1930, Williams made clear that he intended to run the journal 'in the interests of the adult education movement as a whole, and not just those of the Association'. He wanted it to be much more participative, more democratic, and more responsive to its readers' wishes. But he also wanted to take the journal up-market:

> *Highway* is the journal of the movement, and not merely a review of social and literary problems; and I very much want it to be related to the interests of the movement... The WEA is not just a federation of students, but a fellowship of those who believe in education and who wish to make it more and more accessible. It stands above all for the abolition of privilege and of competition in educational systems... I want to provoke opinion and to foster controversy so that we may develop a really vital and constructive influence upon our national educational policy.[19]

Williams somehow persuaded a remarkable collection of luminaries to contribute to *Highway* without paying them much, if anything, for their contributions.[20] Moreover, the schoolteacher and literature specialist, without previous publishing experience, made a financial and critical success of *Highway* without increasing its cover price. He succeeded in part by selling advertising space, offering an exotic range of products and services – from Ruskin College, Oxford, and Cadbury's chocolate, to Pelmanism, 'the mind and memory wizards'. But increased advertising revenues alone cannot explain *Highway's* growing popularity. What brought success was Williams' ability to attract a group of brilliant contributors, who addressed a critical readership with authority but with a lightness of touch, never before seen in the journal. To attract writers such as Ernest Barker, G D H Cole, Olaf Stapleton, R H Tawney and Virginia Woolf, Billy exploited the invaluable network of contacts made during his work as Staff Tutor in Literature at the University of London. It must have taken the full force of his determined personality to secure their active participation. Williams' editorial writing – clear, crisp and totally accessible, with brilliant turns of phrase – put the stamp of quality on the re-invigorated *Highway*. He set and maintained standards of excellence that transformed a prosaic journal into a vibrant and thoroughly readable publication.

In 1934, by another of those twists of fate which marked his whole life, Williams was offered and accepted the full-time post of Secretary of the British Institute of Adult Education (BIAE). That inspired appointment consolidated his position within the adult education movement, enabling him to make vital contacts amongst national education policy-makers, and to bring new vigour and inspirational leadership to the near-moribund Institute. When Williams became its Secretary, the Institute already claimed to be the leading national organisation for the whole of British adult education. In practice, it was a scarcely audible voice in the increasingly clamorous and politicised debate surrounding adult education in the 1920s and '30s – far outstripped, for example, by the more radical and adventurous Plebs League, a Marxist ginger group, which advocated 'independent working-class education'.

There was always something of the missionary in Williams' psyche. In his very first *Highway* editorial, he speaks of 'the movement' and 'the fellowship' of adult students and, above all, of 'the abolition of privilege'. In a much later wartime letter, he confided to Dr Thomas Jones that his true vocation was in adult education, with what he himself called 'the really Common Man' in benighted Britain:

> I may thereby, possibly, fulfil my adolescent desires to be a missionary in Darkest Africa – and fulfil them more usefully than if I had become a colporteur on the Congo![21]

Throughout his work in adult education, Williams came increasingly under the influence of the remarkable Dr Thomas Jones. Here was a man whom he profoundly admired and respected; who combined true intellectual distinction with a highly developed sense of what was politically possible; who had himself abandoned an intended career as a Methodist minister; a sympathetic friend with whom he could share his problems, in whom he could place his trust, on whose sound advice he could always depend, and on whose generous shoulders he could stand. Thomas Jones, or TJ, as he became widely known, was Founder and President of Coleg Harlech, North Wales:

> One of the most remarkable men in Britain in this century; the 14-year-old Welsh clerk who later became the trusted adviser of four very different Prime Ministers, privy to the most confidential business of the state between 1916 and the outbreak of war in 1939... He was a leading figure in the world of education for half a century; he did more to mitigate the ravages of mass unemployment in Britain through his work in the voluntary agencies and by independent initiatives than any other individual; and he inspired many remarkably successful attempts to give music and the arts generally a much wider popular appeal. All these activities, perhaps naturally, were pursued with special vigour and to particular effect in Wales, which was the focus of his strongest loyalty.[22]

A fellow Welshman, equally passionate in his devotion to adult education and the arts, TJ had quickly recognised Williams' talents and did everything in his power to advance his protégé's best interests. At every significant turning-point of his adult life, in every crisis and every triumph, Billy had reason to be grateful for TJ's influential advice and his steadfast friendship. Few young men are able to call on the advice of one of the shrewdest and best-connected men of his generation. Billy exploited that opportunity to the full, never failing to express his appreciation for advice and help given. With the possible exception of Allen Lane at Penguin Books, there was nobody, other than Gertrude, who exerted a more powerful or benign influence on Williams' life and work. Although no substantial evidence has emerged to verify the impression, it seems highly plausible that TJ acted, behind the scenes, in securing the appointment of his protégé as Secretary of the BIAE.

Back in 1924, the British adult education movement had already celebrated its coming of age. But until Williams took over at the BIAE in 1934 and developed the innovative policies which finally put it on the national map, adult education in Britain in the 1920s and '30s was characterised by fragmentation, political in-fighting, and ineffectiveness. Founded in 1903 by two legendary pioneers – R H Tawney and Albert Mansbridge – the Workers Education Association (WEA) had grown from small beginnings to become the country's leading provider of what was then known as 'compensatory' adult education, aimed principally at those who, for various reasons, had missed out on early educational opportunities. Compensatory adult education, later known as 'continuing adult education', has since evolved with changing national needs and fashions into 'lifelong learning'.

At its pre-First World War peak, the WEA could count on some 3,000 regular members. The war saw the catastrophic collapse of its three-year tutorial classes, then the mainstay of the movement, followed by a rapid expansion in the immediate post-war period. By 1919, more than 150 tutorial classes were mounted jointly by the WEA and the Extra-Mural Departments of the more progressive universities. For the first time, the total number of enrolled students exceeded the pre-war peak. That resulted largely from the publication of an influential report of an inquiry into 'Adult Education after the War', chaired by A D Lindsay, Greek scholar and Master of Balliol. There followed the post-war recession, which inflicted massive public expenditure cuts, particularly on all forms of education. The adult education movement was soon threatened with extinction through lack of adequate funding.

In *Highway* for May 1922, an article by Eden and Cedar Paul of the Plebs League exposed the divergent thinking and policies of the WEA and the Plebs:

> The WEA takes for granted the 'fundamental unity' of modern society. It believes 'citizenship' to be a real thing, or at any rate a real possibility, today. We do not wish to be captious, but it seems to be quite content with envisaging a world in which there will

> still be 'rich' and 'poor' provided only the universities are equally accessible to both classes, and are in fact open to all.
>
> The Plebs League holds that 'citizenship' is mythical in the extant form of society which is riven in sunder by the class struggle. For the workers today education can be only a means to an end; a means whereby class struggle can be utilised for the destruction of capitalist society, the overthrow of the power of the master-class, and the establishment of the dominion of the working-class, as steps to the inauguration of a classless society.[23]

In the same issue, Barbara Wootton, the new editor of *Highway*, hit back with a robust leading article – 'Education versus Proletcult' – defending the WEA against this attack from the revolutionary Left:

> When the educational system is organized and administered by representatives of the workers, it will obviously be a different thing and a better thing than it is at present. But the way to bring that consummation nearer is not to cultivate a virtuous isolation from every institution which is touched, directly or indirectly, by 'capitalist' influences, but to follow the course pursued by Labour in other fields of social effort – to win from the existing order all that it can offer – and to work for its transformation.[24]

Those two extracts encapsulate the ideological battle being fought out in the adult education movement between evolutionary and revolutionary socialists. In the winter of 1923, Eden and Cedar Paul launched another fierce attack in *Highway* on what they saw as the lack of political backbone in the WEA. In her self-restrained but astringent response, 'Ourselves and Others', Barbara Wootton indulged in a further bout of critical soul-searching on behalf of the movement:

> The real problem is not a sharp critical struggle of WEA against Plebs... But what we all suffer from at present is anaemia, which is quite the reverse of exhilarating and produces no crisis... We haven't enough people in the working-class movement who are interested enough in educational work of any kind. That's all... Greetings to our new contemporary, *New Standards* [the Plebs journal], which has said of the WEA: "It has no punch, no vigour, no propagandist zeal, no sense of unity" and is run by "a very estimable, but somewhat jaded, bureaucracy of over-worked and ill-paid officials".[25]

That hard-hitting critique was essentially correct: *Highway* reflected the views of more Fabian socialists, middle-of-the-road reformists, who were content to make haste slowly in bringing about the social transformation which they nevertheless claimed to support. From Spring 1925, Barbara Wootton was succeeded as editor of *Highway* by R S Lambert, an educator and journalist, one of Williams' closest allies and collaborators at the BIAE. A leading proponent of educational broadcasting, Ronald Stannard Lambert played a crucial role in encouraging Williams to take the BBC's educational output more seriously, as an ancillary arm of the BIAE. By 1925, the BBC had evolved from a private company to become a public corporation, with

John Reith at the helm, operating under the Broadcasting Act to a Charter that required it 'to inform, educate and entertain' – in that significant order. The Corporation had established a Central Committee for Group Listening, comprising representatives of all the major interests in British adult education, to advise on education broadcasting. In addition, there were Area Councils, to stimulate group listening in their respective regions.

As BIAE representative on the Central Committee, R S Lambert had exercised considerable influence on its policies and become a leading authority in the field. In 1930, whilst visiting the United States, he reported on the growing transatlantic movement to promote discussion or study groups amongst 'wireless listeners'. By then there were already between two and three hundred adult listening groups in Britain, with an average attendance of 25 to 30 in each group. But Lambert warned that such groups were a matter of 'slow experiment' and even slower growth.

In 1929, in his last issue as editor of *Highway*, Lambert, about to take over as first editor of the BBC's new weekly journal *The Listener*, contributed an important article on the future of educational broadcasting:

> To the individual student wireless can be an intellectual tonic; to the class a useful experiment; to the study circle or discussion group it can be an inspiration leading on to all manner of new activities. With a little initiative the enterprising student can help his own WEA branch...by organising a wireless discussion group around a suitable course of talks... It is to be remembered that there is nothing stereotyped about broadcasting, and that there are yet many undiscovered ways of making profitable use of it. Why not be a pioneer in this new field?[26]

Williams succeeded Lambert. His ten-year stint as editor of *Highway*, from 1930 to the outbreak of the war in 1939, gave him his first opportunity for sustained creative writing in the field of adult education. He was always seeking new outlets for his journalistic skills, and was never better as a writer than when working to a tight publishing deadline. Gertrude provides her own account of his apprenticeship to journalism:

> He had no experience either in writing or in producing a journal and he had to teach himself everything from the beginning. Without even a secretary to help him he learned about the layout of pages and how to ensure that the most interesting article should be the first to catch the eye of the reader. Not content with snippets...he began to have long articles on what were then the burning issues of education in general. Most of these articles he wrote himself because it was difficult to persuade others to do it without pay. The circulation went up by leaps and bounds.[27]

Gertrude Williams' memory of this period lets her down, however, when she writes in her memoir:

> All the work he did for *Highway* he did single-handed and it required him to devote to it all his leisure time when he was not actually teaching Tutorial Classes. He gave it up only when he was appointed Secretary of the Institute of Adult Education in 1931 [sic] after which, though it continued to be published, it was never heard of again.[28]

Far from being 'never heard of again', *Highway* achieved major prominence both before and *after* Billy's appointment as Secretary of the BIAE. In October 1934, for example, it re-emerged from a remarkable make-over in a brilliant peacock-blue livery in 9-point Baskerville typeface, claiming no fewer than 14,000 readers. Its contents included an article by Archbishop William Temple on the 'Need for a new culture'; an advertisement for *Adult Education*, a new quarterly for adult students, to be published by the BIAE; a review by Gertrude Williams of Konrad Meiden's *History of National Socialism*; as well as a fascinating review of *The Dorsetshire Labourers, A Play in Two Acts by W E Williams*, adapted from the wireless version by his old friend and collaborator, R S Lambert, and published by the WEA at one shilling and sixpence.

Williams revealed a nice sense of humour in his next editorial, which reported that he was

> ...happy to acknowledge a very widespread approval of the transformation in the appearance of *Highway*. We have received 483 messages of satisfaction and one complaint that we look too 'bourjoys' in our new colour and layout. The dissatisfied correspondent does not debate the issue why the poor should not have the minor pleasures of the better-off. We shall continue to look as nice as we can afford to.[29]

In February 1933, Franklin Delano Roosevelt was inaugurated as 32nd President of the United States, followed shortly by the launch of the New Deal – the Democratic programme for revitalising the ailing American economy with massive government spending, as advocated by John Maynard Keynes. The wider repercussions of the New Deal and its consequences for adult education and State support for the arts on both sides of the Atlantic were incalculable. Those consequences are considered in detail in Chapters 9 and 10.

In 1935 the Institute's Art Education Committee gave its blessing to *Art for the People*, a bold educational experiment, proposed by Williams, to take a travelling exhibition of modern paintings to the outlying areas of Britain. That experiment, discussed at length in Chapter 5, was widely acclaimed as both an artistic and an educational triumph. Williams lost no time in exploiting that success by arranging a further series of exhibitions around the country.

By January 1936, Williams proudly announced that sales of *Highway* had increased from 14,000 to 15,000. In the same issue, he invited students to list their satisfactions and dissatisfactions on joining a WEA class. The quality of responses to that survey encouraged him to undertake the first comprehensive investigation of consumer attitudes to adult education in Britain. The results were published in a BIAE pamphlet *Learn and Live: The Consumer's View of Adult Education* (1936) by W E Williams and A E Heath, Professor of Philosophy at University College, Swansea. Determined to create greater understanding between the providers and consumers of adult education, Williams hammered away at this theme in successive editorials.

The first issue of *Adult Education* appeared in September 1936 with a plea to the membership for their help in deciding the future of the BIAE. In a provocative editorial – 'The Institute: Terminus or Junction?' – Williams spelled out his request in plain language which every WEA member could understand:

> Most of our members know what is going on in adult education and what ought to be going on; and it is their experience and vision which we want them to contribute to the Institute's work.[30]

In another article, using the vivid metaphorical language of the day – *The Storm Troops and the Militia* – Williams initiated a national debate amongst adult educators on how best to reconcile the very different needs of the minority 'storm-troops' of three-year tutorial class students with those of the vast mass or 'militia army' of less able adult education students. He would return to the problem of that reconciliation time and again in his later writings.

In *Highway* for December 1936, Williams published the second of three articles, exploring the pleasures of different kinds of literature in the form of a 'Guide for the General Reader':

> This is the second article of a series whose purpose is to introduce books (other than fiction) which the general reader may have missed. Many of them are the books of yesterday and the day-before-yesterday.[31]

Those articles may well have paved the way for another much later example of Williams' flair for popularising high culture. During his time as Editor-in-Chief of Penguin Books, Williams produced *The Reader's Guide* (1960) – a literary guide for the perplexed on what books to read over a wide range of specialist subjects. He never passed up the opportunity of publicising his connection with Penguin Books, when the time was right. Under the heading *A Wonderful Bird is the Pelican* – Williams' witty variant of the familiar Guinness 'toucan' advertisement – *Adult Education* for June 1937 announced the launch by Penguin Books of Pelicans ('a high-browed Penguin') and another important publicity coup for the Institute:

> It is a venture which deserves to repeat on a different plane the brilliant success of the Penguins; and it ought to get the backing of the thousands of people concerned with or

> about the education of an intelligent democracy. It is pleasant to see that the Institute has a prominent part in the hatching of the Pelicans, for the triumvirate of Advisory Editors includes Mr W E Williams, Secretary of the Institute and Mr H L Beales, a member of the Institute Executive. The third is Sir Peter Chalmers-Mitchell... If the Pelicans can fulfil the promise to bring out modern classics in batches of ten at a time they will become as memorable a bird as Minerva's owl.[32]

In September 1938, *Adult Education* announced that the Institute had established a new high-powered committee 'to consider the adequacy of provision of understanding of art and the prospects for a Popular Art Trust'. The work of that committee later proved a crucial influence on the formation of the Committee for the Encouragement of Music and the Arts (CEMA) at the outbreak of war, examined at length in Chapter 9.

Although the Institute's work mainly centred on the United Kingdom, it also monitored developments abroad and maintained close contacts with corresponding organisations around the world. The international dimension of the Institute's work is reflected in a 1938 book on *Adult Education in GB and the USA, a symposium arranged by W E Williams* – the first major comparative study of adult education in these two countries. In his chapter on provision in Great Britain – 'The Changing Map of Adult Education' – Williams insisted that he was providing only a sketch-map of

> ...the complicated territory which now claims to be adult education, and, to indicate how the newer provinces have grown by a sort of imperial-expansion process, from the small compact movement which adult education was thirty years ago.[33]

The reference to 'a sort of imperial-expansion process' appears to reflect Williams' two-fold interest – first, in spreading the gospel of adult education but second, in developing potentially lucrative markets for both Penguin and Pelican Books throughout the English-speaking world. The chapter encapsulated Williams' keen reflections on his own experience of twenty years of adult education in Britain and his thinking on its ultimate function and purpose:

> It can be said that the main traditional motive of adult education in this country has been the motive of compensation...that vast numbers of the educationally under-privileged ought to be given a second chance, however late, to make up for the opportunities of which they have been deprived by an educational system which at no time has been based upon equal opportunity.[34]

There is nothing remarkable in Williams' commitment to the 'under-privileged' or his attack on unequal educational opportunity. The familiar aspirational language of the 1930s continues to resonate in the so-called 'inclusion' agenda in Britain, more than seventy years later. Having committed himself to the cause, Williams went on to make clear that equality did not mean uniformity – for some students were better equipped than others to take advantage of such educational opportunities:

> Why do we cling to the sentimental fiction that in a democracy there is not only political equality, but also equality of intellectual interest and ability? Why do we retain in University Tutorial Classes, for example, some students who have not yet mastered the alphabet of thought or expression? Equality of opportunity is one thing; equality of intellectual fitness is another... A far more thorough discrimination than we at present practise is needed if we are to attain the standard of intellectual discussion and discovery that the WEA has set itself. We are not taking this standard as seriously as we should.[35]

He followed that with a powerful defence of WEA Tutorial Classes which had come in for strong criticism in the mid-1930s from some adult education tutors, including Gertrude Williams, who protested that such classes were elitist – too academic, too demanding, too far removed from the expressed needs of a working-class membership. Williams set about their defence with characteristic relish:

> There are some who looked to adult education to create a brave new world in one generation, and are inclined to underrate any system which fails to enrol big battalions. But among the few things in this world which cannot be created by mass production is an educated community or a dependable political electorate. Nor is a short superficial educational clean-up in adult years going to put right the mischief already wrought by the imperfect and misdirected ideals which still prevail in our primary school system... There is certainly no need to be disappointed with this spearhead of adult education – the three-year Tutorial Class. The grain-of-mustard-seed principle is more dependable than the beanstalk principle. Only a few thousand each year accept the exacting and intensive study of a tutorial class; yet this student aristocracy, impressing itself on those among whom it lives and works and plays, goes a long way to produce and lead an enlightened community... If the great rank and file of the army of democracy lacks the equipment and endurance for the systematic and intensive system of education, then the next best thing is to see that we create a keen and determined group of NCOs [Non-Commissioned Officers]. And that is precisely what the Tutorial Class system can claim to be doing. It is not a system that will ever appeal to the rank and file of the working class, or any other class for that matter; but it has already created the sergeants who can keep that army steady in the face of cross-fire from the extreme right or the extreme left.[36]

In that extended quotation, we come close to the heart of Williams' thoughts and feelings on his missionary role in adult education, a theme to which he often returned, both during and after the war. As a statement of the aims and the methods advocated by those committed to lifelong learning it could hardly be bettered: 'The grain-of-mustard-seed principle is more dependable than the beanstalk principle'. Williams' adaptation of the biblical metaphor still seems relevant to those committed to lifelong learning. But it is significant for several other reasons: first, it reflects the pervasive influence of his earlier theological training; second, it exactly matches his adherence to evolutionary rather than revolutionary politics; and third, it is a principle to which he repeatedly returns and develops in his later writings. It may also help explain some aspects of his alleged conservatism in administering the Arts Council in the post-war decade. Where others expected mushroom growth, Williams was content to cultivate the mustard-seed.

His chapter on 'The Changing Map of Adult Education' appeared in a book published in 1938 – the year of the Munich Crisis and the phoney agreement between Prime Minister Chamberlain and Adolf Hitler. A European war was almost certainly imminent. Williams deployed military metaphors that reflected the preoccupations of the time. The newspapers and newsreels of the day were filled with images of steel-helmeted, jack-booted Nazi troops, goose-stepping into Czechoslovakia.

Adult Education for June 1939 announced that 'The Carnegie Corporation of New York is conducting in the United States a comprehensive inquiry into such forms of wireless education as Group Listening; and the investigation at the European end is being done at the British Institute [of Adult Education]'. Whether the original inspiration for that project came from the BIAE or from the US Federal Radio Education Committee, Bill Williams worked closely with the BBC in collecting data and writing up the findings of the British field study, whilst his collaborator, F E Hills, took charge of the American end of the research.

Williams was immersed in that project during the summer and autumn of 1939. On 1 September, the German army marched into Poland. Two days later Britain was at war. Given his vast additional workload during the war, it is remarkable that Williams found time and energy to complete the British end of the research by April 1940. Final editing was left to Columbia University Press which published the results as *Radio's Listening Groups: The United States and Great Britain* by F E Hills and W E Williams (1941).

That international comparative research yielded valuable insights into listeners' perception of educational programmes at a critical moment in broadcasting history. In his summary of the British evidence, Williams concluded that group listening was not a panacea but 'only one of a bunch of informal and elementary activities [which] can provide an effective approach to more serious modes of study'.[37] He was in no doubt that 'group listening is often a most exhilarating and illuminating experience'. Having noted with approval the 'massive organization and impressive expenditure by which this movement has been sustained by the BBC', Williams – already an experienced broadcaster and heavily involved in promoting educational broadcasting – pointed out that, if other aspects of adult education had been given the same 'expensive and continuous blood transfusions, their rate of progress would certainly have been more notable'.[38]

In his Introduction to the book, Dr Levering Tyson of the Federal Radio Education Committee singled out one paragraph by Williams as containing 'the most interesting comment' on group listening:

> In some of the most experienced and reliable quarters of adult education there is a reaction against that glorification of discussion which had become a fetish of adult education. There is a kind of discussion which awards prematurely the privilege of an opinion, and which is an impediment rather than an approach to knowledge. The indispensable necessities for effective discussion are that it should be led and directed by someone of incontestable authority, and that it should be based on some preliminary knowledge of the subject. If these conditions are absent, discussion degenerates into a vain beating of the air; it can even have the baneful effect of loosening the toe hold which a thoughtful student is beginning to get on the subject, and thus disorganizing his entire interest and attention.[39]

It would be difficult to improve on that account of the essential pre-conditions for effective adult education through discussion methodology. Williams' views were not theoretical abstractions: they sprang from his personal experience of leading discussions over many years in his Tutorial Classes in English literature. He could not have known, however, that his prescription of 'the indispensable necessities for effective discussion' would be of crucial importance in his future wartime work. The well-led, well-informed, platoon discussion group was to be one of Williams' key recommendations to the War Office in his plan for maintaining military morale during the Second World War. As Director of the Army Bureau of Current Affairs (ABCA – or 'Arguing By Comparing Answers' as he once called it), he insisted that every company commander must lead his troops in a discussion of Allied war aims, and how they were to be accomplished. The use and value of ABCA discussion groups is analysed at length in Chapter 8.

By the late 1930s, Williams' work at the BIAE had established his reputation as one of the most significant figures within British adult education. He had worked tirelessly to unite the disparate political elements within the adult education movement. He had provided clear and courageous leadership. A brilliant campaigning journalist and publicist through his editorship of *Highway* and *Adult Education*, he had commissioned and participated in serious research on adult education. He had stumped the country, instigating, supporting and co-ordinating local education initiatives. He had written, broadcast and addressed countless education meetings. He had organised and taken part in annual education conferences. He had set up and served on many high-powered education committees. He had written or edited several books directly relevant to the work of the Institute. In short, Williams was an educational force to be reckoned with. Yet there were senior civil servants at the Board of Education in Whitehall who were still sceptical of the Institute's achievements:

> The truth is that in the opinion of our Inspectors the BIAE has not succeeded in fulfilling the functions it set out to perform, and cannot as yet be said to be generally accepted as representing the Adult Education Bodies or to have won their full confidence. Indeed the failure of the British Institute to make good has caused concern to the Cassell Trustees who gave it fairly substantial grants. I understand that recently total withdrawal of grant was considered although in the end a reduced grant was continued.[40]

Williams must have been made aware of that negative view within the Board of Education. Whether he took any corrective action is not clear. It is difficult to see what more he might have done to impress the President and the Board. He was 43 years old, intellectually vigorous and physically energetic. He had completed twenty-years' devoted work in adult education and was at the very peak of his powers. With the outbreak of war, the time had come for him to take stock of his career and to discover a more effective way of serving his country. Within weeks, he received an urgent, irresistible summons from Dr Thomas Jones that would provide him with just such an opportunity. We shall explore the outcome and consequences of that summons in Chapter 8 on the Army Bureau of Current Affairs.

The end of another WEA Summer School. Williams as tutor (fourth from right, second row), 1920s.

Five: Art for the People

Long before the Council came into being, Sir William Emrys Williams gave himself to the promotion of general interest in spreading the riches of the world of art, in making it possible for ordinary people to share in the privileges of the few.

Wyn Griffith, Arts Council Annual Report, *1963*

Imagine yourself a young person or mature adult in 1930s Britain, with a serious interest in the arts. You live in any one of ten thousand towns or villages, some distance from the nearest sizeable city. How do you begin to explore great works of literature, music, painting and sculpture? Your appetite for literature has been whetted at school, or stimulated by your local library. You've seen some colour reproductions of Impressionist paintings. You listen regularly to the BBC's weekly broadcast talks on classical music by Sir Walford Davies, Master of the King's Musick, and have heard relays of the Henry Wood Promenade Concerts from London's Queen's Hall. But where do you experience the tingle of live music, the excitement of an original painting, and the dramatic face-to-face encounter with modern sculpture?

In the 1930s, most of Britain's museums and art galleries were concentrated in a handful of cities: London, Birmingham, Manchester, Liverpool, Glasgow, Edinburgh and Cardiff. Most of those galleries were established in the 19th century, often based on major bequests, and maintained by slender Treasury grants. City dwellers therefore had many opportunities of seeing good examples of traditional and modern painting and sculpture in municipal galleries. But what of those living outside the larger cities? Art galleries in Britain's smaller towns and villages were few and far between. How would those living in such places ever come to enjoy art whilst they lacked the opportunity of seeing any?

In 1934, his first year as Secretary of the BIAE, Williams had another of those timely inspirations which allowed him to increase popular access to the arts and to advance British cultural history. For many years, he had shared his enthusiasm for literature with students from humble backgrounds. Rightly or wrongly, that experience led him to conclude that only a small minority of 'ordinary people' would be attracted to the canon of high quality literature. If that was true for literature, it was even truer for the visual arts. Did that mean nothing could – or should – be done for the minority?

In May 1934, Professor W G Constable, Director of the Courtauld Institute, presented a paper on 'Art and Adult Education' at a BIAE conference. Having noted the capacity of adult students to appreciate and enjoy art, he insisted that certain preconditions must be met:

> Nothing can replace direct contact with works of art themselves. It is one of a teacher's first duties to get his students to visit and revisit every kind of fine building, gallery, museum and exhibition. Local art galleries and museums in England are often dull and dreary places, but there is a new spirit abroad, and I know that the curators of most of such institutions would welcome demands for help and co-operation. The local art gallery is beginning to realize the possibility of special exhibitions, and of borrowing from wealthier centres. If those interested in education will indicate clearly what they want, and agitate to get it, they will immensely strengthen the hands of those who are anxious to provide it.[1]

Williams not only published Professor Constable's paper in full in *Adult Education*: he decided to act on those recommendations. He shared the view that many more 'ordinary people' could enjoy the fine arts, *provided* they had sympathetic advisors to show them what to look for, and *provided* they had much freer and wider access to the arts. If the people living in Britain's smaller towns and villages were unable or unwilling to travel to larger cities to see good examples of fine art, then fine art must be taken to the people.

At a meeting of the Institute's Art Education Committee in July 1934, Williams proposed that it should mount a small, experimental exhibition of paintings and drawings in three small English country towns which lacked an art gallery. Since nothing of the kind had ever been attempted before, the proposal represented a significant financial and critical risk for the Institute. The Committee blessed the proposal, taking care to ensure that its motives were not misunderstood:

> The Committee wish to emphasize that this experiment is intended as a definite piece of adult education. Its purpose is not to foist an artificial sense of 'good taste' upon people, but to give them the opportunity of making up their own minds about the pictures they like and of formulating a set of independent opinions about them. Its predominant aim, we repeat, is to give people who seldom see a good picture the chance to see a selection of the best that can be got together.[2]

'Good taste' here is a highly problematic term – hence its enclosure in inverted commas. 'A good picture' on the other hand is a transparent term, here commended as being amongst 'the best that can be got together'. The hand of Bill Williams is clearly visible behind the Committee's statement. His intention is to stimulate the habit of looking at painting and sculpture and so to develop more critical faculties amongst viewers. The first three centres chosen were the mining town of Barnsley in Yorkshire, Swindon in Wiltshire, and Silver End, a village near Braintree in Essex. Each exhibition comprised between 60 and 70 paintings and drawings, carefully selected from English artists of the 18th and 19th centuries, and from 20th century French and English sources, including the Impressionist and Post-Impressionist schools. The works to be displayed were loaned by a number of private individuals, notably Sir Michael Sadler, a well-known art collector, and by the Courtauld Institute in London. Each exhibition lasted one month, with free access not only for adults but also for parties of school children.

In a later issue of *The Listener*, Williams elaborated his motives in creating *Art for the People*:

> If it is true, and I am afraid that it is, that standards of taste are poor in England, then one reason, I am certain, is that we get such few chances to see and understand good examples of art. The appetite for art, like other appetites, grows by what it feeds on… For thousands of those who see good pictures it is just a local attraction like the flower show or the crowning of the beauty queen. But there are hundreds who take it more seriously. It sets their ideas about art fermenting… We are trying to open people's eyes to the pleasures of art. If we can keep it up on a large enough scale, we shall one day make you tired of those pictures in the room where you are now sitting.[3]

Williams was offering ordinary people the opportunity of looking at a wider range of 'good pictures'; not too many people at a time, not too many pictures – and nothing too avant-garde. Visitors were not simply thrown in at the deep end and left struggling for comprehension. On one or two evenings each week, informal talks on the pictures were given by leading art experts. The Institute also provided a number of trained observers, who answered visitors' questions and sought their reaction to the pictures. Four specific questions were asked: Which pictures do you like best? Why do you like them? What opportunities do you get to visit art galleries or exhibitions? In what ways do you think these opportunities could be increased or improved?

Visitor responses were collated, analysed and published by the Institute, attracting much favourable attention. Cultural commentators judged the experiment an unqualified success. It stimulated widespread comment and provoked much discussion in the press and on the wireless about the place of art in modern society and the adequacy of current provision. More than 10,000 adults and an equal number of school children visited the first three exhibitions. Completed questionnaires showed that most visitors favoured representational pictures, but there was also favourable comment on some modern works. Asked to explain their preferences, most visitors said the test they applied to a picture was whether they felt 'they could live with it'.

In May 1938, the Institute announced plans to expand its provision of facilities for art education, including *Art for the People*. The work of the Institute's Art Education Committee would be guided in future by a new high-powered Steering Committee, comprising a list of distinguished art experts, including John Rothenstein, Director of the Tate Gallery and Kenneth Clark, Director of the National Gallery.[4] Funding for the initial experiment, and for its extension, was provided by the York Trust, whose Chairman was the influential and ubiquitous Dr Thomas Jones.

As its name implies, *Art for the People* was partly ideological and partly practical. Williams insisted that adult education need not be confined to the dusty lecture hall or the stuffy classroom. Education was lifelong, multi-dimensional and co-extensive with the whole range of intellectual and aesthetic enquiry and enjoyment. That view derived from his own experience of growing up in the vibrant artistic culture of Manchester in the years before the First World War, and the communitarian values imbibed during his Congregationalist upbringing. Before his family moved to Manchester, he had never visited an art gallery or come under the spell of great works of art – certainly not the more audacious and exciting works of modern art he first encountered in Manchester. He now wanted others to enjoy a similar experience.

In his pamphlet on *The Auxiliaries of Adult Education* (1934), Williams provided an explicit account of how he had come upon his idea of *Art for the People*:

> There is a disposition now showing itself in the Tutorial class movement [of the WEA] to put more emphasis on a training in aesthetics, and to attempt a few Tutorial Classes on aesthetic appreciation. I speak as one who has been a "barker" in this new line of appeal. I have set up my stall at a Saturday school, equipped with a few sample portfolios – a couple of Corots, a Van Gogh or two and a Paul Nash – and have spent an hour suggesting what we ought to look for in pictures or developing a simple study of comparative values. It is a talk which goes down well. It is simple, novel and human; and it has the immense attraction of being in pictorial form. But one swallow doesn't make a summer.

Williams then developed his argument with an elaborate but striking metaphor:

> Adult education is a sort of swimming-pool. And we who provide it are inclined to forget that there is a shallow end as well as a ten-foot end. We stand by and watch the novice plunging out of his depth, and we even encourage him in such hazardous behaviour. Most of those with whom we have to deal are shallow-enders. The ten-foot-enders and the high divers must have all the room and all the apparatus they need; but they will always be a minority. Meanwhile there are in the modern community vast numbers of spectators who are reluctant even to paddle. The most immediate and pressing need in adult education is to turn the spectators into shallow-enders. The deliberate homeliness of this metaphor may itself serve to remind us of the need to think of adult education in terms of greater realism and simplicity than we often do.[5]

That metaphor – no doubt inspired by the boom in swimming pools and open-air 'lidos' in the 1930s – is important for revealing Williams' thinking throughout his work in adult education. He distinguishes the fearless minority, prepared to take the plunge at the deep end of their subject, from the majority, splashing about in the shallows. But his chief concern is to encourage passive spectators to shed their inhibitions and become active participants. Williams had a second, more pragmatic, motive with *Art for the People*: to show the hidden appetite for art amongst ordinary people, some of whom might well be tempted to enrol in an adult education class on art appreciation.

Williams' initial experiment with *Art for the People* exhibitions was an outstanding success. It was quickly followed by further circulating exhibitions at Sawston, Kendall, Harlech, Canterbury, Accrington, Wigan, Morecambe, Blackburn, and St Helen's. Those exhibitions attracted further favourable publicity and led, in the late thirties, to the emergence of a national movement for the promotion of wider access to the arts throughout Britain.

The outbreak of war in September 1939 soon led to the creation of the Committee (later the Council) for the Encouragement of Music and the Arts in Wartime (CEMA), to be discussed at length in Chapter 9. Williams' modest experiment with *Art for the People* provided the crucial evidence needed to persuade CEMA to promote a vast expansion of the Institute's circulating exhibitions of paintings, drawings and sculpture in wartime Britain. Williams was an enthusiastic founder member of CEMA. In addition to his duties at the War Office, he served throughout the war as Secretary of CEMA's Art Panel, enjoying virtual autonomy and taking full responsibility for arranging and supervising a highly popular and successful series of circulating art exhibitions.

As an introduction to those wartime exhibitions, Williams produced a pamphlet, clarifying his reasons for promoting popular access to the visual arts, in war and peace:

> By taking art to towns where there is little or no provision for any kind of leisure occupation a section of the public can be reached which has hitherto hardly been touched... The housekeeper, the shopkeeper, the clerk and the artisan, the docker and the heavy labourer, these as well as the small "intelligentsia" who inhabit the fringe of such work-a-day towns are the people whose reactions are being sought. The implications of this work have become immense, and point clearly to the need for a revival of creative interest in the machine-sated mentality of the average man... But in the desert of bricks and mortar, typical of the major part of our "industrial areas", even this is frustrated and points to the urgent need for the establishment of some sort of centre equivalent to the Public Library and Art Gallery, where not only are there reading rooms and picture galleries,

> but workshops, studios and common-rooms where people can meet to use their hands and minds in some form of creative activity. "Morale" is not only a weapon of war, it is an essential adjunct of peace... One way and another "Art for the People" is constantly extending its range of appeal even in the midst of war.[6]

Where had Williams derived the idea of *Art for the People*? Did it spring from his earlier work in taking literature to the people? Or had the idea emerged from his fruitful contacts with intellectuals in other fields of mass culture? Williams was a political animal, already deeply immersed in British cultural politics. He was also a close observer of cultural developments in other countries. In the United States, President Roosevelt's New Deal had launched a highly ambitious and wide-ranging programme for revitalising the depressed American economy through deficit financing, as recommended by John Maynard Keynes. Thousands of unemployed artists and writers had been taken on to the federal payroll and been given useful work – painting murals, decorating buildings, designing posters and so on – allowing them to play their part in helping to revive the flagging US economy. By contrast, in Fascist Italy, Nazi Germany, Falangist Spain and the Soviet Union, the State had assumed the dominant role, directing the work of artists in support of ideological objectives. In Britain, throughout the inter-war period, the State took an altogether more detached view of the role of the artist in society. Had Williams derived his ideas on *Art for the People* from the Roosevelt New Deal, from the Soviet Union, or from elsewhere?

In April 1930, D H Lawrence had contributed a controversial article to the fashionable magazine *Vanity Fair*. He argued that, whilst most people love pictures and would prefer to have good works of art hanging on their walls, most of us simply lack the opportunity to see good modern works of art:

> Contemporary art belongs to contemporary society. Society at large needs the pictures of its contemporaries, just as it needs the books. Modern people read modern books. But they hang up pictures that belong to no age whatever, and have no life, and have no meaning, but are mere blotches of deadness on the walls... It has no clue to the whole unnatural business of modern art, and is just hostile... The only way to keep the public in touch with art is to let it get hold of works of art... The great reading public came into being with the lending library. And the great picture-loving public would come into being with the lending *pictuary*. The public wants pictures hard enough. But it simply can't get hold of them.[7]

We know that Williams was keenly interested in Lawrence as a major literary talent. He was strongly influenced by Lawrence's ideas on modern literature. He had written enthusiastic reviews of Lawrence's early novels and poetry and went on later to edit an anthology of Lawrence's poetry for Penguin Books. If the Lawrence article was brought to his attention, Williams must have been delighted to discover that his literary hero shared his thinking on the role of art in contemporary society. But the person who probably shaped his thinking most on *Art for the People* was his friend and mentor, Dr Thomas Jones. It was the York Trust, under TJ's guidance, that provided indispensable financial support for the first five years of the circulating exhibition scheme.

Mural paintings in wartime British Restaurants offer another example of Williams' efforts to make art accessible to 'ordinary people' in unconventional settings. In July 1942, in an editorial on *Art and the People, The Listener* warmly commended the scheme, instigated by Williams, and carried out by Lady Jane Clark [wife of Sir Kenneth Clark] on behalf of CEMA. Leading British artists, including Paul Nash, Graham Sutherland, Vanessa Bell and Duncan Grant, had agreed to decorate the walls of several British Restaurants with large, cheerful, mural paintings. One source records that no fewer than thirty of those popular restaurants in Greater London were decorated during the war.[8]

A more colourful, though perhaps less accurate, account of the initiative is provided by Kenneth Clark in his recollection of the wartime spirit of gritty improvisation:

> Somebody [W E Williams] had the idea that [British Restaurants] might be more successful if they were attractively decorated, and asked Jane [Clark] to undertake the task for Greater London. Whatever had been meant by 'decorated', Jane used it as a pretext for employing artists on large schemes of mural painting. I remember Duncan Grant and Vanessa Bell did an enchanting series of 'murals' in North London telling the story of Cinderella, which was brilliantly opened by Maynard Keynes. I don't doubt that they were destroyed long ago. John Piper decorated a derelict church in South London... There were many other such schemes of mural painting, which I have forgotten. How shameful it seems, in retrospect, that we kept no record of them, and did not think of having them photographed. It is a very minor example of how difficult it was to think beyond the end of the war.[9]

Lord Clark's final comment reveals a selective memory of those wartime days. As early as 1941, the Dartington Hall Trustees were already thinking well beyond the end of the war. Under Leonard Elmore's leadership, they acted on an idea, originally proposed by Christopher Martin, for a major enquiry into the state of the arts in Britain, with recommendations for any changes that might be needed in the period of post-war reconstruction. The Arts Enquiry Steering Committee, chaired jointly by Julian Huxley and Christopher Martin, included some of the most familiar names in British cultural circles: Mary Glasgow, R S Lambert, H L Beales, Eric Newton and others. The reports of the Enquiry's four working parties – on The Visual Arts, Music, The Theatre and The Documentary Film – were published by Political and

Economic Planning (PEP) in conjunction with the Office of the Minister for Reconstruction at various times between 1946 and 1949.[10]

Art for the People was entirely Williams' creation and achievement. For him, it was an idea whose time had come. The pre-conditions were already in place for a courageous experiment in 'exposing' Britain's working people to the 'unaccustomed experience of looking at pictures'. Just as they had been denied equality of opportunity for intellectual and vocational development, so they had been virtually excluded from pleasurable encounters with the arts. Some had been 'exposed' to classical music – for example, through the BBC's popular broadcast talks on music; others had learned to enjoy good books through English Literature classes of the kind run by Williams for the WEA. But the vast majority had not been similarly encouraged to attend to the visual arts. British culture has always been predominantly literary, with the visual arts held in lower esteem than either literature or music.

Williams' recognition of the essential need – in all walks of life – for a nucleus of well-trained, well-informed and 'dependable' non-commissioned officers is matched by his concern for 'the great rank and file of the army of democracy' or 'the rank and file of the working class'. He repeatedly hammered home that theme which was at the heart of his thinking about adult education. It underlines his personal philosophy on the meaning and nature of 'lifelong learning' in advanced democracies. Education *alone* can never be relied upon to transform the lives of the masses. But that should never deter us from making education freely available to those who can benefit. The fact that we cannot do *everything* should not deflect us from doing *something*, however imperfect or incomplete. What can be done, *must* be done.

The need to balance the different needs of a well-informed cultural elite against those of the mass of less well-informed citizens is found throughout Williams' mature thinking and writing. It is possible to argue that, with the growing threat of war in the late 1930s, Williams' mind was already formulating the ambition that 'the great rank and file of the army of democracy' could be somehow enrolled into a mass 'adult educational programme'. When war finally came, he succeeded in establishing the Army Bureau of Current Affairs (ABCA) – to ensure that every fighting man and woman understood why Britain was at war. British troops must be informed of how the war was progressing on all fronts; and they must be encouraged to think about post-war reconstruction. A citizen army must be engaged in sustained discussion on the issues underlying a more democratic post-war society.[11] Although Williams created ABCA in response to the Army Council's call for advice on how to maintain army morale, he also exploited that opportunity to spread the gospel of cultural democracy. *Art for the People* is a prime example of Williams' philosophy of cultural democracy in action.

But how much did Williams know about art? He obviously knew less about the visual arts than he did about literature, drama or broadcasting. He was, after all, an experienced practitioner in those essentially literary forms. How much did he care personally about the other arts? How important were paintings and sculpture in his own life? And why was he apparently so keen to promote modern art? He organised, for example, a special 'Moore-Piper-Sutherland exhibition, arranged for more sophisticated centres' in his *Art for the People* scheme.

Williams clearly favoured a fresh, uninhibited approach to the arts in general: witness his remarks on cinema and the modern novel in his critical reviews in *Highway*. Yet we know very little about his commitment to the more abstract experimental paintings that emerged from leading artists during the inter-war years. But what was his attitude to modern music? In all his writings, and in all his voluminous reviews of broadcasting, there is never more than a passing reference to either classical or modern music. The names of the great composers did not spring readily to his mind, as did the names of great writers, or great painters. His wartime reviews in *The Listener* frequently referred to the 'musical qualities' of a broadcast voice when discussing good microphone technique. He hated background music that intruded on the spoken word. But he never embarked on a discussion of the technicalities of musical composition or performance. Some accounts suggest that he enjoyed listening to music; others imply that he may have had a 'tin ear', despite having been brought up in musical Wales. In later years, as Secretary-General, he had free access to the Arts Council box at Covent Garden. But his appearances at the opera seem to have been more of a social occasion than a source of genuine musical pleasure. He may have enjoyed music of the lighter or more familiar kind, but he evidently knew too little about the grammar and syntax of music to offer his uninformed views on the subject. In short, Williams knew when to speak out – but also when to remain silent.

When dealing with the visual arts it was quite another story – though here again, Williams tended to speak as an enthusiastic amateur, playing down his own expertise:

> Where a little learning is dangerous, and this is too often proved by the man who thinks he knows "a bit about art", a desire to know and an enthusiasm for more is all important.[12]

That 'desire to know' – that 'enthusiasm for more' of the visual arts – surfaced amongst 'ordinary people' throughout Britain during the Second World War, thanks largely to CEMA's unstinting support for Williams' circulating exhibitions. With more regular access, people had started to look seriously at works of art. They began to cultivate the art of seeing. They wanted, and expected, to find art in the most unlikely places. One piece of anecdotal evidence of that appetite for art appeared in a letter, published in *The Listener* for 27 April 1944. Although an isolated example, that letter – from an 'ordinary' member of the public – seems to encapsulate the beneficial outcomes of Williams' work over ten years with *Art for the People*:

> **Categories in Art**
>
> I'm a nobody, just one of the great British public, whom these discussions on art and literature are intended to benefit. Still I do want to say that it can't be done – this categorising of art – if it is to live. As soon as it is done – all pictures put into one or another class and hung in a gallery specially built to receive them – then a mausoleum has been made and the pictures are decently interred by the municipal authorities.
>
> Yet collections there must be in some shape or form. CEMA has done a great deal to renew the public interest in pictures. Their small travelling collections give great pleasure. I personally never miss one in Bristol. I always think the few pictures in the foyer of the Theatre Royal, Bristol, are displayed in just the right way, for, after all, the correct place for a picture is where men pass, it is man's work for man to see. If I were one of the great ones I'd have pictures everywhere. In the communal feeding centres, cafes, shops, schools, even pubs and clinics. In the latter I wouldn't have 'Little Children in Many Lands' series, nor even the Infanta Margarita Teresa in red, blue or green; I'd have fully-blooded romantic pictures like Blake's that would take the mother's minds off their duties for a second or two and make them wonder. I'd give them fresh landscape pictures with lots of clouds, and sunshine over grass and hills. Most especially would I have pictures in the home. This is the place for them, where we can live with them intimately and build their beauties into our family life.[13]

Williams was a regular contributor to *The Listener*. He must have read that letter. 'If I were one of the great ones, I'd have pictures everywhere.' That single sentence must have rejoiced Williams' heart, making all his efforts to promote *Art for the People* seem infinitely worthwhile.

Allen Lane and William Emrys Williams, 1960s.

Six:
Penguin Books

Penguin's [sic] is the most constructive and exciting job I know, or am ever likely to know – it's my permanent love.

W E Williams to Allen Lane, 10 September 1948

'We first met, I think it must have been early in 1936', wrote Allen Lane to Bill Williams, some thirty years later.[1] Although its exact date is unknown, no other meeting in their long working lives was more momentous for either man. Without Williams' consistently wise and dependable advice, and his acute literary judgement over thirty years, Lane would not have enjoyed his brilliant critical and commercial success with Penguin Books. Allen Lane invented Penguin Books but, in a very real sense, Williams was the man who made Penguin Books successful. Without the *kudos* of being Editor-in-Chief of Penguin Books, Williams would not have gained the self-confidence that eventually took him to the very top of the British cultural establishment. Like the partnership of W S Gilbert and Sir Arthur Sullivan, or of George and Ira Gershwin, it would be difficult to overstate the interdependence of Allen Lane and W E Williams.

In 1935, when he launched Penguin Books, Lane was an astute and ambitious young businessman who knew a good deal about publishing but almost nothing about literature. He made no secret of the fact that he was simply planning to publish reprints of high quality books. For Lane, books were commodities and therefore the potential source of profit. In his recent biography, Jeremy Lewis records that when the young Allen Lane consulted Kate Murray, a Golders Green astrologer, about his future career, she was remarkably perceptive: 'You seem to need the stimulation of another person's mind and character to do your work'.[2] The man who supplied that mind and character was W E Williams. In the words of another authority: 'A man of limited intellectual stature himself, [Allen Lane] is remembered for his commercial sense and his wise judgment in surrounding himself with intellectuals of great ability'.[3]

Williams knew nothing about business, but was well versed in literary and cultural matters. For Williams, the crucial social and political issue of the inter-war period was cultural democracy, which aimed at providing more equal opportunities for lifelong learning and easier access to the arts for all. Educational opportunity had transformed Williams' own life. It had opened his mind to the stimulating world of ideas, to the healing power of the arts, and to his own cultural and intellectual heritage. Just as science helps us to make sense of the natural world's complexities, so the arts help us to transcend the banalities, the disappointments and the pain of everyday life. Lifelong learning keeps us intellectually alive and the arts help to integrate our lives emotionally – hence the imperative to extend cultural democracy.

For Williams, an outstanding advocate and practitioner of lifelong learning, cultural democracy was more than a personal credo: it was his evangelical mission, his life's work. It dominated his thought, directed his career, and led him to invest all his talents in education, writing and the arts. His early experience as schoolteacher, adult educator and educational administrator stood him in excellent stead during and after the Second World War when he helped to create CEMA; when he directed the Army Bureau of Current Affairs; when he converted ABCA into the post-war Bureau of Current Affairs; and when he later headed the Arts Council of Great Britain. Yet in none of those fields did his personality exert such a powerful or sustained influence on British society as it did with Penguin Books. Without exaggeration it may be said that Williams changed the reading habits and filled the bookshelves of a whole generation. His contribution to the success of the Penguin enterprise cannot, therefore, be overestimated. That claim cannot be assessed without first considering his personal contribution to Allen Lane's decision to take Penguin Books upmarket:

> My idea was to produce a book which would sell at the price of ten cigarettes, which would give no excuse for anybody not being able to buy it, and would be the type of book which they would get if they had gone on to further education. For people like myself who left school and started work when they were 16 it would be another form of education... When we started we only published fiction and biographies and travel and detective fiction, but after a couple of years we realized there was a very great field outside those subjects, and that is when we started Pelicans, which we devoted to the arts and sciences.[4]

Williams always claimed to be the sole progenitor of the Pelican series. On the cover of his 1973 *Personal Portrait* of Allen Lane, there is this unequivocal statement: 'It was he [i.e. Williams] who suggested and supervised the founding of the Pelican list'. In the book, he quotes from a 1943 letter from Lane, which seems to confirm his claim to having 'invented' the Pelican list:

> When we began Penguin's [sic] in the summer of 1935, I hadn't a thought of producing anything but reprints of good quality. When you and I first discussed the Pelican idea my eyes were immediately opened to an exciting new possibility, and I could begin to visualize the expansion of the original idea in many ways. And it all began in that quiet little back-room of yours in 29, Tavistock Square [the office of the British Institute of Adult Education].

> Whoever could have expected such a publishing revolution to begin during these years of turmoil? I hope we'll have a lot more excitement before we've finished.[5]

All this is explicitly clear and independently verified: it was Williams who opened Lane's eyes to the exciting possibility of developing the Pelican list, and who then worked closely with him to turn that vision into a permanent reality. But Krishna Menon's biographer offers a quite different account of those same events:

> Bookish Krishna Menon's dark eyes were wide open for new developments in the publishing world, and he took due notice of the Penguin's progress. Also he had an idea, which he hastened to bring to the attention of the enterprising Lanes. The idea was even more enterprising: to move heavily into the non-fiction field, and to publish not only reprints but also original works by big names.
>
> This was all very well, but the publishers needed some assurance that important schools and other organizations would take note of this venture. Krishna Menon had by then lined up an impressive number of contacts, not only in the political but also in the educational world, contacts which the three enterprising Englishmen lacked as yet. So he introduced the Lanes to influential fellow Britishers whom he knew, and who would be of some help. Among these were the Secretary of the British Institute of Adult Education, W E Williams, and H L Beales, an influential faculty member of Krishna Menon's own alma mater, the London School of Economics. They agreed that the books envisaged by Krishna Menon would be useful in adult education – not the least reason for this being their drastically reduced price – and that therefore they would be ready to lend a hand. This is how the Pelican series of the Penguins came into existence. Krishna Menon became its general editor.[6]

That account raises significant doubts about how and why Williams became involved with Lane in the first place. Having told us of his early involvement in adult education and his appointment at Secretary of the BIAE, Williams offers this persuasive account of how he came to be the lynchpin of the whole enterprise:

> The emergence of Penguins seemed to me a heaven-sent opportunity for making it an ally and collaborator in the mission in which I was so deeply involved... I defected [from his training for the Congregational ministry] to education, I suppose, because in that field I could find scope for my deep social concern and idealistic beliefs.
>
> So when I first met Allen I suggested that Penguin's might join the current cultural crusade by starting a parallel series of cheap books on a wide range of intellectual interests – philosophy, psychology, history, literature, science. He responded immediately and enthusiastically, and off I went to put the idea on paper. At this stage, a colleague of mine joined in. He was H L Beales, then a Reader in History at the London School of Economics, and as deeply involved as I was in adult education.
>
> The books in the new series were to be called Pelicans, and the small editorial board to select them consisted of Krishna Menon, myself, Beales and Sir Peter Chalmers-Mitchell... Within a short time the original editorial board broke up, in 1939, partly through

differences of opinion and partly by Allen's caprice. Chalmers-Mitchell died, Krishna Menon and Beales dropped out. Henceforth the choice of titles was left mainly to me, ably assisted by Eunice Frost who had a wide and perceptive knowledge of books... She was to become a powerful influence on Penguin policy.[7]

Williams' elevated language is noteworthy. He speaks of his 'mission', of his 'idealistic beliefs' and of a 'cultural crusade' – expressions more usually encountered in religious or political contexts than in the world of commercial publishing. Yet those were the passionate metaphors Williams lived by. He insists that it was he who invited Lane to join him in 'the current cultural crusade', rather than Menon who invited Williams to join the editorial team on Penguin Books. The difference is not merely semantic: Williams is here claiming sole credit for persuading Lane to take Penguin Books upmarket by launching the Pelican series – the distinctive Penguin publication of the 1930s.

It is worth noting here that Pelicans were not the first upmarket series to be published under the Penguin imprint. That credit goes to the first six titles in the Penguin Shakespeare series, published in April 1937. Geoffrey Grigson, poet and critic, gave them an enthusiastic welcome in his *Morning Post* review: 'Shakespeare for sixpence, Hamlet for the price of ten Goldflakes [cigarettes], it is pleasant to think of it on the stalls at King's Cross and Paddington, with Dashiell Hammett and Edgar Wallace and Dorothy L Sayers'.[8]

Having secured Lane's enthusiastic agreement to his proposal, it was Williams who assembled Penguin's first editorial board. The subsequent break-up of that board is attributed in part to 'differences of opinion' and in part to 'Allen's caprice'. There is no reference to literary disagreements, professional rivalry, or bare-knuckle in-fighting. The implication is plain: Lane was a capricious fellow but he quickly recognised Williams' superior and dependable talents. Having disposed of the other board members, Lane lost no time in appointing Williams as his sole literary adviser. But Tony Godwin, one of Penguin's younger editors of the 1960s, and later Editor-in-Chief, refused to accept Williams' version of the facts surrounding Menon's departure:

[W E Williams] states that the original Penguin Board broke up in 1939, partly through differences of opinion and partly through Allen Lane's caprice – and that's ALL he tells you. That's a tantle (as in tantalise) if ever I read one! What differences? What sort of caprice? Krishna Menon was one of those original members. I once heard Allen Lane mention his name and though it was some 20 years later, his voice seethed with venom. It gave me goose pimples merely to hear such animosity. I wish I had thought to ask what the fracas had been about. At the time I hurriedly sheered off a subject still so strangely touchy after so many years. Now it's too late.[9]

In a 1963 article in *New Society*, Williams presents an alternative and less egotistical account of those same events – but says nothing of Godwin's alleged 'fracas':

> In the spring of 1937... Allen Lane became animated by a motive reminiscent of another creative pioneer of communication, Lord Reith. Reith was determined from the start that the BBC must enlighten people as well as entertain them. Lane came to a similar conclusion and, following his customary practice of seeking advice, found support for his idea of producing an avowedly educational series... The result was the birth of the Pelican, the Third Programme counterpart of the Penguin. The audience for which Pelicans were intended at that time was mainly the adult student, not least those taking the non-vocational courses run by the Workers' Educational Association and the University extra-mural departments. Two of Lane's associates in this development were men who were deeply involved in adult education and it was they who, so to speak, set the initial target. One was H L Beales of the London School of Economics; the other myself.[10]

Gertrude Williams' own version of the story draws heavily on her husband's account. She confirms that Billy was introduced to Allen Lane by Krishna Menon but leaves the clear impression that Menon was too distracted by his work for Indian independence to give adequate attention to Penguin Books. So he was dropped in favour of Billy.

Jack Morpurgo, whose 1979 life of Allen Lane offers helpful insights, provides his own colourful version of those early events. He tells us that, having secured Krishna Menon as his first editorial director, Allen Lane

> ...set up a panel of three advisory editors: Peter Chalmers-Mitchell, H L Beales and W E Williams. The third Editorial Adviser had been introduced to Allen by Krishna Menon... he seemed to come from the same mould which had shaped both Krishna Menon and Beales. Williams was just forty when he helped to initiate Pelicans... Like Krishna Menon and Beales, he was a Socialist, committed to the view that the masses would never reach the Socialist Nirvana unless their road was paved with solid reading-material. But there the similarity ended. William Emrys Williams was a Welshman to every letter of his unmistakably Welsh name, even if he did come from Manchester. He was mercurial, as eager to make friends as he was quick to find enemies, and his earnest political opinions, like his devout concern for public understanding, was tempered by commercial shrewdness. Unlike Krishna Menon or Beales, he was essentially a polymath. Although his career had been so studiously dedicated to the earnest and generally left-of-centre adult education movement, his enthusiasm for the political, social and economic theorizing that was the staple diet of that movement did not match his zest for the arts. (Eventually almost all of his own contributions to the list were in belles-lettres). He also shared with the Lanes and with Chalmers-Mitchell, but not with the other Pelican editors, an unfettered capacity for hedonism.[11]

Yet a different version of the story is provided by Edmond Seagrave. As editor of *The Bookseller*, he was well-placed to observe, and well-qualified to record, what actually took place:

> In 1936 V K Krishna Menon had introduced the Lane brothers to W E Williams, then Secretary of the British Institute of Adult Education, and H L Beales of the London School of Economics. As a result of this meeting there was planned a new series of books, more serious than the Penguins, and with a definite educational impulse behind them. These were the Pelicans. Krishna Menon was the general editor of the series; Beales and Williams were advisory editors.[12]

What are we to make of all these differing accounts? Morpurgo and Seagrave are certainly accurate in giving Menon historical precedence over Williams as Lane's first editorial adviser. But whereas Menon was first and foremost a man with political ambitions, Williams was not. He was, however, an astute and, above all, a reliable literary critic. In an earlier review, Morpurgo had referred to Williams as Lane's 'enthusiastic, skilful and long-lasting collaborator'.[13] In *King Penguin*, he makes it explicitly clear that Lane dropped Menon in favour of Williams but fails to provide a convincing explanation:

> Menon's fiery politics were fast becoming a liability and his dedicated asceticism a bore, whereas Williams, like Allen, never allowed his social conscience to interfere with his social pleasures and was disinclined to hoist the Red flag if it would write red figures on the Penguin balance sheet. So, out with Krishna Menon and in with Bill Williams![14]

Whilst Morpurgo's suggestion that Lane preferred the sybaritic Williams to the austere Menon as a dining partner and drinking companion may be true, he fails to point out that Menon's primary interest was Indian independence and that he was prepared to sacrifice everything to that end. The fact that he was a devout vegetarian, a non-smoker and a total abstainer was purely coincidental. By contrast, Williams had no other distracting interest. He was committed to literature and to adult education – two causes inextricably linked to Lane's business interests. An unashamed carnivore, compulsive chain-smoker and convivial tippler, Williams could also hold substantial quantities of liquor. In short, he was a man after Lane's own heart. Personal compatibility is often crucially important in publishing. So Lane warmly embraced Williams. They became and remained the best of friends for more than thirty years.

The most recent – but certainly not the final – word on this topic is by Jeremy Lewis, in his recent biography of Allen Lane:

> The truth of the matter was that Lane, mercurial and easily bored, found the austere and unconvivial Menon a far from kindred spirit, and was happy to freeze him out.[15]

In August 1936, Lane received one of George Bernard Shaw's famous postcards. That contact enabled Lane to persuade Shaw to release the reprint rights to a revised edition of *The Intelligent Woman's Guide to Socialism, Capitalism, Sovietism and Fascism*. In May 1937, the book appeared in two volumes as the first Pelican (A1). They carried the names of Menon as Editor, with Beales and Williams as Advisory Editors. By October 1938, Lane had dropped Menon.

It now seems clear what led to Menon's removal; but what about Beales? In the 1930s, Lance Beales was a brilliant, young, social historian at the LSE, a worthy successor to the Webbs and the Hammonds. He was involved in many intellectual projects; he was an early educational broadcaster; and he had advised the editors at Home University Press. Because his long-awaited text on Victorian England never materialised, his intellectual gifts went largely unrewarded. In his *Personal Portrait* of Allen Lane, Williams states unequivocally that Beales 'dropped out' of the editorial team at Penguin Books. Although his name continued to appear in post-war Penguin publications as an editorial adviser as late as 1947, Beales is probably now remembered only in the History Department at LSE and for his time at Penguin Books.[16]

At one time, Williams and Beales were mutual admirers. Both were deeply immersed in adult education; they collaborated in a number of educational initiatives at the BIAE; and there is no question that Beales once held Williams in high regard:

> He is no hot-gospeller. All his experience has taught him that truth is relative, that only unpleasant people claim a monopoly of truth. Williams is a moderate. He knows that no one dogma contains all the truth. He is sensitive. He understands the other fellow's point of view. He is broad-minded. He has a ripe sense of humour and it is always on top... He is in adult education because he believes in it...not because he wants to make people pundits or Marxists... Williams is too knowing an observer of human life, too good-humoured a partisan to want or expect more out of adult education than enabling people to grow up and enjoy life. He dislikes humbug and poverty. He hates the lie that warps and the ugliness that destroys. Vague uplift makes him tired. But Williams is a fine man, and works for sanity, individual and serial... His humour, his sanity, his humanity are never snowed-under by self-infatuation. He has his values but is no prig about them. That's why he has no enemies: that's why he has hosts of friends.[17]

By August 1984, that admiration had gone. In his last recorded interview, Beales had changed his mind about Williams. Aged 95, his memory failing, his mind confused and his speech rambling, he was still sufficiently coherent for some scathing comments on his former close collaborator:

> Yes [Williams] was there [at the Penguin editorial lunches at the Barcelona]. He was never very much use... But he then published the most dishonest book I have ever known...in

> which he claimed he had been responsible for the whole [Pelican] series... A lot of rubbish... He claimed he did the whole thing. He was a liar and a thief.[18]

Setting aside Beales's scurrilous and wholly unsubstantiated remarks, the essential truth about Williams' early involvement with Lane seems to be this: since Krishna Menon had proved his worth as occasional editorial adviser to The Bodley Head, Lane turned to him as his first adviser. Recognising the limits of his own literary connoisseurship, Menon recruited Beales and Williams into an editorial triumvirate for their respective expertise: the first in social science, the second in literature. Sir Peter Chalmers-Mitchell, a former Secretary to the Zoological Society of London, soon joined them as an expert adviser on science. Between them, the members of this four-man team were admirably equipped to advise Lane on the whole range of Penguin and Pelican titles. But Lane quickly recognised that Williams *alone* possessed the necessary combination of professionalism, integrity, literary judgement, and whole-hearted commitment to offer him consistently good advice on the entire range of literary genres. That is the best explanation of why Menon and Beales soon disappeared and why Williams emerged as Lane's sole editorial adviser.

Williams addressed that role – for which his rigorous academic training in English Literature had admirably prepared him – with high seriousness. But what exactly was his role? And how well did he fulfil it? As editorial adviser, and later Editor-in-Chief, Williams was expected to pronounce judgement on the literary merit of a stream of manuscripts presented to him over a period of thirty years. How did he set about that task? How were his literary tastes formed? And how did he maintain his critical edge?

In literature, as in all aesthetic matters, there is no accounting for individual taste. Every editorial adviser, however erudite or sophisticated, deploys some critical apparatus, rarely made explicit, in reaching a judgment: Is this a good book? Does it make for good reading? What makes it good? Should we publish it in its present form, or in some modified form? Above all, will the book sell? The editorial adviser, unlike the literary critic, is required to explain and justify his judgement to his publisher. For some combination of reasons – in part perhaps due his Congregational upbringing – Williams had developed a uniquely valuable talent: he was a superbly successful persuader. But what formed the basis of his literary judgement?

Helen Gardner, distinguished literary critic and Oxford don, giving evidence in 1960 at the Old Bailey trial of Penguin Books for allegedly publishing 'an obscene article, to wit, a book entitled *Lady Chatterley's Lover* by D H Lawrence', described her own approach to forming literary judgements:

> In discussing literary merit one has to give weight to two things. One is, I think, what the writer is trying to say, and the other is his success in saying it. These two are not always commensurate. One can find great literary merit in a piece of writing of a trivial experience, because it is so fully and truthfully expressed. Equally one can find great literary merit in a piece of writing of an experience of great importance and great value, although one may feel at times the writer has not wholly succeeded in communicating what he wishes to communicate.[19]

In short, the critic must consider style and content, intention and execution: What did the writer set out to do? How well does he do it? Was it worth doing in the first place? By following some such consistent sequence of questions, the critic reduces the risk of applying false criteria, thereby mistaking a book's true merit. There is no necessary connection between style, content and literary merit.

Williams shared those fundamental concerns and applied a similar critical apparatus. Through all his textbooks, his book reviews, and his columns of broadcast criticism, he reveals an unusual sensitivity to significant form, style and content. In his 1935 article on 'Style and Purpose in Literature', he defined the primary test of literary merit in a novel as 'mastery of medium' – that is, 'consummate skill of narrative and dialogue'; the ability to 'create characters who seem to live'; and writing which shows 'full control of language'. Those qualities, he argued, were a necessary but not a sufficient condition for great literature, 'in which vibrates some sense of concern for the world's griefs and iniquities'. In other words, there must be something more than the mere reconciliation or integration of form and content:

> The case outlined here is not that of a literary nihilism demanding the assassination of style. It is rather the contention that mastery of medium is not enough to make a full art; and that the quality of purpose is one which cannot be set lower than the quality of skill. Literature at its best has always exhibited a reconciliation of the two; but in our own day there is a rift between them. It is from the novel that many millions of English people get their notions of the values of contemporary life; and the novel today is exceeded only by the cinema in its sterility of purpose. Between them they remind us how inadequate is 'mastery of medium' to make the arts which a great democracy needs.[20]

Williams presented those views in a *Listener* article in 1935, the year in which Lane launched Penguin Books. Over the next thirty years, from 1935 to 1965, the lives of these two men became ever more closely intertwined, as Morpurgo reports:

> Allen's editorial rapport with Williams developed rapidly into friendship and before long Williams' influence spread also to the Penguin list. The frontier between the two lists was not easy to define... Neither Allen nor Williams had any great enthusiasm for rigorous definition...the selection of Pelicans was for all practical purposes merged with Penguin selection.[21]

How well did Williams discharge his duties as editorial adviser at Penguin Books? And how did his performance in that role affect the quality of his relationship with Allen Lane? At the outset, Lane needed somebody with a fastidious taste in literature to offer dependable advice on existing books, worth republishing in paperback form. Within a short while he needed a 'literary taster' – somebody who could advise him on the merits of new manuscript material. Williams easily met both those requirements. If he occasionally missed a literary gem or a bestseller, he picked many more winners than losers. Lane knew all about publishing risk, but he was slow to develop a sense of quality writing. Williams had a shrewd nose for 'good literature' and never lacked literary enterprise. But he was no businessman, and made few claims in that direction. Temperamentally similar, the two men complemented each other perfectly, forming an admirably close and highly successful publishing partnership.

The cumulative evidence, contained in the vast Penguin archive, leaves the dispassionate researcher in no doubt that Williams discharged his onerous responsibilities with vigour and imagination. During his thirty-year tenure as chief editorial adviser, several remarkable new series of books emerged from Penguin, for which Williams must be given principal credit. These included:

Pelican Books, beginning with George Bernard Shaw's *The Intelligent Woman's Guide to Socialism, Capitalism, Sovietism and Fascism*, May 1937

Penguin [County] Guides, beginning with S E Winbolt's *Kent, Sussex and Surrey*, March 1939

King Penguin, beginning with *British Birds on Lake, River, and Stream*, by John Gould and Phyllis Barclay-Smith, November 1939

Penguin Handbooks, beginning with Raymond Bush's *Soft Fruit Growing*, December 1942

Penguin Modern Painters, beginning with Geoffrey Grigson's *Henry Moore*, April 1944

Penguin Classics, beginning with E V Rieu's translation of *Homer's Odyssey*, January 1946

Penguin Poets – perhaps closest to Williams' heart – beginning with his own selection from *Tennyson*, June 1941.

This series of seven imprints sold well, contributing significantly to Penguin's critical and commercial success. The same cannot be said of all Penguin's periodical publications, whose early demise had been predicted by Williams:

New Biology (from July 1945)
Science News (from June 1946)
Film Review (August 1946 – August 1949)
Music Magazine (February 1949 – July 1949)

New Writing (November 1940 – September 1950)
Penguin Parade (November 1937 – November 1948)
Russian Review (October 1945 – February 1948)
Transatlantic (September 1943 – June 1946)

If there is one exception in that list it is Penguin *New Writing*. Still influential and often referred to by contemporary writers, it was certainly not a publishing failure. But it was highly subsidised by other Penguin publications. Edited by John Lehmann, it survived for ten years, with some of the best essays, short stories and poems of a younger, more experimental, post-war generation of writers.

In his appraisal of Allen Lane's overall achievement as a publisher, Richard Hoggart pays this tribute to the founder of Penguin Books, and incidentally to W E Williams:

> To write well for 'the intelligent layman' you have to share with him a particular set of working-values – assumptions about the role of intelligence and of intellectuals, and about possible relationships within the wider life of society. This set of circumstances does not exist everywhere. So, again, Penguin's achievement is by implication telling something to our credit. Not that we always know this ourselves. Most teachers in adult education know it (and no doubt the influence of W E Williams, who had been trained in that hard school, was crucial with Allen Lane and with Penguins for many years)... When you look at the whole Penguin achievement you know that it constitutes, in action, one of the more democratic successes of our recent social history.[22]

In addition to offering meticulously detailed advice on particular books and manuscripts, Williams sustained Lane with sound strategic advice on the development of Penguin Books over thirty years, sharing ideas on a broad range of business issues, from the appointment of key personnel to the opening up of new markets, and from introducing a new series of publications to avoiding costly entanglement in matters outside the profitable core publishing business. Shortly after the Second World War, with the British economy in its familiar fragile condition, Williams wrote to Lane on 14 July 1947:

> As you know, I feel very much as you do about the risks of spreading our wings too far in a period of such increasing uncertainty. World trade is going to be a heart-breaking gamble for the next few years and, in many respects, would-be British exporters have got the dice heavily loaded against them by the USA. One sign that they intend to keep commercial power in their hands is their behaviour in Japan where any prospect of commercial infiltration by anyone else now seems quite hopeless... These are some of the factors which have made me feel increasingly certain that our line should be (a) consolidation at home, and (b) expansion within the Commonwealth. Our policy therefore, on this basis, should be to withdraw in good order from [America] and also from regions which, one way or the other, are bound to be overrun by American expansion... But I

> should try to dig in Australia and India... These are some of the reasons why I think we are right in our long-term campaigns for building up Penguins at home. Our policy of arranging for several long-term series is, so to speak, a system of vertebrae which will give a firm shape to our enterprise. And meanwhile, we shall fill up the areas within the vertebrae with reprints of many species. We have a prospective list which no one in Great Britain can touch.[23]

The strategic advice contained in that letter does not fall within the purview of a literary editor but of a close business associate. It is one letter amongst hundreds in the Penguin Archive in which Williams responds to Lane's requests for advice on Penguin publishing strategy, during their thirty years' collaboration. Time and time again, Williams brings Lane down to earth from some flight of entrepreneurial fancy, reminding him of the distinctive character of Penguin Books, restating its basic business philosophy, pointing out the strengths and limits of Penguin's traditional readership.

On 13 September 1954, for example, Williams wrote to Lane, to dissuade him from going into magazine publishing:

> I very much doubt whether we should venture into the magazine territory, because from what I can glean, the economics of these endeavours have become very difficult indeed. Even a circulation of 50,000 or 60,000 does not attract advertisers in sufficient quantity, and I imagine this situation would be even more acute with a magazine of high aspirations. Anything we should want to produce would bear a resemblance to that which Stephen Spender and John Lehman are now editing, and both of them are receiving substantial subsidies. I have an inveterate belief in the proverb about cobblers sticking to lasts; and not merely on superstitious grounds do I believe that we should adhere to the true Penguin doctrine and produce high class books at the lowest possible prices. I have not, moreover, a great belief in magazines anyway. Even the best of them seem to have to make concessions to the caprice of advertisers, whereas we publish exactly what we please without any obligation to commercial interests. I would not mind your persuading Hutchinsons to try their luck in the magazine field, but I would not like to see Penguin delve into that domain.[24]

Once again, Lane took his Editor-in-Chief's advice on a crucial policy issue. In short, Williams fulfilled for Lane a similar role to that which Walter Bagehot prescribed for a constitutional monarch: to be consulted, to encourage and to warn – except that here the roles were reversed with Lane as monarch and Williams as principal constitutional adviser. The archive evidence makes clear that Williams invariably offered wise counsel, which Lane nearly always heeded. Their strong working relationship was reinforced by ties of deep and genuine friendship, which may help explain why their partnership was so long-lasting and so mutually beneficial in a business notorious for its sudden departures, its bitter quarrels and more bitter recriminations. It therefore comes as something of a shock to discover that Williams was not a Penguin employee and never on the Penguin payroll. Two obvious questions arise: Why was Bill Williams never an employee? And how was he rewarded for his long and loyal service to the firm?

The immediately obvious answer to the first question is that it suited both men for Williams to remain an independent, freelance adviser to the company. In 1936, when he joined Lane, Williams had just completed his first year as Secretary of the BIAE. His star was still rising in the world of adult education when Lane invited him to become one of the two part-time Assistant Editors at Penguin Books. That invitation was flattering and irresistible. But the future of Penguin Books was by no means assured. Lane could not afford to pay his employees very much, and his part-time advisers were, in any case, already in full-time paid employment elsewhere. As the company prospered, the time came when Williams must have considered abandoning his career in adult education to become a full-time Director of Penguin Books. By then he realised that, as one of Lane's salaried employees, he would no longer enjoy the same freedom to speak his mind, and to express strong opinions on policy issues, without the risk of being fired. As a freelance adviser, he could maintain the priceless gifts of intellectual freedom and economic independence – provided Lane continued to compensate him adequately for his efforts. He set out his reasons very clearly in an important letter to Lane on 10 September 1948:

> The full-time option which you first raised with me a long while back, appealed to me very much in many ways. I needn't recite them all, but the foremost was the certitude at which I have arrived, viz. that Penguin's [sic] is the most constructive and exciting job I know, or am ever likely to know – it's my permanent love. Although administration is not my favourite occupation, I do it rather well when I have to, and I even enjoy the compulsion of making a machine work effectively. I believe in time I could have learned to run the office. But two factors to be reckoned with on that point are (a) the similarity of our temperaments, and (b) your fervent resolve – which only abates when you are feeling fed-up – to run the show your way. If I were less mercurial than you (and learned the expertise), I would make a Managing Director all right. But my outlook on that side of the show is too like yours, so that I would become a mere duplicate of your method of management. And that would soon chafe us both, as well as limiting my effectiveness.
>
> The part-time idea seems the right one, and there's no doubt that my range of contacts (and even ideas) depends on retaining many of my present interests and activities. It would please me immensely to continue the relationship.[25]

The facts are assembled, the argument is logical and well presented, and the conclusion irresistible: a characteristic piece of Williams' persuasive writing. In his much later *Personal Portrait* of Lane, written after his friend's death, Williams explained the position in more open terms:

> For many years until 1960, I was the Chief Editor, but never did I have a service agreement or contract of any kind (nor did most of the early series editors). I thus retained at all times a position of detachment and independence which secured me two valuable advantages: I enjoyed special terms of confidence with Allen and I was immune from the tensions which arise among senior management. There were two reasons why I adopted and always maintained this position. The first was my involvement in other activities which were not only remunerative but were also more significant to me even than Penguin's, such as running the Army Bureau of Current Affairs (ABCA) in the war, and later the Arts Council. The second reason was my deep conviction that Allen, who became my closest friend, could well become too invasive and exacting with people whose services he bought. It was on this basis of independence, then, that I was able to assume and preserve a role which brought me so close – but never too close – to this brilliant and unpredictable innovator.[26]

Close friends they may have been but 'never too close' – at least on the subject of financial rewards. We can only speculate on what might have happened if Williams had thrown in his lot full-time with Lane. Williams considered that question in a sadly reflective letter to Eunice Frost, Lane's former personal assistant, and later his most trusted editorial adviser, some three years after Lane's death:

> It is terrible to reflect on how few of us are left. I don't think I am really sorry that Allen never quite got around to making me an offer. I suspect that the cold little shutters would have fairly soon descended and I may have been of more help to him as an outsider than as an insider. I miss him greatly as I am sure many do, but so many of his pals have now joined him that they should be having a pretty convivial time together.[27]

The part-time arrangement also had a strong appeal for Lane. If he could retain Williams' services without having to put him on the company payroll, he would have the benefit of his continuing advice, and his personal friendship, whilst maintaining the freedom to ignore that advice whenever he chose to do so, without the risk of him resigning or being tempted away by another publisher. In that respect, the relationship was mutually agreeable and symbiotic.

We cannot say for sure whether Williams was adequately rewarded for his contribution to Penguin Books because the facts are not fully known and because the answer depends largely on the separate, subjective judgements of both Williams and Lane. At the end of his 1948 letter to Lane, giving his reasons for preferring a part-time role in the firm and which merits quotation in full, Williams set out some of the facts about his remuneration in the late 1940s – when Penguin was enjoying immense commercial success:

> While we are scrutinising our co-operation I want to underline one or two relevant points. I don't think you always realise that my 'homework' is as extensive as it has become. The business of reading stuff, for example, takes many hours a week – as it should. Or, again

> take blurb-writing (in which I claim to have set new standards lately). In many cases it becomes a fascinating but (very often) difficult exercise. Most of my friends think I toss off my bons mots and fashion my sentences on my head, but the fact is that 300 words often takes me a long night from dinner to dawn. And then there are the other additional tasks (like Penguins Progress, or the News Letters) which I also cope with (and enjoy) outside the office. I look forward to doing more, not less, of these things, but I have sometimes felt that you don't entirely recognise what all this adds up to, and that you possibly estimate my contribution solely in terms of our weekly meetings or our lunch-conferences with authors and the like.
>
> The final consideration in my mind is the financial one which we had better examine in the coldest possible blood. The present arrangement – leaving out for the moment such generous extras as the one you organised after my operation is this:
>
> a) Basic [annual] fee £400 less tax
> b) Secretary £250 less tax
> c) Expenses £150-£250 approx.
>
> We assumed when we fixed these items that expenses would be eyewash. But in fact they have proved, literally, out-of-pocket expenses, for I think prestige demands that when I take out a Barbara Ward or a Professor Ayer I should do it in the customary style!
>
> I'd be grateful if you'd think these figures over in the hope, perhaps, that ways and means can be found to 'raise the ante' by a figure which takes into account the range of the contributions I make and am likely to increase. And in considering this point, please do remember how conscious I am of the windfall you contrived last Christmas. But I am looking ahead financially, for I want to shed a few things to make room for a bigger and better reorganisation of my activities![28]

That letter is significant for several reasons. First, it claims that Lane grossly underestimated the extent of Williams' contribution to the success of Penguin Books. Second, it shows that he was slow to express his appreciation of the volume, the nature or the pressure of the work Williams' undertook. Third, it shows the miserably low level of Williams' financial reward for his immense contribution to Penguin Books before, during, and more especially after the war, when Penguin began to make serious profits from the pent-up demand for high quality, low cost books. Lane responded positively to that letter, as he invariably responded to Williams' intermittent requests for more money. But because Lane never took the initiative by offering Williams a more generous reward for his services, Williams appears always as financial supplicant. As the firm prospered, so Williams' editorial fee and his expense allowance were slowly increased. Such facts as we have confirm that, as Chief Editorial Adviser, Williams was paid much more than any other Penguin editorial adviser; that he enjoyed a more generous expense allowance; that his expense claims were invariably met without question; and that whenever he approached Lane for additional payments, his requests were always granted. So whilst money seems never to have been a source of explicit friction between the two men – they exchanged many letters on the subject – that was only because Williams generally concealed his discontent. Throughout their thirty-year relationship, Williams was compelled to plead his cause for additional compensation – not least on the delicate issue of how much he should receive for the books that he himself wrote or edited for publication by Penguin Books, as the following incidents relate.

Three weeks after the outbreak of war, on 20 September 1939, A D Peters, a principal London literary agent, wrote to Williams on behalf of Penguin Books, to commission: 'a volume of Essays of approximately 60-70,000 words in length for which we are willing to pay an outright fee of £30'.[29] Williams accepted the invitation in carefully guarded terms:

> In answer to your letter of September 20th, I am willing to edit a volume of essays of approximately 60-70,000 words in length, and I am willing to accept the terms you suggest, viz. an outright payment of £30. I note that in the event of any copyright material being included this would be paid for separately from the Editorial Fee. I hope to submit my choice of essays within the next two or three weeks.[30]

At first sight, the amount offered seems pathetically small, particularly when one recalls that Williams was already an established author, with six successful titles to his credit, five of which were published by Methuen, a highly reputable academic publisher. On the other hand, we should remember that most publishers notoriously underpaid their authors – both before and after the 1930s. Few authors enjoyed the benefit of an agent to negotiate an advance payment, plus incremental royalties on the volume of sales achieved. Editing an anthology of English essays was less onerous than producing the manuscript of a new book of the same length. The value of money has also changed so much since 1939 that we need to put the offer into some perspective. In 1939, £30 represented the equivalent of ten or twelve weeks gross pay for an average skilled worker. In 1939, the BBC – never generous in its rewards to contributors – paid Williams four guineas (four pounds and four shillings) for 750 words of broadcasting criticism in his weekly column in *The Listener*. Finally, we should note that, in 1935, Williams' annual salary as Secretary of the British Institute of Adult Education amounted to no more than £300. In 1939, you could buy an Austin family-size car for £100. That helps put the fee of £30 into some kind of perspective.

Because of his demanding war work, Williams made slow progress on his book of essays. In spring 1942, as Director of the Army Bureau of Current Affairs, he wrote to Dr E V Rieu at Methuen and to J M Dent, requesting permission to reproduce various essays, of which they held the copyright, in his forthcoming *Book of English Essays* – 'mainly for the use of the Forces'. Given that patriotic motive, both publishers provided the necessary permissions. *A Book of English Essays, selected by W E Williams* (Pelican Books A99) was first published in 1942, reprinted in 1948, with a new and enlarged edition in 1951, to include more essays of a later date. The demand for the book was enormous. It was reprinted no fewer than nine times: in 1952, 1954, 1956, 1957, 1959, 1962, 1963, 1964 and 1965. By then, it had sold something approaching half a million copies – a phenomenal publishing success for a collection of essays.

Williams himself wrote the author biography on the cover of *English Essays*. A comparison of the first edition (1948) and a later reprint (1965) reflects his much-changed position over the post-war period. The 1948 edition provides this impressive, though hardly modest, note on the author, here quoted in full:

> Mr W. E. Williams, who has edited this selection of *English Essays*, has been associated with Penguin Books for many years and is now Chief Editor. He has had a close connection with many enterprises in popular education. Thus in 1934 he initiated the 'Art for the People' plan which a few years later stimulated the formation of the Arts Council. During the war he created the Army Bureau of Current Affairs (ABCA) and subsequently under the auspices of the Carnegie Trust, transformed it for peace-time uses into the Bureau of Current Affairs. He is well-known as the Radio Critic of *The Observer* and, before he took to criticism, was himself a successful broadcaster and televiser. One of his latest activities has been to establish the Projects Division of UNESCO. As an expert in adult education he has participated in many educational schemes developed by such bodies as the Ministry of Education, Home Office, Colonial Office, Air Ministry and War Office; and among the many organisations of which is an Executive Committee member are the Arts Council, the British Council and the London Mask Theatre.[31]

The 1965 reprint contains this significantly modified self-portrait by the author, again quoted in full:

> Sir William Emrys Williams, C.B.E, D.Litt., who has edited this selection of English Essays, has been literary adviser to Penguin Books since its earliest years. In 1934 he initiated the 'Art for the People' plan which a few years later stimulated the formation of the Arts Council. During the war he created the Army Bureau of Current Affairs (A.B.C.A.). He was for several years the Radio Critic of the Observer and Television Critic of the New Statesman, and, before he took to criticism, was himself a successful broadcaster and televiser. He was Secretary-General of the Arts Council of Great Britain from 1951 to 1963 and is a Director of Penguin Books. In 1946 he was given the American Medal of Freedom.[32]

Comparing the two 'brief lives', we discover that Williams is no longer 'Chief Editor' but simply 'literary adviser to Penguin Books'. Where he was formerly 'an expert in adult education' who had 'participated in many educational schemes', he now reports that he has been 'Secretary-General of the Arts Council of Great Britain' and is 'a Director of Penguin Books'. He mentions his brief spell as 'Radio Critic of *The Observer* and Television Critic of the *New Statesman*' but omits all reference to his five consecutive years of radio criticism in *The Listener.* He may have been a successful pre-war broadcaster; but when exactly was he a 'successful televiser'? He had taken part in a couple of pre-war televised broadcasts and makes the most of them. He flags up his knighthood, his CBE, and his recently awarded D.Litt. But why does he drop all reference to his important work at UNESCO? And why does he continue to feature his American Medal of Freedom, awarded almost twenty years earlier? Perhaps he thought it might help boost the book's sales in North America.

It was Richard Hoggart who pointed out that the Penguin format fitted neatly into the knee-pocket of British battle-dress uniform.[33] Many a soldier or airman seems to have gone into action carrying a copy of that first wartime edition of *English Essays*. By 1949, the book had become a favourite anthology amongst many readers. 'As good a pocket companion as can be found' said the *Times Literary Supplement* in 1951. Encouraged by that review, the Penguin editorial board agreed that Williams should prepare a new, revised and more up-to-date edition, including further essays by J B Priestley and Robert Lynd, and some newer essays by V S Pritchett and Harold Nicolson.

Each reprint of *English Essays* prompted Williams to plead with Lane for additional money, as in February 1962:

> On the forthcoming publication of the new edition of *English Essays* I am due for a reprint fee. Last time, in 1959, it was £100. As the price of the book has now gone up from 3/6 to 5/-, and as we have never repeated our reproduction fees since the first printing. I wonder what you think of the suggestion that my reprint fee this time might be £150?
>
> One reason for this suggestion is that my forthcoming operation will run me into the better part of £200, and I am the sort of squirrel who has few nuts in reserve![34]

Allen Lane wrote back to confirm his agreement: 'I am happy to agree to your suggestion to an increase on the reprint fee of the forthcoming new edition of English Essays from £100 to £150'[35] – a miserly increase when we consider the volume of sales and the profitability of reprints compared with new editions.

On 22 November 1965, after the ninth reprint of the 1951 edition, Williams got the bit between his teeth and wrote to Harry Paroissien at Penguin Books in more impassioned terms than he had ever written to Allen Lane:

> I have not been having the merriest time of my life since I last saw you at the Arts Council party. I've kept on working, but with practically no voice it's been useless trying to meet

> friends. I have now reached the sixth week of treatment by cobalt-therapy, and the two eminent quacks who look after me say the prognosis is very good.
>
> I hope that you are in one of those excellent health schemes like BUPA. I, in my foolishness, never joined one of them, so that 1965 cost me nearly £1,000 between the heart and the throat! For that reason I welcome the reprint of *English Essays*, on which, I believe, I receive a modest douceur. I'd be grateful if you'd get your people to send a cheque.[36]

Back in 1960, Williams wrote to Lane complaining that he was being underpaid for various pieces of work he had done. The letter shows how his mind worked in this sensitive area of their collaboration:

> Jack Summers' [Penguin's accountant] contention is that as a 10% royalty has to be paid to Macmillans on the Hardy [*Thomas Hardy*, introduced and edited by W E Williams, The Penguin Poets, 1960], £100 would be a proper payment to me as editor. I think this is a parsimonious and unreasonable proposal, and here are my reasons for thinking so: Hardy is a real scoop, and a Jubilee book at that. After many other approaches had failed, I, single-handed, was able to talk Macmillans into agreement. In other words, this important book would not have come our way at all but for me.
>
> I believe in the principle of 'swings and roundabouts'. My Selections of Wordsworth, Tennyson and Browning did not cost the firm a penny piece in royalties or reproduction rights, and this factor I think should be balanced against the present situation of our having to pay a 10% royalty to Macmillans. It has been our custom, I think, to accept this 'swings and roundabouts' principle. We pay out thundering advances in some cases – e.g. *The Seven Pillars of Wisdom* – knowing we shall not get our money back, but we can offset these cases by others in which we shall do abnormally well. If I may quote one more instance, we paid about £250 outright in reproduction fees on *English Essays* [the new and enlarged 1951 edition]; and having sold about a quarter of a million copies, the firm must have made an extremely handsome profit on that operation.
>
> In short, I maintain that I have put so much into the kitty that the firm can afford to be generous over the *Thomas Hardy*. I think I should get the same fee that James Reeves is having for Georgian Poets, i.e. £200 on first printing, and £25 per thousand on subsequent printings. If an editorial newcomer can command that reasonable rate, then I think that a veteran in the editorial brigade should get no less!
>
> I maintain, too, that this principle should apply to my Lawrence poems, now in their third printing. Here again, the firm has to pay 10% royalty, but that does not seem to me a reason why the editor should be (virtually!) penniless. In this case, then, I think I should receive £5 per thousand for the recent reprint, instead of the £50 that Jack Summers proposes.[37]

A number of points emerge from that letter. First, it confirms that no formal written contract ever existed between Williams and Penguin Books for the publication of his own books. The close personal relationship between Williams and Lane meant that any difficulties that arose in their working partnership could be settled swiftly and informally. That seems to be exactly how they were handled in practice. It was the very absence of a written contract that obliged Williams to write so often to Lane, asking for more money. To be fair to Lane, he always paid up without much argument.

Williams had accepted an outright sum of £30 for *English Essays* back in 1939 but he now rejected the £100 offered by Jack Summers and expected an initial payment of £200, plus a royalty of £25 per thousand for reprints of *Thomas Hardy*. For the reprint of *D H Lawrence: Selected Poems*, he rejected the £50 lump sum offered by Summers, and asked £5 per thousand for reprints. Williams seems to be asking here for no more than his due – but Lane emerges from the story without much honour. Although he agreed to meet each of Williams' demands, the impression remains that he was happy to accept his Editor-in-Chief's literary and business advice down the years without ever ensuring that he got a fair financial return for his exceptional contribution to Penguin Books, more particularly for his own books.

We may speculate just how much of an 'extremely handsome profit' the firm had made on *English Essays*. In the absence of hard facts, we turn to the information that emerged at the *Lady Chatterley* trial in 1960. During the course of his cross-examination, Williams told the court that Penguin had printed 200,000 copies of *Lady Chatterley's Lover*, compared with an average print-run of 40,000 or 50,000. He was quick to point out, however, that, where the firm expected a great success, as with *The Cruel Sea*, or *Room at the Top*, it had printed between 200,000 and 250,000 copies. Compared with such best-selling novels, it is remarkable that more than a quarter million copies of *English Essays* were sold in the new and enlarged 1951 edition alone.

It is interesting to contrast Williams' 1960 letter of complaint with an earlier 1951 letter, offering his thoughts on the subject of reprints:

> We are beginning to fulfil the hope of creating a permanent List, largely in Pelicans, yet the operation still lacks the fluency it ought to possess. My point is that there are some titles which ought never to go out of print, at least for some years to come. By carefully watching the barometer of sales we ought to be able to predict, to within a month or two, the date on which a reprint will be needed – and yet more often than not we fail to achieve this continuity. One current instance is "The Economics of Everyday Life" [by Gertrude Williams], a book in which, I will not deny, I have a special interest. It looks to me as if this will be out of print next month or March – yet no place has been allowed for it in this year's reprints at all; and I am told that, at the best, no place could be found for it before November '51. The consequences of this gap are pretty obvious, I think. Students will be told, in thousands, that the book is out of print and will therefore be inclined to stop asking for it. By the time the book returns to the list the momentum of its first success will have been thrown away, and we shall have to start promoting the book all over again.

> A great deal of our sales energy, I fear, must be going up the chimney in this way, and I feel that our reprint policy at the present is far too happy-go-lucky. I raise the matter as a general principle which, I think, we ought to sit down and scrutinize as soon as you are back. Meanwhile, only your say-so can ensure an earlier reprint of "Economics". Do you feel like insisting that this be found a place in, say, the March list? I wish you would, for it is a book of immense potential success. I observe, incidentally, that it sold nearly 40,000 copies in October alone, a fair indication of its state of health.[38]

That letter provides a further illustration of Williams' exceptional powers of persuasion: the combination of all the essential information, plus a clear analysis and convincing argument, leading to a diplomatically worded recommendation. Although Williams freely admits he has a 'special' (i.e. pecuniary) interest in Gertrude Williams' book – and is clearly unhappy about the lack of a reprint – he maintains a cool tone throughout. Lane acknowledged the force of Williams' argument, conceded the need for a much clearer reprint policy, and ordered an early reprint of Gertrude's book, as requested. That book subsequently went through several reprints to become a Penguin best-seller. It earned Gertrude sufficient royalties to enable her to commission a young woman architect to design a delightful ranch-style house for her in a Buckinghamshire village.

Six years later, in October 1957, Williams responded to a letter from Allen Lane, which suggested extending the Penguin list of books on economics. Once again, Williams made sure that his wife's financial interests were carefully protected:

> I very much doubt whether the Pelican audience could sustain more than three or four Economics titles in print at the same time. While there is a great out-put of Economics books for academic purposes there can only be very few books needed of this kind, suitable for the general reader. We happen to have in our list at present two bestsellers in this field: The Economics of Everyday Life and Facts from Figures...
>
> You will remember that [Alan] Glover from time to time brings up typescripts or suggestions for books on Economics and that we not only examine these ourselves, but put them up to Gertrude for her opinion. But these candidates fail again and again on the ground that they have not got the art of popular appeal or that they refer to the more abstruse parts of the economic field.[39]

In his autobiography, Richard Hoggart recounts a story that confirms Williams' powers of persuasion, and shows how much Lane relied on his advice. In 1964, Hoggart wrote to Lane asking for financial support, through an Inland Revenue seven-year tax-deductible covenant, to help him set up the Centre for Contemporary Cultural Studies at Birmingham University:

> It was inevitable that some people would say he gave the money as a covert thank-you for my evidence in the Lady Chatterley's Lover case. I am sure I would have asked Allen Lane for funds even if I had not appeared in his defence three years before. I knew him

> well enough to be sure the idea would interest him. His reply to my letter was predictable. He would "take Bill Williams' advice"; would I meet him at five-thirty a few days later at Williams' office in St James's Square.
>
> [After some initial fencing] Williams intervened: "Oh, give him what he wants, Allen. You've made a fortune by riding cultural change without understanding it." Lane said: "All right. You'll have the agreement next week".[40]

That was typical of the advice Williams gave his old friend – offered in the kind of language Lane found irresistible. His reliance on Williams' advice derived from their close collaboration over many years – a collaboration based upon mutual respect, shared values and long-established trust between the two men.

Early in 1950, when Lane was taken ill, Williams immediately wrote him the kind of letter he knew Lane would love to receive:

> I'm very sorry to hear of your illness, and as soon as you feel like a gossip, please let me know, and I'll come along and tell you what's cooking. I'm so unused to your having anything more troublesome than a cold (or a hangover) that the idea of your being laid-up is a major intrusion of the planets into human affairs.
>
> I've told T.K. [Tanya Kent, then Allen Lane's Personal Assistant, later to become Tanya Schmoller when she married Hans Schmoller, Penguin's top designer] that I'll gladly take on any engagements from your calendar, so don't let any such matters trouble your mind.
>
> When I hear that you are approaching convalescence, I'll think up some diversions for you, such as an assortment of cut-out books & the like! Meanwhile float as easefully as possible on dream-clouds of association, and let your mind find the relief of discontinuity. Let the clutch out and coast.
>
> I won't bother you with messages, but I hope each day to hear that you are getting better and better – until you surface again with an urgent desire for a cup of sack.[41]

To mark the twenty-first birthday of Penguin Books in 1956, Lane asked Williams to write a history of the firm, from its earliest days in the crypt of Holy Trinity Church in the Euston Road, to its coming of age in the splendid new post-war premises at Harmondsworth. The first half of *The Penguin Story* provided a reliable account of the 'steady and logical process of evolution' of the Penguin imprint; the second half – offered as 'a tribute to the writers of the books' – comprised a 'complete catalogue of every book published by the firm since it began in 1935'. Created by Penguin's brilliant designer, Hans Schmoller, and priced one shilling, the book broke entirely with the standard Penguin or Pelican format. The front and back covers were fully integrated, were not colour-coded in the traditional Penguin house style, and did not carry the familiar Penguin colophon – that most famous of literary birds. Instead, they reproduced a full colour photograph of a young couple choosing Penguin titles in a W H Smith bookshop. The author's name did not appear conventionally on the book's front cover, nor on its spine, but on the half-title page, with a simple note that he 'has been associated with the firm for twenty years'.

In addition to *The Penguin Story*, in 1951 Lane commissioned a celebratory collective portrait of the assembled Penguin Editors from Rodrigo Moynihan, a talented young Royal Academician. Jack Morpurgo, a junior Penguin editor at the time, who appears in the painting as a shadowy and diminutive figure, says of Moynihan's portrait that *After the Conference: the Penguin Editors*, was extraordinary,

> ...not so much because it offered to the viewer a deliberate, solemn and formal interpretation of Penguin as an institution entirely out of keeping with the casual and swashbuckling reality, as because it was intrinsically dishonest... The picture is a fabrication, but it does show all those responsible for Penguin's editorial policies in a period which many have come to see as the golden age. There is Williams, massive in the foreground, and for some reason more prominent than Allen himself.[42]

Despite being a 'fabrication', the painting purports to show the *Penguin Editors* grouped together, as if in conference. That surely puts Allen Lane into proper perspective. He is the creator and genius behind the Penguin enterprise and could hardly be omitted – but he was not one of 'the Penguin Editors' whereas Williams was unquestionably Editor-in-Chief. Shortly after the painting was commissioned, when Williams' knighthood was announced in 1955, he was on holiday in Rome. On 9 June, the following telegram from Allen Lane was delivered to Williams at the Hotel Dinesan:

> THE NEWS IS OUT
> NOW MAY WE SHOUT
> UNTIL OUR ROAR THE TRAFFIC JAMS
> HERE'S TO SIR WILLIAM EMRYS WILLIAMS[43]

This was not very good verse and even worse scansion; hardly up to Williams' own literary standards. But he acknowledged the telegram in a letter that reflects the genuine warmth between the two men:

> In the last days I was rapidly coming to the conclusion that it was all an hallucination. However I beetled off to a news-stand after breakfast today, bought the Times, which I opened with quivering fingers, and found I hadn't been dreaming after all. I confess I felt a little over-awed... After a morning sightseeing round the Forum, I got back to find your telegram waiting. It gave us both great mirth and pleasure, and we promptly knocked the hell out of a bottle of old white Chianti. I'm very happy about it all, & I assure you that I get a most peculiar thrill from the knowledge that two of us, now, can put a pennant on the Penguin. My longest and most rewarding work has been with your operation, and as if that wasn't blessing enough I count you as my oldest and closest friend.

> An hour or two ago, I wandered into the S. Maria Maggiore and found myself in the mood to dedicate a long candle to our friendship, which has given me years of intimacy, & fun and hectic drama. May there be many many more to come.[44]

We may note in passing that when Williams says 'We knocked the hell out of a bottle of old white Chianti' his drinking companion was not his wife, Gertrude, but his long-term mistress, Estrid Bannister, whose crucial role will be examined in Chapter 7.

In 1958, Williams was approaching his sixty-second birthday, as energetic and inventive as ever, still dreaming up ideas for new publications, and new ways to boost Penguin sales. As Secretary-General of the Arts Council, and a Director of Penguin Books, retirement was the last thing on his mind. Throughout his time at Penguin Books, Williams sometimes revisited old ideas that had worked well, to see whether they could be recycled in some new and different form. Twenty years earlier, in the spring of 1936, he had written a series of articles in *Highway*, exploring the pleasures of different kinds of literature. They appeared in the form of a 'Guide for the General Reader', introducing works of non-fiction that the general reader might enjoy. The idea behind those articles lay submerged in Williams' mind until 1958, when it resurfaced as the inspiration for a major new venture. It soon became the most ambitious project he had so far attempted.

Williams set out his ideas for a *Reader's Guide* with meticulous care in a detailed proposal to Lane which merits quoting at length for the light it throws on Williams' method of working:

> The Guide will consist of 18 sections each of which will deal with a category or division of books: Archaeology, Biography, Belles Lettres, Philosophy, History and so on. Each of these sections will be edited by an authority in that particular field who will provide (a) a brief introduction and (b) a selective reading list.
>
> The purpose of the introductions will be to give the general reader a clear and general notion of the content of each field of knowledge: what archaeology, for example, is concerned with; what the novelist is trying to do; why plays are worth reading as well as watching; how psychology can interpret human behaviour...
>
> The second part of each editor's task will be to provide a reading list of not too formidable length, arranged in the order considered to be most helpful, and including a very brief summary or commentary on each title: a sentence or two, no more. Many of the books in these lists will, evidently, be available in several imprints and editions, and the Penguin management will make itself responsible for providing these bibliographical particulars. The Guide is in no sense a Penguin catalogue, and the entries will consist of recommended books from the entire field of British publishing.[45]

The proposal was well received by Lane. Throughout 1958 and 1959, Williams was hard at work with his contributors, driving the project forward. The manuscript that finally emerged was not quite what Williams originally envisaged but it was an impressive compilation. Nothing like it had been attempted before and sales prospects seemed good. Only one question remained: how much should each of the contributors – and the editor – be paid? In October 1958, Williams had sent Eunice Frost the proposed Contents, including a list of the contributions he hoped to gather from a range of distinguished writers, adding: 'I shall get all of them for something comfortably under £1,000'.[46]

Williams then put forward an unusual proposal, on how he should be rewarded for his extensive editorial work on the book:

> I assume that a royalty of 10% will be distributable among the contributors, including the editor. The contributors have all accepted outright payment for their work, and Jack Summers [Penguin's accountant] will be able to tell you what the aggregate of the payment made to them is. My estimate is that this will be a figure which will consume the entire 10% royalty on the first printing. It may even exceed this total of the 10%.
>
> I propose, therefore, that for the time being I draw no fee at all, but leave the whole of the royalty-equivalent on the first printing to the contributors. Thereafter, I trust, things will look up for the editor. On each subsequent printing, there will continue to be a royalty equivalent of 10%. From this there may have to be deducted payments to contributors to bring their material up to date, and this might well cost £250 or £300 per print. But the remainder of the royalty equivalent should then go to the editor. This procedure should be followed in every subsequent printing.
>
> This work has cost me an enormous amount of energy and time. It has been, indeed, the most exacting literary project I have ever attempted. If the project succeeds, I deserve ultimately to get most of the royalty. I would suggest, moreover, that on publication I should receive an advance of, say, £250, to be deducted of course from my ultimate takings on the work. I hope you will think this proposal reasonable.[47]

On that occasion, Lane responded with what seems to have been a more transparently generous offer than Williams had expected:

> I suggest that a more clear-cut arrangement would be to leave the first edition, as you suggest, with all the proceeds and that on all subsequent editions we should pay you a royalty of 5%, and that we should be prepared to pay reasonable sums to the contributors for revising and in some cases re-writing their contributions...
>
> I am perfectly willing to accept your proposal that we should pay you an advance of £250 on account of the first reprint now.[48]

An immediate advance of £250 plus a 5% guaranteed royalty on reprints was much better than 10% less additional payments to contributors, which Williams had proposed. For the first and only time on record, Lane makes a better offer than the original request for money. Perhaps Lane had got the message at last. The *Reader's Guide* was published in 1960 and sold well. A second, expanded and considerably revised edition was published in 1964.

In 1961, after extensive consultancy, protracted internal discussion, and a great deal of soul-searching on Lane's part, Penguin Books was floated on the London Stock Exchange. It was oversubscribed 150 times. Lane, the majority shareholder, became an overnight millionaire several times over. On 11 October 1961, Lane wrote to Williams, thanking him for his advice on how the firm's management structure might be reorganised:

> I found your letter an extremely lucid statement of the situation and as I told you yesterday, I am only too glad to fall in with your proposals which will be put in hand forthwith... We know each other too well to need to write formal letters of appreciation of each other, but I would like you to know what enormous pleasure I have derived from working with you over the greater part of my working life. This is one of the few occasions when one can really feel that something useful has come out of a warm association, and if ever we felt the need for a monument, we could well borrow the inscription which appears on Wren's tomb.[49]

On the thirtieth anniversary of the birth of Penguin Books, in April 1965, Lane wrote Williams a long, reflective letter from El Fenix, his Spanish holiday home, near Malaga. This letter deserves quoting at length because it reflects the mutual reliance of the two men:

> We first met, I think it must have been early in 1936 because at the time I was still at the Bodley Head, at Tavistock Square and both Krishna Menon & Lance Beales must have been around & that was the jumping off ground for the meetings which moved from there, with the Barcelona as an annexe, to the Ministry of Education building, Eaton Square, 117 Piccadilly & to the Arts Council.
>
> The meetings which had started out so informally, happily remained so & although I'm not conscious of any general directive, gradually by judicious pruning, some cross-fertilization and the practice of good husbandry, the growth was controlled until it became the plant which you now and I in two years time hand over to the next generation to tend.
>
> It has taken almost exactly half my life & most certainly the most rewarding part of it, & you know and I know exactly how much you have influenced both the enterprise and me over this period.
>
> I don't think that either of us could have visualized what it was going to become but both of us having a good streak of idealism & a certain toughness of purpose have made it very much in our own image. What happens after our time is beyond our control. As good gardeners or farmers we can only do our best to see that the soil is kept in good heart, free of weeds & that the crops are not forced but allowed a natural growth, in the knowledge that if these principles are followed our successors will continue to have the satisfaction from it that we have had ourselves.

> In conclusion what I have valued most has been the close friendship we have enjoyed over these many years & I look forward to many more years of companionship when we can sit and drink and talk of life and love.[50]

Williams' response to that glowing tribute expresses perhaps more clearly than any other letter the affection that radiated between the two men:

> Your letter of the 14th reached me when I got home tonight, and it has moved me very deeply indeed. The main reason why it has done so, I think, is that what you evidently believe about our long and close relationship chimes so completely with my own feeling about it. We are both civilized, adult and realistic; we have both spent our best years in creative and exacting activity and, although we have had plenty of fun, we have also worked bloody hard. We have enjoyed no social advantages in our formative years – and for all these reasons we have a kinship together, almost (even) a twinship. We have separate identities, but we belong to the same totem, and I believe both of us have always been conscious of that bond. I can truly say that for you, as for no other man, I have always recognized and cherished a profound and abiding affection. Even when things occasionally went wrong – very rarely in fact – the basic thing was never impaired, and I believe that's as true for you as it is for me...
>
> I am prouder of nothing in my professional life than the opportunity I had, for nearly 30 years, of being associated with the momentous and exciting enterprise which you created. Sometimes, like an elderly man, I sit and tell my beads! Those years of excitement and innovation, the enlightened boozing in the old Barcelona, the tantrums, the tears, the perspirations. What a compost we created for the harvest which has since been reaped!
>
> I thank God, in His infinite wisdom, for reminding me recently not to get my priorities mixed. I'm glad that I have the sense to appreciate that there comes a time when you can do no more for an institution to which you are devoted. I felt like that about the Arts Council, and I felt it about Penguins. The poet who wrote the 'Nunc Dimittis' knew what it was all about. So many people, as both of us know, mourn and grieve about what lawyers call the 'effluxion of time'. I am terribly lucky to feel as fulfilled as I do in all the work I have done. I accept the inevitable twilight, and I feel nothing but thankfulness for all the exciting opportunities I've enjoyed. It's been a wonderful and amusing ride.[51]

That remarkable exchange of letters took place shortly before Williams' sixty-seventh birthday, which marked his retirement as Secretary-General of the Arts Council and as Editor-in-Chief of Penguin Books. Between them, Lane and Williams had moulded 'the firm' – as they liked to call it – into a unique British institution. Yet in many ways, its management style and operating procedures were typical of many small, paternalistic, British family firms before the arrival of multinational conglomerates in the 1960s. There was a long-standing tradition of the Christmas staff lunch, at which Lane and his fellow Directors dressed up in chefs' uniform, serving drinks and turkey with all the trimmings to the staff, seated in ranks in the staff canteen, with seasonal music, carols and crackers. There were other social events, like staff cruises down the Thames, when juniors mixed with senior members of staff, drank too much, addressed each other in familiar terms, and lived to regret some of the things said in their cups.

The farewell party for Williams, carefully planned by Eunice Frost and Allen Lane, was a more dignified affair, with appropriate speeches, in which warm compliments were exchanged, with the shedding of an occasional tear amid the champagne glasses. By way of tribute to his long years of dedicated service to the firm, the Penguin Directors invited Williams to choose two works of art as his farewell gift – a permanent reminder of the affection they felt for him. He selected an original Paul Nash painting and a bronze head of himself, commissioned from the young Welsh sculptor, Ivor Roberts-Jones. Many years later it decorated the foyer of the Arts Council premises in Great Peter Street, Westminster.

There was, however, no parting of the ways between Williams and Lane, as their subsequent meetings and correspondence shows. After a five-week holiday in America, and a further month with Gertrude in their favourite stamping grounds in the Basque country of Spain, Williams was ready to take up his new duties as Art Adviser at the National Art-Collections Fund and at the Institute of Directors.

In September 1968, Williams wrote to Lane from Italy, outlining a proposal for what would be his final – and perhaps his most important – book:

> I'd like to do a kind of outline of culture in my time... It's never been done and it makes a significant pattern... I would take, say, three years... I'm better endowed topside (I believe) than ever before, but I now abominate all routine such as offices, committees, fund-raising, memoranda and such. If I could get that job done, in peace and security, I'd reckon I'd fulfilled my life and would settle for the eventide of a Senior Citizen. If and when the spirit flagged, I'd pay a visit to Farmer Lane and swap reminiscences over a beaker of barley-water. The more I think of it, Old Timer, the more I fancy we have something to come... I shall now swallow some cold Soave and go for a ride on a steamer.[52]

We do not have Lane's response to that letter but it was sufficiently encouraging for Williams, then entering his seventies, to set about his retirement task with his customary vigour. He was, however, over-optimistic with his projected time scale. Interrupted by a variety of other calls on his time and energy – such as the Arts Council Theatre Inquiry which occupied him for the best part of two years – he was still working at his last writing project in his final year of life.

In the mellowness of his later years, Williams poured out his feelings for Lane in a series of intimate letters of great lyrical intensity, tinged with autumnal nostalgia. Lane was sometimes moved to respond in similar vein. The following extracts are quoted at some length because they show the intensity of feeling between the two men.

On 20 September 1966, Williams wrote to Lane from his holiday hotel in San Giulio:

> Soon after I return from Italy I shall be 70, the Biblical span of three score years and ten! It's been a wonderful run, and I'm grateful to many friends and colleagues who have made it so. But the trip is nearly over, especially as I am not over-confident about my alleged recovery from the cancer caper. That doesn't worry me, as I've got the get-out capsule. I look forward to the move to Haddenham next spring, and I want at last to get the writing done. I want to do my invented autobiography, In Perspective, which won't be about me but about the things I've been involved in. But then I want to do the Allen Lane Saga, which will be a labour of love and the chronicle of a great humanist endeavour. After that – say three or five years with luck – I'll be ready to sign off.
>
> I've just re-read this letter, and it seems to have come out wrong! I'm not really sad; I'm a realist and I'm reconciled. What's the point in kidding oneself?[53]

Lane replied from The Old Mill House, West Drayton, on 4 October 1966:

> Tomorrow you will be seventy & this letter brings you all my good wishes. I well remember your fiftieth birthday in our drinking days & I've always regretted that I wasn't with you on your sixtieth when you were on one of your capers in Paris. I'm sorry that we won't be seeing each other tomorrow but I much look forward to one of our nights out a week today. As I approach my sixty fifth birthday I have decided to take some action to ensure that I make the most use of the remaining years & to this end I now work only on three days at the office & spend the remaining four at the farm. I find that I am increasingly intolerant of the pace & noise of city life & increasingly drawn to the peace & quiet of the countryside. In this I am sure that we are completely d'accord & I hope that we may spend many contemplative days together in the years to come.[54]

A year later, Williams wrote to Lane, from his holiday hotel in Spain on 14 September 1967:

> And that reminds me of a melancholy event which is only three weeks away – my seventy-first birthday. I can't believe it could ever happen to me. Time creeps up behind one's back, wearing carpet slippers. Although the Bible declares that three score years and ten is man's mortal span, I accept it with bad grace. I seem as bright as ever upstairs, but there's no kidding oneself about the diminution of sundry other powers! There's no good moaning about it, and I have much reason to be grateful for the fulfilment and variety and experience that I've enjoyed for so long. My preferences are changing rapidly. Conventional parties bore me stiff, although I relish even more than ever the company of authentic friends. A play has to be good to get me to go to it, and I hope I'll never again go to a first night in my life. The country lures me more and more. We've now got a pool at Haddenham with high-spirited fountain and a pair of lovely weeping willows. I sit and meditate by it for hours at a time.[55]

On 22 June 1968, Williams wrote to Lane from Haddenham:

> As I get older I feel a deep need for meditation, and the opportunity is hard to find so long as one continues to ride the roundabout of activity. I've been lucky enough to have had an absorbing and happy career – Penguins, Arts Council, ABCA etc. But I want no more except what I must do to keep wolves from doors. I want the last lap to be a reflection upon it all, a 'last look on all things lovely, happy undemanding comradeship, peace and quiet'.
>
> You have had a similar life: creative, successful. We've both managed, without privilege or inheritance, to reach the top of the tree. What better, now, than to talk about the long and often dangerous Odyssey that we have both fulfilled. It's now or never![56]

On 24 July 1968, Williams wrote to Lane in hospital, from Haddenham:

> I've been ringing up the hospital frequently for news about you... But I beg you to stay in low gear for a bit. I'm doing exactly that myself and I accept the cautionary value of an illness. God knows you and I have done a good whack for the world and will do more still. But it has to be in a different way from what we got used to in our more hectic days. We have wisdom and experience to offer – and these commodities are needed by our successors. But we must firmly refuse any executive activities – which isn't easy for the likes of us who have worked so long on our factory floors. What takes it out of us is solving problems of action and detail which are rightly the responsibility of our subordinates. Our contribution must be reserved for operations in the higher altitudes of government. Such is the wisdom of Old Father Williams and I hope you accept it.[57]

On 28 August 1968, Williams wrote to Lane, from Haddenham:

> I am leaving for Italy and I hope I'll be free of tempests and hailstones for a short time. I wish you were coming too, so that we two wise old soldiers could sit in the sun and ruminate upon our campaigns and adventures. We've been shoulder to shoulder for well over thirty years and I want us to stay that way for two or three more laps.
>
> I find myself in very much in two minds when I meditate on my life at the moment. I deplore the decline of some of my powers – such as stamina, mobility, sex and a few others. On the other hand I am grateful for the extent and variety of the fulfilment I've had in work, in fun, in friendship and in bed!
>
> The lesson I am hoping to learn is to be happy with what still remains, and I am discovering some new satisfactions. For the first time in my life I am beginning to like the country more than London (which I have adored in my time); I prefer, now, peace to passion, and meditation to excitement.
>
> I suppose I am also becoming more selective, more demanding. I only want things I trust – an old friend, a well-remembered landscape, a familiar poem or picture or piece of music. I am becoming self-indulgent, I suppose, but not to anyone else's detriment. 'For now I know the things I know. And do the things I do...'
>
> I have much enjoyed coming to see you, for you fortify me in so many ways. No two people can have come so close to each other without creating some vital relationship, and I know how sustained I am by that fact. Sustained, too, by your volatile and courageous endurance of what you have gone through. I'll send you despatches from Italy, and I'll see you soon.[58]

On 28 August 1968, Lane wrote to Williams from the Middlesex Hospital:

> I'm thinking of you now on your way to the warmth and sunshine of Lake Como. I can't tell you how much I have appreciated your visits to this rather dismal cell. Having enjoyed rude health up the present time it comes a bit hard to face some of the problems of mortality.
>
> At the same time being on one's own for fairly long stretches gives one a chance of reflecting on one's life and working out plans for the years that remain.
>
> Here I feel that we are on parallel courses, recognizing the limitations which nature is imposing, we are determined to enjoy the next phase as much as we have its predecessors.
>
> I've had just on fifty years of city life, and that is enough. Now for a bit of peace and quiet. Not that I haven't enjoyed the half-century to the full. I have, but the time has come to give up the daily struggle, and drift with the stream.
>
> There's a new crisis on at Harmondsworth, but I'm far enough away to feel detached from it. I think perhaps the tiredness which comes over one after a go like this acts as a protection against involvement.
>
> I'm now due to go down to the Dr Who [radiotherapy] department. I must say I won't be sorry when all this is over.[59]

On 3 September 1968, Williams, in Italy, wrote to Allen Lane in hospital:

> The letter I got from you yesterday was a most agreeable surprise. I didn't expect that you could yet have the energy to put pen to paper, and it comforts me greatly that you can. I wish you were here, because the place has everything one needs in getting back on to an even keel. One lovely experience is to loll in a chaise longue on the big bedroom balcony with an unread Penguin in the lap, and a euphoric medley of impressions filtering through the drowsy mind – the lake constantly murmuring, the mountain peaks, the lake-steamers bustling about. The hotel is delightful: excellent Italian food including masses of muscatel grapes and juicy peaches and admirable wines at about 12/6 a bottle. The pension is only about three guineas a day each.
>
> Our principal excitement is sailing on the pretty lake-steamers which zig-zag to villages around the lake. You can get a dreamy sun-sozzled two-hour sail, to a place like Como, get off and drink something in the shade and then float back to base in a hot sun tempered by a breeze. These trips make lovely afternoons, from which I return renewed, with bugger-all on my mind. There's no currency problem either, because toffs like you and me, in the top league of illness, get a personal extra allowance of £7 a day, and the wives who look after us, get the same. It gives me quite a kick to watch some poor bloody Briton timidly ordering lemonade while I bellow for another bottle of Valpollicella or Soave. And I know I deserve it! ...
>
> You said there was another crisis at Harmondsworth – and that you couldn't care less. Good for you – and don't weaken. As I get old and crusty I lose patience with our successors: the Godwins of this world, who worship the golden handshake and the bitch-goddess of intrigue. And they aren't even happy in their sham-success. A pox on them!

> I don't know how many years I've got, but I intend to get all I can out of them. Like you, I've done fifty years of hard work and I've enjoyed them. But enough is enough, and I haven't it in me now to carry on at the same old pace or launch out on something new. I will not settle on serenity, and an ever deeper enjoyment of things I've found to be precious. In that category, my boy, is a friendship with you of more than thirty years, a friendship which develops a rich patina with the passage of time. We must take care of each other, amuse and divert each other, and never go long without talking to each other.
>
> I'll be seeing you soon, and I look forward to the day out at the farm that we spoke about. Meanwhile just keep getting better, as you have so demonstrably been doing.
>
> Gertrude sends you love and the best possible wishes. Give ours to Lettice – and mine to you.[60]

On 7 July 1970, Lane died of bowel cancer at Mount Vernon Hospital. Five days after Lane's death, Williams contributed a tribute to the *Sunday Times* of 12 July 1970:

> Every bookstall in Britain testifies to the revolution of our reading habits which Lane inspired, and his name can be bracketed with Lord Reith's as a pioneer of popular culture. Either of them could be called the Moses of Mass Communications… I was one of three people to whom he turned when the heat was on [in the early days], and we all gave him the same advice. We counselled him to raise his sights, not lower them; to begin the Pelican series and to launch those Penguin Specials which, as the World War approached, reminded people what was at stake if the dictators got away with murder… He was, in many ways, not an easy man to work with. He was unpredictable, capricious and sometimes ruthless. If he trusted you he was liable to ask for your advice. But that did not necessarily mean that he would accept it.
>
> But what we shall now remember him for is the abundance and excellence of those Penguin harvests he gathered in for the last thirty-five years. What he created is one of the decisive influences of this century.[61]

Lane's death hit Williams badly. He had lost his best friend and was compelled to confront his own mortality. Having finally given up his responsibilities at the National Art-Collections Fund and at the Institute of Directors, he and Gertrude looked forward to renovating an old mill they had bought at Blockley, in the Cotswolds. He had wanted to spend more time with 'Farmer Lane' and Lady Lettice, reflecting on the good times they had shared, and counting their blessings over a congenial bottle or two. He had intended to devote more time to writing his 'invented biography'. But once 'the maestro' had gone, he was bereft – an elderly stranded editor – a beached literary whale.

On 22 October 1970, Williams wrote a consolatory letter to Eunice Frost, Allen Lane's devoted assistant:

> I feel exactly as you do about what has happened to us this summer, and I cannot escape from the finality and despair of it all. I saw Allen a lot in those last two years and, until he went to Mount Vernon, I thought he was holding his own through the ordeal.
>
> I'm doing very little work and have no stamina for anything. I had a slight heart attack three weeks ago, but the peace of Haddenham is working its spell. Like you, I can summon up no interest in the goings-on of Harmondsworth. For me the Penguin planet has plunged off on a remote orbit and I shall never see it again. It's all the worst grief I have ever known. I can't even think coherently about it all yet, but I suppose that condition will pass eventually.[62]

Before Lane died, Williams had promised to write a full-length history of Penguin Books, to expand what he had written in *The Penguin Story*, back in 1956. He wrote to members of the Penguin survivors club, seeking useful memories or anecdotes. But after Lane died, he changed his mind and wrote a memoir instead. In 1973, the Bodley Head published Williams' *Allen Lane: A Personal Portrait* – a 'personal recollection of Allen Lane as he knew him, giving credit to his virtues but not disguising his faults'. Williams kept writing to his Penguin associates until his own death. There were no more letters from his oldest and closest friend but he found solace in writing that brief memoir as a final tribute to 'an infuriating, mercurial comrade who was dearer to me than any other man in my life'.[63]

An editorial meeting at Penguin Books in London c1950. Left to right – 'TK' Tatiana Schmoller, J E Morpurgo, Richard Lane, Allen Lane, Bill Williams, Eunice Frost and Alan Glover.

Estrid Bannister, on her honeymoon, aged 18, in 1922.

Seven: Bill and Estrid

My beloved, I shall obey you unconditionally, for you are the force and guidance of my life. You see, no claws ever.

W E Williams to Estrid Bannister, 1958

When Estrid Bannister first met Bill Williams, the heavens themselves flashed fire. It was love at first sight and love everlasting – or so Estrid would have us believe:

He and I took one look at each other and fell instantly in love. His name was William Emrys Williams, Bill to his friends, and this amazing 'coup de foudre' which happened between us lasted, in its fashion, for the rest of our lives.[1]

It is poignant to recall that Gertrude Williams used remarkably similar, if less dramatic, language to describe her own first meeting with Billy, twenty years earlier: 'As soon as we met we fell in love and remained so for the rest of his life'.[2]

Neither woman had read the other's story. Estrid's autobiography was published in 1992, by which time Gertrude was ten years dead. Gertrude's memoir remained unpublished until 2000, shortly after Estrid's death. Taken together, those separate accounts of their first meeting with Williams may convey something of his magnetic sexual attraction for women. Gertrude's account suggests an exemplary union. Although they were devoted to each other for almost sixty years, Gertrude's memoir tactfully omits any mention of Billy's extra-marital affairs. Estrid's account is therefore more honest. That telling phrase – 'in its fashion' – hints at the underlying turbulence in their remarkable, long-lasting love affair. Yet, when I finally contrived to meet her, at the very end of her life – stretched out on a day bed, overlooking the blue waters of Glandore Bay in the west of Ireland – her frail hands were clutching a silver-framed photograph of a youthful Bill Williams, taken more than fifty years earlier.

Since there are few independent sources to corroborate her story, we are heavily reliant on what Estrid tells us about her relationship with Bill Williams. We should remember, however, that Estrid was almost ninety when she published her autobiography. It soon becomes clear that her memory was already seriously failing. She tells us, for example, that:

Bill went to Manchester University where he studied theology. He took his vows and was called up for service in the First World War but even Padres get wounded and he was invalided out. After this happened, Bill went into education, especially adult education.[3]

The facts, however, are quite different. The historical record shows that Williams studied English, not Theology; that he never took his vows, was never ordained, and never served as a padre in the First World War. He never joined the army, was never wounded, and never invalided out. Why did Estrid get her facts so wrong? Did she invent her own romanticised version of his early life? Or had Williams sought to impress her with tales of Christian heroism, which she herself wanted to believe? If Estrid's evidence is so inaccurate on Williams' early life, we surely cannot accept at face value every detail of her account of their later life together.

Estrid Bannister was just thirty-three when she was introduced to Williams at the Norwegian Club in London in 1937. Daughter of a Danish sea captain, she was a feisty, curvaceous, Scandinavian blonde, not beautiful in the Garbo or Bergman mould, but certainly an attractive young woman, with a lively personality and a healthy appetite for sexual adventure. She was just eighteen, in 1922, when she married her first husband, Don Bannister, a successful British businessman, with whom she travelled and lived in Shanghai and other exotic places. Having divorced Bannister in 1932, she gathered a sequence of lovers, including Ole Haslund, the Danish antiques collector, Rockwell Kent, the American painter, Baron Wrangel, the Swedish billionaire, Hans Bruun, the Greenland explorer, and Joergen-Franz Jacobsen, the Danish-Faroese author, who embodied Estrid as 'Barbara' in his novel of that name.

According to William Heinesen, his friend and fellow writer, it was Jacobsen's intention 'that Estrid, alias Barbara, should be portrayed "in her inexhaustible charm" and "fundamentally equally fantastic insufficiency", which is justified on the ground of her only possessing "one strength, her sex"'.[4] When Jacobsen was rushed to hospital in 1935, suffering from terminal tuberculosis, Estrid immediately embarked on a new relationship. Jacobsen died tragically young, aged thirty-seven, without finishing his novel, which was completed by Heinesen. Andro Linklater describes the book as

> ...one of the great classics of modern Danish literature. Since its publication in 1939 it has never been out of print. It has been translated into 16 languages, and generations of Danish schoolchildren have read as a set text its story of the compulsively faithless heroine, whose hazel-green eyes, tall, fair figure and electrifying effect on men were all borrowed from Estrid. Yet the portrait he painted of her is not merely affectionate, but almost admiring.[5]

After her divorce, Estrid worked for some time as a freelance journalist, publishing occasional articles in Denmark's leading newspaper, *Berlingske Tidende*. By her own account, there had been many other men in Estrid's life before she met Bill Williams. But they were soon discarded:

> Bill became my whole life. I stopped writing for Berlingske Tidende. They must have wondered what had happened to me but I had only one thought in my head and that was Bill. We decided to make a life together and I went back to Denmark in order to sort things out for my return to London and to Bill, who had promised to find me a job.[6]

What of Bill's feelings for Estrid? He was just forty and had been married to Gertrude for almost twenty years. Within days of meeting – perhaps on the very first day – Bill and Estrid became lovers. The first note he ever sent her, inviting her to dinner, seems to confirm that impression:

> You said you would use up Monday evening with me. So this is what I suggest: We have to eat, whatever else we do, so will you eat with me at the 'Etoile' in Charlotte Street at 7.30? After that we can decide whether to stay in town or drive out somewhere...or else you may decide that you've had quite enough of my inanities. I'll ring you in the morning about 10.30 to hear what you think.[7]

We know from various sources that Williams was susceptible to the attractions of younger women.[8] But Estrid was clearly different from the others, for this was to be no brief, passing affair. She remained Williams' mistress, close friend and travelling companion for the next twenty years. How soon Gertrude became aware of their relationship is not clear; but her response was strangely ambivalent. One member of Gertrude's family suggests that she may have colluded in the relationship because she did not see it as a serious threat to her marriage. Another family member reports that, in the early days, Bill and Estrid were sensibly discreet about their relationship, so that it was not recognised by other members of the family:

> I think it unlikely that the family knew about the relationship before the war (1939) – but after a while then, it would have been, and we all certainly thought something was up [from] 1945 onwards because Billy left Gertrude after tea every Sunday. I think she probably knew, but was determined to keep it private.[9]

Marital relations are nearly always inscrutable to outsiders. One-sided accounts by one of the spouses are notoriously unreliable. It is therefore impossible to be sure exactly when and how Gertrude first became aware of Billy's infidelity with Estrid. It seems unlikely that Billy ever volunteered the information. Did Gertrude perhaps suspect Billy's infidelity, challenge him, and accept his denial? Or did she turn a blind eye, knowing that he genuinely loved her and would never leave her? We may speculate along those lines but can never know for certain.

In the absence of more convincing evidence, we turn back to Estrid, the unreliable narrator, never forgetting that she was already a very old woman when she wrote her autobiography, and that her fallible memory often let her down. She tells us, for example, how their relationship was developing in the immediate pre-war years:

> War was still a while away, its storm cloud slowly gathering over Europe and Bill and I were together and in love. Finally, we took the plunge, so to speak, and moved into a little basement flat in Swiss Cottage, near Hampstead Heath and close to the underground and buses... The place was perfect for my needs and my money... When I had some furniture sent over from Denmark the whole place was transformed into a charming, cosy flat. Bill and I thought our home perfect, as did the many friends who visited us there.[10]

Some of the inconsistencies in Estrid's story are immediately apparent. If the storm cloud was gathering but war was still a while away, the year was probably 1938. Her account suggests that she and Billy acted jointly: '*we* took the plunge... *we* moved into our home'. But she also says that the flat was perfect 'for *my* needs and *my* money' and that she felt sufficiently settled to bring some of her furniture out of storage in Denmark. Nevertheless, the impression she seeks to convey is that she and Bill moved into the flat, sharing a joint household and a settled life together:

> When I first arrived in London, I couldn't boil an egg. All my married life I had had servants and as a child in Denmark mother had always been in charge of the kitchen, so I had never bothered to learn. Now I had to. Obviously Bill and I could not afford to eat out all the time and besides, we wanted to spend our evenings together in our tiny home. For ages we lived on spaghetti and cauliflower with 'cheese topside'... Almost every weekend Bill and I went off into the country in his car, as a result I got to know England, Scotland and Wales quite well.[11]

Where did that cosy picture of frugal domesticity leave Gertrude? Even if she colluded in Bill's relationship with Estrid from as early as 1937, would she have tolerated his absence from home throughout the week and at weekends, too? Gertrude loved her husband and was determined to preserve her marriage for personal, professional and social reasons. If we ignore his infidelities, Billy was a highly intelligent, supportive, and congenial husband and partner. Who could know how long his affair with Estrid might last? Gertrude may well have reasoned that, if she refused to acknowledge Estrid, or legitimate her existence, she could ignore her status as Bill's mistress. But how far could Estrid ignore Gertrude? How well did she grasp the hidden strength of Bill and Gertrude's marriage and their mutual commitment? According to Estrid,

> Bill had told me that he was married. It had come as a shock even though I had no plans in that respect. I felt that I had had enough of marriage. I couldn't have any more children, although I would like to have had Bill's child, marriage or no marriage. It was a hot summer day when Bill dropped his bombshell... I borrowed a little dinghy and rowed out on the Oresund [between Denmark and Sweden] to think things over. After a while I rowed back to the shore where poor Bill was anxiously waiting. My mind was made up, I would stay with him no matter what.[12]

On a later occasion, when Estrid went on a short trip to Denmark, probably to visit her mother, she was pursued by a *News Chronicle* journalist. As Estrid recounts the episode, Bill wrote her a witty, mock-threatening love letter:

> I have the constant worry that I mightn't be around (even on paper) when you need me and that finding me absent, you run away with the captain of the HMS Courageous, or the bastard from the *News Chronicle*. Jealous...no, because I know you love me, and because it's one of the corrosive diseases that I've got through for good, many years ago. Possessive... again, no, because you can't hold love in any kind of a net. But for all that, I flinch a little because you are with other people and I mope a little when I remember how inevitably men will want to seduce you. It would be easier to be jealous, to be engulfed in one consistent mood of green...
>
> Darling, this sounds as if I'm a pig. I'm not really; I just can't pretend that I'm the same separated as I am united. I grudge everything we don't do together and I scowl at everyone who has you when I can't...man, woman, child or dog alike. And now I'll behave, and mostly I do: and when we are together I will have none of these undercurrents.
>
> But Estrid, darling, NOT the *News Chronicle*, NOT a penny paper. Be raped by The Times if you must, but not by a vulgar, democratic organ. Tell the bastard that if he makes a pass at you, I'll choke him with his own infamous paper; I'll stuff it by the yard down his lewd and licentious throat. Tell him I'll create a first-class sensational murder, which he won't be able to scoop because he'll be in the mortuary. And tell him in soft accents, that I will distribute his guts for garters among the whores of Piccadilly.[13]

That letter – frivolous, amusing, yet expressing genuine feeling in Williams' characteristic style – is full of the whimsical word-play which he loved. He was probably incapable of committing murder but was fortunately never put to the test. According to Estrid, it was just one of hundreds of letters that she claimed she received from him: 'From the start of our relationship, Bill and I wrote to each other every day when we were apart. I still have all his wonderful letters'.[14]

The declaration of war on Sunday, 3 September 1939 found Bill and Estrid spending the weekend together in the Cotswolds. Their first two years had been a heady mix of sexual excitement and subterfuge. As Secretary of the British Institute of Adult Education (BIAE), Bill was in the habit of spending considerable time away from home on business without arousing Gertrude's suspicion. He was therefore able to meet Estrid at secret locations, initially well away from London, where they could conduct their relationship without risk of intrusion or discovery. Gertrude was, in any case, heavily pre-occupied with her teaching and research at Bedford College, and her many extra-mural activities.

Back in London, where the lovers were more vulnerable to discovery, they exercised more discretion. Estrid's basement flat in Swiss Cottage was ideally located within easy reach of Bill's office in Tavistock Square and of the Williams' flat in

Westbourne Terrace, Paddington. As Chief Editorial Adviser at Penguin Books, Williams had arranged for Estrid to be retained as a part-time 'advisor and translator from the Danish'. There was no reason why they should not be seen together in public. But once installed in Estrid's flat, they were safe from prying eyes and free to express their true feelings.

At an earlier stage of their marriage, Billy and Gertrude loved getting out of London, walking in the countryside, and exploring the rural scene. So there was a strong tradition of weekends in the country. By the time he met Estrid in 1937, Williams could afford the modest luxury of a weekend for two at a small country hotel.

According to Estrid, they were staying at Burford, near Oxford, over the first weekend of September 1939. On Sunday morning, 3 September, they gathered round the hotel wireless with other guests to hear Prime Minister Chamberlain's 11am broadcast, announcing that Britain was at war with Germany. Bill listened attentively to that broadcast, not only for its historic importance, but because its style and content formed the basis of his *Critic on the Hearth* column in the following week's edition of *The Listener.* As soon as the broadcast ended, they lost no time in implementing their precautionary plans. As Estrid reports:

> Bill went back to London and I went to nearby Bath. We had been discussing for some time what I should do in case of war. For some strange reason I imagined myself as a 'land girl', doing good work in the country and driving a tractor... There was a recruiting office in Bath and I volunteered...but they very politely refused my offer. I drew a sigh of relief and headed back to London.[15]

The air-raid sirens had sounded before Estrid reached London but some months were to pass before the war impacted their lives directly. Having spent considerable time in the late 1930s reflecting on the prospect of war, Williams was better prepared than some of his contemporaries for the practical steps he must take, once war was declared. As Secretary of the BIAE, he knew he must initially stay at his post, with a reduced staff, re-organising the work of the Institute to cope with wartime conditions. There was much talk of air raid precautions. Government policy decreed that school-age children, nursing mothers, and major government departments should be evacuated from urban centres in anticipation of heavy bombing raids by the Luftwaffe. That mass evacuation was already under way. How long would the Institute be able to continue with its normal activities? Meetings of its Executive had already been arranged. A National Conference was due to begin at Cambridge in mid-September. The Institute's *Art for the People* exhibition was due to open shortly at the City Literary Institute.

It was in this atmosphere of gloom and uncertainty that Williams received an unexpected and welcome morale-booster: a commission to prepare an anthology of English essays for Penguin Books. He accepted the commission and in due course produced his *Book of English Essays*, his best-selling publication, discussed earlier in Chapter 6.

Estrid spent her first wartime Christmas with friends at a country cottage near Colchester, some forty miles from London. Bill was spending Christmas, as usual, with his family. His father, Thomas Owen, was by then seventy-nine years old. Bill and his sister, Edith, recognised that they might not all survive the war. Who knew whether they would ever spend another Christmas together? A few days after Christmas, Bill travelled to Colchester to be with Estrid, despite the bitter weather that engulfed south-east England. The cottage was well provisioned: the food was plentiful and the drink flowed freely before blazing log fires. They brought in the New Year with a flourish.

On returning to London, Estrid discovered her home was flooded after the frozen pipes in her house had burst:

> When I got home there was seven inches of water on the floor. Pictures had fallen out of their frames and were floating about. Books and furniture were ruined. It was a sad end to a lovely holiday, everything had to be sent away to be dried. [Friends] very kindly put me up... until I found my lovely house in Harbin Road, just around the corner from Belsize Road. [16]

According to Estrid, Williams spent most of his free time with her at Harbin Road where they settled down happily, hosting many congenial wartime parties, despite the frequent shortage of food and drink, and heavy bombing during the London blitz. She obviously loved her new wartime home. It comprised the lower half of

> ...a four-storeyed Victorian house, with a wonderful south-facing walled garden [which was] truly lovely and had obviously been planted by someone with a great love and knowledge of gardening. There were mulberry trees, red and white horse chestnuts and many more. In summer I couldn't see any other houses for the green canopy provided by my trees. The garden walls had roses of every description trained against them so that all through the summer there was an abundance of blossom and fragrance.[17]

Early in 1940, Bill was seconded from the Institute to undertake a special assignment for the War Office. Within a year he accepted the post of Director of the Army Bureau of Current Affairs (ABCA). That took him away from London and around the country for weeks at a time. But it had advantages for Estrid:

> By rights, Bill should have been in uniform but then I should not have been able to travel with him. He also should have carried the rank of brigadier and driven in an army car with an army driver. It was fun to see the reactions when we drove up to military headquarters where Bill was due to speak about ABCA, most irregular![18]

Back in London, Bill spent several nights each week with Estrid in Harbin Road, travelling daily to his work at the War Office. The house remained undamaged throughout the war. When its owner died, the bank put the house up for sale at £350:

> We bargained and bargained until I eventually got it for £50! Even more amazing was the fact that Bill had won the £50 on a horse called 'My Love'. What actually happened was that I bought the tail end of a lease with just seven years left on it...I didn't understand any of this but got a good bargain for my money because I managed to get my lease renewed for another 14 years.[19]

Bill and Estrid shared exciting times in wartime Britain, visiting army depots and camps, being entertained in officers' messes, spending time in Cardiff, Edinburgh and Belfast. They even contrived a visit to Dublin:

> It was fabulous, going from completely blacked out London to a city where the street and houses were lit up... We could even have a light on in our hotel room and the food was out of this world. We bought dozens of eggs and had them raw for breakfast and we ate steak twice a day.[20]

But there were darker times, too. The war was going badly. France had capitulated, the Low Countries were overrun, and Denmark was occupied by the German army – a terrible blow to Estrid, whose mother was living in Copenhagen. Then came the long-promised German bombing campaign. Londoners took to their underground shelters, night after night, and woke each morning to widespread death and destruction. There was heavy property damage; roads and pavements were frosted each morning with broken glass. On 12 September 1940, Bill and Gertrude's top-floor flat in Westbourne Terrace was fire-bombed and destroyed. On Friday 13 September 1940, Bill threw himself down on the pavement in Euston Road to avoid the blast, when a stick of bombs fell near King's Cross.[21]

Throughout the war, in addition to his ABCA duties, Bill wrote his weekly column for *The Listener* as an independent reviewer of the BBC's output of 'The Spoken Word'. Night after night, he and Estrid sat by their wireless, in her Harbin Road flat, listening to the speeches, talks and features broadcast on the BBC Home and Forces programmes. Bill often worked late into the night, drafting and polishing his manuscript for publication in the following week's edition of *The Listener*.

When the European war eventually ended in 1945, and Denmark was liberated, Estrid lost no time in returning to see her mother, family and friends. Meanwhile Bill was touring British army camps in Germany on ABCA business. According to Estrid, at the beginning of August 1945, he turned up in Denmark in a large open car, which had formerly belonged to Hermann Goering.[22]

Back in England, Bill and Estrid continued to celebrate the return of peace with a hectic round of parties and functions. But they were soon forced to face up to life in post-war Britain. Bill left the War Office and began work on plans to convert the military form of ABCA into the civilian Bureau of Current Affairs. Estrid, for her part, undertook translation work for various publishers, including Penguin Books, where Allen Lane had become a close personal friend. Douglas Rust, formerly Royalties Manager, and before that Payroll Manager, at Penguin Books, describes how and when he first heard of Estrid:

> It was about this time [the early 1950s] that Allen Lane asked me confidentially to set up in the pay-roll a new editorial person by the name of Estrid Bannister. The charge was to be made to WEW's current account in the company's books. Whilst he was telling me this he raised his head and said, with a slight wink and a nod: "This must not get back to Lady Williams. I know I can trust you with it". It was some years later when I read an article in one of the Sunday papers ['The Naughtiest Girl of the Century' by Andro Linklater] that the truth came out.[23]

In addition to advising Penguin Books on Scandinavian literature, Estrid selected and edited a collection of Scandinavian Short Stories, published as early as August 1943. She later translated two books by the Danish anthropologist, Jens Bjerre: *The Last Cannibals* (1957) and *Kalahari* (1960).

Soon after the war ended, the newly-established Arts Council backed Estrid's proposal to organise a small travelling exhibition of Danish furnishing design, and related products such as silver, pottery and wallpaper. The exhibition, which opened at the Geffrye Museum in Bethnal Green, was a great success, leading to a second, expanded exhibition at the RIBA headquarters in Portland Street. As Estrid tells us, she began to earn regular money of her own: 'I got my wages from Penguin Books and the Arts Council at the beginning of every month'.[24]

The immediate post-war years were crammed with exciting new projects and adventures for Bill and Estrid. They went to Aldeburgh for the first Britten-Pears concerts; they attended the opening of the Edinburgh Festival; and they celebrated the 1951 Festival of Britain in London and at St Davids in Pembrokeshire. Foreign travel restrictions were lifted soon after the war but there were strict limits on the amount of currency allowed for foreign travel. They nevertheless shared some holidays abroad, including visits to Rome, Venice and Delphi.

Tanya Kent – who worked closely with Allen Lane at Penguin Books in the immediate post-war years and who later married Hans Schmoller, chief designer at Penguin – stayed for some time with Estrid at Harbin Road. She remembers Estrid as a very good cook, and an excellent hostess. There were memorable parties in the basement flat, with some distinguished guests, much drinking and regular sing-songs, including 'Men of Harlech' in honour of Bill Williams. Most revealing of all, she recalls Estrid as 'the nearest thing to a nymphomaniac I've ever met'. She was, however, not just a 'sex kitten' but a highly intelligent woman, with a very good eye and a keen interest in design.[25]

Early in 1947, Williams accepted an invitation from Julian Huxley, Unesco's Director-General, to undertake an assignment on adult education. He spent the next few months at Unesco headquarters in Paris, working with other leading European specialists, developing its future education policy. In June, he wrote from Paris to Lane at Penguin Books, expressing his frustration over the long drawn-out assignment, tempered by the compensatory pleasures of Paris in early summer:

> Of Unesco as a whole my opinion, from close quarters, is even lower than it was. But Paris continues to be Paris & Estrid and I are enjoying its June beauty, an occasional evening at a fairy-tale restaurant in the Bois & many agreeable gastronomic discoveries on the Left Bank. Many Unescans enquire about you and seem to have had their lives brightened by a drink and a word with the Archiepiscopal Penguin.[26]

During the summer of 1948, Bill was juggling his work priorities between Paris and London, where he was struggling to establish the Bureau of Current Affairs, and serving as Lane's chief editorial adviser at Penguin Books. But he found time for a short holiday with Estrid at Pramousquier, in the South of France. From there, he invited Lane to share a few days with them in Paris, combining work with pleasure. When Lane failed to appear, as previously arranged, Williams wrote him a frantic letter, full of concern for Lane's well-being, with instructions on where to obtain the necessary hard currency to survive in Paris:

> Absolutely devastated with disappointment that your caravan has failed to turn up... I can only assume something's gone awry, and I hope it's nothing serious... Any minute now I must give you up and wander away to weep on my desolate pillow. The hell of it is that I leave for London in the morning... However let me collect my shattered wits sufficiently to say that I have left an emergency fund of 15,000 Francs for you, if necessary, at Unesco. They are in the keeping of a nice little man called Flann who does my chores. He can double the figure at a pinch. Ring Kleber 5200 and ask for him.
>
> Secondly, if you have any petrol coupons to spare (at any price) would you send some to Estrid, whose current boy-friend cannot bring her back to Paris unless he gets enough to do about 150 miles = 30 litres. If by God's grace you have any surplus, would you mail them thus:
>
> Madame Estrid Bannister, chez Monsieur H O Guignard, Ecueille, Indre.
> Christ Jesus Almighty, what a tangled web we all do weave.[27]

Whether Lane ever mailed spare petrol coupons to Monsieur Guignard, enabling him to drive Estrid back to Paris, we do not know. The archives are silent on the matter. Lane certainly called on Flann for the 15,000 francs, which Williams later reclaimed. But if Williams thought his life in France with Estrid and her 'current boy-friend' was a tangled web, which merited that powerful expletive, there were more exotic tangles to come – not in France but in Ireland.

Estrid was now approaching fifty, and showing signs of restlessness. Once more, she went off to France, a country she had always loved, with the idea of finding a place of her own in Provence or the Dordogne. She eventually found an affordable, run-down chateau:

> I told everybody I had found a dream castle and everybody got very excited about it. The plan was to buy and run it as a guesthouse but obviously this wasn't meant to be and everything fell through... The restlessness haunted me... What was wrong with me? Life was interesting and challenging but I was always looking for something else. The problem was that I didn't know for what I was looking. I had been delighted with my house in Harbin Road, now I wanted to move. I loved Bill very much but I had lovers too. All the travelling and excitement didn't fill the void that existed within me. Then in 1954 I went to Ireland again. This time it was to the south-west of the country and I fell completely in love with it.[28]

When Estrid fell in love with something, she was determined to have it. At Easter 1955, she persuaded Bill to return with her to Ireland, where they explored the south-west coastal area, in search of a suitable property. By chance, they found an empty fisherman's cottage, near the village of Rosscarbery, and bought it outright for £47. It was connected to the electricity supply but lacked such modern amenities as heating, running water and indoor sanitation. That did not deter Estrid who was thrilled with the prospect of refurbishing the cottage. She devoted many months of hard physical work to directing and supervising local workmen, who undertook the structural tasks, demolishing walls, rebuilding the fireplace, installing a new bathroom. When the building was complete, she did all the decoration herself, before giving the cottage a final touch of Danish style with her new furnishing:

> One of the many charming features about my cottage, Rose Cottage, was the fact that it was so near the sea. Bill came over as often as he could and we spent many happy hours swimming and sunbathing on the lovely sandy beach. Allen Lane had, of course, heard about this idyllic place and he came to visit. Between the house and the sea was a tract of land called 'The Warren'... Allen Lane was horrified at the thought of this unspoilt place falling prey to property developers so he bought it. Rosscarbery should be forever grateful to him as it is still unspoilt today.[29]

Estrid was fully absorbed by her project. Where others might have feared to tread, Estrid relished the challenge. It engaged all her energy, as well as her undoubted artistic and creative skills. In her autobiography she explains that she wanted her cottage as a retreat from London, somewhere she could work and relax at the same time. She also welcomed a stream of visitors, many of whom came to stay, or to rent Rose Cottage, when she was in England. She was also able to let the Harbin Road house, and so had some additional income. Her life must at last have seemed almost complete. But neither Estrid nor Bill could have foreseen the bizarre events that were about to transform her life. She tells the story in dispassionate and remarkably frank terms:

> In the summer of 1958, Bill and I were back there again and one day a fisherman came round selling fish. Much later this man told me that he had made up his mind then and there to marry me. His name was Ernest Good... This was the start of a quite remarkable romance... The physical side of my relationship with Bill had dwindled over the years; perhaps if we had had the chance of marriage things would have been different; as it was I suppose I never felt married. There had been many lovers but I was never promiscuous, I simply hadn't found what I was looking for until Ernest came along. Bill was the best friend I've ever known and he accepted everything. He wrote me the following letter:
>
> "Darling... On my way home in the train, I thought a lot about our discussions and I am absolutely certain that your wisdom and honesty have once more brought us to a 100% right decision. I see that we reached our milestone when you had the world to yourself and were able to think things over.
>
> Darling Puss... I have never seen you so calm and collected as this time after so many weeks of undisturbed peace. When you have weighed the case alone, your decisions have always been brave and dramatic. My beloved, I shall obey you unconditionally, for you are the force and guidance of my life. You see, no claws, ever..."[30]

How do we explain Estrid's apparently irrational and impulsive behaviour in abandoning Bill Williams in favour of an unknown local fisherman? In one sense, she provides an honest answer to those questions. She was still only 55, whereas Bill was now 62. She wanted to settle down and be married again. Bill was not free to marry her, or did not wish to do so. She had fallen in love with Ernest, just as she had fallen in love with Bill, and her many other partners. There were no half-measures with Estrid. But she had known Bill Williams for more than twenty years – and was certainly not ready to give him up simply because she intended to marry Ernest. Like Bill, she wanted the best of both worlds. Her forthcoming marriage did not inhibit her from making special demands on Bill:

> Ernest was ten years younger than Estrid, almost twenty years younger than Bill. His father, a strict Methodist, had sent him to public school in Dublin, hoping that he would

eventually take over the family milling business. But Ernest had other ideas. He was not academy material and soon dropped out of school. For the next 18 years, he earned a precarious living doing casual work in and around Rosscarbery. He then became a fisherman, spending three or four days a week at sea, and a couple of days on the road, selling his catch. That was how he had come to call on Estrid at Rose Cottage.

> Ernest wanted to marry me. I was in rather a state of shock; everything seemed to have happened so quickly but somehow it seemed the right thing to do and I agreed. It was important to Ernest that we were married in church. His father told him that no minister would marry him and was absolutely furious when no less than two men of the cloth offered to perform the ceremony. We were married on 27th September 1958 by Reverend Ritchie in Clonakilty Methodist Church. Ernest's brother, Ronnie, and my sister were the witnesses and Bill gave me away.[31]

Estrid casually drops in that last comment, as though it was perfectly reasonable to tell her lover of twenty years that she intended to marry another man – and then to ask the lover to give her away at her wedding. Being the man he was, Williams agreed. But how did he feel when carrying out his ceremonial duties? It was apparently not until the wedding breakfast that Estrid realised the pain she had caused him:

> Suddenly my eyes were filled with tears, I pretended I had got mustard in them but really it was because I knew Bill would be walking up and down the beach in tears. It was a terrible wrench and yet we were still as close, in spite of everything. 'I have been faithful to thee Cynara, in my fashion'. Ernest understood perfectly how I felt and was always loving and caring to me and a good friend to Bill. Bill and I still kept up our daily correspondence as we had done for the last 21 years, it was as necessary and as natural to us as breathing.[32]

It may have seemed 'necessary and natural' to Estrid. But are we to believe that her long-standing and once passionate relationship with Bill was now transformed into a mere platonic friendship, which Ernest had no difficulty in accepting? Ernest must have known he had married an unconventional and high-spirited woman, who kept her former lover closely informed of her new life and did not hesitate to turn to him when she ran out of money.

The newly-weds settled down to enjoy married life in Rose Cottage – for a short while, at least. Estrid then decided that the cottage was too small and realised she could make more money by investing in a larger home and converting it into a guest-house. By chance, they discovered a suitable property in the attractive neighbouring village of Glandore:

> It was a great rambling Georgian house and was called Shorecliffe House – I was in love again! I was still working for Penguin [Books] and doing translating so, with the help of Bill and Allen Lane, I got a loan to buy Shorecliffe. The lease on Harbin Road was at an

> end so I had all the rest of my furniture and things moved over. Shorecliffe cost £2,500, complete with the 16 acres and the outbuildings. We put in central heating and redecorated... We couldn't really afford to put all our visitors up for free so we charged them. This was the birth of our guest-house.[33]

Estrid acknowledges the help she received from Williams and Lane but gives no real indication how difficult she found it to fund the purchase. On 6 October 1958, Williams wrote to Lane, suggesting ways in which the loan might be secured. The sum required was duly provided and Shorecliffe House was bought outright. In its first year, the guest-house was a great success. Estrid brushed up her cookery skills. She made a Danish-style 'hay-box' and used nothing but fresh garden produce and local provisions. The Irish, Danish and English press gave Shorecliffe House some valuable publicity. The *Cork Examiner* described Estrid as the 'Danish Invader in Cause of Good Food'. To her many Danish and other foreign visitors she became 'Denmark's Cultural Ambassador'. She and Ernest worked hard to restore the neglected grounds. They rebuilt dry-stone walls, re-laid paths, and planted a new lawn. Members of Ernest's family were enlisted to work in the gardens, growing vegetables and flowers of all kinds in great profusion. The summers were long and hot. They installed bee-hives in the lower garden.

Ernest then invested in 200 lobster pots. He had identified and recorded all the best fishing grounds for miles around. Estrid helped him haul in his daily catch of lobsters, pollock and conger, which they sold at good prices to French buyers. There was good salmon fishing in the local rivers and mussels to be collected along the sea-shore. The sun seemed always to be shining. Family and friends – including Bill Williams and Allen Lane – came from near and far to meet Ernest and to admire their new home:

> There was never a dull moment at Shorecliffe. I worked hard and loved very minute of it, whether it was fishing or gardening, entertaining guests or cooking, it didn't matter. There was such pleasure to be had from going out into the garden and picking the first bunches of asparagus, artichokes, strawberries and all the other wonderful things we grew. I was always aware of the beauty around me, of the scents and sounds that were the essence of Shorecliffe... It seemed to me that all my years of searching were at an end, I had found Nirvana.[34]

In 1962, Ernest secured a grant from the Irish Tourist Board to help them buy and renovate 'Richard', an old trawler which he intended to use on more extended fishing trips. They found the cash deposit and borrowed the balance from the bank. At first, all went well. The fishing was good and Ernest's takings enabled him to start paying back the loan. Then they were hit by severe gales. The trawler broke her moorings, was badly damaged, and laid up for several months for repairs. Ernest put the trawler up for sale and went back to salmon fishing in the rivers and to collecting mussels along the sea-shore. And he continued to go to sea in his small boat. He loved his fishing trips. As long as he could get on with his work and was not interrupted, he was happy.

At the end of each tourist season, Estrid tried to take a holiday. She had frequently asked Ernest to accompany her on her overseas jaunts, but he was never happy away from home. He even hated going to London, a regular trip to which she always looked forward. Having travelled extensively with Bill as her companion, Estrid found Ernest's lack of interest in foreign holidays difficult to grasp. But she got used to it. In 1963, she booked herself a late holiday in Egypt. Shortly before she was due to depart, President Kennedy was assassinated in Dallas. Estrid was so distressed, she felt like abandoning her holiday. But Ernest insisted that she should stick to her plans.

Her itinerary took her first to Copenhagen, where she visited family and friends. One night, whilst dining out, Estrid received an urgent message to call home. She collapsed on hearing the news. It seems that Ernest had been driving home from Cork during an exceptionally violent storm. He stopped his car in Rosscarbery to look at the sea, when a huge freak wave broke over the pier, sweeping the car out to sea. His body had been washed up the following morning. Estrid was given sedation and put to bed. When she had got over the initial shock, she began the long, sad journey home. She spent one night in London, where she was met by Bill and taken to stay overnight with a close woman friend. Early next morning, Lane saw her off at London Airport. Knowing her precarious financial situation, he slipped her an envelope containing a cheque for £1,000.

Estrid brings the narrative of her colourful and tragic life down to Ernest's death in 1963. She tells us that she resumed work at her guest-house, but leaves many questions unanswered. Did she continue to see Bill after her marriage to Ernest? There is no reason to believe that he stopped visiting her in Glandore. Gertrude never once mentions Estrid in her memoirs but she must have been relieved to learn of Estrid's marriage to Ernest in 1958. It was therefore not unreasonable for Gertrude to assume that Billy had returned to her for good. Although he had by then retired as Secretary-General of the Arts Council, and given up his work for Penguin Books, there is documented evidence that Estrid continued to turn to him whenever she ran into difficult problems.

Immediately following Ernest's death, Williams wrote to Lane, explaining Estrid's precarious financial situation:

> She needs a short-term loan of £1000 and asked me whether she dared ask Penguins for one. I rang her and told her I would talk to you. My thought is this. The firm holds the

> policy for the insurance it has on me, up to the age of 70. Would the firm accept that policy as collateral for a loan of £1,000 to Estrid forthwith? It seems to me a cast-iron affair. She'll be able to repay within a few months, especially as she is booked solid [with holiday visitors] after Easter.[35]

If Estrid got that money as a loan – or perhaps another gift? – and wrote to thank Lane for his exceptional generosity, that letter has disappeared – together with the hundred or so letters that Estrid claimed Bill had written to her every day they spent apart. It seems likely that her son, Geoffrey, destroyed them to avoid further embarrassment.

Estrid outlived both Lane and Williams, finishing her days in Shorecliffe House as the *grande dame* of Glandore. Journalists continued to pester her for interviews, well into her nineties. In January 1993, the *Telegraph Magazine* published a five-page feature article on Estrid by Andro Linklater, describing her as 'The Naughtiest Girl of the Century'. Towards the end of her life, she produced *Smørrebrød and Cherry-Blossom*, her colourful, vanity-published autobiography. She slowly succumbed to Alzheimer's, losing all those precious memories that had sustained her for so long. When she finally died, aged 95, on 31 December 1998, the silver-framed photograph of Bill Williams was on her bedside table.

Estrid and Ernest Good, who gave her a fishing outfit for a wedding present.

Estrid and her sister Marie in Aporta Café – lots of coffee and very little money.

Estrid Bannister – lectures in lecturing – the beginning of her journalistic career.

Sir William Emrys Williams, c1965.

Eight:
Army Bureau of Current Affairs

> It was ABCA which first attracted national attention to Williams. Today's argumentative, uninhibited, open-ended society must find it difficult to appreciate what an explosive idea the project of educating the army in wartime about public affairs could be... Williams [engaged] all his Welsh passion in asserting that the fighting men and women had a right to basic information, to political curiosity, and to a feeling of partnership in deciding what kind of country Britain should be after the war had been won.
>
> *Obituary of Sir William Emrys Williams,* The Times, *1 April 1977*

In the first year of the Second World War, Britain suffered disaster upon disaster. By Spring 1940, the German army had swept through Belgium, Holland and France, trapping half the British army on the beaches of Normandy. Hundreds of troops were killed or captured. Thousands more were lifted off the beach at Dunkirk by a flotilla of small ships and brought safely back to England. For the next twelve months, until Hitler's invasion of the Soviet Union in June 1941, Britain stood alone. Half a million British and Commonwealth troops licked their wounds and kicked their heels, impatient for the chance to re-engage the enemy. Until December 1941, when the Japanese attacked Pearl Harbour, America remained neutral.

It was against that background that Lord Croft, Under-Secretary of State for War, addressed a confidential letter on 3 August 1940 to Dr Thomas Jones, seeking his advice on the crucial issue of army morale:

> I have been asked to appoint a Director of [Army] Education [and] am anxious to get someone who is a sound educationalist and good administrator and dynamiser with a military background (not necessarily an ex-regular)... I wonder if by chance you know of anyone who might very successfully fill the post? It is of great importance to keep the Army "on its toes" during the coming black out and I want to supply the mental stimulant in the educational line which will help to prevent the soldier getting stale with a Maginot complex! [1]

TJ immediately consulted W E Williams, who was likely to know some of the more promising candidates. There is no surviving record of Williams' advice or of TJ's recommendations but they may be inferred from Lord Croft's response:

> I will certainly see [Williams], if possible, and your views would certainly influence me. He certainly seems to be to be much alive. I only fear whether the fact that he was not in the army last war or this may be a disadvantage as I find there is a very general feeling that the soldiers would prefer someone who has shared their kind of life. I do not mean as a 'professional' soldier but to have served in some military capacity even in the ranks.[2]

In due course, Williams wrote to TJ, telling him what subsequently took place at his interview with Croft:

> I discovered that he is ex Sir Henry Page Croft, but he didn't at all seem or sound the reactionary he is imputed to be. We talked a long time, very agreeably, and he then took me along to Sir James Grigg [Secretary of State for War].
>
> I'll do anything I can for this particular cause, and there will be many things one can do from the outside. In bed last night I had the mad idea that Tawney (ex-Sergeant Tawney!) would be the man for directing Army Education with me as his adjutant. Is it an impossible idea? He is very fit, and when I last saw him was (I thought) conscious of not being used for something.
>
> I have got a date with Ernest Bevin to discuss a big series of art exhibitions in factories. Our first series has gone so well that I want him to back it on a bigger scale.[3]

Sir Henry Page Croft was the Conservative MP who once described General Franco, in a House of Commons debate on the Spanish Civil War, as 'a great Christian gentleman'. Williams' first impressions of Croft were somewhat premature, as later events would show. Although he never achieved his ambition to become Britain's first Director of Army Education, Williams had clearly impressed Croft. In a lengthy memorandum, dated 8 January 1943, Croft explained why he rejected Williams in favour of Colonel F W D Bendall. Whilst acknowledging that Williams was 'a very vital personality and undoubtedly a man of ideas as well as push and drive', he had not served in the forces in the last war and was therefore not in touch with the tradition of keeping politics out of the army. As a Director and Joint Editor of Penguin Books, he had published 'all the most extreme Left Wing literature' and as Secretary of the British Institute of Adult Education and an executive member of the Workers' Educational Association, 'he was associated largely with Left Wing politicians who happened to predominate in these circles'. 'His life was so largely wrapped up in music and art that I doubted his capacity to keep the morale of the army as a fighting force in the forefront':

> With the temptation before me to appoint one who is undoubtedly a very live wire my instinct told me that political trouble was inevitable if he was appointed Director, although he is good in a subordinate position. I accordingly chose Mr Bendall who had the advantage of having been a fighting soldier and knew the Army from within, having commanded two different battalions with success, and who was most warmly recommended to me by the Board of Education as one likely to get the machine working smoothly and efficiently.[4]

Williams had good cause to reflect that his failure to enlist in the army in the First World War might well have cost him his appointment as Director of Army Education in the second. Croft and Grigg nevertheless recognised Williams' exceptional talents and decided to harness them. They despatched him on a 'fact-finding mission' to army establishments in Home Command, to assess troop morale and, in particular, to report on the progress made in implementing army education, as proposed by the Haining Committee Report on 'Education in the War Time Army', published in September 1940. The Report recommended that, in addition to formal military instruction, all ranks in the army should be offered three kinds of less formal education, all on a voluntary basis, to take place in the men's free time:

> (a) the humanities – to cover the familiar curriculum of adult education – e.g. history, geography, international affairs, economics, either in single lectures or in short courses.
>
> (b) the utilities – designed to enable soldiers to begin or to continue some training in the vocations they hoped to take up when the war was over.
>
> (c) the arts and crafts – intended to give men constructive hobby interests.[5]

The voluntary approach, advocated by Haining, did not meet with universal approval in the British Army. General Sir Ronald Adam, General Officer Commanding, Northern Command, wrote:

> Like other Army commanders, I was horrified at the utter lack of knowledge of the average man as to the war, what we were fighting for, and what we were fighting against. I decided that officers ought to discuss these things with their men, and asked the Director of Military Intelligence if he could get out some information pamphlets, which he said was impossible. So I wrote out a training instruction suggesting that officers should get their notes from the daily papers.[6]

To implement the Haining Report, the War Office set up a small Directorate of Army Education, under Colonel Bendall, reporting to Major General Harry Willans, Director-General of Welfare and Education. Haining recognised that, to cope with its immense new task, the army must supplement the local supply of civilian instructors by identifying officers and other ranks capable of giving informal talks, lectures and instruction. A cautious start was made during the winter of 1940/41 but during his tour of Home Command, Williams noted two important factors that handicapped progress:

> The first was that there were nothing like enough civilian lecturers to go round the Army if the Haining Scheme were to be developed. The second was that at least 80% of the Army's demand was for enlightenment about Current Affairs. Talks and discussions on themes within this field were more popular and in more urgent demand than anything else. This fact confirmed in broad terms the opinion at which most observers of the new Army had arrived, namely, that the men were usually keen to know and appraise the reasons why they were in arms and anxious to see day-light about the post-war world. The soldier of 1941 was potentially, if not already, the type which Cromwell recruited for his crack squadrons – the man 'who know what he fights for and loves what he knows'. These considerations deeply impressed the Director General of Welfare and Education,

> the late Major General Harry Willans, who became convinced that a drastic revision of the Haining Plan was necessary. He concluded that steps must now be taken to meet the Army's urgent demand for instruction in Current Affairs and that this instruction must be an authorised element in the Army's training.[7]

Whilst Major General Willans is credited with the creation of the Army Bureau of Current Affairs (ABCA), it was clearly Williams, the War Office liaison officer attached to General Sir Ronald Adam, who provided the original inspiration. In his own later account of the birth and development of ABCA, and writing of himself in the third person, Williams makes clear that he was

> ...invited to prepare a scheme which would enable Current Affairs to be introduced into the Army time-table on the widest possible scale. Mr Williams accepted the assignment and produced [in three days] the outline of a plan which was duly approved by the Army Council. His proposal was to set up, independently of the Directorate of Army Education, an Army Bureau of Current Affairs to provide a new species of military training.[8]

In August 1941, in an historic policy statement, General Sir J G Wills, Chief of the Imperial General Staff, announced a new campaign to raise the British Army's awareness and understanding of what the war was about and what the troops were fighting for:

> Interest in Current Affairs, including the events of the war, induces confidence; confidence is one of the ingredients of unshakeable morale. The success of this project depends upon the ability and enthusiasm of Commanders of every rank; I wish them to do their utmost to ensure that success.[9]

In his later more informal account of ABCA, Williams explained the thinking behind his creation:

> The new plan was to be compulsory. It was to specialize in Current Affairs and was to employ an educational process for the purpose of making good soldiers. This new venture, promoted by ABCA, got under way in the Autumn of 1941. The rules, though obligatory, were simple. Once a week, in the King's time and not their own, soldiers were to sit down, under the leadership of their regimental officer, and discuss some topic of the day.[10]

In September 1942, the Army Council approved 'The Winter Scheme of Education' for the months of November 1942 to February 1943. It authorised three one-hour periods a week of training-time to be devoted to education but left discretion to commanders in dovetailing these periods into training programmes:

> The hard centre of the Winter Scheme proved to be...the civic period. As a syllabus for this education citizenship there were prepared in the War Office a series of "British Way and Purpose" booklets, each devoted to a full consideration of the main elements in our government, our industrial structure, our social institutions and so on... The earlier experiences of ABCA brought to light what its architects had foreseen – the lamentable lack of background knowledge in the average platoon discussion. It was a common

experience for discussion to peter out because there was no one present to confirm or contradict reputed matters of fact. To consolidate and reinforce the ABCA bridge-head it was necessary to devise a method of instructing the Army about the background of Current Affairs, and for this purpose the "British Way and Purpose" booklets were admirably adapted.[11]

The 'Winter Scheme' did not begin well. On 5 November 1940, Basil Yeaxlee, Secretary of the Central Advisory Council for Adult Education in H M Forces (CAC), and a specialist in adult education, addressed a confidential Memorandum to the Council, criticising policy development in relation to the Haining Committee's recommendations:

[In addition to concern about the lack of sufficient staff to implement the Haining Committee's proposals] I am even more concerned about the direction and purpose of the whole undertaking. We have established the principle that no "programme" or "curriculum" should be pressed upon either Commands or troops. The general procedure of Regional Committees has been to draw up a list of lecture topics...and to offer these to the Education Officers... The net result at present, however, is provision of a very miscellaneous lot of lectures and talks... This lack of purpose may well continue indefinitely unless the drift is arrested and a very thorny problem handled courageously.[12]

Tension between the Army Council and CAC continued throughout the early years of the war. Matters came to a head in September 1941, when the Executive Committee of CAC met under the Chairmanship of Sir Walter Moberly, to review progress. The newly-appointed Director of ABCA was invited to give a first-hand account of his stewardship of that office:

Mr Williams said that every effort would be made to promote free, full and fair discussion. The scheme would be applied throughout the Army and in a few instances the plan of talks by capable NCOs would be tried out. No specific time for each talk had been suggested though in casual conversations half-an-hour had been mentioned, to include both talk and discussion. He recognised that this was insufficient to allow of a really thoroughgoing discussion, but the training timetable was less rigid than formerly and it was hoped that officers would make use of their discretionary powers to extend the time for discussion whenever desirable and possible.[13]

Although determined that ABCA should promote 'free, full and fair discussion' of the issues raised in its fortnightly *Current Affairs*, Williams was keenly aware that he was engaged in a form of psychological warfare on behalf of the War Office. In that context, it is interesting to note his response to Dr Thomas Jones, who sought his advice early in 1941 on the choice of a new head of propaganda at the Ministry of Information (MoI):

I have pondered a lot on the problem you put to me last Friday about the M of I. If it was simply a matter of finding a technical expert in controlling propaganda & publicity...

> A very good gamble would be Professor Lindley Fraser (Aberdeen Political Economy). He has revolutionised our wireless propaganda to Germany, & is also a man of mind. Aged 45+, not a bit academic, very alert & easy to get on with. I'd fancy him for the job.[14]

Lindley Fraser was eventually appointed to the post and emerged as a master of the black arts of wartime propaganda, broadcast to Germany and the rest of the world throughout the Second World War. But Dr Jones was not the only person to seek Williams' advice in matters of appointments to top jobs. In February 1942, Major-General Willans asked Williams to help him find a successor to Bendall as Director of Army Education. Following his familiar practice, Williams consulted TJ on how he should respond to Willans. Having disclaimed any personal ambition to take the job himself, he made clear that he felt better qualified than any of the other candidates:

> Honestly, I've no ambition to combine Army Education and ABCA. Yet such an amalgamation seems logical, and would (I believe) be generally acceptable... There is a case for combining the roles of Director of Army Education and the Director of ABCA... ABCA can be said to be responsible for the Army's basic educational rations; moreover 80% of the Army Educational Courses and Discussions are on Current Affairs. The present Director of ABCA has been a functionary in Army Education since the scheme began. He knows the Army Education Council very well, and is probably palatable to the Civilian Organisations.[15]

We do not know how TJ responded to that letter, or what advice Williams offered Major-General Willans, but the War Office awarded the post to Burgon Bickersteth, a well-qualified and forceful Canadian education specialist. His relationship with Williams was far from amicable. In an important letter to Dr Jones, dated 12 July 1943, Williams brought him up to date with ABCA developments and outlined his longer-term plans:

> In general we are going well. The Eighth Army have become ardent ABCA-addicts, a fact which pleases me particularly – because I always felt that our most important job was to get into the front line. At home, too, ABCA is getting its roots deeper, and we are beginning to get results from the protracted spade-work. Everywhere I go I hear Coleg Harlech referred to in the warmest terms; and I think it will be as deep a satisfaction to you as it is to me to know that Harlech has become a significant name to hundreds of men and women who knew nothing about it before...
>
> One way and another I am convinced that the most vital necessity for Adult Education after the war is that it should come down off its high horse and fraternise with the really Common Man. Most of my own work has been in the more primitive areas of adult education – and after the war it will be even more so. I may thereby, possibly, fulfil my adolescent desires to be a missionary in Darkest Africa – and fulfil them more usefully than if I had become a colporteur on the Congo!

> There's been another ABCA brawl, due to a complaint lodged to the P.M. about us by Ernest Bevin, a complaint based on one of our Reconstruction Posters which that doughty Socialist couldn't swallow. P.J. [Grigg, Secretary of State for War] stood by us 100 per cent, and demanded an investigation of ABCA to silence the carpings. The investigation – by John Anderson – is proceeding, but what will emerge I have no idea.
>
> We have numerous minor worries and irritations, and the dyarchy between Bickersteth and us is the source of much untidiness and crossed cables. But I suppose it will endure until the war is over. He really is the most muddle-headed, garrulous ass I have ever encountered![16]

Sir John Anderson's investigation vindicated ABCA and the complaint was dropped, only to reappear in different guises at intervals throughout the war. Williams' reflections on the post-war period show that he was already thinking of converting ABCA into some civilian equivalent, which might allow him to invest his wartime experience into a more vigorous form of adult education for 'the really Common Man'.

In September 1943, General Sir Ronald Adam, the Army's Adjutant-General, addressed a memorandum to his senior commanding officers. Having reviewed progress with the War-time Scheme of Education and ABCA, he came to the heart of his message:

> I am afraid that there are still some officers, although they are in a diminishing minority, who look upon education as, at best, an unnecessary frill and, at worst, an infernal nuisance. They think that "it is not the Army's business", that "we have plenty to do to win the war without going in for all that sort of thing" and so on. Such officers are often heard to say that there is so much training to be done that there is not time to get in education as well. They must be taught that education is part and parcel of training. Any experienced officer knows that the better educated the recruit, the quicker and easier it is to train him. Moreover, they must learn that to win a war of this character, when we are up against two of the cleverest nations in the world – the Boche and the Jap – it is not enough to use our hands and our bodies – we have to use our minds as well.[17]

Despite General Adams' clear instructions, Williams experienced real problems in making a success of ABCA. The entire venture was surrounded by intense partisanship and controversy from the outset. First, the way in which the scheme was launched – with the appointment of a civilian Director – was bound to upset many brass-hats at the War Office. The British Army, like all armies, was an authoritarian institution, which strongly suspected any form of democratic control. To stand any reasonable chance of success, Haining's proposals for broadening army education needed not only ardent champions in every unit but some form of Unit Education Committee to provide support, to maintain momentum, and to ensure success. Despite strenuous efforts on Williams' part, that support was not always forthcoming.

Second, ABCA got off to a poor start because CAC was not properly informed in advance of the launch. According to one source, the first intimation of the new plan came from the press or the BBC. Major-General Willans informally consulted the Chairman of CAC on the proposal a few months before the launch. But neither the Chairman nor the Secretary was formally asked for his views. The CAC was therefore not responsible for the scheme it was then asked to help deliver.

The third factor which hampered ABCA's success was the uncomfortable and mutually distasteful dyarchy, with two Directors of nominally equal status, both civilians, both strong personalities, each wanting – and used to getting – his own way on policy matters. John Burgon Bickersteth was a formidable personality. Fourth son of the Rev. Dr Samuel Bickersteth, Canon of Canterbury and Chaplain to King George V, he completed his education in Britain before emigrating to Canada, where he served as Warden at Hart House in the University of Toronto. Back in England, Bickersteth was appointed in September 1940 as Educational Adviser to Lieutenant-General A G L McNaughton, GOC 1st Canadian Army in Britain. In June 1942 he succeeded Colonel Bendall as Director of Army Education, where he remained until 1944, when he returned to Canada to prepare for the post-war influx of ex-servicemen in the University of Toronto.

Colonel A C T ('Archie') White VC, who served as Williams' Military Adviser (Education), offers this account of army education during the dyarchy:

> Burgon Bickersteth's appointment as Director of Army Education was an unusual, perhaps a uniquely extravagant, appointment as Director of Army Education. The fact that he was Canadian was less of a problem in itself than the fact that he seems to have been a prickly and difficult Canadian, difficult to know, prickly in his response to any initiative which appeared to challenge his omniscience and omni-competence in all matters of education and training... Bill Williams, on the other hand, had made an excellent first impression on his service colleagues during his tour of army establishments in the Home Commands, immediately prior to his appointment as Director of ABCA. His ideas on what the army needed by way of current affairs training were refreshingly crisp and clear and even-handed as between the responsibilities of ABCA at the centre and Commanding Officers in the field.[18]

Another major source of difficulty for Williams was the repeated charge by right-wing critics that ABCA's fortnightly publication, *Current Affairs*, was politically slanted in favour of the extreme Left. After reading *Current Affairs* for 31 July 1942, Lord Croft was provoked to write to Sir James Grigg, Secretary for War, complaining in impassioned terms about some dangerous left-wing influences on the troops:

> Discussions and material provided by ABCA, and to an extent by British Way and Purpose, on all home affairs have tended all the time in the following directions:
>
> (a) the promotion of criticism upon financial, economic and social structure existing in this country at the outbreak of war
>
> (b) the suggestion that all soldiers should regard material considerations as they concern themselves as the most important factor in life
>
> (c) the suggestion that the pre-war way of life must never be consented to and that something much better is coming
>
> (d) that the old kind of job in which the man was serving is possibly inadequate and unsuitable and not one to which he would wish to go back to.
>
> Whereas these efforts to promote critical discussion upon the Government of Great Britain can none of them be described as openly vicious, the cumulative effect must tend towards revolutionary ideas, and what is equally undesirable a grave sense of disillusion, heart-burning and anger if and when it is found that the State is not able to implement all the promised boons that soldiers are encouraged to demand as a right.[19]

In their history of *Adult Education: The Record of the British Army*, Hawkins and Brimble tell of the great storm which blew up, involving ABCA and the Beveridge Report (Report on Social Insurance and Allied Services, 1942), which later formed the basis of the post-war Welfare State. Published on 1 December 1942, and known popularly as 'The Beveridge Plan', the Report proposed benefits for those experiencing unemployment, sickness or old age, to be financed by National Insurance contributions, as well as certain income-related non-contributory benefits (later called supplementary benefits). The Report was greeted cautiously by both Churchill's wartime National Government and the public but almost all its recommendations were later adopted and given statutory form:

> Knowing the tremendous interest that the troops were taking in this subject, the enterprising Director of ABCA approached Sir William [Beveridge] and persuaded him to write his report in popular language so that it could be published as an ABCA bulletin. This Sir William did, and on December 19, 1942, the fortnightly number of *Current Affairs* was issued to regimental officers in the usual way. Within a few days a hasty teleprint message was sent round to all units ordering these copies to be called in and returned to the War Office. Then the storm broke.[20]

With the storm raging, the progressive line was strenuously argued by Kingsley Martin in his editorial 'Blimps and Beveridge' in the *New Statesman and Nation*:

> Who said Blimp was dead? The Ministry of Information hailed the Beveridge Report as the best propaganda yet produced in the war. But the War Office Blimps are apparently not interested in morale. They keep up the pretence that common soldiers do not think... Officers tell us that they regarded the Beveridge Report as at length offering a way of removing from their soldiers the haunting fear of post-war poverty and unemployment.

> If this document is withdrawn, soldiers will draw the inference that their rulers do not intend voluntarily to concede any change... We urge that this issue be resolutely taken up by all progressive persons.[21]

Williams' political sympathies were undeniably on the Left. He had grown up in a poor Welsh home, with few advantages in life. He had seen the effects of economic and social deprivation in Manchester before the First World War and in the East End of London in the inter-war period. In the 1930s, he had watched the rise of fascism in Italy, falangism in Spain, and national socialism in Germany. With a Jewish wife, it would be remarkable if he had not been implacably hostile to all three totalitarian regimes. But did he deliberately set out to politicise the British army through his work with ABCA? There was inevitably some political bias amongst members of staff at ABCA. But how widespread, how influential, and how far to the Left was that bias? To what extent did any such bias influence British political life in the broader sweep of history?

Writing of the civilian contribution to army education during the war, Scarlyn Wilson offers this balanced judgement:

> There was the risk of propaganda. But the pamphlet which outlined the scheme clearly recognised the principle of free discussion so, unless there was bad faith, which there was no reason whatever to suspect, the danger of a propagandist element creeping in seemed slight... Propaganda did occasionally creep in, though seldom or never was the person guiding the discussion directly responsible for it. Usually he had at his command little information on the topic of the week apart from what the bulletin supplied. Now, a pamphlet of four or five thousand words...however closely packed with facts, cannot contain all the facts, and a book or pamphlet may be coloured by the facts it leaves out as well as by those it puts in. The anxiety over propaganda which had exercised the minds of many members of the CAC, when their attitude towards ABCA was being considered, did prove needless.[22]

In *The Story of Army Education*, Colonel 'Archie' White gives his own view on political bias in ABCA:

> It is surprising that misgivings should have existed over a serious attempt to teach citizenship. The root of them was perhaps the dislike of seeing soldiers discussing public affairs, a practice of which Wellington once said, "It is not objectionable in itself." Discussion, as the promoters of ABCA pointed out, was going on all the time, on railway stations, in public houses, in sergeants' messes. Much of it, through ignorance of facts and want of logic, was interminable and inconclusive; and these were the qualities that it was hoped to eliminate. At all events, no one has ever quoted an actual case of indiscipline arising from an ABCA discussion; and Sir Ronald Adam, who as Adjutant-General from 1941 to 1946, was responsible for the discipline of the Army, has confirmed that he never heard of one.[23]

On 6 June 1944, General Eisenhower, Commander-in-Chief, Allied Forces Europe, launched the long-awaited invasion of mainland Europe. The greatest fleet ever assembled, carrying tens of thousands of men, and a prodigious mass of armoured equipment, moved under cover of darkness across the English Channel where they established an initial bridgehead on the shores of Normandy. Within one month, having suffered heavy initial casualties, Allied armies were strongly entrenched and slowly advancing along a broad Second Front. At times, it was touch and go whether the invasion would succeed. German Army Commanders threw their crack armoured corps and thousands of troops into repulsing the invasion force and driving it back into the sea. It was a turning point in the Second World War, a moment when the training and morale of the Allied armies were put to their severest test.

Back in Britain, those concerned with army education turned their minds to the problems of sustaining morale during the long run-up to the end of the war and the demobilisation period. Williams had for some time been considering his own role in the post-war world. On 10 February 1944, he addressed a confidential letter to Dr Thomas Jones, containing a bold proposal for his possible future employment:

> When we last talked at Harlech, you took me some distance into your confidence about the future of the Pilgrim Trust... Most of what I want to say amounts to the suggestion that I should like to be considered for the long-distant succession. For these reasons:
>
> (1) In more ways than you realise I have served an apprenticeship to you, and I now consider myself a journeyman in your trade.
> (2) I have a good knowledge of the geography of the region the P.T. serves and ought to serve, including some of the semi-explored territory to be developed after the war.
> (3) My contacts are considerable and varied – much more so than people who have lived the cloistered life of the Civil Service.
> (4) I have been brought up frugally, and I know that good work can be done on modest resources. I should not be a prodigal dispenser of money, and I should not be captivated by South Sea Bubbles.
> (5) As a hardened poacher of Trust funds I ought to prove an implacable game-keeper.
> (6) As an administrator (of low degree) I am methodical without being fussy.
> (7) I have always managed to escape the Procrustean bed of a career.
>
> And after the war I want to maintain that freedom, because I work best that way. In the sector of popular education where I've served these last 20 years there need to be a few people who have a roving commission; and I think that, at my level, I could manage to do almost as many good jobs as you continue to do. Those are the main reasons why I should like to go on your short list.

> My limitations you know so well that I won't indulge myself by enumerating them. Beyond the ones you know is the fact that I have no experience of the mysteries of finance and investment.
>
> I've tried to put these points as detachedly as I can, for I want to be considered on nothing but my merits and record. Yet a personal factor comes into the business too; for I so deeply admire the way you have wielded the P.T. that I would like a shot at it some day. It's perhaps the temerity of the novice contemplating the bow of Ulysses. Anyway there it is, and I wanted you to know how I felt.[24]

Dr Jones replied to that suggestion in a letter that was somewhat discouraging, but not altogether unflattering to its recipient:

> I am glad to have your letter of 10 Feb and to know how you regard the P.T. post. I have no sort of doubt of your first-rate qualifications for the job & I have told the Chairman [Lord Macmillan] so, when discussing possible successors. But I have also said to him that this work can be well done by a sexagenarian & that you have far bigger national tasks in hand and ahead of you in the next ten or twelve crucial years.
>
> I shall put your letter & my reply 'on the record' for submission to the Chairman when my departure is imminent, so that the Trustees can exercise their own independent judgment in the matter. Meanwhile, as the hymn says, I go on at this 'poor dying rate'.[25]

Nothing came of that initiative. When Dr Jones retired as Secretary of the Pilgrim Trust, Sir Ben Bowen Thomas of the Welsh Board of Education took his place. By then, the war was over, Labour had swept to power in the 1945 General Election, and Williams had embarked on his mission to establish the post-war Bureau of Current Affairs (BCA). He fervently believed that the generation of servicemen and women who had taken part in ABCA discussions had developed an appetite for adult education and current affairs which they would carry over into civilian life. In the words of W O Lester Smith, Chairman of the Council of the BCA, Williams was 'inspired by an ardent belief in discussion as an essential of the democratic way of life'.[26]

Having secured initial funding from the Carnegie Trust, Williams set about recruiting staff, devising publicity, organising and holding meetings, and preparing the first BCA Bulletins. Amongst his first tasks was the acquisition of well-located premises at Carnegie House, Piccadilly, to serve as headquarters for the new organisation. The rental was high, but Williams calculated that the demand for the BCA would soon enable him to recoup the initial costs. The Bureau was eventually launched but did not last. Whether that was due to inadequate planning, poor administration, a lack of secure funding, or to an excessively ambitious programme, is difficult to say. Whatever the reasons, Williams' assumptions were over-optimistic. The Bureau failed to attract and retain sufficient members to pay its way. Many ex-servicemen and women enrolled in courses of adult education provided by local education authorities. But the vast majority were happy to return to private life, to resume their former careers, or establish themselves in new careers. They wanted, above all, to marry, settle down, and raise a family. They resumed their leisure interests and tried to make up for lost time in a wide range of new post-war opportunities for personal enrichment and enjoyment. Membership of the BCA was nevertheless sufficiently high in the first few years to encourage Williams and his colleagues to organise meetings and seminars, and to produce a stream of bulletins and newsletters, building on the experience of wartime ABCA. Within five years of the BCA's launch, Williams was forced to admit defeat. When the Bureau finally closed its doors in 1951, Williams was disappointed and dejected. He went briefly into retreat to re-think his future. Once again, fortune favoured the prepared mind. Within a short while, he turned his attention to Penguin Books and the post-war Arts Council.

The Carnegie Trust's *Annual Report* for 1950 summed up the work of the Bureau in these words:

> We regret that the Bureau has not been able to establish itself as a self-supporting institution; but we do not regret our experiment in creating it. The purpose of that experiment was to discover whether a method which, at considerable cost to public funds, had proved outstandingly successful during the war, could be made economically self-supporting in time of peace, and to this question we have received a definite though negative answer. On the positive side of the account, we can point to an educational service which has been consistently maintained at a high level of quality for more than five years, and we have ample evidence to show the esteem in which the Bureau is held by those who have made regular use of what it had to offer. Our thanks are due, and they are given very warmly, to all members of the administrative, editorial and other staff who have been associated with this venture.[27]

Some historians claimed that ABCA had contributed to Labour's electoral victory in 1945. In a correspondence that flared in the *Sunday Telegraph* in October 1970, a letter from Mr George A Short of Manchester concluded:

> In domestic affairs the vigorous Leftist educational campaign of the movement was to work against Churchill, providing the seed-bed for the radical Army Bureau of Current Affairs (ABCA), which helped to swing the Services' vote to Attlee in 1945.[28]

In the following week's issue, Colonel 'Archie' White rushed to ABCA's defence:

> I have for some time been trying to investigate the rumour, which your reader George A Short has revived, that the wartime Army Bureau of Current Affairs engaged in a campaign against Churchill. Churchill himself went into the matter, and after strong initial doubts, declared himself satisfied ("Second World War": vol.5 p.581). What Mr Short perhaps

> does not understand is that every ABCA publication was approved, before issue, by the Minister into whose field the subject fell; and Churchill's Ministers included Attlee, Alexander, Morrison, Bevin, Cripps and Dalton. If any specific instance of propaganda can be alleged, I should be glad to have details of it.[29]

We do not know whether White was in touch with Williams before drafting that robust reply; but on 11 October Williams contributed his own response to the allegations. His letter provides a rare example of Williams' use of the personal pronoun in describing his achievements over thirty years in public life:

> ***The truth about ABCA***
>
> *From Sir William Emrys Williams*
>
> On evidence he fails to produce, Mr George Short declares that the Left Book Club provided "the seed-bed for the radical Army Bureau of Current Affairs (ABCA) which helped to swing the vote to Attlee in 1945". This assertion is arrant nonsense.
>
> I created ABCA, and was its sole director throughout the war. I was invited by the Army Council to devise a simple portable system of keeping the troops in touch with current affairs, and I built up the entire organisation – discussion-groups at platoon level, "brief" for regimental officers, training courses by the thousand, maps and visual aids, a film unit and a "live" theatre of current affairs.
>
> I was picked for the job because I was a pioneer of adult education and Chief Editor of Penguin Books. And I suppose the fact was taken into account that I had no political affiliations whatsoever, a form of virginity which remains unsullied.
>
> ABCA was an entirely military organisation, and I was its only civilian member. My staff, all in the Army already, included a former assistant editor of Picture Post, two feature-writers from the Daily Express, two professors, five directors of education, a film producer, a West End theatre producer, and several well-known writers. My military boss was the Adjutant-General, that humane and far-sighted soldier, General Sir Ronald Adam. My civilian boss was the Secretary of State for War, most of the time, Sir James Grigg, for many years a close colleague of Churchill's, a true-blue Tory of strong mind and resolute character.
>
> We had no civilian attachments except one with the Royal Institute of International Affairs (Chatham House) who laid on specialist courses for us. Our organisers were the Royal Army Education Corps, and the men who led the discussion groups were the regimental officers in their thousands, to all of whom we managed to give a basic training in chairmanship.
>
> A body like ABCA, however scrupulously conducted, roused suspicions amongst feather-brained bogey-hunters. But these were shot to pieces when Churchill instructed Sir John Anderson (later Lord Waverley) to investigate us. John Anderson, a great man of penetrating intelligence and wide experience, not only gave us a clean bill of health but praised our work unreservedly.
>
> Where Mr Short gets his evidence from about ABCA helping to swing the Services' vote to Labour in 1945 I cannot conceive. If it were true, Attlee's Government proved very

> ungrateful, for one of its immediate economies was to dismantle the Army Bureau of Current Affairs. I suppose I was lucky to escape the Tower – W. E. Williams, Haddenham, Bucks.[30]

Witty and persuasive as that letter was, there is convincing evidence elsewhere to show that ABCA had been brilliantly successful in training servicemen and women to think for themselves, politically as well as socially. When their votes were counted, they showed an overwhelming preference for Labour over the Conservatives. In effect, the services vote swelled the civilian vote and so decisively returned Labour to power at the 1945 General Election.

Despite the failure of the BCA, Williams' achievements with ABCA in the war did not go unrecognised. In 1946 King George VI was 'graciously pleased to admit W E Williams as a Companion of the British Empire', an award in which he took justifiable pride. The letters CBE were regularly attached to his name in all official documents after that date. Williams was also awarded the American Medal of Freedom, the highest award given by the United States to foreign nationals. Dated 7 August 1946, promulgated by command of General McNarney, and signed by Major General H R Bull, the citation reads as follows:

> William E Williams, British Civilian, for exceptionally meritorious achievement which aided the United States in the prosecution of the war against the enemy in Continental Europe, as Director, Army Bureau of Current Affairs, War Office; Secretary, British Institute of Adult Education; Joint Editor of Penguin and Pelican Books; BA Manchester University. From July 1942 to May 1945 he distinguished himself by his tireless energy and outstanding devotion to the Allied cause. Through his wide knowledge of educational policies in the British Empire, his timely and expert advice and his close cooperation with the American Army Education Service he rendered invaluable aid to the United States Army and contributed in large measure to the successful accomplishment of their educational campaigns.[31]

Nine: Encouraging music and the arts

> I do not believe it is yet realised what an important thing has happened. State patronage of the arts has crept in. It has happened in a very English, informal, unostentatious way – half-baked if you like.
>
> *John Maynard Keynes,* The Listener, *12 July 1945*

On Monday 18 December 1939, three months into the second World War, a group of thirteen men and one woman gathered at Kingsway House in London to discuss cultural activities in wartime Britain. Summoned by Lord 'Buck' de la Warr, President of the Board of Education, they included Lord (Hugh) Macmillan, Minister of Information and Chairman of the Pilgrim Trust; Dr Thomas Jones, Secretary of the Pilgrim Trust; Sir Walford Davies, Master of the King's Musick; Sir Kenneth Clark, Director of the National Gallery; and W E Williams, Secretary of the British Institute of Adult Education. Representing the Board were the Parliamentary Secretary and six male colleagues, plus Miss Mary Glasgow, one of the Board's Inspectors of Schools, who acted as conference secretary. That meeting was destined to re-shape the course of British cultural history by leading to a permanent change in the relationship between the State and the arts. This chapter aims to substantiate that large claim.

At the outbreak of war, the fear of heavy casualties from German bombing raids led the War Cabinet to order the immediate closure of all theatres, cinemas and other places of mass entertainment. For security reasons, every city, town and village was blacked-out. The country was approaching its darkest hours, in every sense of those words. School children were evacuated from major conurbations that might come under air attack at any time. Families were dispersed, with children sent to foster homes in the country, men mobilised into the armed forces and women directed into the factories and offices to take their place. Against that highly disruptive and demoralised background, those attending the Kingsway House conference faced a difficult agenda.

Lord Macmillan was present in a dual capacity: as Minister of Information, he carried prime responsibility for civilian morale; as Chairman of the Pilgrim Trust, he was concerned about the arts in wartime. He defined the purpose of the conference:

> first to discuss in principle the problem of cultural activities in war-time; and then to decide how the needs of the various organisations and individuals might be met. The discussion was confined to what have been termed "practical" activities: music, drama, the arts and handicrafts generally, as distinct from other activities which are on the fringe of academic adult education. The problem, therefore, goes beyond the mere subsidising of the arts, and beyond the entertaining of the depressed evacuees. It is one of helping voluntary societies, and possibly in some cases individuals, to give leadership and inspiration to the many people who, it is certain, are only too anxious to take part in worth-while musical and artistic activities.[1]

For Macmillan the problem was urgent. It was essential 'to begin any scheme at once and proceed by trial and error rather than delay matters by preparing too detailed an organisation'.[2] In a significant intervention, Lord de la Warr suggested that 'if anything effective were done, the Board would wish to consider the whole matter as more far-reaching and of more lasting importance than a wartime emergency'.[3] Buck de la Warr, in company with others present, appeared to recognise a long-awaited opportunity for converting the State from its traditional abstentionist role in British cultural life, into a more active and continuing role, in supporting or encouraging – if not exactly sponsoring – the arts. As for the immediate action required, Lord Macmillan announced that

> ...the Pilgrim Trust would be prepared to put up £25,000 if a suitable scheme were presented to the Board, or by the present Conference. He understood that the Treasury 'might be prepared to put up £ for £ in such an arrangement'.[4]

By the end of the conference, a small committee – comprising Sir Walford Davies, Sir Kenneth Clark, Dr Thomas Jones and W E Williams – was set up to consider practicalities. Recording the events of that day, Dr Jones made the following entry in his diary:

> Gave Kenneth Clark £25,000 to start a scheme with the Board of Education to carry out W E Williams' dream of helping music, drama etc... I have got him summoned to the talk at the Board of Education on Monday [18 December] with De la Warr, Walford Davies and TJ.[5]

There is no reason to doubt the accuracy of that diary entry. As often remarked, success has a thousand fathers, whilst failure is an orphan. It comes therefore as no surprise to find any number of claimants to authorship of state support for the arts in wartime Britain: J M Keynes, Sir Kenneth Clark, R A Butler, amongst others. But Dr Thomas Jones's diary note seems definitive: it was 'W E Williams' dream of helping music, drama etc' that prompted the wartime experiment with CEMA which in turn led to the post-war Arts Council. Many others talked about the need 'to do something'; Bill Williams got something done. He made the difference.

His modest scheme for promoting the arts in 'the current emergency' was launched in 1940 as the 'Committee (later Council) for the Encouragement of Music and the Arts in Wartime' (CEMA) which evolved in 1944 into the 'Arts Council of Great Britain' (ACGB). News of the initiative soon reached the press and the wider world. On 4 January 1940, *The Times* reported the emergence of CEMA, with an accompanying leader that looked forward to the post-war period and helpfully suggested 'dropping the last two words' from its cumbersome title. That suggestion was soon accepted.

In his biography of Dr Thomas Jones, E L Ellis provides this commentary:

> The state, which before the war had been adamantly laissez-faire in its attitude towards funding cultural activities, now hastily recognised their supreme importance in sustained morale in a people's war. Some time later the Treasury came forward with matching grants and a promise of conditional sums, but not before the arts relief work supported by Pilgrim Trust funds had evoked widespread response... TJ's part in the pioneer stages of this great pioneer adventure was, by general consent of those most closely involved, crucial to its success... He believed passionately in the importance of the quality of life of the people, and had insisted since early manhood that aesthetic considerations were as relevant to the everyday life of ordinary people as they were to that of the privileged, educated minority... He has often been driven to the verge of despair by the cultural deprivation and the poverty of aspiration of the mass of the people. Here was a great new opportunity. TJ meant to take it.[6]

By coincidence, in the same week as the inaugural meeting of CEMA, the text of John Maynard Keynes's broadcast on 'The Arts in War and Peace' was published in *The Listener*. Keynes identified 'the most dreadful heresy that has ever gained the ear of civilised people' – namely, that the economic ideal was the 'sole respectable purpose of the community as a whole'. Humane values, he argued, were far more important.[7] Keynes had put down a marker, which would become more significant as the war advanced.

At CEMA's first meeting, on 9 January 1940, those present included Dr Thomas Jones, Professor Sir Walford Davies, Sir Kenneth Clark, together with Mr Reginald Jacques, notable conductor and musical educator, Mr Wilkie, representing the Carnegie Trust, and W E Williams. Mary Glasgow had by then been seconded from her Civil Service duties to act as full-time Secretary to the Committee. CEMA operated throughout the war with a minimum of paid staff and a large number of unpaid volunteers. The Committee lost no time in developing a scheme to sustain civilian morale by taking orchestral music to the people of blacked-out Britain. Dr George Dyson, Principal of the Royal College of Music, proposed that the London Philharmonic and London Symphony Orchestra should put on concerts, with at least 25 per cent of tickets priced at one shilling or less. They would be given in industrial areas and housing estates within fifty miles of London but not in larger towns where facilities for hearing good music were already available. Observers were appointed to report back on the reception given to those sponsored concerts – an obvious parallel with Bill Williams' *Art for the People* scheme of the 1930s.

In January 1940, the Committee approved an interim report by Williams on 'The Circulation of Art Exhibitions in War-time'. He reported that he had already received eighty-three applications for exhibitions from different parts of the country. There was clearly an unsatisfied appetite for visual art as well as for music in wartime Britain. Given its broad remit and limited resources, CEMA was soon overwhelmed by grant applications from every corner of the United Kingdom. Having reviewed its spending commitments, it soon agreed the following order of priorities:

(i) the encouragement of interest, and the maintenance of a high standard in all branches of art by whatever means were found to be most appropriate

(ii) help and encouragement for the general public

(iii) help for unemployed professionals.

At the end of January 1940, *The Times* published a letter from Lord Macmillan, explaining why the Pilgrim Trust had made a grant of £25,000 for the encouragement of music and the arts. In an accompanying leading article – 'The Arts in War-time' – *The Times* welcomed the Pilgrim Trust's 'generous intention towards the arts of peace in time of war' and noted 'some flutterings in artistic dovecotes'. But it warmly supported the initiative and was quick to identify the longer-term implications of the scheme:

> So far so good. But the announcement gave presage of greater things to come, of further assistance from other sources, including the Treasury, and of an organization which might become permanent.[8]

In its first three months, CEMA found its feet and established a distinct national identity. It set up a wartime organisation, defined its own clear objectives and policy, and devised its priorities and methods of working. After six meetings, CEMA had disbursed its first dozen grants. Among its early beneficiaries were the Rural Music Schools Council; £500 for the appointment of a Music Director, Scotland; £500 to the National Council of Social Service to pay the salaries of two music organisers for a period of twelve months; the National Federation of Women's Institutes, the Religious Drama Society, the Scottish Community Drama Association, and no less than £2,750 to Bill Williams for the British Institute of Adult Education's art exhibitions for one year.

In April 1940, CEMA transformed itself from a Committee into a Council, a more practical executive body of just eight persons, comprising Dr Thomas Jones, Vice-Chairman; Sir Kenneth Barnes, BBC; Miss Thelma Cazalet, MP; Sir Kenneth Clark, Director of the National Gallery; Sir Walford Davies, Master of the King's Musick; Miss Margery Fry, author and journalist; and Mr J Wilkie, of the Carnegie UK Trust; plus three representatives of the Board of Education, including Mr Davidson, the Accountant-General to the Board. The Council would henceforth be serviced by a small staff, plus a team of five Honorary Directors, experts in their respective fields, to advise on the initiatives required and the merits of the many claims for financial and other forms of assistance: Mr Lewis Casson, the distinguished actor-manager, for professional theatre; Dr George Dyson, Principal of the Royal College of Music, for professional music; Dr Reginald Jacques, for amateur music; Mr L du Garde Peach, the playwright, for amateur theatre; and Mr W E Williams, originator of *Art for the People*, for art.[9]

An important document, dated 10 April 1940, offered Guidance Notes on the Council's *Policy and Structure*:

> The central policy of the Council is to maintain the highest possible standard in our national arts of music, drama and painting* at a time when these things are threatened and when, too, they mean more in the life of the country than they have ever meant before. An essential part of the plan is to carry the arts to those places which, for one reason or another, are cut off from their enjoyment. Thus it is hoped to give encouragement and refreshment to people suffering from the strain and anxiety of war while, at the same time, substantial help will be given to the professional artists engaged. The Council is helping our great national orchestras...to give concerts in drab industrial areas where so far there have been no opportunities for such things... It is sending exhibitions of original paintings to minor villages and suburbs which have as yet no cultural roots and these will be accompanied by expert guides who are ready to talk about the pictures and encourage comment and discussion.[10]
>
> * later extended to include sculpture, drawings, architectural plans etc.

The hand of Bill Williams is clearly visible in those notes, which built on the experience of arranging his pre-war *Art for the People* exhibitions. Sending 'original paintings to minor villages and suburbs' and the use of expert guides 'ready to talk about the pictures and encourage comment and discussion' were ideas taken directly from Williams' pioneering BIAE scheme. Attached to the Guidance Notes was a crucial Board of Education Memorandum, which set out some of the Board's considerations on the Council's work:

> It is not cynical but rather realistic in the true sense of the word to say that while the actual encouragement of music and the arts and even the preservation of the people's

> morale in war time might indeed be left to individual initiative and be paid for out of trust funds, it is essential to the whole idea of the Committee which the President has called into being is that it should be a Government concern. It is of practical importance to show publicly and unmistakably that the Government cares about the cultural life of the country. This country is supposed to be fighting for civilisation and democracy and if these things mean anything they mean a way of life where people have liberty and opportunity to pursue the things of peace. It should be part of a national War policy to show that the Government is actively interested in these things. Such an assurance needs to be given equally for the sake of our own people and for the sake of British prestige abroad.[11]

In short, whilst waging the most ferocious, unremitting and costly war, Britain's wartime Government had decided to show 'publicly and unmistakably' that it intended to play a more active part in caring for 'the cultural life of the country'. CEMA's expanded role in preserving, maintaining and disseminating cultural life in wartime Britain is a complicated story which cannot be compressed into a few paragraphs. This chapter does not pretend to be a history of CEMA. Instead, it seeks to bring out the main features of CEMA policy and to illustrate some of its major achievements, with specific attention to Bill Williams' vital contribution to its work.

At the first meeting of CEMA Council, on 23 April 1940, the Chairman read a letter from Prime Minister Winston Churchill: 'I warmly approve this project which is excellent in every way'. Council then formally approved its operating procedure:

> Agreed that the most effective method of working would be for the Directors to be free to frame their own programmes, which they would then submit, with estimates of cost, for approval by the Council at its monthly meetings. Between meetings, they would be responsible for the administration of their schemes to the limit of the grants allocated. They would also be responsible for advising the Council in regard to applications from societies and individuals falling within their respective fields.[12]

Lord Macmillan stressed the emergency nature of the Council's work:

> The Treasury grant [of £50,000] had been given on the understanding that it was to be used for dealing with special war-time conditions. It was an example of how on rare occasions good may come out of evil, and help be given through the pressure of tragic events to activities which, in addition to their war-time urgency, have permanent peace-time value. He expressed the Council's gratitude to the Government for its timely action.[13]

The grant-in-aid of £50,000 promised by the Treasury would be passed by Parliament as a supplementary vote on the Board of Education estimate. Of that total, some £6,000 would be allocated to Scotland. The Treasury representative stressed that the grant was a special wartime measure, not an annual one, nor was it given for any specific period. No pre-war British Government had considered establishing an 'Arts Council', let alone appointing a Minister of Culture. Nor was there widespread public demand for such extraordinary public expenditure. In 1940, when the

Treasury announced its first grant to CEMA, the *Daily Express* had thundered: 'The government gives fifty thousand pounds to help wartime culture. What madness is this? There is no such thing as culture in wartime'.[14]

Fortunately for Britain, there were those who thought differently. In May 1940, the Carnegie United Kingdom Trustees reported that they 'were unanimously in favour of granting the full sum of £25,000 for the Council's work' and asked 'that Dr George Dyson be made a member of the Council to represent the music policy of the Trust'. Dr Dyson was replaced by Dr Reginald Jacques, who was invited to supervise its music policy. A skeleton scheme was approved for sending musicians at short notice to play to groups of people who might be stranded for long periods during or after a crisis – such as a severe air-raid, when many hundreds of civilians might be temporarily housed in an empty school or hotel awaiting re-housing.

CEMA's policy of taking art and music to some of the remoter parts of Britain soon attracted the envious attention of London's newspapers. In August 1940, the Secretary reported suggestions that the Council ought to abandon its original policy of excluding London and other large cities from its scope. The criticism was two-fold: first, that larger cities were as much in need of refreshment as more remote places and were sometimes suffering more acute war strain; and second, that it was easier and cheaper to help the arts in bigger places. The Council agreed that a strong case would be made to the Treasury for an extension of grant to cover the larger towns. The issue of metropolitan versus regional bias was destined to figure largely in later criticism of State support for the arts.

Meanwhile, Williams' touring art exhibitions continued to attract favourable attention wherever they appeared. In October 1940, Sir Kenneth Clark reported that the Circulating Exhibitions Scheme

> ...gave real hope for the future because it was laying the foundations of a popular understanding of living Art and living artists. At present, it was the one channel open for getting into touch with ordinary people and creating among them a new and genuine appreciation of painting.[15]

In January 1941, Williams, the 'Honorary Director for Art', was congratulated on his report for the previous year. A well-timed request by the Ministry of Information for a section of the War Artists Exhibitions to be circulated under the *Art for the People* scheme, prompted Williams to seek Council approval for the purchase of a lorry to ensure the quick and safe transport of art exhibits. Later that year, as Director of ABCA, Williams obtained Council's permission to take CEMA's touring exhibitions, particularly those concerned with post-war town planning, to the armed forces, the cost being fully met by the War Office.

The courageous quality of CEMA's decisions derived from the independent-minded members of Council, spurred on by its five Honorary Directors. It also reflected the skill and devotion of its Secretary, Mary Glasgow, in presenting and summarising the complex and often difficult policy options. Mary Cecilia Glasgow plays a key part in this narrative. Born in 1905, she studied French language and literature at Lady Margaret Hall, Oxford. Having served for a year as Organising Secretary for the League of Nations Union in Oxford, she then became an Assistant Librarian at the Board of Education from 1927 to 1932. After two years' research and teaching abroad, she returned to her job as a civil servant, working for six years as a Board of Education Inspector of Schools from 1933 to 1939, when she was seconded to serve as Secretary of CEMA. In the early years, Mary Glasgow was uniquely responsible for ensuring that State policy on the arts was put into practice.

With the passage of time, membership of Council gradually changed. In July 1941, Dr Ralph Vaughan Williams, Britain's most distinguished symphonic composer, succeeded Sir Walford Davies. In September of that year, Professor B Ifor Evans, representing literature, was welcomed to Council. Sir Lewis Casson resigned as Honorary Director for Professional Drama and was replaced by Mr Ivor Brown, with an honorarium of £100pa plus £250 expenses.[16] In the same month, Council heard of an anticipated deficit of £7,000 at the end of March 1942, due largely to over-spending on factory concerts. There had already been heavy cuts in the Council's expenditure on music and only a small part of the demand was being met. Lord Macmillan suggested that the time had come to review the future position of CEMA in relation to the Treasury grant, and the policy of the Board of Education. At the conclusion of formal business, members of Council were presented to Mr R A (RAB) Butler, newly-appointed President of the Board of Education, who expressed a strong personal interest in CEMA's work, and in its future.

Butler's arrival at the Board of Education in March 1942 is a refreshing example of the right man in the right place and the right time. By his personal commitment to its long-term future, Butler may well have prevented the disappearance of CEMA as an interesting but extravagant wartime experiment. It is difficult to think of anyone in Britain better qualified by temperament, taste or experience to oversee the future of CEMA, whose survival largely depended on the goodwill and enthusiastic support of a Cabinet Minister with clout. In 1942, Butler was a politician on his way to the top. Co-author of the 1944 Education Act; Chancellor of the Exchequer in Churchill's 1951 Government; tipped for the premiership after Prime Minister Anthony Eden's resignation; Foreign Secretary under Alec Douglas-Home, who beat him to the prime ministership after Macmillan's resignation, RAB finished his days as Master of Trinity College, Cambridge, when his long political career ended.

CEMA was not, however, without its well-informed critics. On 19 September 1941, shortly after attending his first meeting of CEMA Council, Professor B Ifor Evans, academic and Chairman of the British Council, wrote an impassioned letter to Sir Robert Wood, Permanent Secretary at the Board of Education, complaining bitterly at the direction in which he saw CEMA moving. The crucial question was whether the time had come for government to assume total financial responsibility for CEMA's work. By liberating itself from even part-dependence on the Pilgrim Trust, CEMA would have greater freedom of action and so regain the decisive voice in determining future policy. The matter was happily resolved over the next few months by the apparently independent, though perhaps not entirely coincidental, decision of the Pilgrim Trust to end its financial support. As a consequence of that decision, Lord Macmillan and Dr Thomas Jones, both Trustees of the Pilgrim Trust, tendered their resignation as the longest-serving members of CEMA Council. Having been advised of their imminent departure, Butler lost no time in recruiting a suitable successor to Lord Macmillan. In a letter to Professor John Maynard Keynes, dated 17 December 1941, here quoted in full, Butler used his familiar powers of persuasion to secure the new Chairman he wanted:

> I have no doubt that [CEMA] has met a real need and has found a quite remarkable response, and while the Council's work will still remain emergency war work it does, I think, point the way to something that might occupy a more permanent place in our social organisation. The Treasury are ready to continue their subvention, which is now at the rate of £60,000 a year, and I hope that they may increase it.
>
> I am wondering whether you would be willing to consider taking on the Chairmanship. I know how fully occupied your time is already and I have indeed some hesitation in approaching you with any further request which might add to your load... With your knowledge of, and sympathy for, the Council's objectives, your guidance at this stage of its development would be invaluable, and I should be only too glad if you could see your way to accept an invitation to become its Chairman.[17]

Having considered the matter carefully, Keynes responded to Butler on 14 January 1942:

> After discussing the very interesting proposal which you sent me in your letter of December 17th with yourself, Miss Glasgow and Ivor Brown (also with Kenneth Clark), I should like to accept, and am ready to succeed Lord Macmillan in the Chairmanship of CEMA after March next, if you ask me to do so.
>
> I was considerably consoled as regards the amount of work and responsibility likely to be involved in the near future by my talks with Miss Glasgow and Ivor Brown. It is evident that CEMA is a well organised, well run affair, moving on its own wheels, and I found very

> little I wanted to criticise or should feel moved to endeavour to change. Meanwhile I feel that I could do what you suggest without involving myself in an amount of work to which I should be unable to do justice in view of my other preoccupations.[18]

Delighted with this acceptance, Butler wrote Keynes a personal note of thanks: 'I feel that the future of something rather important depends on your influence and I could wish for no better'.[19]

On 19 January 1942, Dr Thomas Jones also thanked Keynes on the occasion of his taking over from Lord Macmillan:

> I must send you a line, which requires no reply, to say how glad I am, and I am sure Macmillan also will be, that you have agreed to take over the care of CEMA. It does need someone who is in London oftener than I am for though a healthy and promising plant it is still somewhat tender & could easily be 'blown upon' in the House. With you as Head Gardener it should grow strong and flourish in all three branches. The staff at the Board you will find are very devoted to its welfare & will support you most loyally.[20]

Keynes replied immediately in a letter dated 22 January 1942:

> I much appreciated your note about CEMA. I hope I shall do nothing to hurt the good beginning which has been made.
>
> Since I am not likely to have any leisure worth mentioning during the war, I much hesitated in taking over this new responsibility, and only did so after I had made sufficient enquiries to convince myself that the affair was so well and efficiently run and moving forward on its own wheels that there was little, or nothing, I should feel moved to criticise or seek to change. You have done a splendid job in getting this organisation going. I am hopeful from what R A Butler told me that it may conceivably form the beginning of something more ambitious after the war. But without private enterprise to start the ball rolling, no balls get rolled.[21]

At CEMA Council on 17 February 1942, the acting chairman announced that Keynes had accepted Butler's invitation to be Chairman of CEMA and confirmed that the Treasury had increased its grant from £60,000 to £100,000 for 1942/43. At the same meeting, CEMA Council considered a Memorandum by Bill Williams on the circulation of Art Exhibitions:

> Mr Williams underlined the point that he had made in his paper that the first purpose of the "Art for the People" Exhibitions initiated by the BIAE had been pioneer work among unsophisticated communities. Of recent months, however, there had been a heavy increase in the number of requests for exhibitions from the larger provincial towns with art galleries. The Institute could not hope to meet these demands by foregoing its own special work. He therefore felt that the time had come for CEMA to expand its activity in the field of art and, in particular, he suggested that the existing machinery and resources of the Victoria and Albert Museum should be employed in provincial galleries.[22]

The wheel had come full circle. Having set out to provide a taste of art to people living in the more remote towns and villages of Britain, Williams now had the gratifying experience of receiving so many requests for his circulating exhibitions to visit Britain's larger provincial cities that he felt compelled to call on the resources of the V & A to help meet those requests.

Within a week of that meeting, *The Times* carried the following story:

> CEMA has become an established national institution in the two years since it was founded ...By its work CEMA has dissipated scepticism about the public response to unaccustomed forms of beauty in sound, thought and design. In all, some 60,000 people have visited its art exhibitions; CEMA playgoers number 1,500,000; and there have been about 8,000 concerts... The "Art for the People" exhibitions of paintings, drawings and reproductions, and of industrial and architectural design, are taken out by CEMA in collaboration with the British Institute of Adult Education. Collections of all kinds are being sent out to the Forces, and particularly to the more remote Army and RAF stations. They are also lent to factory canteens, workers' hostels, clubs, and churches.[23]

At Council meeting on 14 April 1942, Sir Robert Wood welcomed J M Keynes as the new Chairman of CEMA. As the first item of business, Keynes informed Council that the Pilgrim Trust had made CEMA a parting gift of £25,000. The Minutes of that meeting also record that:

> Mr W E Williams had become so fully occupied with his new duties at the War Office that he wished from now onward to resign his position as Art Director to CEMA. The Council accepted Mr Williams' resignation with an expression of gratitude for the indispensable pioneer work which he had performed for them but were glad to understand that Mr Williams proposed to continue in effect to act as a link between CEMA and the BIAE.[24]

It was agreed to appoint Philip James as Art Director, responsible to Sir Kenneth Clark in questions of policy. In arrangements affecting the *Art for the People* circulating scheme, James would co-operate with the BIAE through W E Williams.

At Council meeting on 27 May 1942, it was agreed to invite Williams, as Secretary of the BIAE, to meet members of the Council to discuss details of the Council's art policy as a whole and the appropriate division of functions as between the BIAE and CEMA. Williams immediately agreed the Council's financial arrangements for his *Art for the People* exhibitions but refused to accept any modification of the system of guide lecturers to accompany them. Not everyone agreed with this. But all his experience confirmed Williams' belief that visitors to art exhibitions welcomed the presence of guide lecturers to stimulate their enjoyment of art, and especially of modern art.

On 2 July 1942, in its leading article on *Art and the People*, *The Listener* warmly commended a scheme, instigated by Lady Clark on behalf of CEMA, whereby two leading British artists, Paul Nash and Duncan Grant, had agreed to decorate several

British Restaurants with large colourful mural paintings. The article went on to discuss the possible long-term effects of 'State interference' in the arts:

> There is much to be said against State interference in the arts; but, as we observed recently in discussing the state of Kultur, State support for the arts, as opposed to State control, is an excellent thing; and it may be that in CEMA, whose members are independent people appointed by the President of the Board of Education and who as a body have no political axe to grind, there exists the germ of a movement which is to have a great and beneficial effect on the study and appreciation of the arts by the people of this country.[25]

In short, by 1942, informed opinion in Britain had discovered that, far from being a sinister instrument of State control, government support for the arts was playing a valuable part in maintaining wartime morale and might be worth preserving in the post-war period.

As time passed, Williams' relationship with CEMA became increasingly fraught. Having taken up his appointment as Director of ABCA in August 1941 and resigning his part-time position as CEMA's Honorary Art Director in April 1942, he continued to take his circulating exhibitions to the armed forces but frequently found himself in conflict with Philip James, his successor as Art Director. For James had developed his own ideas on CEMA's art policy. Williams let Kenneth Clark know that he was unhappy with his anomalous position outside CEMA and coveted a seat on Council itself, where he could directly influence its policies.

On 22 September 1942, Butler wrote to Lord Keynes (created 1st Baron of Tilton in 1942), first expressing his gratitude 'for your excellent and encouraging direction of CEMA', and then raising the delicate matter of Williams' position:

> All my information goes to show that it would go far, if not all the way, to solving the present discontents if he could be invited to join the Council. He feels, justifiably, that he has done as much as anyone to establish CEMA in the early stages, and I think it would be an advantage to the Council, as well as frankly his due, if I were to issue this invitation. I can see the difficulties, and I understood your objections to taking action earlier, but I am convinced that this is a right step to take.[26]

Butler later clarified his request. He was asking for Williams to be appointed to the new Art Panel and not to Council. Williams thus found himself working alongside some of the most prestigious personalities in modern British art history – like Henry Moore, Duncan Grant and John Rothenstein.

Speaking at the official opening of a CEMA exhibition at the National Gallery in October 1942, R A Butler, by then Minister of Education, predicted that CEMA would survive the war to become 'an instrument of collective patronage'.[27] But there was nothing inevitable about CEMA's future nor any guarantee that it would survive the cultural and financial storms that lay ahead.

At Council meeting on 8 December 1942,[28] the Chairman announced the re-organisation of CEMA and RAB's acceptance of the members of three specialist panels to advise on policy issues:

Music	***Drama***	***Art***
Sir Arthur Bliss	Mr Ashley Dukes	Mr Samuel Courtauld
Dame Myra Hess	Mr Herbert Farjeon	Mr Duncan Grant
Mr Constant Lambert	Miss Athene Seyler	Mr Henry Moore
Sir Thomas Wood	Mr Emlyn Williams	Dr John Rothenstein
		Mr W E Williams

On 11 May 1943, with allied armies fighting in North Africa and the Russian army driving the German army out of Stalingrad, Rostov and Kharkov, Lord Keynes contributed an important signed article to *The Times* on the occasion of the reopening by Dame Sybil Thorndike of the Theatre Royal, Bristol:

> The functions of CEMA are evolving rapidly, and an account is soon out of date. If it thought fit to preserve after the war any part of the organization and experience that CEMA, which is on a temporary basis will have acquired, this, I believe, is the fruitful line of development. If with State aid the material frame can be constructed, the public and the artists will do the rest between them. The Muses will emerge from their dusty haunts, and Supply and Demand shall be their servants. To begin the good work, let us build temples for them as our memorial to the gallant endurance of Plymouth and Coventry and the rest, and of old London herself... At any rate, do not let us lose what we already have.[29]

At Council meeting on 20 July 1943, in a discussion of Theatre Building Policy, the Chairman sought members' views on the possible acquisition by Council of two 19th century buildings which might shortly come onto the market at a total cost of £50,000. Dr Vaughan Williams protested strongly against spending money on buildings rather than on fostering the arts and artists themselves. Lord Esher supported the proposal while Sir Kenneth Clark expressed his doubts. Mrs Cazalet Kerr said that while she hoped Council would not forget the main wartime purpose for which it was created, she regarded the proposal as 'a step towards the permanent policy of State help for the arts, and one which would establish the Council's claim for generous funds after the war'.[30]

By the autumn of 1943, Mary Glasgow had served as Secretary of CEMA for four years. It was assumed that she was content with her position, her civil service grade and pay scale. But at Council meeting on 19 October 1943, Mrs Cazalet Kerr formally proposed that:

> in view of the importance and responsibility of the Secretary, her present status is inadequate and should be raised.[31]

Following delicate negotiations, the Chairman reported to Council on 14 March 1944 that the Board of Education could not accept the view that the position of Secretary to the Council warranted an officer of higher rank than that of Principal. They hoped that, in due course, the Secretary would be directly employed by the Council. Meantime, it might help if the Secretary were in future to be known as General Secretary. The suggestion was agreed and Mary Glasgow did not contest the Board's decision.

One of the most difficult problems for a wartime organisation like CEMA was that, whilst it succeeded in managing its day-to-day affairs with reasonable efficiency, and whilst it pioneered many outstanding new ventures – like its midday concerts at the National Gallery, its commissioning of new work by war artists, its public displays of imaginative plans for post-war reconstruction and mass re-housing – it had no resources to devote to re-thinking the position of the arts in the post-war Britain.

As President of the Board of Education, Butler was known to be formulating his ideas for post-war education policies, including art education. As Chairman of CEMA, Maynard Keynes had independently developed his own ideas for the visual arts, theatre and ballet. As Director of the National Gallery, Kenneth Clark held strong views on how the great national collections should be re-housed and revitalised. Dr Thomas Jones and Bill Williams, like others in the field of adult education, had developed their own thoughts on the appropriate policies to be pursued when peace returned. Many hundreds of arts practitioners in the field knew what they wanted. But there was no systematic attempt by the Council of CEMA to bring these ideas together, to confront the divergent views, and to seek some common policy objectives for the post-war arts in Britain.

Others recognised the existence of such conflicting views and were sufficiently concerned to initiate discussion on how they might be reconciled. In November 1941, with the war just two years old, the Trustees of Dartington Hall, an independent arts promotion and educational body, together with Political and Economic Planning (PEP), set up The Arts Inquiry under the Chairmanship of Professor Julian Huxley. The Inquiry appointed a number of panels that met frequently over the following three years and, in due course, presented their separate Reports between 1943 and 1945. One key issue was whether overall responsibility for the arts should remain with the Board (later the Ministry) of Education; whether it should be handed over to a new Ministry of Culture, as in other European countries; or whether another, less bureaucratic, solution should be sought. For example, should CEMA be allowed to continue in some modified form, independent on policy matters but still dependent on the Board of Education for its budget? 'Education and the arts' had become so conflated in British cultural discourse that it was difficult to see any easy and practical way of de-coupling them in the post-war period. So long as the arts continued to come under the aegis of a government department, it seemed impossible to remove the dead hand of the Treasury from Britain's cultural development.

The debate came to a head at The Arts Inquiry in February 1944, when the Director of the Inquiry, Christopher Martin, wrote to Kenneth Clark, enclosing a letter from Jasper Ridley, challenging the conventional idea that the proposed new Arts Council should be put under the Board of Education:

> If the Arts Council is to be established somewhat in the BBC dress, and if it is to be entrusted, directly or indirectly, with the serving of grants, is it really certain that the Minister of Education is the right Minister to sponsor them in Parliament and elsewhere? Might it not be – how shall I put it? – a more adult system to get away from him and have in the place of sponsor (as I ventured to suggest at the meeting) one of those independent and amorphous people like the Lord President of the Council or the Lord Privy Seal?
>
> Our reasons for putting the Arts Council under the Board were, I think:
>
> (1) The Board is already responsible for CEMA, the V&A, the Royal College, Art Schools, etc.
>
> (2) No other administering department seemed suitable.
>
> (3) The indeterminate people such as the Lord President and the Lord Privy Seal would not take the job.
>
> Possibly a fourth reason is that in a new and better world education is, we hope, not going to carry the rather tiresome connotation which at present it undoubtedly does carry and which is probably at the back of Ridley's mind.[32]

Lord Keynes was unable to attend Council meeting on 26 September 1944, having returned to the United States to continue negotiations on the Lend-Lease Agreement. In his absence, Mary Glasgow presented a short Memorandum by Lord Keynes on CEMA's future. He had discussed the Memorandum with the Minister of Education who had welcomed it and agreed it in principle. The main lines of the proposals were as follows:

> (i) The new CEMA should be established by Royal Charter.
>
> (ii) Its name should be changed to the Royal Council of the Arts. (There was no finality about this name and another might prove more suitable. It might also be desirable to keep the well-known name of CEMA for popular use.)
>
> (iii) The new Council should have considerably increased funds at its disposal.
>
> (iv) Whatever the nature of these funds, whether given under statute or as a grant-in-aid, they should be made available by the Treasury in advance, over a reasonable period of years, to enable the Council to make long-term promises.

(v) The Council's income might be given, as at present, on the vote of the Ministry of Education or it might come direct from the Treasury, in which case the Chancellor and not the Minister of Education would represent the Council in the House of Commons.

(vi) Lord Keynes did not contemplate any immediate change in the activities or the personnel of the Council. A small executive committee of the Council, meeting often and regularly, would probably be necessary.

(vii) It would not be necessary in the first place to define the Council's exact functions for the purposes of the Charter. It was, however, very important that the Council's exact relations with Local Authorities, as well as with art galleries and with professional colleges, should be worked out.[33]

Keynes's pioneering work behind the scenes had evidently been a well-kept secret. He had taken advantage of his periodic meetings with R A Butler to try out his ideas before completing his Memorandum. It seems likely that Kenneth Clark was another member of Keynes's inner circle of advisors. On 11 December 1944, Clark addressed the following letter to Butler, which shows how little had been leaked to wider circles of British artistic life about the post-war rebirth of CEMA:

> A few nights ago I was asked round to Dame Myra Hess's house on the pretext of hearing some music, but, as it turned out, in order to hear an harangue from Stafford Cripps. He said that the work of CEMA must be continued after the war and that not enough was being done either in public or Cabinet circles to urge this point of view. It seems that he and Dame Myra had formed the fanciful notion that I might in some way organise opinion in support of this end. I told Cripps that you and Keynes had already given much thought to the subject and had already prepared a plan that was already with the Treasury.[34]

Clark ended his letter by quoting Sir Samuel Courtauld's suggestion that

> ...a few of the people who believe in State support for the arts...might form themselves into a kind of dining club...to put some ideas about State patronage into [the politicians] heads at the present moment.[35]

In a letter, dated 12 January 1945, Lord Keynes sent Members of Council the full text of his suggestions for the re-organisation of CEMA as a permanent peacetime body. The document, on 'The Royal Council of the Arts', was discussed at length at Council's meeting on 30 January 1945. The Chairman's proposals fell into three main sections, dealing respectively with legal aspects (notably the acquisition of a Royal Charter); financial aspects (which the Treasury must decide); and the executive organisation (which dealt with the Council's own power). Council reviewed in detail the composition and working of Specialist Panels, and the functions of the proposed Executive Committee. As to the name of the new Council, the Minutes record that:

> Numbers were almost equally divided between the full title proposed, "Royal Council for the Arts", and the shorter "Arts Council". There was some feeling that the accepted name "CEMA" should be allowed to go on in popular use, because of the goodwill attached to it.[36]

It was finally agreed by Council

> ...that the Minister of Education should be urged to press for the incorporation of the new Council under Royal Charter at the earliest possible moment. It should be made clear to him that the financial position was appreciated and that, if no quick decision under this head were forthcoming from the Treasury, the Council would be content to continue on the present year-to-year basis for the time being.[37]

Immediately following that meeting, Lord Keynes wrote to Butler, urging him to press the authorities to 'let us have a decision on the issue of incorporation at the earliest possible date'. Members of Council wished to suggest that the draft aims and objectives of the proposed Royal Council of Arts should be re-worded to run somewhat as follows:

> The scope and purposes of the Royal Council of the Arts will be stated in the Charter as being in general terms to encourage the knowledge, understanding and practice of the arts, and in particular:
>
> (a) to increase the accessibility of the arts to the public throughout the country
>
> (b) to improve the standard of execution of the arts
>
> (c) to encourage and aid proficiency in the arts
>
> (d) to improve and maintain the status of artists
>
> (e) to advise and co-operate with Government Departments.[38]

All this essential but time-consuming preliminary work was carried out with the greatest possible secrecy, to avoid premature disclosure of an official announcement by a Government Minister. But Lord Keynes and R A Butler were by no means the only public figures pre-occupied with these matters. At its meeting on 15 May 1945, when Mrs Ayrton Gould and Mr W E Williams were welcomed as new members, Lord Keynes told Council, in confidence, 'that the Chancellor had agreed to the continuance of CEMA' which would be known, in future, by the name he had finally submitted: 'The Arts Council of Great Britain'. The Council immediately adopted that title unanimously.

In a first discussion of the total amount of Treasury Grant for the period 1946-1951, Lord Keynes said that he regarded the sums offered (£320,000 in 1946; £360,000 in 1947; and £400,000 in each of the following three years) as 'reasonably adequate' for current needs. There was no provision for non-recurrent expenditure, but he felt the Treasury would 'not be unsympathetic' to an appeal for special allocations outside the main programme.

On 12 June 1945, Sir John Anderson, Chancellor of the Exchequer, announced to the House of Commons that the government had reviewed CEMA's experience in maintaining 'the standard and the national tradition of the arts under wartime conditions' and had decided to incorporate the Council with this object and with the name of 'The Arts Council of Great Britain' and with J M Keynes as its first Chairman.

In its leading article, 'The Arts in Britain', *The Listener* of 21 June 1945 welcomed the establishment of the Arts Council:

> Many have long held that it was a reproach that we have had nothing in this country equivalent to the ministries of the fine arts established elsewhere. Others believed that to put the arts in charge of a special ministry would not accord well with British habits and traditions. In the event, the method of a central body directly under the State had not been chosen, but CEMA, which has done good work in war conditions for the theatre, music and (in lesser degree) for some of the other arts, will be separately constituted under a charter, receiving a Treasury grant, but keeping independent management of the ordinary conduct of its affairs.[39]

On the night of 25 July 1945, the results of the first post-war general election became known: Labour was returned to power with a large majority. With the disappearance of CEMA, the new Minister of Education, Ellen Wilkinson, now faced the task of nominating new members of the Arts Council for approval by Hugh Dalton, the new Chancellor of the Exchequer. How far would he go in confirming former members of CEMA as members of the Arts Council? In a letter, dated 30 October 1945, Mary Glasgow wrote to Dr Thomas Jones:

> May I consult you about another matter? The Council, as you know, is being legally set up, with a Charter and what not. New members are under consideration and, in particular, our Minister wants there to be some "representation" of "adult education". (Please reassure yourself: Lord Keynes is as fierce as ever you were about keeping the Council small and about non-representation.)
>
> I have told the Minister [of Education] that she ought to put W E Williams on the Council. Keynes agrees. But I think I ought to find out what I don't know for sure: Is he leaving the British Institute? If not, then the old difficulty remains, that the BIAE is a grant-aided body. Can you inform me? And, anyhow, what do you think? We must have him, mustn't we? [40]

Dr Jones replied to Mary Glasgow on 2 November 1945:

> The future of WE is uncertain. The plan in which I am interested is moving slowly, but I think surely, and the BIAE is involved in that plan. I am afraid that is all I can say at the moment.
>
> Why not suggest Philip Morris, the new Vice-Chancellor of Bristol University? He is deeply devoted to the cause of adult education. How soon must you decide this? I think WE would feel bad being off the body which he had so much to do in creating.[41]

On 19 November 1945, Mary Glasgow addressed another letter to Dr Jones:

> I have delayed in answering your letter of Nov 2nd about Mr W E Williams. Let me hasten to say that there is no question of cutting him off. He is a member of the Art Panel and there is no suggestion whatever that he should cease to be. What I am so anxious for is that he should become a full Council member. That was not possible before, because he was identified with the BIAE which is a beneficiary of CEMA assistance. I want to find a way round that now, but from what you say it may prove difficult. I do so strongly agree with you that he ought to be a member of the Council.[42]

At the Arts Council meeting on 21 February 1946, it was agreed that the 'Secretary-General, Miss Mary Glasgow, to be placed on the establishment of the Arts Council for an initial period of five years at a salary of £1,600 a year'. She was the Arts Council's first employee, and had served the Council and its forerunner, CEMA, for over six years.

Early in 1946, Lord Keynes suddenly collapsed with an undisclosed condition and was ordered to rest. He died on Easter Sunday 1946, worn out by his heavy wartime responsibilities. Lord Keynes was a towering figure in the British cultural establishment. Had he lived to steer the Arts Council through its later years, State support for the arts in Britain might have been more generous and its subsequent history rather different.

At its meeting on 5 June 1946, Sir Ernest Pooley, the Arts Council's new Chairman, moved the following resolution, which was carried unanimously with a request that a copy should be sent to Lady Keynes:

> The Arts Council of Great Britain, meeting now for the first time after the death of Lord Keynes, place on record their sense of the profound deprivation which all connected with the arts have suffered by this loss, and more particularly their realisation of the great and distinguished services generously given by him to the development of this Council, whose deliberations he guided with his wisdom during years when the nation made so many claims on his varied talents.[43]

The death of Lord Keynes, and the appointment of Mary Glasgow as first Secretary-General of the Arts Council, marked a turning point in State support for the arts in Britain: an appropriate point to cite some contemporary assessments of CEMA and the Arts Council's early achievements.

In *The Observer* in May 1945, Ivor Brown, a member of Council, offered an insider's reflections on the experience of CEMA:

> The Arts Council will have more status and durability: it can plan with more confidence: it inherits much good will. CEMA, like every stripling, may have erred and strayed, but continued Government recognition is as good proof as may be of steady achievement. It will come in, rightly, for criticism; and, less rightly, for all the grumbling and snarling so popular with artists whenever somebody tries to help the arts.

> CEMA was always exposed to two forms of attack: one, that it messed about humbly and drably in the provinces and lacked prestige and panache; two, that it didn't stick to the provinces but swaggered about in St James's or the Haymarket and cultivated the pomps of theatrical Tennentry. He who gets slapped north and south in this manner is probably in the right, and the Arts Council will doubtless receive the same kind of contradictory and reassuring attacks...
>
> My immediate point is that the Arts Council should be closely linked with national education as CEMA was from the start... It will surely be a primary duty of the Arts Council, while being associated with the high lights and top flights of the metropolitan Muses, to make sense of education up and down the country by providing cheaply, gaily, and to good advantage, those human pleasures of reason and the senses which have so often been mere raw material of pedagogy, exam-fodder, tasks and torments.[44]

A second judgement is by another CEMA Council Member, Professor B Ifor Evans, who threw out this sharp challenge in *The Observer* in October 1946:

> The organs of culture at the disposal of the State should be at least as well organized as the holiday camp, the dirt-tracks and the 'dogs', so the Government and municipalities should immediately face their responsibilities and not be fobbed off with excuses about 'difficulties'. What commerce can arrange, the community with all its 'priorities' could certainly achieve.[45]

A third and final judgement is taken from an article by Adrian Forty, a cultural historian, writing of the 1951 Festival of Britain, more than twenty-five years after the events he describes:

> Although it is hard to put any precise value on the political effects of the Festival, it did represent an important step in the policy of state support for the arts. In 1940 the Government had set up CEMA to organise concerts and exhibitions round the country and help break London's monopoly of artistic activity... After the war CEMA changed its name to the Arts Council and carried on the same kind of work, while a new organisation, the Council of Industrial Design was set up. The decision of the Labour Government to finance these two bodies indicates that there was a strong belief in some quarters that the arts in Britain both deserved and needed official support in peacetime as much as in wartime, if they were to survive and grow in modern society. The Festival itself was the apogee of this policy, since it provided the money and the occasion for architects, composers, painters and sculptors to work on a scale much larger than was normally possible.[46]

CEMA's wartime achievements were crowned by its transformation into the Arts Council of Great Britain. The fact that the Arts Council has survived into the 21st century – despite several further make-overs – testifies to the remarkable solidity of CEMA's foundations. Bill Williams had played a crucial role in CEMA's success. But he was destined to play an even more active role in its successor body, the Arts Council of Great Britain.

Literary event, with William Emrys Williams (second left) chatting with poet Stephen Spender.

Ten:
The Arts Council of Great Britain

England does not have a philosophy of cultural subsidy. Indeed to have one might to some extent violate the philosophical principles which have helped create a very great culture here... The English ethos is empirical, pragmatic, historical and contextual. Things happen, people act; there are consequences, not always logical ones, which lead on to other happenings and actions. A culture is a mixture of minerals and detritus of things that have come down to us from upstream... As with the culture, so with the development of the State's intervention.

Lord Gowrie, Chairman, ACGB, Arts Council Annual Lecture, 1995

He faces you directly, as you cross the threshold of the Arts Council: the self-confident head of a handsome man in later life; the thinning hair over a lightly-furrowed brow; the gaze of those interrogating eyes; the hint of a smile about the mouth; those fleshy ears – listening, learning, interpreting. This fine portrait bust in bronze by his fellow-countryman, Ivor Roberts-Jones, introduces us to Sir William Emrys Williams. A simple plaque identifies him as 'Secretary-General of the Arts Council of Great Britain, 1951-1963'.

This chapter is not a potted history of the Arts Council. There are already several good histories and some critical commentaries.[1] Instead, it sets out to examine Williams' personal influence on Arts Council policies and activities during his twelve years as Secretary-General from 1951 to 1963, by considering how well he discharged his responsibilities for directing and supervising State support for the arts in Britain in the 1950s. It begins by tracing the curious path by which Bill Williams came to occupy the powerful and prestigious office of Secretary-General and asks how well he served the Arts Council.

At the end of the Second World War, the Council for the Encouragement of Music and the Arts (CEMA) transformed itself into the Arts Council of Great Britain, whose Charter required it to raise cultural standards and to spread the arts throughout the land. In the words of John Maynard Keynes, State sponsorship of the arts had been smuggled into Britain through the back door, in a wartime crisis, under cover of blackout. It had all happened in an informal, unostentatious and, above all, 'a very English way'.[2] As the Council's first Chairman, Keynes was to exercise a dominant and not always beneficial influence on its later development.

At the Arts Council meeting on 9 August 1950, it was noted that:

> The Council, being unanimously of the opinion that the office of Secretary-General should not be a permanent one, and having considered a Report from the Chairman on the discussions which the Executive have had, and having heard a statement from Miss Glasgow that she had come to the conclusion that it would be in the interests of the Council for her appointment to be terminated in March, 1951. Resolved, by a majority, that Miss Glasgow's appointment as Secretary-General, which expires on the 31st March 1951, be not renewed.[3]

So much for the official record. But why did Mary Glasgow resign and depart without a fight? Had she fallen from grace, or was the ostensible reason for her going the real reason? Mary Glasgow was certainly not reticent about expressing her feelings. But in those now far-off days, before the advent of investigative journalism, all concerned observed a decent silence.

In his critical history of the Arts Council, Richard Witts makes a number of uncorroborated claims, including the following:

> Williams dominated the Council as a member from its inception in 1939 until he retired as Secretary-General in 1963. He hated his predecessor, Mary Glasgow, and had her pushed out.[4]

Those assertions are made without any supporting evidence. Although Williams' views were certainly influential, he did not dominate Council. Nor is there a shred of evidence that Williams 'hated' Mary Glasgow or contrived to have her 'pushed out'. We know that she was urged to remain in office but was determined to resign. Williams did not emerge as Mary Glasgow's successor until December 1951, five months after her resignation, and after over one hundred other candidates had been considered and rejected for the post.

Writing about the history of Covent Garden, Norman Lebrecht gives further credence to the idea that Mary Glasgow was deliberately disposed of to make room for Bill Williams:

> Mary Glasgow, the Council's Secretary-General, refused to mask her contempt for Keynes's successor [Sir Ernest Pooley] and paid for it... Pooley replaced her in 1950 with W E Williams, one of Tom Jones's antediluvian Taffia. In her memoirs, Glasgow reported that she was once told by a drunken civil servant that Pooley was a 'safe little shit' who would not demand money or make trouble, because 'we've got something on him'.[5]

Despite such wild speculation and distasteful name-calling, cultural historians have failed to provide a satisfactory explanation of exactly why a popular and, by general consent, a highly efficient Secretary-General, left her post at the unusually early age of forty-five. As her successor, Williams was a vigorous fifty-five – so hardly antediluvian. And there is no specific evidence to show that Dr Thomas Jones had a backstage hand in Williams' appointment. In the files of the Public Record Office, however, there is a note that throws refreshing new light on Mary Glasgow's departure:

> ***Statement by Miss Mary Glasgow, Secretary-General***
>
> I understand that it is the view of the Chairman and the majority of the Executive Committee that my appointment as Secretary-General should not be renewed, at least for more than a nominal period. I had myself hoped that my appointment might be renewed, not permanently, but for a reasonable time; but after the talks I have had with the Chairman and Executive members, informally and in Committee, I am no longer anxious to continue in office.
>
> I have come to the conclusion that it would be in the interests of the Council for my appointment to terminate in March 1951.[6]

That document seems to effectively dispose of the myth that Williams was behind Mary Glasgow's resignation or that he engineered her departure in order to take her place. Prominent members of Council worked hard behind the scenes to persuade Mary Glasgow to stay. When Council refused to provide her with a longer-term contract, she resigned of her own accord. But it lamentably failed to find a suitable successor in the eight months between her resignation and her departure. Finally, at Council meeting on 10 January 1951, it was agreed 'to invite Mr W E Williams to take up the position of Secretary-General with effect from 1 April 1951'.[7]

Mary Glasgow was present for the last time as Secretary-General at Council meeting on 28 February 1951. Having noted that Treasury grant for the years following 1951/52 was likely to be maintained at the pre-1951/52 level of £575,000 p.a., the Chairman invited the Secretary-General to comment on the Estimates:

> The Secretary-General said she thought that wherever possible savings should be effected by cutting down the expenditure on directly provided activities rather than on grants to independent bodies... She thought there was a real danger of an eventual State dictatorship of taste, fostered unwittingly by some of the Council's best friends; and that the safeguard lay, in the principle of "State support without State control", whether in London or in the remote places which the Council endeavoured to serve.[8]

Mary Glasgow's departure was marked in dignified fashion by placing on record an appreciation of her outstanding contribution to the Council and its predecessor body, and she disappeared without fuss. At Council meeting on 18 April 1951, Sir Ernest Pooley 'extended good wishes to Mr W E Williams on taking up his appointment as Secretary-General'. It was also agreed that a gratuity of £1,850 should be paid to Miss Glasgow.

A formal account of Williams' appointment as Secretary-General of the Arts Council appears in its Annual Report for 1950/51:

> Miss M C Glasgow CBE relinquished the post of Secretary-General on March 31st 1951. When the Committee for the Encouragement of Music and the Arts was formed in 1940 Miss Glasgow, then an HMI in the Ministry of Education, became its Secretary, and subsequently served more than 11 years as chief executive officer. She devoted herself enthusiastically to its affairs and made a notable contribution to its development. The post was advertised but, failing to find a suitable candidate, the Council, with the approval of the Chancellor of the Exchequer, invited Mr W E Williams CBE to accept the office and, after resigning from the Council, he did so.[9]

That single paragraph, written by Williams, at the end of his first year as Secretary-General, appears entirely innocuous. A more revealing story emerges in a Report dated 10 January 1951 from the Special Committee on the Appointment of Secretary-General:

> Your Committee had before it a list of 127 candidates from which the Chairman selected 45 for consideration by the Committee. [It] then made a list for interview of seven, of whom one withdrew before the interviewing day. The Committee, after discussion with each candidate in turn and after careful consideration of their claims, was unanimously of the opinion that none of them was suitable. The Committee then agreed to invite Mr W E Williams to submit his name for consideration, which he did, giving details of his career and his present appointments. After discussion with Mr Williams the Committee unanimously agreed to recommend his appointment as Secretary-General in terms of a letter of appointment which will be tabled at the Council meeting on January 10th.
>
> It was resolved:
>
> (a) That the Chancellor of the Exchequer be asked to approve the appointment of Mr W E Williams, CBE.
>
> (b) That, subject to such approval being given, Mr Williams be offered the appointment in the terms of the following letter:
>
> Dear Mr Williams,
>
> The Arts Council offer you the appointment of Secretary-General for a period of five years, as from the 1st April 1951, at a salary of £2,500 per annum.
>
> It is understood that before taking up this office you will resign your present appointments, including your office as Director of the Bureau of Current Affairs, your Editorship of Penguin Books, and your various journalistic commitments, and will devote your whole time to the service of the Council.
>
> The Chancellor of the Exchequer approves your appointment.
>
> Yours sincerely, Chairman[10]

That report raises a number of important issues. First, why did the very large initial field of 127 applicants fail to produce a single suitable candidate? Was the salary too low to attract better-qualified candidates? Second, why was Williams offered a starting salary of £2,500 pa – almost one-third more than that paid to Mary Glasgow in her final year? Third, would Mary Glasgow have stayed on as Secretary-General if her salary had been raised to that level, even if she was denied a long-term appointment? Fourth, was Williams seriously expected to relinquish all his 'present appointments', some of which he had held for almost twenty years? Or was that requirement a mere formality?

By 1951, the Bureau of Current Affairs had virtually collapsed. As Robert Hewison, a leading cultural historian of the period, perceptively notes: 'Bill Williams faced the prospect of a new decade without a significant position, other than as an adviser to Penguin Books'.[11] But Williams was much more than 'an adviser to Penguin Books'. He was Chief Editorial Adviser and surely never intended to surrender that position. The suspicion remains that there was 'something irregular' about Williams' appointment. That played directly into the hands of those who later sought to denigrate his achievements as Secretary-General.

Amongst the voluminous Treasury files at the Public Record Office are two documents that throw further revealing light on Mary Glasgow's resignation and Bill Williams' appointment. The first, dated 12 January 1951, is a tantalisingly terse letter from Sir Ernest Pooley, Chairman of the Arts Council, addressed to the Chancellor of the Exchequer, Hugh Gaitskell. Its final paragraph hints at some potential conflicts of interest in Bill Williams' affairs that remained unresolved at the time of his appointment:

> I write on behalf of the Arts Council to ask for your approval to the appointment of Mr W E Williams CBE as Secretary-General for a period of five years from 1 April 1951, at a salary of £2,500 per annum.
>
> Mr Williams has placed in my hands his resignation of membership of the Arts Council which I have accepted.
>
> The Council intend to require Mr Williams before taking up his office to resign his present appointments, including the Directorship of the BCA, the chief editorship of Penguin Books, and his various journalistic commitments, and to devote his whole time to the service of the Council.[12]

In other words, before seeking the Chancellor's formal agreement to the appointment, the Chairman had told Williams that his appointment was conditional upon his giving up his specified outside interests once the Chancellor had ratified his appointment.

The second document, dated 13 January 1951, is an internal Memorandum, written by Eddie Playfair, Under-Secretary at the Treasury, to his Permanent Secretary, Sir Edward Bridges, offering advice on how the Chancellor should respond to Sir Ernest Pooley's letter:

> Please see Sir Ernest Pooley's letter below. As you know, the nomination of Mr Williams as Secretary-General has given us a good deal of anxious thought. It may be rather a contentious one and its manner is unusual, but I have no doubt at all that it is the right appointment.
>
> The Council advertised the appointment in the ordinary way. Mr Williams, who was a member of the Council, was known to want to be Secretary-General, but was not willing to put in his nomination competitively, given his position on the Council. The Council appointed a sub-committee of seven members to examine the applications. They went through them, picked out a short list and interviewed this short list. They were satisfied, at the end of it, that none of them were up to standard. They then invited Mr Williams to put forward his candidature, which he did... The Committee decided that he was the only man for the job, and recommended accordingly to the Council. At that point Sir Ernest Pooley told me of the proceedings, and I asked him whether, when they came to the point of rejecting all the people who had applied for the job, they had considered asking not only Mr Williams, but any other people in the circumstances. They had not formally done so, but they had discussed the matter among themselves, and had found nobody who would be both suitable and available, except Mr Williams...
>
> The whole proceedings were unusual, but I feel no doubt that it is the right choice. It is a guarantee of honesty that the Committee held very divided views at the start on Mr Williams' merits, and one or two members were pretty strongly opposed to his appointment. But all their decisions were unanimous (as was the Council's approval of them) and at the Council meeting which I attended one member said that he entered the proceedings with a strong feeling that Mr Williams was the wrong man, and ended with an equally certain feeling that he was much the best, and indeed the only available candidate. I therefore have no hesitation in recommending the Chancellor to approve the appointment.[13]

That Memorandum exemplifies a senior British civil servant's pragmatic approach to such matters. It makes no mention of the potentially embarrassing circumstances of Mary Glasgow's departure. Without making specific allegations, it hints darkly at an unsavoury deal behind the scenes. It draws attention to the irregular methods followed but finds no fault with the final outcome. In short, Williams' appointment might be contentious but it was the right decision. The Permanent Secretary is assured that he may safely advise the Chancellor to ratify the appointment. If questions were asked in high places, the evidence on file would show that impartial justice had been done. Nothing had been rushed. Everything had been done to find the best candidate. The Selection Committee's work was thorough. Other departments had been consulted. The Committee had found 'much the best' man. Finally, with sublime realism, Playfair recognises that the deed has been done. It was too late to go back on it, even if the Treasury had any serious doubts about the appointment.

Sir Edward Bridges responded two days later with a brief note in his own hand:

> The appointment of Mr W E Williams may cause some eyebrows to be raised. But I think it is a good appointment. Anyhow there are no grounds on which we can object. No other comments.[14]

In the Arts Council's 6th Annual Report for 1950/51, the mind and voice of Williams come through with exceptional clarity. Having given a factual retrospective report on that year's work, he develops his argument on the Council's future policy:

> The Arts Council's predecessor and, indeed, begetter, was CEMA, that celebrated wartime improvisation which gaily embodied so many worthy if not wholly reconcilable motives [but] CEMA had small opportunity, in those precarious times, to insist that high standards should be maintained in such impromptu presentation of the arts as war conditions imposed.
>
> The Charter of the Arts Council, however, enunciates a double purpose: (a) that the Council should seek to elevate standards of performance in the arts; and (b) that is should endeavour to spread the appreciation of the arts. The Council has sought to observe both those injunctions. But the size of its budget in a period of rising costs may require it to re-examine how far both these objects may be simultaneously secured...
>
> Might it not be better to accept the realistic fact that the living theatre of good quality cannot be widely accessible and to concentrate our resources upon establishing a few more shrines like Stratford and Bristol Old Vic? Is it good policy to encourage small, ill-equipped expeditions to set out into the wilderness and present meagre productions in village fit-ups? These are the questions to which the Council must address itself earnestly and dispassionately in the immediate future. In reconsidering the exhortations of its Charter to 'Raise and Spread' the Council may decide for the time being, to emphasise the first more than the second word, and to devote itself to the support of two or three exemplary theatres which might re-affirm the supremacy of standards in our national theatre...
>
> High standards can be built only on a limited scale. The motto which Meleager [a hero of Greek antiquity] wrote to be carved over the door of a patrician nursery might be one for the Arts Council to follow in deciding what to support during the next few straightened years – 'Few, but roses – including, of course, regional roses'.[15]

The debate initiated by Williams in his first Annual Report has continued to the present day – namely, whether State support for the arts should be concentrated on a few metropolitan and provincial centres of excellence, or spread more thinly over a much wider range of less prestigious but no less deserving projects. Should the Arts Council – 'for the time being' – that is, until funding was significantly increased – nurture a few superlative roses, like Covent Garden, the National Theatre, and other great cultural institutions? Or should it spread itself thinly by encouraging and assisting a thousand blooms to flourish in some of the remoter cultural wildernesses of Britain?

As mentioned previously, Ivor Brown, a respected critic of the arts, and a former member of CEMA Council, was amongst the first to identify its vulnerability to attack from both sides of the cultural divide.[16] Williams had worked long and hard in the 1930s to bring high quality painting and sculpture to the galleryless towns and villages of Britain through his *Art for the People* scheme. His wartime experience of taking circulating art exhibitions around the country had demonstrated the appetite of ordinary men and women for the arts, including the performing arts of live music, theatre and ballet. His fundamental instincts were democratic rather than elitist. Whilst 'the great rank and file of the army of democracy' might show little interest in high culture, he was convinced that should not deter the Arts Council from ensuring much easier access to the arts for all those people whose appetite would grow by what it fed on. In principle therefore Williams favoured spreading money on arts spending rather than concentrating it on a few centres of excellence. But if he could not do both whilst maintaining or better still by raising standards, he would be forced to concentrate rather than spread.

Williams developed and illustrated his policy argument on 'Raise or Spread?' with particular reference to the performing arts, more specifically the theatre. In that context, it is instructive to consider an analysis by Ruth Shade, a recent academic commentator, which holds Williams' personally responsible for promoting elitism rather than popular culture. Reviewing the history of theatre funding in Wales, Ruth Shade argues that:

> The Arts Council functions as a panoptic, or disciplinary, body and it is this panopticism which provides the conditions for hegemony, or cultural domination… The Arts Council was established, like the panopticon, for ostensibly utopian purposes. It was founded after the war but its framework was essentially that of CEMA…[which] was a radical move towards organisation and regularisation, arguably the most major historical shift towards a national, cultural policy the UK has seen…
>
> From the outset it was recognised that there would always be too many calls on the limited supply of money and, consequently, there was always the need to disqualify and invalidate. The important questions in relation to panopticism and the arts relate to the means by which disqualification and invalidation have been exercised…
>
> Theatre forms were being hierarchised and differentiated. By 1945, a panoptic structure for the surveillance of the performing arts had already been established… "Dr Jones…saw (CEMA's) work as an extension of the 'social service' of pre-war Pilgrim Trust activities (Robert Hewison)". However, Jones's interest in cultural democracy was replaced by (John Maynard) Keynes's insistence on the pursuit of excellence…[but] there has to be some mechanism which enables the thinking of Dr Thomas Jones to be superseded by the Keynesian ethos, and this might be found in the shape of…William Emrys Williams – 'one of the most powerful cultural mandarins in the country'… However inconvenient

> it may be to recognise this, it is the case that the policies of quality, professionalisation and centralisation, which have been so damaging to a distinctively Welsh arts practice, were manipulated by a Welshman [William Emrys Williams] when he muses in 1952: "might it not be better to accept the realistic fact that the living theatre of good quality cannot be widely accessible and to concentrate our resources upon establishing a few more shrines like Stratford...".
>
> After Keynes's death, it was Williams who enacted the Keynesian philosophy of the arts. What this demonstrates is that professionalisation and a particular notion of 'high' standards were not inevitable, but rather the consequence of one set of imperatives being followed and not another.[17]

Since Williams cannot defend himself from that assault, it seems only fair to quote from 'The First Ten Years', the 11th Annual Report of the Arts Council for 1955/56, in which Williams reviews the lessons derived from the experience of CEMA:

> First, that the size and the ardour of the audiences which its activities attracted far exceeded all expectations – many little places were offered plays and concerts of a calibre far above their normal expectations – [so] that CEMA immensely enlarged the popular audience for plays, music and paintings and, in doing so, also enabled hundreds of artists of all kinds to keep in active employment and practice for several critical years.
>
> Second, CEMA had established...the necessity to distinguish between the professional and the amateur practice of the arts. Both are supremely important, but for different reasons... and early in its experience CEMA discovered the manifold difficulties encountered by an administrative body which seeks to act simultaneously as the trustees for both movements. Hence its decision to withdraw virtually from the amateur field...[an] action [which] in itself is a further affirmation of the belief that the primary obligation of such a body as CEMA or the Arts Council is to preserve the arts on their most vital and vulnerable level, which is the level of standard.
>
> Third, the relative paucity in the country of buildings worthy of and suitable for the reputable performance of music and drama... Ten years after the war we are little better off... If music and drama are to be revealed at their best we must provide them in suitable settings, with buildings (old and new) in which the mystique of the arts can be properly communicated.[18]

Williams' words leave no doubt that, when forced to choose, the Arts Council felt compelled, under the terms of its Charter, to support professionals rather than amateurs; to sustain the highest rather than modest standards of performance; and to emphasise the need for suitable buildings for the performing arts:

> The primary responsibility imposed by its Royal Charter is to preserve and improve standards of performance in the various arts. The Arts Council interprets this injunction, in relation to its income, as implying the support of a limited number of institutions where exemplary standards may be developed...
>
> The Arts Council believes, then, that the first claim upon its attention and assistance is

> that of maintaining in London and the larger cities effective power-houses of opera, music and drama; for unless these quality-institutions can be maintained the arts are bound to decline into mediocrity...
>
> The most fundamental change of policy which has occurred since CEMA developed into the Arts Council concerns the actual provision of the arts. CEMA was heavily engaged, most of its time, in the direct provision of the arts, in promoting theatre tours and concert tours. In England this direct provision has diminished year by year since 1946, and will ultimately cease altogether. It is better that music and drama should be promoted by separate individual organisations than that they should be centrally and officially provided.[19]

Throughout his twelve years as Secretary-General, Williams succeeded in persuading Council to pursue clear, intelligible and coherent goals – namely, the pursuit of excellence, and making the arts increasingly accessible to more people, outside the limited number of urban centres of excellence. Since the Council lacked the necessary resources to diffuse the arts on a massive scale, and since better local methods of diffusion already existed, it seemed wiser to concentrate its limited resources primarily, but not exclusively, on the maintenance and enhancement of standards:

> Faced with the problems of choice and a limited budget, the Arts Council must seek to consolidate rather than enlarge its own particular responsibilities to the arts in Britain.[20]

At the start of the 21st century, fifty years after the event, it is easy to highlight the early errors and modest achievements of both CEMA and the Arts Council. But those immediately involved were grappling with unprecedented problems, under the most adverse wartime and immediate post-war conditions, without the benefit of historical experience to guide them. If they had decided to spread limited resources more thinly across the whole country, they would almost certainly have faced the serious charge of diluting standards. What seems to be true is that they could not achieve both objectives simultaneously.

Anthony Everitt, who was Deputy Secretary-General and then Secretary-General between 1985 and 1994, believes that the modest achievements of both CEMA and the Arts Council reflect the dominant influence of Keynes, and his obsession with high culture and professional standards of performance:

> The key figure was Maynard Keynes, who chaired both bodies [i.e. CEMA and the Arts Council] and steered CEMA away from its broad approach to the arts and support for amateur participation, on the grounds that it was too concerned with the welfare side of things. His interest was essentially in professional excellence, as his draft objectives for the Council's royal charter show... Keynes's opinion was decisive. For many years the Arts Council concentrated on the high or the old arts. The fact that it did so with considerable success should not blind us to the limited nature of its achievement.[21]

In carrying out his onerous responsibilities, Williams obviously encountered resistance, if not direct opposition, to some of his ideas. It is therefore important to consider his working and personal relationship with the three Chairmen of the Arts Council whom he served.

When Lord Keynes died suddenly on Easter Sunday 1946, he was succeeded by Sir Ernest Pooley, an obscure and colourless personality, a former President of the Honourable Company of Haberdashers, with no significant interest or previous record in the arts. According to Robert Hewison, 'Pooley's one significant action at the Council was to set himself to get rid of his Secretary-General, Mary Glasgow, who had been faithfully preserving the policies set by Keynes'.[22] Hewison does not amplify that statement; nor does he explain why Pooley took five years to achieve that objective. If Hewison is correct, why was there no break with those policies when Pooley finally succeeded in replacing Mary Glasgow? The policy of 'Few, but roses' was developed and defended by Williams, who not only preserved but significantly extended Keynes's so-called 'elitist' philosophy, thereby opening himself up to the charge that he was essentially conservative, wishing to concentrate resources and control standards.

Williams had himself identified the 'streak of donnish superiority' in Keynes's make-up and 'his singular ignorance of ordinary people' – whose cultural emancipation and access to the arts Williams had worked so hard to promote. Kenneth Clark remarks of Keynes that: 'He was not the man for wandering minstrels and amateur theatricals. He believed in excellence'.[23] Robert Hewison picks up that theme by noting that Williams made a useful ally of Sir Kenneth Clark, but he made an enemy of Keynes. He also tells us that Keynes had once expressed an earlier wish to bring about 'a gradual winding-up of our relations' with Williams:

> In 1943 Keynes halved CEMA's grant of thousands of pounds for [Bill Williams' circulating art] exhibitions, although with Clark's help Williams got two and half thousand of this reinstated. Keynes kept further grants down, and CEMA began to mount its own touring shows [but] Williams, never one to remove a finger from a pie, stayed on the Council.[24]

Hewison further notes with approval that, 'while defending the unprofitability of the sort of work [the Arts Council] supported, and the need for public subsidy, Williams argued that it could only be carried out in the larger concentrations of populations'. But he is explicitly critical of Williams for failing to pursue a more aggressive, pro-active policy:

> Until the sixties, the Arts Council held to a purely "reactive" policy, responding as it saw fit to requests for funds, but taking no major initiatives of its own.[25]

What more could Williams have done – or done differently – to promote the arts in Britain in the early 1950s? Hewison fails to suggest what realistic pro-active policies he might have pursued, given the paltry levels of government subsidy. Above all, Hewison fails to acknowledge that Britain had just emerged from the most devastating and costly war in its history, with many competing priorities for government expenditure, and severe limits on what government was willing to spend on the arts. Throughout Williams' time as Secretary-General, he was confronted by a succession of cheese-paring Chancellors of the Exchequer in the Conservative Governments of Winston Churchill (1951-55), Anthony Eden (1955-57) and Harold Macmillan (1957-63). When Chancellor Selwyn Lloyd finally relented and began to loosen Treasury purse-strings after 1960, Williams immediately liberalised Arts Council policies and initiated many more creative projects. Throughout his time in office, he cut his cultural coat according to the subsidised cloth that government provided. He could do little more, given the composition of the Council which he inherited, and the kind of Chairmen with whom he was required to work.

During Williams' first two years as Secretary-General, Pooley caused him few, if any, problems. But Pooley was by all accounts not the kind of Chairman to support fresh initiatives. In 1953, when Pooley retired, he was succeeded by Kenneth Clark, who had felt betrayed when not appointed, eight years earlier, as Lord Keynes's successor:

> Most people imagined that I would succeed [Keynes] as chairman of the Arts Council. I confess that I expected to do so, and rather looked forward to the prospect. I still thought of myself as a 'public servant' and enjoyed having to make decisions. I was not so foolish as to imagine that such positions give one what is known as power. Even a cabinet minister has very little power... But the Treasury have a principle that a volatile chairman, and in Keynes's case a brilliant one, should be succeeded by what the eighteenth century used to call 'a man of bottom'; and they discovered an admirable example in Sir Ernest Pooley... Having no interest in the arts he could be relied on not to press their claims too strongly. After a moment's disappointment I felt relieved at not having on my hands the tricky juggling with human relationships, which I thought would be inevitable.[26]

Clark was shrewdly perceptive in anticipating human relations problems at the Arts Council. But it was Williams himself who presented Clark with one of his trickiest juggling acts. The two men knew each other very well. They were both founder members of CEMA from its inception in 1939. They were close friends and frequent collaborators. They had worked together on *Art for the People* in the 1930s and again during the Second World War, when Williams directed the circulating exhibitions of paintings, for which Clark loaned paintings from the National Gallery. In his autobiography, Clark wrote of Williams in glowing terms:

> I had opened one of these exhibitions ['Art for the People'] in the first weeks of the war, and been much impressed by Williams' enthusiasm and intelligence. Under his guidance the new CEMA virtually continued the 'Art for the People' scheme on a wider field. Such were our first faltering steps towards state support for the arts.[27]

In her biography of Clark, Meryle Secrest identifies the principal source of the friction between Clark and Williams:

> Kenneth Clark discovered that he had taken on the role of figurehead [as Chairman of the Arts Council]. Previous occupants of the position hardly ever appeared and the real work was being done by the Secretary-General, a flamboyant Welshman, Sir William Emrys Williams, who wrote the reports, directed policy, and appointed staff. Although Kenneth Clark does not say so, the implication is that Williams took steps to ensure that his chairman would not meddle in Arts Council affairs. He decreed, for instance, that Kenneth Clark did not need a secretary. He would be brought whatever correspondence it was thought safe to show him. A younger Kenneth Clark would have taken about two months' worth of such frustration and then left. Surprisingly, he lasted seven years.[28]

In the *Dictionary of National Biography*, David Piper notes of Clark's time as Chairman of the Arts Council that:

> [He] underwent a frustrating experience. He felt little more than a figurehead, and his own commitment to the validity of state support of individual creative artists was ambivalent.[29]

It was for that reason, amongst others, that Williams was determined to keep Clark from interference in policy-making. From his personal observation of the Arts Council at work, Richard Hoggart adds this perceptive note:

> W E Williams was the last dominant Secretary-General. He saw himself as a public servant but not a civil servant; with his Royal Charter, he could distance himself from parliamentary control. He looked to his chairman for support outside, especially in the corridors of power. He knew his chairman would see himself as a guide and friend, and would not hesitate to take him for a talk over a drink if things seemed to be going wrong; or at the limit, might advise him not to seek an extension of his contract. It was Williams who said, to a chairman he thought too interventionist and too often around: 'You are the admiral, I am the captain. Now please get off my bridge.' Those days had gone.[30]

In his waspish history of the Arts Council, Richard Witts offers yet another commentary on the Williams-Clark partnership:

> If anyone had truly thought about it for a second, they would not have put Williams and Clark together at the head of the Council... Clark has been the only Council Chairman who we could say was himself involved in the arts, if only at the level of interpretation and patronage. It might therefore be thought a pity that Bill Williams blocked K's ability to make an impact on policy. Yet Clark was a little like Keynes in his artistic taste, endorsing the classical canon, relishing the distractions of the unruly and eccentric, but disengaged from creative experiment.[31]

There was one subject, however, on which Williams had no compunction in calling for Clark's direct intervention and support: that of his own salary. Williams was appointed Secretary-General in April 1951 at a salary of £2,500 plus £250 expenses. At that time, the Directorate operated with less than twenty headquarters staff and an annual budget of less than £20,000. In addition, there were twelve Regional Directors, with their clerical and secretarial staff, bringing the grand total to £770,000. Early in 1955, Williams told Clark that he was unhappy with his salary, in relation to relevant comparators and the volume and complexity of his work. Clark immediately consulted Council members, seeking their support for his decision to seek an increase in Williams' salary. Oliver Lyttleton (later Lord Chandos), an influential member of Council, pledged his unequivocal support:

> Of course your proposals will have gone through about Williams, and I need hardly say I would have given them every possible support if I had been [at the meeting]. I look upon him as a pillar of perfection in his job of Secretary-General, and it will be a sad day for the Arts Council if he ever leaves it. Surely it is a golden rule that on the rare occasions when you get the right man in the right place, 'fetter him to your soul with hoops of steel'.[32]

That statement, by a respected and independent-minded member of Council, demonstrates the high regard in which Williams was generally held. On 5 February 1955, Clark wrote to the Treasury, proposing that the Secretary-General's salary, which had not moved since 1950, should be increased from £2,500 to £3,500 p.a. In due course, Sir Alexander Johnston, the 'Treasury Assessor to the Arts Council', referred the matter to the Permanent Under-Secretary, Sir Thomas Padmore, saying that Williams was 'a little sore with us over the way we are handling his own salary and there may be trouble about his staff if we are not careful'.[33] A Treasury Minute notes that:

> There is the added complication that Mr Williams appears to have outside activities... When the post was advertised at the time of his appointment [in 1951], no reference was made to the fact that it was full-time, and Mr Williams himself, in accepting the appointment, said that, while he would give up most of his other activities, he intended to retain one or two of them, notably that of Chief Editor of Penguin Books which at that time (5 years ago) brought him a salary of £500 a year. There is a pencil note...to the effect that Mr Williams would give up the Penguin Books, but this does not seem to have materialised, as he described himself in Who's Who as 'Chief Editor of Penguin Books'. I have been told that this takes at least one day a week.[34]

When Padmore replied to Clark, seeking his comments on Williams' 'outside activities', he received this spirited response:

> I am greatly surprised at your statement that you did not know whether 'in form or in practice' the Secretary-General of the Arts Council has a full-time occupation. I did not

> know that this had ever been in doubt. Certainly the present Secretary-General gives a good deal more than a full working day to his duties on behalf of the Arts Council. It is, of course, true that, like the rest of us, he does a number of unpaid public services, such as the trusteeship of the National Gallery and membership of the present Treasury Committee on the Queen's Hall [considering whether to replace the old Queen's Hall destroyed in the London Blitz of 1940] but these are indirectly connected with the work of the Arts Council... Williams is no longer Chief Editor of Penguin Books: the entry in 'Who's Who' is wrong, for he resigned this post in 1951. At the same time he gave up his journalistic work.
>
> I am afraid I can only say that I suspect he is getting rather more than he would if his salary were regulated by the standards prevailing in the Government Service or in bodies coming directly under the Treasury's wing...
>
> Taking one thing with another, I think we could agree to increasing the Secretary-General's salary to £2,850, but more than that we should find embarrassing. I very much hope that, on reflection, the Council will find this acceptable.[35]

By another simple twist of fate, on 18 March 1955 the *Times Literary Supplement* published a photograph of Rodrigo Moynihan's painting of 'The Penguin Editors after Conference', with a caption showing Williams as Editor-in-Chief. A senior civil servant sent the press cutting to Sir Alexander Johnston with the acid comment: 'Also four years out of date, I suppose?' Nevertheless, on 13 March 1956 Williams' contract was renewed when he was re-appointed Secretary-General for a further term of five years to March 1961, by which date he would have attained the age of sixty-five.

On 14 June 1957, Clark wrote to Sir Alexander Johnston, raising for the first time the question of payment to members of Council – and, by implication, to the Chairman. By that time, Clark had also been Chairman of the ITA for three years but had let it be known that he wished to step down as Arts Council Chairman. Unfortunately no suitable successor could be found. Lord Robbins had been considered eminently qualified, though perhaps too much like Clark – a 'pictures man' rather than a general arts man. So Lord Cottesloe was smuggled onto the Council in preparation for Clark's departure.

Williams returned to the Treasury, on 23 July 1957, for a lengthy discussion with a senior official, who minuted the meeting:

> W E Williams said that he did not think that the Arts Council involved Sir Kenneth Clark in more than half-an-hour a week, apart from the periodical meetings of the Council and its Executive Committee. He took no part in the ordinary office work and merely came in to be briefed on general points for meetings. I pointed out that Sir Kenneth Clark had said that the Arts Council involved, or could involve, the Chairman in as much work as had to be done by the Chairman of the ITA and that it was difficult to question this statement, at least directly.

W E Williams then made the unexpected statement that he did not think that Sir KC was prepared to go on as chairman after April next. He admitted that Sir KC had given as one of his reasons for abandoning the chairmanship of ITA that he would give more time to the Arts Council, and that he (Sir WW) had been proceeding on the assumption that Sir KC would continue with the Arts Council. Sir Kenneth Clark's talk was now all about retirement and about the things he wanted to do which he was prevented from doing through his public duties. Sir Kenneth Clark had gone on to say that the obvious course was to make Sir William Williams Chairman of the Arts Council, under an arrangement by which he would in effect double the duties of Chairman and Secretary-General. The eyes of the blind were opened and I understood why Sir William Williams [sic] was prepared to open up on the subject.

Sir William Williams has, of course, had an odd career on the Arts Council. He was a member of the Council and then was appointed Secretary-General in succession to Miss Glasgow. I have always had the impression that the process by which Sir William Williams supplanted Miss Glasgow as Secretary-General would not bear too close scrutiny. There was a vast amount of intrigue. It would be necessary to take a number of soundings before we entertained any suggestion that Sir William Williams should become chairman of the Arts Council. He has his detractors, but that is true of everyone in the cultural field. Our real difficulty is that, if Sir Kenneth Clark goes, we have no obvious successor and we certainly want to have plenty of time to think out how we are to fill the vacancy.[36]

Such persistent references to Williams having 'supplanted Miss Glasgow', and the 'vast amount of intrigue', strengthened the Treasury impression of Williams as a devious and manipulative character. The implication is clear: Williams had raised the issue of Clark's salary and his imminent departure to bolster his own chances of succeeding him as Chairman, whilst continuing to serve as Secretary-General. High-minded senior civil servants at the Treasury seem to have been embarrassed by Williams' canvassing and evidently took decisive steps to thwart any such ambitions. When Clark departed in 1960, he was succeeded by the Chairman of the Tate Gallery, Lord Cottesloe, with whom Williams worked constructively until he retired as Secretary-General in 1963. According to Richard Witts:

His time with Cottesloe was spent wiping the babies' bottoms of the National Theatre and the Royal Shakespeare Company. Cottesloe backed the National, while the Council staff rather liked the look of [Peter] Hall's Royal Shakespeare Company. The survival of both of them is a testament either to Williams' skill in keeping them alive if underfed, or to a lack of skill in failing to pick one or the other.[37]

In 'A Brighter Prospect', his Annual Report for 1961/62, Williams continued to defend the Council's policy of concentrated spending in pursuit of excellence:

The essence of Arts Council policy nowadays is to sustain the best possible standard of performance at a limited number of permanent institutions... This group of priority institutions are the trustees of high artistic standard, the main line of defence against the debasement of values in public entertainment, and the Arts Council recognises a paramount responsibility to them. Even if its income were larger it would still prefer to consolidate these priorities than to dissipate its resources upon an extensive provision of the second-rate. If the power-houses were to fail there would be a black-out of the living arts in Britain.[38]

In his reflections on British philistinism, Arnold Wesker (now Sir Arnold), playwright and polemicist, captures the disillusion of those who had once looked to the State to ensure that the arts would be made accessible to the masses:

I try to console myself with the fact that all art is an aristocratic pursuit. I agree with John Whiting and Ben Levy that only a percentage of society has aristocratic tastes; the rest will always be philistines. Then I am nagged by another doubt – do we really know how large that percentage could be? Have we the right to organize society on the assumption that there are only a few aristocrats?

The answer might have been in the work of the Arts Council had this Council been able to rely on its income from any but a philistine government. Even then I am not convinced that they would have known how to clothe themselves in any but the most foreboding and rarefied garments. As it is this Council receives only one and half million pounds to spend on the arts which remain – in the words of their 1959-60 report – a 'novelty' of this country... The Arts Council, through no fault of its own, is powerless. By 1961 it had thrown control to the wind and used a language which clearly indicated its plight. Consider the first sentence of their 1960-61 report: 'An encouraging feature of the effort to sustain the arts in Britain...'. What a humiliating picture that conjures up – the effort to sustain the arts! What happened to the protesting voices? Had the seductive germ reached them or had they humbly learned and accepted the lesson that they were powerless to take over the authority of the status quo?[39]

In 1962, Williams submitted evidence to the House of Commons Arts and Amenities Committee, presenting a powerful case for more generous government funding of the arts. The Chancellor of the Exchequer, Selwyn Lloyd, agreed to increase the government's grant by almost half a million pounds, bringing the total grant to £2.25 million.

Williams publicly acknowledged the Council's gratitude for the Chancellor's beneficence in his final Annual Report for 1961/62.[40] Richard Hoggart notes the immediate change of atmosphere in the Council's disbursement of funds after that date:

From the beginning of the Sixties, the Arts Council had been given more or less continuous increases in grant, some of them very high. W E Williams' motto 'Few, but roses' as a guide to the choice of clients could be forgotten, and was against the 'let's not make distinctions between' mood of the time. Judgments on quality could be fudged: 'You never know how they may turn out. Let's give them a chance'.[41]

So much for the crucial policy issues. But what kind of Secretary-General was Williams? How well did he discharge his day-to-day responsibilities? How did his immediate staff regard him? How did the local worthies with whom he had to deal in his travels around the country, promoting local arts provision through Regional Arts Councils, see him? Tony Field, who worked closely with Williams as his Finance Director, gives some examples of his Secretary-General's management style:

> Bill interviewed me for my job at St James's Square and I am sure the only thing which impressed him was that my formative years and schooling were in Manchester! He certainly left all financial matters in my hands and I was horrified to find, as a young and newly-qualified accountant, the money decisions were all delegated to me...
>
> Bill chaired the weekly Directorate meetings every Tuesday morning with tremendous zeal, good humour and sound common sense...
>
> There is one vivid memory I have of my first month with Bill when he asked me to sign a cheque for £250 for a bursary for a young dramatist and I expressed horror that there were no conditions attached to the offer. Bill said: "Well, what conditions would you set? To have a certain number of pages submitted each Friday? And if they are not forthcoming what action would you take? Request a refund? Don't ever think of imposing conditions which you cannot enforce!" I signed the cheque and Shelagh Delaney took it away and wrote *A Taste of Honey*.[42]

According to Tony Field, Williams was 'the best Secretary-General ever':

> He had a fantastic brain, and he'd use it to help you see the flaws in your own reasoning, Some found this intimidating, but it was always constructively offered.[43]

Sir Hugh Willatt, a distinguished Regional Arts Director, based in Nottingham, and a later Secretary-General, left this vivid impression of Williams at work in the provinces:

> He was not, and this was one of the reasons for his effectiveness, what people outside London expected an Arts Council representative to be. The North-county accent, the lack of any precious touch in speech or in manner, the handsome, solidly-built Welshman who had lived and worked in Manchester, took many people by surprise. Aldermen and Councillors, Town Clerks and Borough Treasurers among whom he moved very easily, felt that here was someone who talked practical sense and with whom they could do business. He always had a funny story to tell, and he never made the mistake of pushing the case for the arts too soulfully or intensely. Whether in his speeches or in private conversation, the method was under-statement, a few telling and easily understandable facts (whether wholly accurate or not didn't much matter) and a friendly down-to-earth manner... He didn't hesitate at times to say abrasive things, and his gift for the right phrase made many a local philistine sit up. "We like our art glossy" was a remark – I am sure apocryphal – he attributed to Queen Victoria. There was also a touch of recklessness in his comments on people and institutions, refreshing in a public official, though as often as not calculated... In other words, as a salesman for the Arts Council, and for what was going on in the region he visited, he was very good indeed.[44]

Gabriel White, who served the Council for many years as Art Director, writes of the strong support that he, and other Directors, invariably received from Williams in their often controversial work:

> W E was a model as Secretary-General to the various Directors of Departments. I could see enough of his workings of the Council as a whole to appreciate this, but I found this especially the case as far as the Visual Arts were concerned. Here I think I can speak for my predecessor, Philip James, as well as for myself. If he had someone as Director in whom he could have confidence, he gave it unstintingly and let him get on with his job with the help of his panel... If his advice, help and support was needed in the various difficulties that cropped up, he was always ready to give them unstintedly [sic]. If Chairmen might at times be difficult, he would be sympathetic and his tact and ability was generally able to ease the situation.[45]

Sir Roy Shaw, a former Secretary-General drawn from the ranks of adult education, notes one significant deficiency in Williams' discharge of his duties:

> More surprising is the fact that even W E Williams, who in the 1950s became a most distinguished Secretary-General of the Council, seemed to leave his educational zeal behind him when he took the post. I found no record of his trying to encourage the Council to take up the educational responsibilities implied in its charter. Indeed, towards the end of his period in office he reacted strongly against the playwright Arnold Wesker's brave but unsuccessful attempt to bring serious arts to trade unionists in his 'Centre 42' organisation. Writing in the *Daily Telegraph*, Williams, a former champion of 'art for the people', claimed that Wesker's attempts were unnecessary. Of course art was the privilege of the minority, he argued, but the minority which wants and enjoys the arts is a classless one. Whether a man is a stoker or a stockbroker, he has today equal opportunities of enjoying or practising music, painting, or drawing.

Sir Roy found it difficult to comprehend Williams' outright opposition to the Wesker plan:

> How could Williams be so unaware that the minority of art lovers is predominantly middle class? How could he have forgotten his adult education experience and his clash with Keynes? Did he really not know that the stoker had less of the necessary education and far fewer cultural opportunities than the stockbroker? Perhaps Williams, who spent longer in the seductive atmosphere of the metropolitan arts world, found it more difficult than I did to remember the social and cultural situation in which most people live...[and which] most Council members had never known.[46]

The idea that Williams had been seduced by 'the metropolitan arts world' is, however, totally unconvincing. Williams was certainly aware that art-lovers constituted a minority of the general public and were essentially middle-class. For that precise reason he devoted his life to democratising culture by bringing the arts to ordinary people. There is, however, another more obvious and legitimate objection to Wesker's ground-breaking proposal of 'theatre for the masses' – namely, the risk of deliberate fragmentation and hence dilution of arts provision. The Arts Council was certainly under-funded during most of Williams' term in office. Any attempt to set up an alternative arts centre, along the lines suggested by Wesker and others, would have weakened and undermined what the Arts Council was seeking to achieve with its policy of 'Few but Roses'.

Wyn Griffith, Vice-Chairman of the Arts Council 1952-61, gave this account of Williams' management style:

> At the Council meetings, he was silent unless asked for his opinion, content to keep his finger on our pulse, aware of the significance of what was left unsaid, always able to bring order out of the clash of minds. The three Chairmen under whom he served would, I am sure, agree that his unflinching devotion, his stubborn persistence in pursuit of the best, his sanity and his integrity, are largely responsible for the success the Arts Council has achieved during his stewardship.[47]

Williams' twelve years at the Arts Council were marked by some momentous events in his private as well as his public life. In 1953, he was appointed a Trustee of the Shakespeare Birthday Trust. In 1955, he was awarded a knighthood. In 1957, he celebrated his sixtieth birthday. In 1958, his long-time mistress Estrid Bannister married Ernest Good. In that same year, Williams was made a Director of Penguin Books. In 1960, he gave evidence in the Lady Chatterley Trial on behalf of Penguin Books. By then he had almost certainly begun an intimate relationship with Joy Lyon and had dedicated his 1960 anthology of Hardy's poetry to her. In 1962, he entered hospital for a major operation. In 1963, before leaving the Arts Council, he agreed to take up two new part-time appointments: first, as Secretary of the National Art-Collections Fund, and second, as Art Adviser to the Institute of Directors. Shortly before leaving, he was awarded the honorary degree of Doctor of Laws in the University of Wales. In the same year, his wife, Lady Gertrude Williams, was elected Emeritus Professor at Bedford College, and awarded a CBE.

On Williams' retirement in 1963, Wyn Griffith paid his close friend and fellow countryman this fulsome tribute:

> It had fallen to the lot of few in our country to show so long and thorough a devotion to the underlying purpose of the Arts Council. Long before the Council came into being, Sir William Emrys Williams gave himself to the promotion of general interest in spreading the riches of the world of Art, in making it possible for ordinary people to share in the privileges of the few. A founder-member of the Council and one of its progenitors, he undertook the office of Secretary-General in 1951, to the great satisfaction of its members. They knew that he brought with him a continuity of purpose, strong convictions, an understanding of people, the gift of speech – and, rare in a Welshman, the gift of silence.[48]

From its earliest days, the Arts Council and its predecessor, CEMA, had come under severe attack from those who wanted to keep the arts free from State interference. Cyril Connolly, an influential commentator, mounted a powerful attack as early as 1942 on further attempts to make the arts more accessible to the masses:

> We are becoming a nation of culture-diffusionists. Culture-diffusion is not art. We are not being true to art. The appreciation of art is spreading everywhere... But war-artists are not art, the Brains Trust is not art, the BBC is not art, all the CEMA shows, all the ABCA lectures, all the discussion groups and MOI [Ministry of Information] films and pamphlets will avail nothing if we deny independence, leisure and privacy to the artist himself.[49]

Philip Hope-Wallace, a distinguished music critic, continued that attack in 1944:

> I am an enemy of mass, state organized culture; muddling-through to art, as to other things, seems to me the good way; the hand of CEMA, the cautious benevolence of commercial risk means the integrity of the critics will play their part.[50]

In his 1999 narrative history of the arts in Britain, Sir Roy Strong notes that:

> At the outset in 1946 the [Arts] Council's role was clearly to be conservative, resolutely British, and fiercely anti-American. In the face of what was regarded as the cultural threat from Hollywood, the Arts Council retreated from the things which CEMA during the war had pursued, like direct management, a deep concern for the regions, and a commitment to art education. Under its secretary-general, W E Williams, the Council...set about creating what others later would denounce as bourgeois cultural imperialism, trying to make the masses appreciate arts which had never been intended for them in the first place.[51]

That denunciation ignores what Williams himself wrote at the time: that whilst the broad mass of people might never come to love high art, that was no reason why they should not enjoy greater access to all the arts; for in time, some would come to love them, every bit as much as members of the middle class. Sir Roy concludes by noting the moral dimension in the Arts Council's policy:

> In general it stood for excellence against populism, for the metropolis as the showcase for the great national art institutions, and was against commercialism, viewing the arts as a social activity which bore with them a moral as well as an aesthetic dimension in what was an increasingly agnostic age. The commitment was firmly to the middle ground with a distaste for extremes, perhaps summed up as a combination of native neo-Romanticism with neutered modernism.[52]

Williams fully subscribed to that conception of the arts. He was an unswerving advocate of the middle way, as he made clear in his writings some sixty years before Sir Roy Strong. Williams deserves full credit for pursuing policies to preserve the best in British culture against the increasingly clamorous claims of brutal (native) amateurism on the one hand and crass (imported) commercialism on the other. He was the longest serving and arguably the most successful and innovative Secretary-General of the Arts Council at the most formative stage of its development. He no doubt made mistakes, for which he may legitimately be criticized. But, all things considered, he served the Arts Council and the nation with distinction.

By the summer of 1963, when preparing to stand down as Secretary-General, Williams may well have reflected on some words he had written during the Second World War, in a 1942 ABCA pamphlet on post-war Britain:

> We are fighting not to win, but to win something, and the more we clear our minds here and now about the world we want after the war, the more likely we are to attain it.[53]

Williams' pioneering work with ABCA had certainly helped to clear his own mind about the post-war world. He formulated a clear vision of post-war Britain as an aspiring cultural democracy. At the Arts Council, as elsewhere, the strength of his arguments and the force of his personality helped turn that vision into an enduring reality. His achievements, through his twelve years as Secretary-General, are amongst his finest monuments.

Gertrude and Bill Williams, c1965.

Eleven: *Broadcaster and critic*

> [W E Williams] is one of the best broadcasters in the country – would you like to broadcast when you know you stammer?
>
> *H L Beales: 'Penguin Personality',* Penguins Progress, *1940*

For members of the 'information generation' – enjoying virtually unlimited access to terrestrial and satellite global communications – it is almost impossible to imagine the intoxication of the earliest days of wireless broadcasting. The launch of the Internet offers perhaps the nearest contemporary analogy. For those like Bill and Gertrude Williams, who lived through the birth of broadcasting, who scratched a primitive 'cat's whisker' to obtain their first, faint radio signal from a crystal set, and who later clustered round a low-output speaker to catch the first reliable broadcast output, 'wireless' epitomised modernity.

In 1927, when the British Broadcasting Company was granted its Charter, with the statutory duty 'to inform, to educate, and to entertain', Williams was working as a schoolteacher in Leytonstone. He was amongst the first to recognise the potential of broadcasting as a powerful instrument of mass education and a potent means of promoting cultural democracy. He was an avid listener, a compulsive commentator, and a tirelessly constructive critic of the BBC's serious output. In particular, he soon realised that the audience for serious broadcasting included those who also enjoyed books and reading. That prompted him to write frequently to the BBC, in the early years of broadcasting, offering stringent criticism of their book programmes.

In November 1933, for example, Williams wrote to the Talks Department, offering to deliver a series of broadcast talks under the title *What shall I read?* As Staff Tutor in English Literature in the Extra-Mural Department of London University, Williams was well qualified in his subject matter. His lecturing experience and academic credentials were impressive. But what did he know about broadcasting technique?

The BBC accepted his proposal and he delivered his first talk on the National Service on the evening of Tuesday 20 February 1934, with succeeding talks on five following Tuesdays. For those six broadcasts, each lasting 15 minutes, he was paid in total £45, the equivalent of roughly one month's salary as a schoolmaster. Over the next five years, Williams broadcast regularly on a variety of themes, mostly but not exclusively concerned with education. By April 1939, senior managers at the

William Emrys Williams at the BBC microphone, March 1934.

BBC recognised that Williams had developed into a skilful broadcaster, but decided he would be even better employed as a perceptive and probing independent critic of BBC broadcast talks.

In February 1934, the BBC's prestigious weekly publication *The Listener* commented on Professor Sir Ernest Barker's lecture on 'The Constitution of the BBC':

> Professor Barker finds the touchstone in the effect of broadcasting on culture and politics, and he formulates certain standards – advancing education and culture, encouragement of free political discussion, and the promotion of the sense of citizenship – by which the contribution of broadcasting to the community can be assessed. Judged by these standards, the BBC comes well out of a comparison with France, Germany and the USA.[1]

Given his serious interest in the new medium of broadcasting, with its untapped potential for adult education, Williams must have read that article. Broadcasting had become increasingly important in the 1930s as the BBC raised the technical quality of its output, as reception improved, and as producers became more professional and inventive. Radio – as it later came to be known – soon replaced the printed word as the primary source of immediate news, as well as more general information and entertainment.

Broadcasting presented Williams with a serious intellectual challenge as well as providing a welcome addition to his modest income. He was soon engaged in analysing and discussing radio as a powerful new medium for shaping the social, political and cultural dimensions of national life. On 10 April 1934, he sent the BBC an analysis of listeners' responses to his first broadcasts, noting their interest in both his content and delivery. Half a dozen responses were sentimental – 'including one which declared that I was bracketed with the Bishop of London as her Favourite Voice'. The rest fell into three categories: those desiring more information; those giving their own experience of reading literature; and those requesting further guidance on their reading. But he noted with regret that there was 'no communication at all' from any of the adult education Listening Groups, whose members met regularly to hear and then discuss a particular broadcast, and whose attention he had hoped to attract.

Williams went on to give his first impressions of 'being a broadcaster':

> After the first baptism I enjoyed the talking very much; and at present I feel it is by far the most congenial way of discoursing. There is quite obviously a radio technique but it takes nearly six sessions to learn about it. Beginners, at any rate, would, I think, profit by more extensive rehearsal – or rather, by more prolonged acclimatisation to the rigours of the studio climate! It would comfort some people too (myself included) to have the same studio week by week. I had three changes, and they don't encourage acclimatisation. These are trifles, but they are part of that general experience which you asked me to describe.[2]

Although he dismissed these 'trifles', Williams' comments were taken seriously by his producer and passed on to the Talks Executive, with an explanation of what had gone wrong:

> Williams had to sit in the studio after 11 o'clock with the red light flashing and no announcer. This is always likely to happen in the morning in my experience but it is exaggerated when the 11 o'clock talk is four storeys away from the preceding item. And it is a devastating experience for any speaker unless very experienced which Williams certainly is not.[3]

In the BBC's eyes – and in listeners' ears – Williams had been reasonably successful, even if his microphone manner left something to be desired. But he had put down a clear marker: he was determined to demonstrate his ability to master this demanding new medium of communication. In this context, it is instructive to compare Williams' initial experience of broadcasting with that of his friend and mentor Dr Thomas Jones:

> Put into Studio 3B… The red light quivered, then stopped and before I knew it, I was away. Up to the moment I had been thoroughly at ease, but then I began to feel very 'artificial', as if the voice did not belong to me at all. At the end of my first five minutes, I could see I was about eight lines behind and about this time I rested my hand on the table and it bumped away, up and down, at a great rate and I could not keep it still… I tried hard to get out of the reading manner to a more natural speaking key, but for the life of me, could I? But I saw I was keeping fairly to my time until the last five minutes when I realised I was going to be a trifle behind. In fact I ended a minute over – which the announcer thought was very good for a first go off.[4]

Following his 1934 broadcasts, Williams listened with renewed interest to the BBC's output, paying special attention to book programmes and to broadcasts concerned with education in general. In January 1935, he wrote to Mary Adams, Head of Talks, enclosing a two-page critique of *Bookshelf*, a new book review programme:

> I felt that tonight's *motif* was too abstract. Decisions seemed to me too amorphous a theme altogether to provide any instigation to reading. Doesn't it need a sharply-defined and concrete motif? It needs to be pitched, of course, in relation to the books available; but I should think that a group could readily be chosen which did afford a more tangible sort of common interest. Shouldn't it be *Dictators* or *Nomads* or *Country Life* or things like that?
>
> Tonight's defect, all the time, seemed to me a loose and indecisive *motif*. And I thought the compère sounded very depressed. Wouldn't a genial tone to the whole thing, plus a cinemagazine treatment get this excellent notion across more completely? A few scenarios would be worth experimenting with, I think.[5]

Williams' letter is noteworthy for its sharp analysis, its frankness and its constructive tone. It is perceptively detailed, intelligent and well written. It probably did no harm to his reputation amongst senior staff at the Talks Department of the BBC, always on the lookout for well-informed and constructive criticism of its broadcasts. Within a month of that letter, Mary Adams gave Williams the first opportunity to present his own reviews in the *Bookshelf* broadcast in February 1935, for which he was paid eight guineas – twice the amount he had been paid in the previous year.

Throughout the 1930s, Williams submitted a stream of suggestions to BBC producers on the kind of programmes he thought they should be broadcasting. In May 1934, for example, he proposed a series about the many little-known cultural clubs and societies in and around London. In April 1935, he suggested a series of pre-election talks, to be given by Evan Durbin of the London School of Economics, with debates on such subjects as the five-day week, compulsory annual holidays, and state medical services versus voluntary hospitals.[6]

But there was another way in which Williams impressed the BBC. In January 1929, R S Lambert, one of Williams' close collaborators in adult education, was appointed Editor of *The Listener*, the BBC's new flagship publication, which printed a selection from the best of the previous week's broadcasts, as well as current book reviews and other relevant articles from independent contributors. Lambert was an accomplished journalist, a former editor and regular contributor to *Highway*, a member of the British Institute of Adult Education's policy-making committees, and an influential figure in broadcasting politics in the 1930s and '40s.

In *The Listener* for 1 August 1934 Williams reviewed the Central Council for Schools Broadcasting prospectus on Broadcasts to Schools: 1934/35, which he found 'as excellent as it is comprehensive':

> As an auxiliary on the imaginative side the School Broadcasts are of indisputable value ...[but] is there not a growing opportunity for the BBC to play its part in breaking down the false antithesis which we are inclined to make between education and entertainment?[7]

In March 1935, Williams wrote to Lambert, offering to contribute a series of articles on literature and broadcasting. That letter resulted in five articles by Williams in *The Listener* in the summer of 1935. They dealt in different ways with one central issue: Could the written word survive in the face of the renewed challenge from theatre, and from the relatively new media of radio and cinema?

In the first article, 'Style and Purpose in Literature', Williams presented his anatomy of contemporary fiction. Having noted that the primary test of a good modern novel was 'mastery of medium' – that is, 'the consummate skill of narrative and dialogue; the creation of characters who seem to live; and a full control of language' – he concluded that 'mastery of medium', while necessary, was not sufficient of itself:

> More and more, intelligent readers are looking for a greater purposiveness in their novels. They want an 'attitude' in the novelist; they want contact with a mind which is aware of the conditions and beliefs of the times. In a sense, all they want is that a novel shall be up-to-date, not in its description of the inessentials, but in its revelation of social values.[8]

For Williams, the best modern novels expressed a strong sense of purpose: 'They are novels in which vibrates some sense of concern for the world's griefs and iniquities'. He did not favour propaganda literature whose characters were 'ventriloquists' dolls, mouthing the lines of their manipulator':

> I am not asking for disguised dissertations on the totalitarian state or on the economics of planning. I am asking that the novel should concern itself more with the impulses and experiences of the men and women who live against the background of these phenomena, and who are in large part moulded by them.[9]

Two further articles analysed the perennial appeal of biography, with clear and persuasive distinctions between different kinds of biography. Having used the first article to offer some answers to the question 'Why Do We Like Biography?' Williams turned in his second to 'The Art of Biography':

> There are two alternatives. There is the anonymous assembly of anecdotes, incidents, letters and sayings – the biography of commemoration; chemically pure, yet tasteless as distilled water. And there is the impressionistic interpretative literary biography which is as much the release of the personality of the living author as it is the chronicle of the dead man's life and habit. It is this quality above all which gives the new biography its kinship with the novel.[10]

In his two remaining articles, Williams speculated on the chances of the novel surviving against competition from the cinema, and on the challenge presented to live drama by cinema and broadcasting.

In 1936, public attention in Britain was preoccupied with the worsening political situation in Europe, with the outbreak of the Spanish Civil War, and General Franco's challenge to the elected Republican Government. Those events did not disturb the BBC's normal programme schedule. Earlier in the year, N G Luker, a Talks producer, had invited Williams to give a series of five weekly talks, at eight guineas each, on *Books that made History*. Discussion brought swift agreement on the first four books: Machiavelli: *The Prince*; Rousseau: *Social Contract*; Marx: *Capital*; and Darwin: *Origin of Species*. But there was sharp disagreement over the choice of the fifth and final book. When Williams turned down Adolf Hitler's *Mein Kampf*, Luker proposed

Nietzche's *Will to Power* as an alternative. On 9 November 1936, Williams wrote to Luker:

> *Will to Power* seems to me the utterest of dry bones. I plead on my knees for a reprieve from this particular fate! ... I do not say that I refuse Nietzche outright; but as Mr Justice Swift told Counsel for the Defence the other day, "I am getting restive".[11]

He suggested instead Captain Cook's *Voyages* – which was eventually accepted. Following *Books that made History*, Luker sent his Head of Department this frank assessment of Williams as a broadcaster:

> W E Williams puts his scripts together well. They show occasional pomposities and left-wing anti-clerical prejudices, but were, on the whole, fair and entertaining. He was very willing to alter his script from literary to broadcasting style where necessary, and was interested in the technique and rehearsed each time. Much improved by playback. Occasionally parsonic and didactic, sometimes stutters badly. With careful training would make an admirable stand-by but perhaps never a front liner... 12.45pm on Saturday is not so absurd a time as it looked; thirty-eight responses to the first talk, one describing it as a pleasant interlude in lunch-time music.[12]

'Parsonic and didactic' he may occasionally have been but, despite Williams' intermittent stammer, Luker was quick to spot his potential as a reliable 'second-liner' if not exactly a true 'front-liner'. BBC producers sent periodic reports to their Head of Department, giving their views on the type of programme they wished to make and the kind of audiences most likely to enjoy them. In November 1938, Norman Luker wrote to his Head of Department on the standard of broadcast talks. His report divided listeners into three groups: Group A were 'intelligent and well-informed' and therefore needed to be catered for only occasionally. Group B – the 'intelligent and not so well-informed' – were identified as the most important target for BBC Talks. Discussing the characteristics of this group, Luker pointed to the increase in secondary, adult and university education, the huge sales of Pelican and Left Book Club publications devoted to serious issues, and the success of the newly-established magazine *Picture Post*. All this suggested that there was now a 'considerable serious-minded public anxious for mental pabulum which we are well placed to give them'. Group C, the largest part of the potential audience, included the 'not-so-intelligent and mostly uninformed' who would only listen to 'adventure' or 'personality' talks. In Luker's view, the Talks Department should continue to educate unobtrusively by using its most eminent broadcasters.[13]

Luker's report was sympathetically received by his Head of Department and he was earmarked for early promotion. In his history of the BBC, Asa Briggs notes that Luker was amongst a group of people seconded by the BBC to the Ministry of

Information in 1939 to advise on psychological warfare. In the post-war era, he became BBC Director of Talks.[14]

In March 1939, Williams received a letter from R S Lambert at *The Listener*, to confirm a verbal understanding they had just reached:

> I gather you would be willing to undertake as from the beginning of May the talks criticism column in *The Listener*. The number of words per week is about 750. Your first contribution would cover the week April 28th to May 5th inclusive, and copy should reach us if possible on the last-named day; or if not, by the first post on the 6th. The fee we could offer would be £4.4.0. There will be the need for close consultation with Alan Thomas, Editor.[15]

In her 1940 Sixpenny Pamphlet, 'Reviewing', Virginia Woolf caused a minor furore when she described reviewing as a form of 'intellectual harlotry'.[16] Such considerations did not inhibit Bill Williams, who gratefully accepted the invitation. But why, after five years' growing maturity as a professional broadcaster, was he so ready to become a regular columnist and independent professional critic of other people's broadcasts? First, it was a highly flattering invitation. *The Listener* had emerged over the previous decade as the BBC's most prestigious publication, well able to stand comparison with other cultural weeklies. Its panel of independent critics included such eminent journalists as Grace Wyndham Goldie, Scott Goddard and Herbert Farjeon. Second, broadcasting had established itself as an exciting new medium of immense potential for cultural democracy, and audiences were growing rapidly. Above all, a regular column in *The Listener* provided Williams with a national platform from which to advocate higher standards in broadcasting. Third, reviewing radio broadcasts was highly congenial work, offering a refreshing counterpoint to his full-time work at the Institute of Adult Education. Fourth, it would provide him with another useful string to his bow, alongside his editorship of Penguin Books, his own published books, and his work at the British Institute of Adult Education. Finally, it added a steady trickle of supplementary income.

Williams would probably have made a success of his new role, as *The Listener's* 'Critic of the Spoken Word', in any historical circumstances. But he was immensely helped by the outbreak of war within a few months of accepting that role. As Paul Fussell has pointed out:

> In a way not easy to imagine in the present world of visual journalism, the war was mediated and authenticated by spoken language, whose conduit was the radio. For those at home the sound of the war was the sound of the radio. Actually, wartime was a special moment in the history of human sensibility, for in those pre-television days the imagination was obliged to fill in the missing visual dimension, and in those pre-tape days, there was in addition all the excitement of live transmission, when anything could happen. It might not be going too far to say that in those days the audience's "creative imagination" was,

willy-nilly, honoured as seldom before or after, by the very conventions of radio. Besides inviting listeners to imagine the appearance of speakers and scenes, broadcasting seems to confer on utterance both intimacy and authority.[17]

Williams had worked as a freelance journalist for more than ten years, contributing book reviews and short articles on literary themes to *Highway* and *The Listener.* Book reviews were a long-standing feature of the political weeklies and the cultural monthlies. Reviews of broadcasting, by contrast, were still in their infancy with few outstanding practitioners. Radio talks were certainly not given the same thoughtful attention as literature, drama or music. In accepting Lambert's invitation, Williams recognised that he could now exploit a unique opportunity to develop a more reflective, analytical and constructive type of radio criticism that might contribute in the long run to better broadcasting.

Williams was amongst the first to recognise that radio broadcasting was a new art form which called for a new kind of criticism. He was concerned with how it sounded as well as what it said. As broadcasting technology improved, wireless audiences became more discriminating. Williams recognised that the microphone was an exacting taskmaster. It detected insincerity and amplified pomposity. Microphone technique was not easily mastered. Radio criticism had to develop its own criteria, its own standards of judgement. In his reviews of broadcast talks, Williams often referred to himself as 'the assiduous fireside listener' in much the same way as Virginia Woolf had referred to 'the common reader'. Style, tone and balance were as important as content when discriminating between good and better broadcasts. But Williams never lost sight of the needs and responses of 'the ordinary listener', 'the common man' or 'the man or woman in the street' as he often referred to them without embarrassment.

Williams soon settled down as a regular member of *The Listener's* team of part-time contributors, on easy terms with its editorial staff. On 4 May 1939, Williams filed the copy for his first column of The Spoken Word, due to appear in the following week's issue of *The Listener*:

Here is my piece. The Political Debate was really worse than I say, but I have toned down my first comments. The whole thing is not 750 words, but I have marked a possible cut on page 2. The final paragraph, again, is easily detachable. Perhaps you can give me a ring...to say whether this is the sort of thing you want. We aim to please. PS: I've cut it out on second thoughts.[18]

In his early contributions, Williams went out of his way to meet his editor's requirements by not exceeding his word limit; by toning down his first thoughts; and by sacrificing his final paragraph. He aimed to produce exactly what was required, with little or no need for editing. He displayed a genuine willingness to moderate harsh criticism – a far cry from his later, more self-confident and outspoken reviews. Given its significance, his very first piece merits generous citation:

> ***Why Call It a Debate?***
>
> A few weeks ago my predecessor on this page found fault with the first of the new monthly series of Political Debates. After listening to the third of these last week I felt that a great opportunity had been lost... In the first place the performance was not a debate: it was a symposium of party opinion on the topic of unemployment: and only, it seemed, by accident did the three spokesmen ever touch upon each other's contentions. From each of the trio we had an impeccable statement of party policy, but at no point did the three arguments dovetail into each other.
>
> Do the organisers who sponsor this item really give their spokesmen a chance to discuss? Or does their method tend to pin the speakers down to a set piece? Does it discourage the use of those devices of debate which broadcasting has brought to such a fine art – well-timed cutting-in, incisive cross-examining and so on? This example of how not to do it is a reminder of what is really involved in 'producing' a debate or a talk. The back-stage gang responsible for broadcasting the spoken word seldom gets its due; its work is taken for granted in the same sense as we forget the back-stage gang in the theatre, the Press or the cinema. But the fireside listener who know nothing of those patient and elaborate processes by which a skilful presentation transforms the raw material of debate into microphone discussion could not fail to be conscious of the difference between the average wireless discussion and this unskilful imitation which the politicians provided...
>
> Now and then, alas! the faders-out spoil a beautifully built-up bit of broadcasting. When 'Bartimeus' was reaching the climax last Wednesday someone turned the knob on him; so we shall never know how the old woman summed up human experience for him during his caravan wanderings in Ireland.[19]

It was surely not by chance that the topic he chose for his first column was radio discussion. It was a subject to which he would often return – not least because discussion and debate were forms most favoured by the BBC when dealing with contentious issues. Williams had already reflected long and hard on discussion methodology during his work with WEA Tutorial Classes, as shown by his reported reflections in Chapter 4. He gave much closer attention to the subject in his broadcast reviews whilst promoting well-led platoon discussion in his work with ABCA during the Second World War, discussed in Chapter 8.

Several noteworthy points emerge from Williams' first column of criticism which help to characterise his style: his passing reference to taking over the column; his specific criticism, with sharply-defined examples; his broadening of the review to address some deeper, underlying political or social dimension; his generous tribute to 'back-stage gangs' in radio and other media; his devastating use of 'how not to do it'; and the original and witty tailpiece. His column frequently followed a similar, well-defined pattern. Taking a specific programme as his starting point, he would broaden his comments on the theme of that particular programme with some bold generalisations about the emerging art of 'the broadcast talk', offering constructive ideas for improving its quality, with some sharper, brighter, contrasted material in his concluding paragraph. Each of his articles is an essay in the difficult art of broadcast criticism. The body of Williams' work as the BBC's critic of the spoken word represents a unique historical document, which traces the emergence of one of the most powerful ideological forces of our time: the spoken word, broadcast to the nations of the world.

Williams was never constrained by the BBC in peace or war on the choice of programmes he chose to review. Although he recognised the need to cover a broad range of subject matter, he had his favourite topics – microphone technique, radio discussion and debate, the voice of ordinary people, poetry on air – and his favourite broadcasters – John Hilton, Walford Davies, Richard Dimbleby, Commander Anthony Kimmins, Winston Churchill, J B Priestley and others – as well as his favourite dislikes – intrusive background music, excessive and contrived sound effects, Welsh ranters, Sandy Macpherson at the theatre organ. He returned to these matters time and time again, without embarrassment or apology. Sometimes he would recall his earlier remarks on the subject. At other times, when his wartime duties took him away from home and from his files, he might unconsciously repeat – but never knowingly contradict – himself. Above all, he was at all times honest and open-minded.

Williams delivered his 750 words of weekly criticism on The Spoken Word for five full years, or 250 consecutive weeks – from May 1939 to June 1944 – with the exception of just one week, when his column was 'pulled' by the BBC for reasons discussed later in this chapter. It is clearly impossible to do justice to the full breadth, depth and quality of this body of criticism within the limited scope of this chapter. The range of subjects covered, the originality of the ideas presented, the critical apparatus deployed, together with the issues of impartiality, fair comment, balanced judgement, sincerity and integrity – all these are relevant to an exhaustive account of Williams' radio criticism.

Some of Williams' most effective writing emerged in his weekly column of radio criticism, honed to a fine edge over a period of five years. Comparing earlier and later columns, we find a growing depth and maturity in his writing, with a much surer grasp of what was needed to capture and hold his reader's interest in his comments on the previous week's broadcast talks. After a tentative start, Williams soon discovered how to swoop down, like some genial bird of prey, on a single broadcast as the point of departure for a surgical dissection of some general issue of special concern to both broadcasters and listeners. He never avoided difficult subject matter or muted sharp criticism, where he deemed it appropriate. His comments were never vicious but always tempered by his penetrating intelligence. Wit crackles through every paragraph; irony irradiates every column. There are some beautifully crafted passages, which demonstrate his capacity to think aurally, to write under severe time pressures, and to turn an exact epithet or precise phrase, with few opportunities to revise his copy.

Amongst Williams' broadcasting heroes, none stood higher in his estimation than John Hilton, a neglected figure in British broadcasting history, whose name and voice were as well known to listeners in the 1930s as those of the Dimbleby brothers, John Humphrys or Jeremy Paxman today. Hilton was a Cambridge don, Professor of Industry, a man with wide-ranging sympathies and exceptional skill at the microphone. The subject matter of his talks was catholic and always life-enhancing.

'How Hilton Does It' was the title of Williams' first column on a broadcast by the legendary John Hilton. Published in *The Listener* on 18 May 1939, it opens with an apology for 'this bare-faced and perhaps clumsy dissection of his methods, but there are not very many broadcasters who set one off on this effort to discuss how they do it'. The subject of Hilton's talk – 'the disease of literary style called jargon' – was close to his reviewer's heart. According to Williams, the substance of the talk comprised:

> a repetition of an old and excellent lesson on the right and wrong use of language. But as a piece of broadcasting it revealed more skill than you will hear on the air in a month of Sundays [suggesting that Hilton had] pondered deeply on the question of getting the spoken word across. One of his methods is the use of vivid images – for instance, 'a difference as big as a mosquito's eyelash', or 'all goggle-eyed with admiration'. Another of John Hilton's characteristics is an unabashed and full-blooded use of alliteration – another trick which makes the genteel wince but which has a powerful value in oratory and drama. John Hilton uses it with relish... The well-timed, well-prepared repetition of a word or a phrase is another of his resources; and yet another (equally familiar to students of literary style) is his neat alternation of longish sentences and short... To reinforce the 'literary' devices, moreover, he seems to use many appropriate artifices of rhetoric – or are these again part of an unconscious natural gift? Whichever they are, he excels, for instance, in that sudden pause to rivet your attention on an impending pictorial phrase.[20]

Williams is concerned with both content and delivery. His analysis is incisive and illuminating. Above all, he recognises and acknowledges an exceptional, perhaps instinctive, broadcasting talent – a subject to which he returned many times in his later reviews.

The BBC published *The Listener* every Thursday. Contributors were required to submit their copy seven days before publication date, which meant that Williams usually posted his material to his editor, Alan Thomas, on the same day as his previous week's copy appeared in print. On the day his first piece appeared in *The Listener*, Williams sent Thomas his second piece with this accompanying plea:

> Here is the Spoken Word stuff. If in the mercy of your heart you can spare the knife – even at the cost of despoiling my colleague on the page – I'll be grateful. I've cut and cut and cut. But I know the difficulties, & I'll leave myself in your hands.[21]

The editor spared the knife and printed the piece in full. It was a review of a talk by the distinguished drama critic, Sir Desmond MacCarthy. Williams had a passionate interest in the function of criticism in general and of literary criticism in particular. But instead of dwelling on the drama critic's trade, Williams focussed on the script and its delivery, as an example of broadcasting at its best:

> I found nothing so engrossing during the whole week as Desmond MacCarthy's talk on 'The Dramatic Critic's Function'. To my mind he is the most serious critic of the theatre now writing in England, yet no one could have more effectively lured the man in the street to an austere theme as MacCarthy did the other night... Here then was a model script; a perfect example, on paper, of this new art of microphone oratory – the opening cajolery, the translation of precepts into imagery, the beautifully-timed climax of the organ simile, and the quick and friendly drop-down to home truths at the end. If anyone ever compiles an anthology of broadcast scripts for the use of embryo broadcasters, this script will be a first choice.[22]

MacCarthy soon became one of Williams' favourite broadcasters. What he admired most was the art behind the apparent artlessness that made MacCarthy an entirely 'natural' broadcaster:

> What first commands one's attention to Desmond MacCarthy is the quality of his voice, low-pitched, deliberate and sympathetic... In many ways, his script resembles one of his literary articles or reviews, but in delivering it he takes care to make concessions to the requirements of the Spoken Word. By a sensitive use of pause and emphasis and parenthesis he attains flexibility of speech without any sacrifice of his invariable sense of literary style... His motto should be pondered by everyone who accepts an invitation to deliver a talk – the condensed language of the pen adapted by its rhythm to delivery by the voice.[23]

Once again, Williams was as interested in exploring the essential ingredients of successful broadcasting technique as he was in the substance of the broadcast talk. Here, for example, are two extracts from his review in *The Listener* dated 23 January 1941:

> The microphone is a very curious filter of undertones: it discovers, and magnifies any self-consciousness, artifice or insincerity. And it is particularly ruthless to any forcing of an effect or an emotion. If you *try* to be yourself, the microphone mocks you and parodies you; if by some miraculous good luck you can *be* yourself, without any effort, then the microphone transmits you without distortion.[24]

He does not leave the matter there, but applies his theories to one particular broadcaster, his fellow-countryman, the actor and playwright Emlyn Williams:

> After his first postscript I cried him up to the skies. But after his last I like him less. Partly, perhaps, because, as his fellow countryman, I begin to discern that too-easy mastery (and wireless adaptation) of the art of rhetoric. Is he becoming the equivalent in postscripteers of the notorious Welsh pulpiteers? Is he fingering the stops of sentiment too brazenly? Is he going a bit Wurlitzer? The Welsh have this pull over the Irish – that they can do their blarney without kissing a stone: they can bamboozle you with the rope-tricks into seeing a stone that isn't there. It is for such incoherent reasons as those that I hope Emlyn Williams will abandon virtuosity and resist temptation.[25]

Williams loved good broadcasting. He enjoyed high quality drama, he was fascinated by vivid field reporting, and relished a wide range of lighter entertainment, from favourite magazine formats – such as 'Monday Night at Eight', and 'In Town Tonight' – through the situation comedy of Tommy Handley, to the crooning of Bing Crosby. He could not avoid broadcast music though he rarely named a composer or mentioned his musical preferences. He never lost an opportunity to lambast programmes that embellished the spoken word with any kind of background music and always sought to tease out the essential ingredients of successful microphone technique. Few other commentators on radio broadcasting took the trouble to analyse the qualities that a handful of highly successful broadcasters brought to the microphone. He was equally persistent in discovering why any number of successful orators, especially politicians, failed to 'come across' on radio broadcasts.

Williams' conception of his role as critic of the Spoken Word was firmly rooted in his understanding of the role of criticism in the arts in general. Over several centuries, that role had developed along lines prescribed in the ancient world: to identify and to analyse beauty, and to expose fraudulence. From the aesthetic revolution of the 18th century, the professional critic's task was to explicate and to explain, to pass judgement, to commend the best, to encourage the good, and to condemn the worst.

As critic of The Spoken Word, Williams began with a clear distinction between ends and means. If the role of broadcasting was to inform, to educate and to entertain, in that order, the critic's first question must be: What were the broadcaster's intentions in this programme? Having established the aims, the second question followed: How well did the broadcaster succeed in achieving those aims? What means were employed in achieving them? And, finally, how far were they successful?

Williams drew a sharp distinction between scripts intended for reading and those meant for speaking, a theme which he frequently revisited. Since non-professional broadcasters had few opportunities to practise their art, many script-readers carried over into radio some of the oratorical tricks of the trade learned in politics or the theatre: the verbal flourish, the expansive gesture, the inflated rhetoric. Williams was amongst the first to see that this was the very antithesis of what the new medium required:

> It is my favourite thesis about broadcasting that the microphone is a filter which never fails to discover the personal attribute of the speaker. It magnifies every virtue and every vice; it is a reminder of what the blind have always known – that the voice is a rare revealer of personality.[26]

The essential point here is that, whilst many of today's radio broadcasts are live and unscripted (e.g. interviews, quiz programmes, phone-ins, chat shows) the invariable rule in the 1930s was that *every* BBC broadcast was scripted. The art of the radio talk was to deliver a script in such a way that it *appeared* spontaneous, whereas in fact it was highly contrived. Professional broadcasters and their producers slowly mastered this technique, mostly by trial and error. Williams was amongst the first to note that some script-readers seemed 'natural' broadcasters: their technique appeared effortless; they were comfortable at the microphone; and they sounded as if they were speaking directly to their listeners, impromptu. Later critics and commentators made it their business to analyse more precisely what the new medium required for good broadcasting. As Paddy Scannell, historian of radio broadcasting, records:

> The art of radio talk as it came to be understood by the Talks Dept is easily summarized. Since it was received by family groups it should be conversational in tone rather than declamatory, intimate rather than intimidating. The personality of a speaker should shine through their words. But because broadcasting was live, talks needed to be scripted. Otherwise what they gained in colloquialism and personal idiom they would lose in clarity and succinctness. As Briggs put it, 'what was natural had first to become artificial before it would sound natural again'.[27]

Williams was quick to detect and applaud experiments with unscripted broadcasts but even he wished to set sensible limits to this 'revolutionary' approach:

> There's somebody in the Talks Department who from time to time promotes an ambitious experimental programme. He doesn't always get away with it – and he has had his share of well-merited buffets in this column – but when he does the triumph is positively

> reverberating... Well, this man is a fanatic in search of the impromptu. He believes that one of the most sincere kinds of broadcasting is the kind which dares to let people speak their unrehearsed minds on some serious matter... He got his reward last Friday. He had previously sent four people a copy of the same book and then he got them into the studio, recorded their extempore discussion and gave us the untouched version of their talk. No method could have produced a more honest and engrossing debate.[28]

Whilst he appreciated the polished delivery of so-called 'cultured' voices, like those of Desmond MacCarthy, Richard Dimbleby or Harold Nicolson, Williams was always encouraging BBC producers to risk more regional voices, such as J B Priestley, John Laurie, or Emlyn Williams. Above all, he urged the BBC to find space for the voice of the man and woman in the street, discussing everyday topics that directly concerned them, like employment and unemployment, war and peace, hobbies and habits.

In July 1939, within two months of taking over his column, Williams nailed his colours to the critic's mast in a piece which gave clear notice of what, to his mind, constituted one of the essential components of effective radio. This piece announced another important theme to which he reverted on many occasions. Because of its importance, the complete column – of which this is an extract – is reproduced as an appendix to this chapter:

> ***The Voice of the Masses***
>
> To my mind the BBC has never rendered a more valuable national service than when it gave these four men the air to speak, in their own words and their own way, the sentiments of their class. It is no new thing to hear on the wireless the more-than-average working man, their warrant officers so to speak, who have learned the niceties of debate in some kind of adult education or social service. Here at last was the real rank-and-file, the proletarian foot-slogger saying his piece out loud – with his cap on. We must hear him again.[29]

In the early 1930s some programmes produced by Olive Shapley in the BBC's Manchester studio had allowed the voice of the masses to be heard in the land. But in London, there was a reluctance to bring members of the working class, with their proletarian vowels, to the microphone. In the words of the mould-breaking BBC producer, D G Bridson:

> That the man in the street should have anything vital to contribute to broadcasting was an idea slow to gain acceptance. That he should actually use broadcasting to express his own opinions in his own unvarnished words was regarded as the end of all good social order.[30]

Within a few months, Williams returned to this favourite theme:

> For some weeks I have grumbled on and off because we so seldom heard on the air the spokesmen of the working class... Whether any battle was ever won on the playing fields of Eton I very much doubt, but this war will be won in the workshops of Britain. And in the last week or two the BBC has given the men and women in those workshops a chance to record their activities and their opinions... 'Go to It!' reported progress on the armaments drive...I found it fresh and invigorating.[31]

A few weeks later, Williams was banging away on the same drum:

> What I want to hear on the air is not only what the workers do but what the workers *think*: their opinions, their antipathies, their grievances, their affirmations. It is exhilarating to hear what the workers are doing: it is no less vital to hear what they are thinking about the conduct of this war. I plead again for their liberty to speak their minds. What they say may prove unpalatable in parts but it will be salutary on the whole. They are the people of England – and they have not spoken yet.[32]

Within three months, Williams returned to the same theme, this time on the subject of the voices of working-class women:

> One of the differences between the wireless and the press is that whereas certain newspapers claim to speak particularly for 'the People' the wireless needs no transcriber or interpreter of the People's point of view. It brings the People to the microphone and allows them, in their own idiom and accent, to say what they have to say... These reflections and assurances are prompted by listening to 'Women in War', one of the best programmes so far in a series which has kept a very high level of interest as well as a high level of integrity... although for an Edwardian like me it's piquant to hear girls bandying such words as 'calibration' and 'monometer'.[33]

Williams' sustained campaign to promote the broadcasting of working-class voices is highly significant. First, it reveals where his deepest sympathies lay: with the excluded 'ordinary people' of Britain rather than the educated middle class. Second, he was a decade ahead of his time in insisting that working men and women had things to say and should be allowed to say them without intermediaries. Third, by advocating more democratised broadcasting, he helped make the BBC's output more widely acceptable and popular to a mass audience. Fourth, his campaign may be seen as yet another example of his lifelong and wide-ranging crusade to bring art to the people.

As well as closely scrutinising broadcast voices, Williams paid close attention to what those voices said and how they said it. He could be lacerating in his witty attacks on unsympathetic voices, as shown in these extracts from *The Listener* at various dates:

> ***Trenchard Cox:*** The speaker had a curious mannerism which caused him to put a violent and quite irrelevant emphasis on every fourth syllable or so. Moreover, he spoke in the sort of long-haired drawl which music-hall comedians use to mimic the highbrow.[34]

John Middleton Murray: He delivers long reverberating sentences in which the meaning perishes half way through. He had no bony structure; it was nothing but adipose literary curves, elaborate parallel sentences, for example, sonorous cliches.[35]

Sir John Rothenstein: Much literary ability, of an orthodox kind, but not a solitary broadcasting quality.[36]

Sir Clive Liddell: He lacked rhythm, he frequently planted an emphasis on the wrong word, and he sometimes appeared to mistake his commas for full stops.[37]

Stuart Hibbert: He has the sensitive temperament which is bothered and betwattled by the peculiar responsibility of reading a news bulletin.[38]

For all his hard-hitting criticism, Williams was also generous in his praise – for producers as well as broadcasters. The programmes he singled out for praise reflected the catholicity of his taste as well as his shrewd judgement.

Richard Dimbleby: [His] front-line sound despatches, if we can judge by this example, are going to make broadcasting history.[39]

Brian Vesey-Fitzgerald: [His] five-minute explorations of fields and coppices and hedgerows are wireless miniatures of a rare and enchanting quality. Apart from anything else, I confess, it is agreeable to forget war-potentials for a time in favour of the revelation that the fur of the poor blind mole is inhabited by equally poor blind fleas.[40]

Thomas Woodroofe: It is some time since I heard a piece which I would choose on the spot as a recording for the Anthology of the Spoken Word. Woodroofe's eye-witness narrative of those nine hours off the beaches of Dieppe would be an instantaneous selection.[41]

Marching On is magnificent. It vitalises the news with a skill unmatched by any newspaper or newsreel… Whoever writes the words knows to a hair's breadth what language can do on the air. Whether it is dialogue or narrative or commentary he knows, in syllables and synonyms, exactly how many beans make five. He never puts an adverb wrong, he never fumbles for a verb.[42]

J M Keynes: He put his case the other night with an authority and a clarity which was as exhilarating as the conclusions he presented. He did not confuse the art of popular exposition with the device of talking down to his audience.[43]

Desmond MacCarthy: If anyone ever compiles an anthology of broadcast scripts for the use of embryo broadcasters, this script will be a first choice. It will read so well that some pedantic grammarian will annotate it, as I am doing now, and obscure its excellence in a cloud of footnotes. But he will probably forget to say that this script depended, too, on MacCarthy's equal skill as a speaker.[44]

A Couple of Winners: In that attractive talk which Emlyn Williams gave on the theme 'I'm not English', he had the wisdom to put the spotlight not upon the triumphant elements of his life but upon that part of it which had a particular social significance… So ardently and persuasively did he generalise from his own experience that one forgot, for the moment, that in our unequal educational system very few clever little Welsh boys ever get to college.

> The corn may be green, all right, but it does not always get a chance to ripen… There were many passages in this talk in which he spoke for all Welshmen. One was his account of his racial susceptibility to language – which he illustrated by absolutely vibrating examples. Another was his candid admission of the dexterity with which a Welshman can turn black to white. As a broadcaster, Emlyn Williams has got everything the microphone takes: an individual manner of talking, a beautifully-paced rhythm and an artful sense of impromptu…a better all-round talk than this I have not heard in a long time.[45]

An expatriate Welshman, Williams always turned an attentive ear to examples of Welsh voices on the air. Here he introduces his distinguished fellow-countryman and friend, Dr Thomas Jones:

> I doubt whether Dr Tom Jones has been on the air half-a-dozen times in his life, but even listeners who have a poor memory may recall the occasion when, out of his long back-stage experience of Downing Street, he broadcast some memorable comments upon the political scene of the last twenty years. He is another example of a principle I have often emphasised in this column – that the off-normal voice – not necessarily the 'regional' voice – is nicer to listen to than the standard English accent. His voice has the Welsh qualities of colour and vibration; it is decisive, yet responsive to each turn of thought. It is what you might call a gesticulating voice. I do not mean to suggest that he waggles his spectacles or waves his arms at the microphone; I mean that he brandishes his sentences rather than delivers them. He has that rarest of microphone gifts, one which even such aces as Churchill lack, the gift of rhythm. He has something else rarer still, something which the microphone never fails to detect and magnify. The only word for it is 'sincerity'. And, as I have said on this page once before, one of the mysteries of the microphone, that poor mechanical contrivance of wires and whatnot, is that it never fails to discover the difference between the genuine and the phoney sentiment. There is some power of divination in that little black box – and Dr Tom Jones is the sort who can look it in the face and speak what is in his heart.[46]

That article was read by Gunner Keidrych Rhys, stationed at an anti-aircraft gun site on the cliffs of Dover. Well known in Welsh cultural nationalist circles, the young Welsh poet sat down and wrote to Williams:

> I was glad to read your notes on Dr Tom Jones and the Welsh in this week's Listener; they are interesting and raise several points with which you might or mightn't agree! But I think every real Welshman appreciates your remarks. I notice that J Roberts Williams of Y Cymro always draws attention to them. And that is something to be thankful for these days because most of our 'New Wales Society' feel that the Principality doesn't get her due share of 'attention' in papers and periodicals! This is not due to lack of writers I may assure you… So you see I don't entirely agree with you when you boost up the Anglicised Welshman… There are some amazing younger people – Commonwealth-scholars etc who write in both Welsh and English, and have lived on next to nothing for years.[47]

Williams sent Dr Thomas Jones a copy of Gunner Rhys' letter, adding this illuminating comment: 'Latterly I have felt a need to be a Welshman in more than blood and association; I'd like to help in the cultural movements in Wales'.[48] Williams was never reluctant to remind his readers of his Welsh origins; yet nowhere in his mature writings did he devote more than a few sentences to his Welsh cultural heritage, which had contributed so much to his personality.

Williams often allocated his entire column to a single theme, but rarely to a single broadcast. One favourite device was to get his readers to think more critically about one or two specific talks as examples of good broadcasting in general. In the following example, having designated a group of outstanding broadcasters as 'Aces of the Air' he goes on to anatomise the art of J B Priestley:

> Priestley's way of talking would make him a microphone success in any case; but a popular manner is only half the battle. The history of broadcasting is full of examples of men who were popular broadcasters but who lost their grip on us because they had nothing momentous to say. Their winning ways were not enough. When all Priestley's merits have been added up they are irrelevant beside the fact that he has something he passionately wants to say about this disordered world. His vision of the post-war world is already giving the men of privilege a belly-ache, I believe; but it is putting new heart into the common man.[49]

Faced with the challenge of reviewing seven days of broadcast talks in 750 words, Williams concentrated his attention on two or three programmes, often brought together through some ingenious metaphor or other literary device. Here, for example, he introduces his comments on Schools Music Broadcasts with a striking railway simile:

> On and off during that last few weeks I have given a good deal of my listening time to what I shall call 'wheel-tapping'. Like the man-with-the-hammer at a railway terminus I have been tapping some of those regular wireless-features which have been running a long time. To my ear there are serious cracks and flaws in one or two of them; they are due to be taken off the track for overhaul and renovation...
>
> The Schools Broadcasts strike me as being in excellent running order, and I can well understand why they have such a large 'unofficial' audience of adult listeners. One of their regulars who rings as true as ever is Sir Walford Davies, whose methods of persuasion, I believe, could get music out of a mummy. It sounds so very easy, that casual informal method of his; but although he gives you the illusion of having plenty of time for a gossip or a joke, he is putting something over all the time.[50]

With the outbreak of war in September 1939, Williams resumed his pre-war practice of firing off a string of letters to influential figures at the BBC. They offered ideas, criticism and suggestions for maintaining a stream of cultural broadcasting to entertain and uplift listeners during the darkest days of the war. In November 1939, Williams wrote to Frederick Ogilvie, Director-General of the BBC, on the subject of broadcast poetry:

What I wrote last week, after being deeply moved by Felix Aylmer [reading Tennyson], was that some of the inevitable short intervals in the programme should be filled, not with gramophone records, but with reading three-minute poems... It would probably be sensible to suggest that records of him speaking short poems might be kept handy; or, even better, there are several of the announcers themselves who could read a poem most admirably. I do strongly believe that if such a poem as Monroe's Milk for the Cat (one of those Aylmer read) were introduced into the programme without warning, it would persuade many listeners that poetry is not a high brow and forbidding thing, but something which is just enjoyable to hear. Is this kind of experiment worth trying? I doubt if you will get large numbers to listen to poetry on set occasions. The idea is to ambush their interest.[51]

Ogilvie responded positively to Williams' suggestion. Poetry began to appear more frequently in BBC programme schedules, read either by the poets themselves, or by professional actors, or even by BBC announcers, who discovered a new and exciting outlet for their talents. 'Poetry on air' was a subject that Williams addressed repeatedly throughout the war and on which he was often at his most eloquent. For his love of poetry was deep and genuine. His thinking on 'poetry for the masses' was entirely consistent with his earlier thinking on *Art for the People*. Whilst he doubted whether large numbers would ever listen to poetry regularly, that was no reason why the BBC should not try 'to find ways of making poetry popular to the ordinary listener'.

In June 1940, Williams again urged the BBC to provide more poetry on air, with the bold but serious suggestion that Lord Reith, former BBC Chairman, should be invited to read Milton's *Paradise Lost* – a suggestion that the BBC diplomatically rejected. Later that month, when the BBC succeeded in persuading Duff Cooper, Minister of Information, to come to the microphone to read a poem, Williams could not contain his enthusiasm:

The BBC's answer to a critic's prayer... I have been arguing that in these times we should call up the poets to bear witness on the wireless, for their testimony and their inspiration can match the history which is being made...thereby helping to break down the illusion that poetry is a ritual for the few... If Duff Cooper's excellent example is followed up, we may live to hear Lloyd George declaiming Chesterton's 'We are the people of England, and we have not spoken yet' or Ernest Bevin beating 'Drakes's Drum' in the authentic West Country accent... So I say it again: Cut out this 'production' business, the team of actors, the musical fanfares, and give us more unpretentious ten-minute sessions of poetry spoken by a single voice.[52]

When the BBC acted on that suggestion, they apparently still did not manage to get it quite right, providing Williams with an opportunity to rehearse another favourite theme: the need to lead listeners gently towards poetry:

> No one applauds more vociferously than I the BBC's decision to put on short poetry reading after the news. But I found many faults in the three-part reading from Tennyson last week. The producer neglected one essential preliminary to such a programme: *he did nothing whatever to coax or acclimatise his audience to poetry* [WEW's emphasis]. We were taken straight from the news to the poetry: there was no sort of introductory comment, no timely suggestion that we should change the key of our listening, no hint of an intimation why such a programme was being presented.[53]

Finally, on the subject of broadcast poetry, there was the vexed question of poets reading their own poetry:

> I dislike all poetry reading which is incantatory, for nothing (to my ear) so completely drains the lifeblood of a poem as the practice of chanting it in a monotone. That treatment seems to land poetry in no time in a dim lugubrious region where pale hands weave and spirals of sickly incense ascend. There are many sincere devotees of poetry who must make it a ritual before it becomes a rapture. I don't feel it or like it that way. I prefer poetry to be read without settings or trappings and genuflexions so that by its own incandescence it can set our minds and senses alight.[54]

Williams' freely acknowledged the strongly didactic tone in many of his ideas and suggestions for improving the standard of broadcasting. In a letter to Sir Richard Maconachie, Director of Talks, he wrote: 'I take my jobs with appalling seriousness'. In an earlier letter to Luker, he apologised for being 'such an incorrigible educator'. His underlying purpose was nearly always serious; but his method avoided pomposity. He maintained a brisk and breezy tone, even when discussing matters of high seriousness. Nowhere is that better illustrated than in his columns devoted to his pet aversion: background music to talk programmes.

> The announcement in the *Radio Times* said that Laurence Olivier would 'read verses on the theme of Britain'. What could be more attractive? But the specification proved misleading. While Olivier tried to read some of the poems a gang of musicians plied their instruments with such vigour that I could catch not more than one word in three. Sometimes they played the poem in, sometimes they played the poem out; and more than once they played right through it. Now what is the idea of this monkey-business? ... What can justify the intrusion of music into the actual reading? To my mind the only service can be to cover up deficiencies in the poem itself, to distract us from noting some mediocrity in the lines. But on such an occasion as this why read a poem which has faults to be concealed? I don't mind how much tuneful trellis-work is erected round second-rate verse but I wish the BBC would leave great poems to speak for themselves.[55]

In April 1940, when Williams had completed his first year as independent critic of The Spoken Word for *The Listener*, his producer, Alan Thomas, sent him a letter of appreciation:

> You have been our Talks Critic for just a year now. I take this opportunity of saying how much I, personally, have appreciated the way you have been doing the job. In order to

> give practical expression to this feeling I am arranging for your weekly payment to be increased from four guineas to five guineas.[56]

That fee increase must have pleased Williams, though perhaps not half as much as the letter he received early in August 1940 from Sir Richard Maconachie, Head of Talks, inviting him to act as 'interlocutor' in 'Taking Stock', a new series of twelve weekly discussion programmes, for which he would be paid ten guineas per programme, inclusive of all expenses. The invitation was tempting but he declined. The first year of the war was an exceptionally hectic time for Williams. In addition to his enlarged duties at the British Institute of Adult Education, and his weekly reviews for *The Listener*, he was heavily involved in the formation of CEMA and had been sent by the War Office as a civilian adviser on a tour of army camps to report on troop morale. 'Taking Stock' went ahead without Williams – and he seems to have had no regrets with his decision. He soon found himself in conflict with BBC top brass following his outspoken remarks in *The Listener* on the broadcasting abilities of Cabinet Ministers:

> ***Wireless Bores***
>
> Wherever the responsibility lies, the plain fact is that too many of these Big Pots are not worth listening to. Consider, for example, Lord Lloyd's broadcast on the War Effort of the Colonies.
>
> First there was the drab language, which fairly crawled with cliches [then] his accent is hard and unsympathetic. He lacks both rhythm and colour... My second exhibit is Mr A V Alexander. He, at least, has an agreeable full-blooded voice, but he, too, has no gift of tongues. His after-dinner patter last week was full of such phrases as 'the great waters' and 'the defence of liberty and freedom'. (Two words for one, in the careless fashion of those who don't know the value of words). His language has neither resource, exactitude nor dignity... It is not enough for wireless purposes to say that Mr Alexander is a brilliant First [Sea] Lord: all that matters is his command of language, his ability to navigate his metaphors, his timing of a climax. And it is in all these qualities of composition and utterance that Mr Alexander is a lubber. That is why I keep saying to whoever it is who inflicts these boring speechifiers upon us: pick them for their broadcasting abilities and forget their eminence in Another Place.[57]

Williams considered that to be fair comment on a matter of public interest. He not only speaks his mind: his commentary is unstuffy, irresistible and irreverent. The logic of his argument is incontestable, though his choice of language might imply a loss of public confidence in what Government Ministers had to say in time of war. There is no evidence that the Ministers he criticised complained to the BBC. Much more significant was the level of sensitivity of BBC senior managers to outspoken criticism of individual Ministers.

On the day *The Listener* appeared with Williams' offending article, the Director-General addressed an angry Internal Memorandum to the Controller (Home Service):

> I read Williams' article 'Wireless Bores' last night. This morning in your absence, and after consulting the chairman, I told Thomas to cut Williams' article out of the forthcoming number, and on reference to Thomas, I told him to keep the articles on Drama and Music... I told Thomas that Williams should not be invited to contribute again without reference to you.[58]

The Listener for 28 November 1940 appeared without Williams' regular column. In its place there appeared this bland notice: 'The Spoken Word, which does not appear this week, will be resumed in our next issue'. Williams' column had been 'pulled' for the first and only time during his five years as Critic of the Spoken Word. By chance, the one issue from which he was ejected included a review of Desmond MacCarthy's broadcast on John Bunyan and *Pilgrim's Progress*. It quoted Mr Valiant-for-Truth's proud exclamation 'My sword I shall give to him that shall succeed me in my Pilgrimage, and my courage and skill to him that can get it' – words that Williams might with justice have spoken himself.

In his history of the BBC, Professor Asa Briggs offers his own commentary on prominent public figures as broadcasters:

> Broadcasting was considered to be such an effective medium that it was easy to forget that a radio audience is not necessarily a captive audience and that a minister or a civil servant, however urgent his message, is not necessarily a star broadcaster. That good speakers were chosen and that some of them established their reputation as a result was largely a tribute to producers inside the BBC... Thus George Barnes wrote bluntly in January 1942 that "the success of talks depends not upon the decision of a Board but the enthusiasm which the producer is able to impart to his speaker."[59]

Although he used his weekly column to lavish both blame and praise on BBC broadcasts, Williams also wrote directly to senior members of BBC management whenever he felt particularly strongly on any broadcasting matter. In November 1941, for example, he wrote an ecstatic letter to George Barnes, Director of Talks:

> For two years and a half I've been criticising the Spoken Word for *The Listener*, and sometimes I've begun to feel a cynical battered old bastard who'll never know exaltation any more. Well, last night I got it back again; the most perfect broadcasting, on its level, that I've ever listened to – 'The Living Image'. I hope I'll get my ecstasy sufficiently under control to express it in my weekly column; but I'm still rather possessed and bemused by last night's quartet. It deserves a plaque in the lobby of your marble hall.[60]

In less than a year, Williams was again in trouble, this time for his comments in *The Listener* for 10 April 1941, on Mr A P Herbert, an influential, popular and independent backbench MP:

> When the announcement was made that A P Herbert was to give some of the Sunday evening postscripts, an official explained in a Press interview that J B Priestley was 'not being sacked'. "It's just a change of bowling for a bit", he said. The cricketing metaphor will serve well enough for some preliminary comment on the new man...
>
> What surprised me most in the first of this new series was its lack of shape. Although it included many just and keen-edged comments there was too little relation or consequence between them; the design of the whole piece seemed desultory. Mr Herbert was half-way through before I could discern what he was driving at.[61]

Without waiting for his next column to be pulled, Williams wrote immediately to the Director-General, Frederick Ogilvie, offering his views on 'some fundamental issues' of concern to 'independent' critics:

> I try to conduct my column according to the caption which now appears at the top of 'Critic on the Hearth' page – 'Comments on BBC programmes by independent critics'... I have sincerely adhered to the rule you and Ryan imposed on me some time ago, not to criticise Front Bench speakers; and I am willing to consider any further modifications you wish to make about the rules of the game... Without these restrictions I am doing my best to fulfil the tradition which this page of *The Listener* has built up: viz. a tradition of serious broadcasting criticism which is not to be found anywhere else in the British press. Nothing has encouraged me to continue in this difficult job more than the opinion so widely held inside and outside the BBC that, because of its integrity, 'Critic on the Hearth' is a feature of considerable value to broadcasting... I am a reasonable and realistic person. I could still conduct my column with as much honesty as these foul times afford if some one would make it his business to tell me where 'policy' may cut across criticism. Thus, if someone, through [Alan] Thomas [Editor, *The Listener*], had told me to keep off Herbert I should have kept off Herbert. As it is I am once more put in the stocks for an offence which is none of my fault.[62]

The combined logic and charm of that letter are quintessential Williams. The Director-General's reply assured Williams that his article had not breached any BBC rules or conventions and that he was not under criticism for any lack of discretion or good taste. Williams was greatly relieved and lost no time in acknowledging that relief:

> I am grateful for your assurance about a matter which had been worrying me very much. My only fear now is lest you should feel I have been bothering you about nothing. But I take that Listener column so seriously that I hate the risk of any misunderstanding about it, and this time I was certainly left with the impression that I had unwittingly displeased someone at Broadcasting House.[63]

A few months earlier, in December 1940, Williams had launched a major attack on the BBC's Forces Programme, (a service aimed directly at an armed-services audience). He was by then actively involved with the War Office, helping to maintain the morale of servicemen and women in the desperate winter of 1940. Having set out his credentials, he accused the programme of offering the troops a relentless diet of mindless listening matter, without the balance of more serious and thought-provoking material:

> ***The Stuff to Give the Troops?***
>
> One afternoon last week I found twelve soldiers listening to an item they had deliberately picked out from the Home Service Programme on 'Art and the Nazi'. Although it was not one of the talks planned for Listening Groups...it set the twelve soldiers off into one of the most thorough and intelligent follow-ups I have ever listened to: and they seized no less upon the limitations of our democratic usages than they did upon the despicable values of the Boche approach to art.
>
> Here, in a nutshell, was a novel and very important revelation of war-aims, and in the presentation of war-aims this country has a lot of leeway to make up, especially in the Army, where (as I know from experience as well as from hearsay) the troops are very willing to be enlightened upon the issues of the war... So why does a programme labelled For the Forces fail to provide even a modest proportion of the kind of talk which sets the troops talking and thinking? ... The thoughtful soldier resents that assumption on which the Forces Programme seems to be based.[64]

It took several years of sustained effort by Williams and others to persuade the BBC to convert the lightweight Forces Programme into serious-minded Forces Educational Broadcasting. In 1944, before the war ended, Williams was invited to chair the Inter-Services Committee on Educational Broadcasting. On publication of its report, the BBC went ahead with the formation of a special Services Educational Unit. If he did nothing else in the field of broadcasting, this was an achievement of which Williams could be justifiably proud. BBC education broadcasters of today owe an enormous, unacknowledged debt to Williams' pioneering work on educational broadcasting, in war and peace.

Williams' final broadcasting review in *The Listener* appeared in June 1944. In a characteristically gracious and witty farewell, Williams saluted his readers, the broadcasters, and the BBC back-room teams who had made it all possible. That final review deserves to be quoted here in full:

> ***Curtain***
>
> I have occupied this column for more than five years, and with this piece I take my leave of *The Listener*... I have been permitted in this column to say what I think about policies and programmes, even when my observations were a flat contradiction of BBC dogma and belief. Once and only once, in my lengthy tenure of 'The Spoken Word' have I been hauled over the coals by the Corporation; and even then, I am glad to say, no timorous half-measures were taken. They slung me out of the paper for a week – and subsequently allowed me to repeat, many times over, far worse misdeeds than the one for which I was brought to book. In thus applauding the BBC for the liberty of comment it allows to the

> three 'Critics on the Hearth' I am doing no more than endorse the opinion of many readers who have corresponded with me on these matters. This page could easily become the resort of 'house-boys', a conventicle of BBC stooges committed to the glorification of their lords and paymasters. My own experience has been that they give one so much indulgence that, from time to time, one feels compelled to say a good word about them.
>
> What has made it equally worthwhile to keep on writing this column so long has been the attitude of those who read it. The problem of the critic is to strike a balance between amusing his customers and giving them something to think about. I could never resist a bit of verbal somersaults, and my cartwheels in this column have rarely, I am glad to say, passed unnoticed. But in my voluminous correspondence with readers the emphasis has always been upon doctrines I advocate rather than upon the witticisms I have used in advancing them. I realise, beyond a doubt, that *The Listener* is read by people who have a deep concern for broadcast values and methods, and not by people whose listening is a mere surge of emotional response. It is the constructive reader who puts ideas into the mind of the critic, and many of the themes which I have sought to interpret week by week have been proposed to me by those who read this paper. Their contribution has, I hope, made this column a forum rather that than a pulpit.
>
> My final pleasure in these five years has been the forbearance of those wireless professionals on whom I have enjoyed so much target-practice – that is to say, the Talks Department. There have been occasions, rare and widely-spaced, when I fancied that my pleas had been attended to at their staff conferences. But on a more modest reckoning I am content to believe that they have grown to accept my good faith without altogether appreciating my good sense. Somehow or other, you observe, I have landed on the wrong foot in what I intended to be a graceful goodbye. But there's no time to adjust the posture.[65]

That review marked Williams' final appearance as a regular contributor to *The Listener*, but it was not the end of his reviewing career. Having completed a five-year stint as Critic of the Spoken Word for the BBC, he then spread his wings by reviewing a much wider range of programmes. *The New Statesman and Nation* gave him the opportunity to contribute a column of general radio and television criticism every other week during 1945/46. He later transferred to *The Observer* for a few more months as television critic. By then, his life as a regular reviewer was over; his life as a figure of the first rank in British cultural life was about to begin.

Appendix to Chapter Eleven:

The Voice of the Masses – The Listener, *6 July 1939*

One broadcast last week made radio history in a double sense – the discussion of 'Re-armament' by a quartette of working-men. Its more amusing but less important significance was that it went on with the salutary job which Bernard Shaw began thirty years ago – the introduction to polite society of popular but forbidden language. Eliza Dolittle in Pygmalion put one of these super-charged words on the map; and it was a man from Bow, appropriately and alliteratively, who introduced its first cousin the other night.* And, by all that's wonderful, the member of the quartette who used it was called – if I am not confusing the four – he was called Kipling! We have been told since that he used the word because he was carried away by a 'mood of spontaneity'. Could there be a better assurance of the integrity of this discussion than this – that the debaters were so completely at ease in the studio and so engrossed in the topic that one of them used the language which, as we all know, is the clear and vigorous speech of everyday use? Those listeners who seem to have been scandalised by the incident were barking up the wrong tree; they mistook honest speech for a deliberate and offensive audacity. So much for that.

But this broadcast moved me by its complete integrity. As a technical performance at the microphone it could scarcely have been worse. It was a shapeless discussion. The performers kept getting in each other's way, as unskilled amateurs do on the stage; they seemed to have run dry more than once. That didn't matter a bit, for they gave us something far more valuable than a neat and shapely exhibition of broadcasting skill. Theirs was the eloquence of the inarticulate. They stumbled about among unaccustomed turns of phrase until, every minute or two, one or other of them managed to put over in some vivid phrase the convictions of the class for which they spoke. The whole dialogue was the kind you can hear in a Bermondsey pub any night; or if you prefer it in pastiche, the kind O'Neill wrote for such a play as 'The Hairy Ape'.

They got down to the very bone of working-class feeling in what they had to say about Re-armament. It didn't matter how oblique and irrelevant their argument became for behind it all was an honest and stubborn testament of their faith and experience. And when they threw off the unaccustomed effort to make a nice water-tight argument of it their words came out surely and triumphantly. 'We've let too many countries down lately'. Or 'The masses pay for the war before it comes and the masses pay for the war when it's over'. They managed above all to express the biggest of the working-man's dilemmas. He knows there are things he will defend and die for; but he also knows he will probably pay an exorbitant price for his patriotism – 'I broke an apprenticeship to go to the last war and afterwards I couldn't get a job'. He is willing to serve his turn in the militia, but he doesn't like his mother going on short commons for six months. He will put his back into munition-making but he doesn't relish industrial conditions in which 'he's merely a number in a factory: he ain't a human being'. Between them they revealed those qualities which make the British working-man as vital a raw material in any plan of re-armament as the steel he works: his endurance, his sense of justice, his supple and incorrigible humour. If their evidence is representative of the spirit of Bermondsey and Bow – and I have never listened to more convincing witnesses – there's nothing wrong with the morale of the working-man.

To my mind the BBC has never rendered a more valuable national service than when it gave these four men the air to speak, in their own words and their own way, the sentiments of their class. It is no new thing to hear on the wireless the more-than-average working man, their warrant officers so to speak, who have learned the niceties of debate in some kind of adult education or social service. Here at last was the real rank-and-file, the proletarian foot-slogger saying his piece out loud – with his cap on. We must hear him again.

* "Yeh – that's bleeding right – thirty bob a week jobs, that's about it".

William and Gertrude Williams, out on the town, 1970s.

Sir William and Professor Lady Gertrude Williams attend a Mansion House dinner.

Twelve: Art adviser

> Before I could say any more my first visitor had arrived. This was Sir Robert Witt, who came to tell me that anything I did must be attributed to the National Art Collections Fund; he was immediately followed by Sir Eric Maclean, who came to tell me that, whatever I did, I must have nothing to do with the National Art Collections Fund. I was fully launched on my new career.
>
> *Kenneth Clark, on taking over as Director of the National Gallery in 1933.*

Bill Williams was a fortunate man, endowed with exceptional reserves of physical, intellectual and emotional energy. Other men were content with one career; Williams had six or seven. Other men were exhausted by one important project; Williams often ran several concurrently. Despite Treasury objections, he contrived to defer his retirement from the Arts Council until 1963, when he was sixty-seven. At that age, most men are glad to take things a little easier. Not Bill Williams. Before leaving the Arts Council, he had secured two new appointments that kept him gainfully employed for the next five years.

From his early days in Manchester, when he first entered the city's art galleries, Williams had enjoyed looking at paintings, drawings and sculpture. His first great passion was English literature but his second great love was the visual arts. Both loves remained with him throughout his life. If literature was his metier, art was his refreshment. As his friend and confidant, Dr Thomas Jones, is said to have once remarked: 'Great artists are not merely decorators, they are the creators of civilisation'.

Williams devoted the final years of his career to consolidating his earlier work – that of promoting 'art for the people'. His renewed involvement with painting, sculpture and art of all kinds enlivened his old age. But it also continued his life's work of introducing 'ordinary people', less visually aware people, to the enjoyment of great art. How could that be achieved in a mass society, increasingly in thrall to a rampant, commercial, international 'pop culture'? Perhaps there were lessons from across the Atlantic.

New Society for 4 April 1963 included Williams' review of *The Public Happiness*, a new book by August Heckscher, White House consultant on the arts:

> Mr Heckscher's diagnosis of the malady is admirable, but his remedies are debatable. He proposes as a curative treatment for citizens of an affluent society a massive scheme of public works calculated to make them art conscious [and] to bring the visual arts into

> our daily lives. The trouble about this sort of advocacy is that it so easily leads to the measurement of culture in terms of how many people went to look at the Mona Lisa on its recent visit to Washington and New York, or how many of us went to gawp at the Leonardo in the National Gallery... But these short cuts are fallacious. The Kennedys may well make the arts respectable and desirable, but a fashion or a habit will not touch the source of our malaise. If there is a cure, it will be a slow and painful one. In the last resort, the people who get the 40 hour week must learn the hard way what to do with their leisure, and that process is as arduous and prolonged as the time it takes a coral reef to build itself up... A sudden, voracious and artificial passion for the arts is not the remedy for our restlessness and our sense of impotence.[1]

Once again, Williams reverts to the parable of the grain of mustard. Slow, patient, educative nurturing will achieve more in the long run than any 'sudden, voracious and artificial passion for the arts'. Over the next five years, Williams transformed that philosophy into practical action through his work with the National Art-Collections Fund (now known as the 'National Art Fund') and the Institute of Directors.

Shortly before his retirement from the Arts Council in June 1963, Williams accepted an invitation from the Earl of Crawford and Balcarres, Chairman of the National Art-Collections Fund (NACF), to become its Secretary. The Fund came into existence in 1903 through the efforts of a small group of art lovers, concerned to preserve and improve Britain's national art collections, by acquiring great art treasures that might otherwise be sold abroad and lost to the nation. Using the income from member subscriptions, donations and bequests, the Fund did not itself buy works of art but made selective grants to national and provincial galleries and museums to help them acquire such works by topping up local funds. Paintings, drawings, sculpture, furniture and precious objects of importance were thus retained as part of Britain's national heritage.

Between 1913 and 1953, England had lost to overseas buyers no fewer than forty-five paintings by Rembrandt, forty by Rubens, twelve by Holbein, and ten by Velasquez, amongst others. Those that left the country included Gainsborough's *The Blue Boy*, Holbein's portraits of Henry VIII and Edward VI, and van Eyck's *Three Maries at the Sepulchre*. Those losses occurred because, whilst the world price of art objects soared during the first half of the 20th century (and increased even faster in the second half), Fund membership and subscription income slumped catastrophically in real terms. Amongst works of art saved for the nation were the *Rokeby Venus* by Velasquez, and the great Leonardo Cartoon in the National Gallery, for which an urgent appeal by the National Art-Collections Fund, at short notice, raised no less than £450,000, or one-third of the total amount of £1,200,000 needed to retain it in Britain.[2]

In 1903, when the Fund had 550 members, the annual subscription was set at one guinea (i.e. twenty-one shillings, or the rough equivalent of £65 in today's purchasing power) and remained at that level for the next sixty years. With an annual income of around one thousand pounds, the Fund's early ambitions were appropriately modest: it made only limited grants and saved comparatively few works of art. Membership grew steadily before and after the First World War to a peak of 12,500 in 1930. By the outbreak of the Second World War in 1939, membership had dropped to just over 10,000. During the war, it fell to less than 6,000 but recovered in the post-war period to around 10,000. There was no question of the Fund collapsing but its scope was severely constrained by the lack of adequate resources. As with the national economy, it took considerable time for the Keynesian revolution in economic thinking and management to take effect. Eventually the State and Local Authorities intervened to make up some of the deficit in private investment in the arts.

Williams took up his post as Secretary of the NACF in October 1963, for an initial period of three years. Brought in to refresh the Fund with new ideas, he soon identified the Fund's key weaknesses and came forward with proposals for reform. Under the chairmanship of Lord Crawford, Chairman of the National Galleries of Scotland and a Trustee of the British Museum, the Fund's Executive Committee included the ubiquitous Sir Kenneth Clark; Professor Sir Anthony Blunt, Surveyor of The Queen's Pictures and Director of the Courtauld Institute; and a dozen other distinguished art historians, practitioners and gallery specialists. They gave immediate backing to Williams' ambitious plans to improve the NACF image, raise its national profile, increase membership, and boost income.

Williams' specific proposals included re-locating the Fund's headquarters from its dingy headquarters, in the basement of the Wallace Collection, to a new, attractive and accessible location, where the provision of a 'showcase' would allow members of the general public to view new acquisitions. Williams also hoped to establish branches of the Fund in provincial cities, so increasing corporate membership, and to give NACF publications a new look with wider readership appeal. Other men might have seen this as a challenge that demanded their full-time attention. Williams agreed to tackle it on a half-time basis.

To assist him in this work, Williams brought with him from the Arts Council a young woman who acted as his secretary and personal assistant. Born in Luton in 1929, Joy Maudie Lyon was the daughter of a hat manufacturer. She trained as a musician and graduated from the Royal College of Music but soon recognised that she lacked the temperament for a successful career as a professional musician. She therefore settled for secretarial work at the Arts Council, where she could still feel part of the contemporary arts scene. We may reasonably infer from subsequent developments that she not only assisted Williams in his demanding workload but that she brought a burst of late vitality and happiness into Bill Williams' life. In 1960, whilst still at the Arts Council, he dedicated his edition of Thomas Hardy poems to her. She was his close companion for almost twenty years, collaborated with him in most of his final projects, and played a dramatic role in the events surrounding his death.

Williams and Lyon worked well together. Within a few months of arriving at the NACF, Williams had made his mark. Reporting on the Fund's work during 1963, Lord Crawford told the 61st Annual General Meeting, on 10 June 1964, that Williams was 'our main acquisition this year':

> We welcome our new Secretary, Sir William Emrys Williams, who, as you know, was for many years Secretary-General of the Arts Council, to which his contribution was outstanding, and who has his finger in more pies than almost anyone else. We are delighted, proud, and very fortunate that he has joined us.[3]

Williams had precious little time to rescue the Fund from further financial decline. He set about his task with characteristic energy and enthusiasm, exploiting his wide range of contacts, and using the full force of his personality to bring about the changes he thought necessary. His impact on the NACF was immediate, wide-ranging and long lasting. In the 1965 issue of *Review*, the Fund's annual report to members, and the first for which he was responsible, Williams introduced his own column of 'Notes and Comments'. He used that platform to report on past activities, to comment on major acquisitions, to acknowledge significant donations and bequests, to publicise forthcoming events, such as overseas visits, but above all to try out new ideas and suggestions for boosting membership and generally to ginger up the membership. The rest of this chapter chronicles his more significant contributions to the NACF, as reflected by documents in the Fund's archives.

In his first 'Notes and Comments' for May 1965, Williams challenged the suggestion that official patronage of the arts had eclipsed the private patron. Public subsidies to the arts in 1964 from central and local government were still modest, amounting to less than £4 million annually, with a further £1 million from charitable trusts and corporate donors. The only other source of income was the paying public. In 1964, the Arts Council gave Covent Garden a grant of some £800,000 towards its running expenses, but the public paid over £1 million at the box-office. In short, the aggregate contribution of private patrons was bigger than ever before:

> This is surely a healthy condition, and not only on financial grounds. It is good for the arts that many thousands of individuals should feel and express their concern for their nourishment, for it is a concern which has far more than a cash value.[4]

Williams reminded members that the Fund's primary function was to assist galleries with their acquisitions by offering timely 'topping-up' of local funding. To that end, the Fund needed to increase membership, subscription income and donations. Between 1962 and 1964, membership income had increased by £5,000 and donations by nearly £6,000:

> These are encouraging figures, but we want to improve on them. We appeal for more support not because we are a declining body but because we are an expanding one. The cost of works of art increases year by year, and the needs of our public collections do not diminish.[5]

He made three bold suggestions for immediate implementation: first, that from 1964, the annual subscription for new members should be increased to £2; second, that *existing* members should increase their subscriptions *voluntarily* to the same amount; and third, that every existing member should seek to recruit one new member, and so double overall membership. *Apollo*, the famous international art magazine, had just produced a special number on the work of the NACF. As an inducement to recruitment, Williams offered a free copy of *Apollo* to any member who used it to recruit one new member.

On his appointment as Secretary to the Fund, Williams made a personal donation of £10 to the Fund – and made sure it was publicised, as an example to others. But it was behind the scenes, in his daily dealings with staff, in his regular discussion with Lord Crawford, and at monthly meetings of the Fund's Executive Committee that he made his most important contributions. During his first year as Secretary he persuaded the Committee to accept a bold target of doubling membership; of arranging ambitious overseas visits for members and friends to galleries and museums in Italy, with later planned visits to Spain, Germany and the Soviet Union. He used his continuing influence at Penguin Books to secure Allen Lane's personal commitment to underwrite the entire costs of a Penguin Special on *The Anatomy of Patronage*, which would include an account of the work of the Fund. Most ambitious of all, Williams proposed the launch of an appeal for a £1 million Development Fund to meet the cost of urgent and unique projects – such as the great Leonardo Cartoon – that lay outside the scope of the normal budget. The impact of Williams' ideas was clearly reflected in successive annual reports to Fund members.

At the general election of October 1964, just one year after Williams' appointment, Labour was returned to power, replacing Ted Heath's Conservative

Government. Prime Minister Harold Wilson's incandescent rhetoric on the 'white heat of the technological revolution' did not detract from his concern for wider quality of life issues. He established an entirely new and fashionably named 'Department of Education and Science', and appointed Jennie Lee, widow of Aneurin Bevan, as the country's first ever 'Secretary of State for the Arts'. Her appointment was widely acclaimed as a triumphant and long-overdue break with the tradition of government non-intervention in the cultural life of the nation. In the words of Michael Foot:

> She was, in effect, Britain's first 'Minister for the Arts', and thereafter no government could abandon the idea.[6]

There was however a negative aspect to her appointment. It emerged at the 62nd Annual General Meeting of the Fund, held on 9 June 1965, when Lord Crawford welcomed the Minister's appointment with these words:

> The Government has published its 'Policy for the Arts'. I opened it with great excitement, but this evaporated when I found that the great museums and galleries for which we work, which house the nation's collections, and which are the essential basis of any appreciation of the fine arts, are hardly even mentioned. This is profoundly disheartening.[7]

Even more disturbing was the radical change imposed by the government on the organisation of all the national museums and galleries. Before the change, they were all responsible in England (in Scotland and Wales the position was somewhat different) directly to the Treasury. In future, they would be responsible to the newly created Department of Education and Science, which meant they were one degree further removed from those responsible for government spending. As Lord Crawford bitterly complained:

> In London it was possible to go to the right man in authority at the Treasury, to put the case for more money (or whatever it was) directly, and always to get sympathetic understanding – and sometimes even what one wanted... All the museums will now have a Ministry placed between them and the Treasury. That has been decided, and there is nothing we can do about it but to make the best of a bad job, and also to thank a long series of Treasury officials, whom I have bullied for thirty-five years, for their patience, support, and, on the whole, for the wonderful help that they have given to our work.[8]

In his 'Notes and Comments' for May 1966, Williams reminded members that the Fund welcomed applications for grants from museums and galleries throughout the country. It would always give sympathetic consideration to requests to meet a proportion of the cost of any works of art they wished to purchase. The major national collections in London and other great cities consisted in the main of works of art beyond the financial reach of most local galleries, whose purchase grants remained 'pathetically paltry'. They could seldom find more than a few hundred pounds from their own resources, so were obliged to set their sights at a modest level. By contrast, the cost of acquisitions by national collections tended to be much higher which meant that the Fund generally paid out larger amounts in grants to national institutions. Williams took particular pleasure, therefore, in reporting that, during his first full year in office, the Fund had assisted no fewer than twenty museums and galleries outside London, so helping to produce a more equitable balance of expenditure between metropolitan and provincial collections – a balance which Williams had failed to achieve during his time at the ACGB.

Williams' major and continuing concern, however, was the inescapable need to increase Fund membership and income. With a large proportion of older members, the society lost more members each year than it gained. How could the Fund enlarge its support? The cost of publicity – press-advertising, professional fund-raising, postal appeals – was unaffordable and the results unpredictable. A charity devoted to art was significant only to a minority, as compared with such good causes as animal welfare or cancer research. The Fund had less than 11,000 members compared to the National Trust with fifteen times that number. Williams said he would rejoice if the Fund achieved one-fifth of that total (i.e. 30,000 members). In Williams' view, personal recruitment was the best way to achieve that target. If each member could persuade one friend to join the Fund, it could double its subscription income and greatly increase its effectiveness. To that end he produced an attractive new illustrated pamphlet, explaining the Fund's aims and activities, to assist in bringing in new members – another example of Williams applying his skills as a writer and publicist for the benefit of the Fund.

At the Fund's 63rd Annual General Meeting, held on 22 June 1966, the guest speaker was the Right Honourable Jennie Lee MP, Secretary of State for the Arts – a publicity coup quietly engineered through Williams' personal contacts. In her address, the Minister freely acknowledged that her revolutionary appointment had caused 'a certain amount of alarm and despondency' amongst those in artistic circles who believed that it could only lead to political pressure on the arts:

> Artists might be told what subjects they should paint and producers told what plays they were to stage. Such fears were soon seen to be mythical. The function of the post to which she had been appointed was clearly defined. She was the advocate of the arts to her ministerial colleagues, and one of her vital duties was to make the best possible bargain with the Treasury. It was her business to be advised by expert bodies such as the Arts Council... On the basis of the policies and the budget of these advisers, she had then to secure the best possible support, both moral and financial, from the Government.[9]

In thanking the Minister for her encouraging speech, Lord Crawford said her enthusiasm for the arts and her work to date deserved warm praise. He had never been slow to chastise the previous Conservative Government, and to press them hard, especially for the increased gallery and museum grants. When, at last, the grants were substantially raised three years earlier, he had been quick to praise them. When the present Government did as much in that direction he would praise them too.

At the same meeting, Sir Trenchard Cox, Director of the Victoria and Albert Museum, expressed the great pleasure the Fund had given members by the visit it had organised to the Soviet Union. He thanked Sir William Emrys Williams and everyone concerned in making it possible for members to see the historic treasures of the Soviet Union:

> Never have I been offered a more beautifully organised or more enjoyable journey in all my professional life.[10]

In his 'Notes and Comments' for May 1967, Williams reported some £41,000 in grants over the previous year, slightly less than half of which had gone to London galleries and slightly more than half to galleries outside London – a pleasing result for the man who had sought to boost local galleries by promoting *Art for the People* more than thirty years earlier. But his efforts to recruit new members were grievously disappointing. In a society sixty-three years old, there was inevitably a high mortality rate. The Fund had lost no fewer than 800 members over the previous year. He renewed his appeal to existing supporters to bring the Fund's work and needs to the attention of their friends. He went on to note that 300 members had taken part in the Fund's arranged visit to the Soviet Union in 1966, which had been an emphatic success. Members were generously welcomed and entertained by the USSR-Great Britain Society:

> The most memorable of the social gatherings was, perhaps, the one at which a most eminent Scottish member of the Fund rose to his feet and recited a poem by Robert Burns, the famous proletarian poet. The Russians could no more understand the language than most of our party could, but they cottoned on enthusiastically to the symbolic significance of the performance. Libations were copiously dispensed.[11]

For the 64th Annual General Meeting of the Fund, held on 14 June 1967 in the Great Hall of St Bartholomew's Hospital, Williams invited his old friend, Sir Kenneth Clark, a member of the Fund's Executive Committee, to give the formal address. Sir Kenneth Clark – 'Kingfisher' or 'K', as Williams called him – graciously accepted. Following his established practice of breaking the rules, Clark offered a pungent and idiosyncratic view of the Fund's activities from the inside. Having ranged far and wide in his comments on the current state of the arts in Britain, he brought matters nearer home by reminding those present that the Fund did not initiate gifts:

> It acts solely to requests of museum or gallery directors. This is a great limitation on its power of choice and I must say that there are times when we are sorely tempted to tell the directors that we could find them something better of the same kind for half the price. I think that our limitation is a wise one and for the guidance of future applicants who may be present I wish to distinguish between those proposals that give us pleasure and those which fill us with gloom and embarrassment. I think we are always grateful to a director who is not too much influenced by fashion. I know how difficult it is for him, because local enthusiasts will certainly wish their director to bring home the kind of prizes that they have seen illustrated in art magazines... Nevertheless, I think a director would do well to risk a little unpopularity and to look attentively at what is unfashionable, because only in that way can he still get things of high quality. The proposals that make our hearts sink are second-rate examples of a fashionable genre, either old or new. If they are old, they are sometimes in very poor condition and it is difficult for us to explain to a disappointed director why we have been unable to support him.[12]

In his 'Notes and Comments' for May 1968, Williams posed an uncomfortable question: *What Good is a Guinea?* Of the Fund's 10,000 members, no fewer than 6,000 had increased their subscriptions *voluntarily* to the new minimum rate of £2; but 4,000 had still not done so. A guinea a year did not go far in running the Fund. He earnestly pleaded with as many as possible of those who were paying a sub-standard subscription to raise it to £2. He knew the Fund had some devoted supporters, living on fixed incomes, who could not afford to give more than a guinea, and he hoped they would remain members. But the figure of 4,000 must include a majority who could afford to increase their subscription to £2, and he hoped they would immediately do so. He barely disguised his impatience in the anecdote that rounded off his column:

> There seems to be among us a miniscule minority who set too much store on the 'privileges', private views and soirees we provide. One subscriber wrote to say he found he could not get to the last soiree at the Royal Academy and so he was returning his (free) invitation card and would we, he added, send him the refund?[13]

The 65th Annual General Meeting of the Fund, held on 14 June 1968 at The Mansion House, welcomed the Right Honourable the Lord Mayor of London, Sir Gilbert Inglefield, who addressed the meeting on the subject of civic virtue in the arts. Sooner or later, he argued, one must decide how to assess the greatness of a community or a country. When a country's artistic output was at its height, then that country was at its greatest. The City of London was not populated by a group of reactionary fuddy-duddies. It was 'a corporation of energetic fellows, whom age could not wither nor custom stale, who organised that place as efficiently, indeed more so, than their opposite numbers in any town or city in the United Kingdom'. He cited the examples of the Barbican Centre and the proposed Shakespeare Theatre to show that the City had at last become a real patron of the arts. But the public in general remained deeply indifferent to contemporary arts. Britain had great architects, painters, sculptors and composers in abundance, yet we had developed an almost morbid fascination for the past:

> Seldom before has England been more virile in world affairs or the creators of its native arts more vigorous. Never before had patrons, civic or individual, been more timorous. I reverence deeply all manifestations of great art. But art, sometimes great, is being produced today, and in preserving what must at all costs be preserved, discrimination must be exercised. The wheat must be sifted from the chaff. I regard the National Art-Collections Fund as a benevolent kennel of vigilant, discerning, indeed I hope savage, watchdogs. Long may they continue to bark and, if necessary, bite to preserve our heritage.[14]

In his 'Notes and Comments' for May 1969, Williams presented a table showing twelve years of the Fund's growth from 1957 to 1968. It revealed that whilst grants to galleries had more than doubled over that period, annual subscriptions had failed to keep pace with expenditure. The Fund's membership had reached its peak of 12,500 in 1930. Between 1939 and 1962 it never rose as high as 10,000. From 1962 it had remained fairly stable at a figure comfortably above 10,000; but it seemed to be stuck in that region. Although he was reluctant to admit the fact, all his efforts to increase membership had so far failed. He had therefore produced a new poster showing forty-nine details taken from works of art that the Fund had helped the national collections in London to acquire. He wanted members to display the poster in public places where it would attract maximum attention – public libraries, universities, art centres and the like, in the hope that it would help to bring in new members.

At the 66th Annual General Meeting of the Fund, held on 11 June 1969 in the Drapers' Hall, the Right Honourable Lord Goodman, Chairman of the Arts Council, addressed the meeting. He began by paying tribute to 'your remarkable Secretary, an old friend of mine, whose talents I have come to know and respect over the years'. The Fund was itself a remarkable organisation, which made a massive contribution to a task of primary importance to society – namely, to make 'more available to more people the artistic treasures of this and other nations, so that people can come to know what constitutes beauty, what constitutes art, what makes civilisation':

> It is for this reason that the work you are doing seems to me of such vital and crucial importance. It is for this reason that we must go on making things available not in a controversial spirit, nor in a debasing spirit, but simply in the spirit of amassing human knowledge. If a man, young or old, is determined to arrive at his conclusions without study, without knowledge, and without regard to the treasury of human knowledge available to him, that is his own silly fault, but we must not be in the position of being open to the reproach that we did not give him the key to that treasury of human knowledge, and it is on this account that associations such as yours, selflessly and with dedication, doing the sort of work which provides with great difficulty the mammoth sums of money that your splendidly drawn annual accounts have indicated to me are found year after year with obviously increasing difficulty in times of increasing taxation and estate duty and the like – societies such as yours are doing work of unequalled importance.[15]

If some members attending the AGM had difficulty following every twist and turn of that splendidly serpentine sentence by one of the keenest forensic brains in the kingdom, they had no difficulty in applauding Lord Goodman's concluding remarks:

> I believe the notion that has been engendered in some quarters that London is splendidly endowed with museums and art-galleries and theatres and the like, and that the regions are horribly deprived is an extremely artificial and false notion. I do not know of any city that is more pitifully endowed than London as to the greater part of its geographical area. If you took a motor car and drove over the greater part of London you would not find a single theatre, art-gallery, or intellectual activity serving any one of the millions of people who reside in those drab colourless areas.[16]

Whether by good fortune or by Lord Goodman's influence behind the scenes, Williams was able to announce in his 'Notes and Comments' for May 1970 that the Fund had enjoyed a record year. For the first time in its history, grants exceeded £53,000, compared with an average of £30,000 in each of the previous ten years. More important was the fact that 60 per cent of that total had been given to galleries outside London. But membership still hovered stubbornly around the 10,000 mark:

> We must recognise that a body devoted to securing works of art for the nation will only appeal to a small section of public interest. It lacks the emotional appeal of the many charities involved, for example, in the fight against famine, or the care of paraplegics. But even when such relevant considerations are taken into account there must be many more than 10,000 people in this country who feel some concern for our public art collections and would like to see them fortified by new acquisitions. The immediate question is: can these 10,000 double their number? And the immediate answer is: by selective methods, yes.[17]

Williams made no secret of his disappointment at failing to double membership during his first six years as Secretary. It must nevertheless have come as a complete surprise to many readers of the *Review* to find this short paragraph at the foot of Williams' column:

> Our Secretary, Sir William Emrys Williams, resigned at the end of the year and has been succeeded by Miss Mary Shapland who has been with the Fund for seven years. Sir William however remains with the Fund, having accepted the invitation of the Executive Committee to become our Hon. Appeals-Secretary.[18]

No further explanation followed, either immediately or later. Members may have assumed that Williams had resigned for personal reasons, rather than on grounds of age or ill health, for he still appeared vigorous and in full possession of his creative faculties. In fact, his health was no longer robust. In October 1970, he was due to celebrate his 74th birthday. He had suffered a mild coronary in 1965, followed shortly after by cancer of the throat for which he had received extensive cobalt therapy treatment. On 16 November 1969, Williams received a hand-written note from Lord Crawford, which effectively brought his appointment to its natural end:

> We thought it right to 'regularise' your position, as I told you, at our last meeting. Two-thirds of the second triennial period of your appointment have already passed. So what we decided was – if you agree – that we should ask you to continue till the end of the period to which we should have appointed you, if we had noted the passage of time!
>
> This means, I think, that you have now about a year to run? Please let me know the date. And please let us know in very good time to take any decision, say some 6 months before the end of this second triennium. It is awful how time has flown! And during this time, we have been very lucky and very happy to have you looking after us.[19]

For six years, from 1964 to 1970, Williams never worked more than half-time as Secretary of the National Art-Collections Fund. The balance of his time was devoted to a quite different post as Art Adviser to the Institute of Directors (IoD) – which, by coincidence, was also established in 1903. Throughout the events described above, Williams' working life as Secretary of the NACF was interwoven with that as Art Adviser to the IoD – a two-sided relationship that seems to have benefited both bodies.

In 1953 the Institute had appointed Sir Richard Powell MC and Bar, director of a substantial building company and a merchant banker, as its first Director-General. That appointment was itself a major innovation, an indication of greater professionalism in the world of business and commerce. Amongst the many changes introduced by the new Director-General was an annual IoD conference at which a distinguished practitioner – in a field unconnected with industry or commerce – was invited to address conference on a subject of his own choosing.

At the Institute's 1963 conference, Sir Kenneth Clark, former Director of the National Gallery and Slade Professor of Fine Art in the University of Oxford, explored 'some of the ways in which commerce and industry can have a fruitful relationship with the arts'. His address was well received and stimulated a great deal of interest.

Within a few months, the Institute's monthly publication, *The Director*, for May 1964, announced the establishment of an Arts Advisory Council to serve those of its members who wished to have some stake in the arts. By October 1964, well over 2,000 members had registered their names with the Arts Advisory Council. A specially commissioned 20-page booklet – *Investing in the Arts* – explained the objectives of the programme as

> ...putting the relationship between business and the arts into strictly practical terms, to provide answers for the man who is conscious of the agreeable responsibilities of industry, but is uncertain about where to begin. Choosing a picture for the boardroom, getting advice on sculpture or antique furniture, exploring the possibilities of a works theatrical society – these are the everyday problems which the Arts Advisory Council can help to solve. And what better guarantee of impartial, seasoned advice could there be than the names of those on the Arts Advisory Council? They are all pre-eminent in their own sphere. Sir William Emrys Williams CBE, the distinguished former Secretary-General of the Arts Council, agreed to act as the Institute's General Adviser on this programme.

In the same publication, Williams explained why he had agreed to serve as General Adviser on the programme:

> I welcomed this assignment for two reasons. One is that I wholly share Lord Clark's conviction that business and the arts might develop a fruitful alliance of benefit to them both. My other reason is that for over 39 years I have been closely associated with him in many endeavours and experiments designed to make the arts more accessible and acceptable.

Among the services offered by the Arts Advisory Council were:

> 1. Advice on buying or commissioning pictures, sculpture, applied art, antiques, etc, whether for board-room, foyer or canteen.
>
> 2. Advice on developing works-activities: how to set up music, dramatic, operatic societies, or how to organise an arts festival.
>
> 3. Advice on party-visits of employees to concerts and plays in the neighbourhood.
>
> 4. Advising firms objectively and confidentially on the merits and prospects of institutions which appeal to them for support.
>
> Amongst the luminaries who had agreed to serve on the Advisory Council were Lord Clark, Sir John Rothenstein, Henry Moore, Sir Arthur Bliss, Sir Adrian Boult, Lord Olivier, and Peter Hall, Dame Ninette de Valois and Dame Marie Rambert.[20]

The booklet posed two fundamental questions: Why should businessmen bother about the arts? What responsibilities or obligations does a firm have towards the town in which it operates? Williams sought to persuade sceptical as well as sympathetic company directors and businessmen and women to become more actively involved in the arts of all kinds, and in many different ways.

Williams' essential argument was three-fold. First, the arts already played an important part in business. Industry and commerce used the arts, in varying degrees, in designing, creating and selling themselves and their products. Second, the arts, notably the visual arts, were used to embellish and humanise places of work. Third, many firms were already 'good citizens' in their local communities and patrons of the arts by sponsoring music, drama and opera. Business could help further in the arts by organising industrial concerts, by sponsoring productions of drama and dance, Music and Youth, the National Youth Orchestra, or a local arts festival; or by becoming 'Friends' of the arts (e.g. by supporting such voluntary bodies as the National Art-Collections Fund). Amongst companies already actively supporting local art activities were: Rolls-Royce, Whitbread, Fisons, Esso, Shell Mex, Harvey's of Bristol, Wedgwood, English Electric, Oxo, Hovis, Littlewoods, Schweppes, Heinz, ICI, Martin & Rossi, and Gillette.

Williams noted that, as far as the arts were concerned, many parts of Britain were as arid as the Sahara. Cumberland, for example, was one such desert until Sir Nicholas Sekers, textile designer and manufacturer, created an oasis there. With his keen interest in drama and music, and his wish to contribute to the local community, he had set about building the Theatre at Rosehill, which served as a flourishing focal point for the arts in and around Whitehaven.

Over the following six years, from 1964 to 1970, Williams produced a succession of pamphlets, bulletins and newsletters, reporting new developments and business initiatives in the arts; publicising visits to overseas art collections and galleries; promoting special exhibitions and displays by local arts associations and others. An illustrated booklet – *How to Commission a Portrait* – written by Williams and published in October 1964, offered company directors advice on all aspects of the tricky business of commissioning a portrait for themselves or their company. One article by Williams explained the work of the Artist Placement Group, whose function was to place artists in industry, not as decorators but as technicians, working alongside other company employees on their own lines of research and development. Many talented artists had already entered into experimental partnerships with leading industrial firms, to their mutual benefit. Another article described the work of young artists who were producing very large pictures, often using spray paint, to decorate big empty spaces, such as factory walls, industrial canteens, airports, railway stations, hospitals and schools. In 1969, a special exhibition of 'Big Pictures in Public Places' was organised by Williams at the Royal Academy, with the approval and support of the Arts Council.

In 1968, the Estimates Committee of the House of Commons conducted a prolonged enquiry into the financing of the arts in Britain. Many witnesses, including the Arts Council, Local Authorities, and others, were summoned to explain and justify the use of public funds. The enquiry also considered other current sources of patronage, such as the contributions of industry and commerce. As Art Adviser at the Institute of Directors, Williams was invited to elaborate his views – the only witness asked to do so. The Estimates Committee published its 600-page Report ('The Arts and Industry') at the end of 1968.

In the course of his evidence, Williams explained that, despite his best efforts over twelve years as Secretary-General of the Arts Council and his five years as Art Adviser to the Institute of Directors, he had found it impossible to obtain precise figures on the extent of industrial and commercial assistance to the arts. He had nevertheless formed an opinion on the volume of industrial patronage which took many different forms: for example, prestige advertising in arts brochures and programmes; welfare programmes in company operatic, drama and art societies; contributions to arts festivals in local communities; private trusts and foundations which gave generously to the arts; industrial and commercial commissions for sculptures, paintings, mosaics, murals, engraved glass, applied art, etc. At a conservative guess, he estimated annual industrial patronage to be worth between £1 million and £1.5 million; plus industrial purchases of art at around £1.5 million. In addition, many art students became commercial artists, many composers wrote music for films, documentaries and television; and writers were in regular demand to prepare scripts and presentations. In short, the value of industrial patronage and their role as consumers of the arts was grossly under-rated. As patrons alone they did far more for the arts than Local Authorities, and came an easy second to the Arts Council.

From the autumn of 1967, Williams chaired a high-level, two-year inquiry into the condition of the theatre in England and Wales, commissioned by the Arts Council. Members of the 30-strong inquiry team included such theatrical luminaries as Lord Bernstein, Hugh Beaumont, Sir John Clements, Richard Findlater, Frank Hauser, John Mortimer, Kenneth Tynan and Max Rayne, as well as two Members of Parliament. The final report, *The Theatre Today in England and Wales* (1970), written by Bill Williams, assisted by Joy Lyon, his Research Assistant, stated the problem in unequivocal terms:

> The theatre in Britain today presents a confusing spectacle. In London...the situation causes a good deal of concern... Outside London the theatre of private enterprise is on its last legs, physically run-down and morally disheartened... What are the causes of the dry-rot which afflicts the commercial theatre? Are they eradicable? What remedies or

> palliatives exist? Can the theatre continue as a mixed economy of private enterprise and public ownership? Is the subsidized theatre justifying the public money it receives? Should subsidies be also given to the ailing commercial sector? Is there a case for Government investment (rather than subsidy) in the theatre?[21]

The Main Report, published early in 1970, and widely acclaimed at the time, recommended twenty 'first priorities' for immediate adoption, including the need to maintain substantial grants to the National Theatre and the Royal Shakespeare Company; assistance for specialised touring companies and major repertory companies; an increase in subsidy from both central and local authorities; and a more ready and rapid response by both national and local government than in the past, 'to an artistic and social need which is keenly and increasing felt by a large and enlightened section of the community'.

In an important Memorandum of Dissent, one member of the committee, the Conservative MP Sir Harmar Nicholls disagreed with the Main Report's 'underhand disparagement of the commercial theatre, as compared with the treatment it gives to all subsidized theatres'. But he went on to pay a handsome tribute to Williams' conduct of the enquiry:

> The wealth of information and constructive advice contained in the Main Report confirms without question that the Arts Council are to be commended for instigating this Enquiry. It also confirms the wisdom of inviting Sir William Emrys Williams, CBE, DLitt, to preside over the Enquiry and, as it transpires, to become the author of the Main Report. He was painstaking, courteous and unequalled in his knowledge of theatrical history, as well as being well versed in contemporary Art forms and in the thinking of the Arts Council itself.[22]

In June 1970, shortly before his seventy-fourth birthday, Williams made his final appearance as Art Adviser to the Institute of Directors, where he was warmly thanked for his services. After a well-earned holiday, he retired to his home in Buckinghamshire to resume work on his memoirs of fifty years' continuous involvement with the arts. Seven years later he was dead. *The Times* published a generous obituary. But it was left to the retired Director-General of the Institute, Sir Richard Powell, to pay this exceptional personal tribute:

> I first came up against Bill Emrys Williams in 1942 when, as a dedicated junior officer in the Brigade of Guards, I was training my guardsmen, as I thought, to win the war. An order came from the War Office, to say that all company commanders should spend at least two hours a week lecturing their men on 'current affairs'. I remember thinking at the time that 'they' hadn't got their priorities right, and pushed on with teaching 'the object of all bayonet instruction'. This seemed more important than learning about politics from Bill's weekly ABCA pamphlets. Quite a few of us thought the same – and how wrong we were! Bill – and it was he alone who initiated this curious and unique experiment –

gave tens of thousands of fighting men an exciting glimpse of what they were fighting for. What England would be like after we'd won. Those who survived, lived to be deeply grateful to this great educator.

It wasn't until I asked him to become Director of the Institute [of Directors'] Arts Council that I got to know him as an individual – and to love him for the warm, generous, witty, brilliant fellow that he was. And what a 'trouble taker'! Nothing was impossible! Whatever one put to Bill was met with enthusiasm, searched into and made the best of. The value of the work he did for the Institute was incalculable – and, in a way, not dissimilar from what he achieved for the Army. He brought education and culture to a band of men and women who all too often confined their interest to their day-to-day business affairs.

Together, he and I planned – and he executed – a score of exciting exhibitions of paintings, sculpture and gold and silver craftsmanship. Perhaps the most ambitious and successful of these was the occasion when he persuaded Sir Thomas Monnington, the Royal Academy's president, to lend us the Academy itself for an exhibition entitled 'Big Pictures for Public Places'. He organised cultural tours, too; magnificent in their scope, to Italy, Russia, Austria and Brazil, where we saw the finest works of art – ancient and modern – that the world has to offer. I can see him now giving his inaugural talk to the not undistinguished group of company directors setting off for Leningrad – erudite, modest, funny and, in spite of the slight, but endearing stammer, always and supremely articulate.

Bill Williams had a crusading zeal to spread knowledge of the Arts to those whose cleverness was restricted to their own professional field. He succeeded in his crusade. And his lovable enthusiasm brushed off a bit on every one who was lucky enough to sit at his feet.[23]

Grenville Paddock, Haddenham, Buckinghamshire – Bill Williams prunes his roses, c1968.

Bill and Gertrude relaxing at Grenville Paddock, 1970s.

Epilogue: In perspective

I look forward to the move to Haddenham next spring, and I want at last to get the writing done. I want to do my invented autobiography, *In Perspective*, which won't be about me but about the things I've been involved in.

W E Williams to Allen Lane, 20 September 1966

David Riesman, the American sociologist, described two contrasting personality types: 'inner-directed' and 'other-directed' people – those with a mission in life, with their own inbuilt motivational clockwork; and those more reliant on external stimuli. Bill Williams was unquestionably an 'inner-directed' personality – a man with a mission. As noted earlier, he often used the vivid metaphorical language of the missionary to describe his work and his ambitions. In a letter to Dr Thomas Jones in 1943, Williams wrote:

One way and another I am convinced that the most vital necessity for Adult Education after the war is that it should come down off its high horse and fraternise with the *really* Common Man. Most of my own work has been in the more primitive areas of adult education – and after the war it will be even more so. I may thereby, possibly, fulfil my adolescent desires to be a missionary in Darkest Africa – and fulfil them more usefully than if I had become a colporteur on the Congo! [1]

Here is clear evidence of a mature man, looking back on his early life, who long nourished an ambition to do some good in the world – perhaps as a Congregational Minister, perhaps as 'a missionary in Darkest Africa'. Notices of Williams' death, as well as later tributes to his life, clearly bring out the strong missionary strain in his make-up, as the following examples show.

Of his pioneering editorial work for Allen Lane at Penguin Books, *The Times* obituary noted that

...Lane was not a publisher with a mission like Joseph Dent. Williams was. In creativity, in originality, in scope, he surpassed Dent. The arts, sciences, classics, politics, sociology, not only in Britain but throughout the world – Williams was anxious to spread knowledge and comprehension about them all.[2]

In creativity, in originality and in the broad sweep of his interests, Williams was 'a publisher with a mission'. That crusading spirit is clearly identified in the generous appreciation by Sir Richard Powell of Williams' work at the Institute of Directors. He noted that Bill Williams had 'a crusading zeal to spread knowledge of the Arts to those whose cleverness was restricted to their own professional field. He succeeded in his crusade'.[3] The determined nature of that crusading spirit was echoed by Robin Huws Jones, who knew both Gertrude and Bill Williams over many years. He captured Bill Williams' character in three carefully-chosen adjectives: 'brilliant, sullen and ruthless'.[4] He went on to explain how that ruthlessness manifested itself: 'Billy was a complex character with robust hatreds and a certain fierce ruthlessness – without which he would hardly have achieved all that he did, I suppose'.[5] In his 'alternative history' of the Arts Council, Richard Witts underlines that reputation for ruthlessness. He describes Williams as 'a resolute operator, a bit of a bruiser' – but without offering specific evidence.[6]

Peter Cox, Secretary to the wartime Arts Inquiry at Dartington, provides an entertaining example of Williams' 'fierce ruthlessness'. In April 1956, the Arts Council announced the decision to do away with regional directors, as a cost-cutting exercise. Those most closely involved protested vigorously:

> After some rather acid correspondence between the Secretary-General and Colonel Perry Morgan, Sir William agreed to receive a deputation himself on February 17 and six of us set off for London... Sir William kept us waiting for quite a time but once seated he set off with immense Welsh volubility to justify the Council's decision and tell us how well we would fare under the new dispensation [until] the marvellously dramatic moment when Perry Morgan, feeling he could stand this flow of talk no longer, suddenly interrupted the Secretary-General and said *"Sir William, please stop. We have come here to do the talking."* It was a perfect tactic and allowed each of us to make the contribution we had hoped to make... We came reeling out of that meeting into the wintry sunshine of St James's Square having brought to birth the first regional arts association in the UK.[7]

In a letter to the author, following up that story, Peter Cox wrote:

> I guess WEW is quite a person to be writing about – I can hear him breathing volubly down your neck to be sure that you had got him right and were doing justice to all his achievements.[8]

Sir Hugh Willatt, another close observer of Williams at work, offers further evidence of his tactical skills – or cunning – in pursuit of his objectives:

> He was an effective plotter not only because of tactical skills and what some people called cunning. There was also a warmth and a quite genuine response to people and to ideas, and this combined with his other qualities enabled him to get his way and get things done.[9]

Enthusiasm, ruthlessness, cunning: these words all suggest a 'driven' personality, but Williams did not conform to the pattern of the compulsive personality and he was certainly no fanatic. His determination to achieve his objectives was always informed by a keen, moderating intelligence. Those who encountered him, in one of his many public roles, recognised a considerable measure of charm to set alongside his 'fierce ruthlessness'. In his entry for Bill Williams in the *International Biography of Adult Education*, Edward Hutchinson observed that:

> His early working experience, communication skills, and personal charm helped him to enlist essential support for new projects.[10]

Sir Richard Powell emphasises the effects of Williams' warm personality on everybody he met and worked with:

> It wasn't until I asked him to become Director of the Institute [of Directors'] Arts Council that I got to know him as an individual – and to love him for the warm, generous, witty, brilliant fellow that he was. And what a 'trouble taker'! Nothing was impossible! Whatever one put to Bill was met with enthusiasm, searched into and made the best of... And his lovable enthusiasm brushed off a bit on every one who was lucky enough to sit at his feet.[11]

Professor Boris Ford, who worked closely with Williams as Deputy Director of the Bureau of Current Affairs, remembered him as 'a man of quite extraordinary intelligence, charm and imagination'.[12]

In the Penguin Collectors' Society edition of *Educator Extraordinary*, Gertrude Williams' memoir of her husband, Clare Morpurgo, Allen Lane's daughter, paid this glowing personal tribute to her late godfather:

> Although I did not know him at all as the brilliant and persuasive educator and administrator – something of his charm and integrity also touched my life... Certainly I was blessed with an extraordinary godfather in Bill Williams...he could not have helped me more... How many people, how many lives must he have encouraged and helped in this way? Thousands I suspect.[13]

In her scholarly account of *Penguin Modern Painters*, Carol Peaker makes repeated reference to Williams' 'visionary spirit', his 'intellectual breadth', and his 'passion for adult education'. But she also notes the gentler side of his personality – his 'affection' and 'deep paternal fondness' for Eunice Frost.[14]

Anthony Field, who served as Williams' Director of Finance at the Arts Council, describes him as 'the best Secretary-General ever':

> He had a fantastic brain, and he'd use it to help you see the flaws in your own reasoning. Some found this intimidating, but it was always constructively offered.[15]

In his warm tribute to Williams, on the occasion of his retirement from the Arts Council, Wyn Griffith said this:

> Sir William Emrys Williams gave himself to the promotion of general interest in spreading the riches of the world of Art, in making it possible for ordinary people to share in the privileges of the few...he brought with him a continuity of purpose, strong convictions, an understanding of people, the gift of speech – and, rare in a Welshman, the gift of silence... The three Chairmen under whom he served would, I am sure, agree that his unflinching devotion, his stubborn persistence in pursuit of the best, his sanity and his

> integrity, are largely responsible for the success the Arts Council has achieved during his stewardship.[16]

'Strong convictions', developed early in his life, combined with 'a fantastic brain' and a steely 'continuity of purpose', were precisely the qualities which took Bill Williams from his modest origins in a Welsh carpenter's family to the very top of the cultural tree in Bloomsbury, Mayfair and St James's. Those qualities were not devoted to self-aggrandisement but, as Wyn Griffith indicated, to 'the promotion of the general interest' – thereby 'making it possible for ordinary people to share in the privileges of the few'.

Allen Lane knew Williams better than any other man. He recognised two characteristics in his friend and collaborator which they shared – 'a good streak of idealism and a certain toughness of purpose'.[17] Williams was rather more brutal in his own assessment of Lane, in whom he identified a degree of 'moral cowardice' and 'a decided streak of sadism'.[18] Williams had his detractors, but no one ever accused him of displaying either of those particular character defects.

Bill Williams was certainly an unfaithful husband – though he was hardly unique in that. Women held a special fascination for him, but he was neither a serial adulterer nor a compulsive womaniser. From what we know, he remained 'faithful' to Estrid Bannister, his mistress for the middle twenty years of his married life. How far Gertrude Williams colluded in her husband's infidelity is an open question: we simply do not know whether she decided to tolerate it, knowing that 'her Billy' would never totally abandon her for another woman; or whether she did her best to conceal her grief at his betrayal. There were episodes in Gertrude's middle life that suggest she found it difficult to cope with Billy's extra-marital affairs. There seems little doubt that she was fully aware and mostly tolerated his long involvement with Estrid Bannister. There were times, however, when she seriously doubted Billy's devotion and made herself ill with anxiety on that score. According to her late nephew, John Crammer, a psychiatrist, she sometimes experienced severe anxiety and was obliged to seek professional help. In that context, it is interesting to note that, shortly after Lord (Jeffrey) Archer was sent to prison for perjury and perverting the course of justice, his wife, Mary Archer, was asked about her husband's infidelity. Her reply was diplomatic and to the point: In modern marriage, she said, loyalty is more important than fidelity. In her more rational state of mind, Gertrude might well have agreed. But even if she colluded in her husband's long-standing relationship with Estrid Bannister, Gertrude could neither comprehend nor condone his suspected infidelity with Joy Lyon, whom she had trusted and welcomed into her own home.

Many commentators have remarked on the warm, generous and considerate side of Williams' personality – the side that appealed so much to women. Yet those tributes cannot altogether erase the impression that he was also an arch-manipulator of people and situations – not to promote his career, and rarely to line his own pocket. He was no moral paragon, but neither was he notably corrupt, venal or grasping – as shown by his modest financial demands on Allen Lane at Penguin Books. If Williams had a major character flaw, it was his determination to exploit every beneficial opportunity that came his way. In short, he was a sublime opportunist. But there is no evidence that he used people simply as means to his own ends, or refused to accept personal responsibility for his actions. In that respect, he was quite unlike Allen Lane, who regularly opted out of difficult situations:

> Many good men came to grief through Allen's summary and capricious decisions... When he made up his mind, sometimes hastily, to sack someone on the staff, he often flinched from breaking the news himself and delegated a senior colleague to fire the victim. This habit was not due to any feelings of delicacy but wholly and visibly due to a lack of moral fibre.[19]

If compelled to encapsulate Bill Williams' complex, many-layered, and sometimes contradictory character in a single phrase, we might describe him in paradoxical terms as an ethical manipulator. Like most people, Williams was a bundle of contradictions. On the one hand, he was a man of considerable intelligence, charm and warmth, as his admirers generously testify. On the other hand, he was a man of great enthusiasm, energy and determination – even ruthlessness – as his critics have not failed to point out.

Despite his frailties and contradictions, Bill Williams was highly disciplined and focused in his working life. His projects in one field – adult education, for example – complemented and overlapped his work in other fields – such as broadcasting, or the Pelican publications of Penguin Books. To maintain his exceptional productivity in so many different fields, over so long a period, he conducted his life in fairly segregated compartments. Those who worked alongside him in one field often knew little or nothing of his work in other, closely-related fields. In a letter to the author, Professor Boris Ford confessed that, despite working closely with Williams in ABCA and at the Bureau of Current Affairs, he never really got to know what else he did:

> Although I worked with Bill Williams for a number of years during and after the war, I don't believe I am competent to answer questions about the factors that led him into promoting the arts... I know nothing of his work at the Arts Council: he kept his multifarious commitments in separate compartments.[20]

That thematic segmentation of his working life, coupled with his intense powers of concentration, enabled Williams to get through an enormous workload, to engage simultaneously in highly divergent projects, and to work to very tight deadlines. During the Second World War, for example, whilst directing the Army Bureau of Current Affairs for the War Office – a more than full-time job – he was also running his circulating exhibitions on behalf of CEMA, and still advising Allen Lane on the wartime publications of Penguin Books. Yet he somehow found time and energy to prepare and present a daily news bulletin for schools for the BBC and to write his weekly column of radio criticism in *The Listener* for five consecutive years. Such dazzling virtuosity and commitment to the task in hand is found in very few individuals.

In *Penguin Special*, his 2005 biography of Allen Lane, Jeremy Lewis describes Williams as 'endearingly idle, a man for the broad brushstrokes who left others to fill in the details'.[21] That is not simply a misjudgement but a gross distortion of the truth. Throughout his working life, Williams was a stickler for detail who ensured that the final touches were correct in everything he did – from his fastidious appearance to his carefully crafted prose. That was both his policy and his practice at the British Institute of Adult Education in the 1930s (where he wrote, edited and administered *Highway* and *Adult Education* for the WEA); with his hands-on management of the Army Bureau of Current Affairs during the war; throughout his thirty years with Allen Lane; and later during his twelve years with the Arts Council. Endearing he may have been – but certainly not idle.

Lewis goes on to say that Williams 'wanted to write, but his contribution to the printed page amounted to little more than brief introductions to collections of essays or anthologies of poetry'.[22] Yet the British Library catalogue shows Williams as sole or joint author of twenty books, as well as editor of a large collection of booklets, monographs and pamphlets, to say nothing of his voluminous journalism. Lewis seems not to have done his homework.

Above all, Lewis's biography of Allen Lane fails to bring out that whereas Lane devoted his entire adult life to making a success of Penguin Books – which he did brilliantly, with Williams' considerable help – Williams always had larger, nobler, more wide-ranging objectives in his sights. As Beatrice Warde has pointed out: 'We are all used to thinking of the Penguin adventure as an instance of broadening out, *the democratization of culture in our generation*'.[23] Unlike Lane, Williams was passionately engaged in a crusade to democratise British cultural life: hence his lifetime's work – with the WEA, the British Institute of Adult Education, *Art for the People*, ABCA, CEMA, broadcasting, *The Listener*, UNESCO, the Arts Council, the

National Art Collections Fund and the Institute of Directors. As this biography has shown, Williams was a far more interesting, important, energetic and productive man than Allen Lane ever pretended to be.

Williams' productivity was in part attributable to the sublime opportunism already described. He regularly exploited his contacts and connections in one field to help him achieve his objectives in another. His long-standing friendship with Kenneth Clark is a case in point. Clark was appointed Director of the National Gallery in the summer of 1933, when still only twenty-nine years old. When Williams was appointed Secretary of the BIAE, in 1934, he was already thirty-eight. The two men met and the personal chemistry worked. They became friends, and collaborated on projects of joint interest for more than forty years. Having recognised that their broad aims were not merely compatible but closely convergent, they developed a highly symbiotic relationship, exploited to their mutual advantage. In 1934, Williams involved Clark in his first *Art for the People* exhibitions and enjoyed his unstinting support. As Carol Peaker points out, Clark possessed a gift for 'presenting culture in an entertaining and edifying way'. Williams quickly recognised that gift and ensured that Clark's work reached the widest possible readership through Penguin Books. Carol Peaker goes on to explain: 'What Clark had above Williams, however, was a network of friends and acquaintances and connections that ranged from Queen Elizabeth to Vivien Leigh',[24] connections which Bill Williams was only too ready to exploit to advance his own aims.

Both men were midwives at the birth of CEMA in December 1939. They worked together closely at CEMA and later at the Arts Council. Clark backed Williams against Keynes during various crises over the Council's circulating exhibitions, which Williams organised. In 1942, in the darkest days of the Second World War, Williams persuaded Allen Lane to invite Clark to edit *Penguin Modern Painters*. In 1953, as Secretary-General of the Arts Council, Williams was instrumental in ensuring that Clark succeeded Pooley as Chairman of Council. In return, Clark brought influence to bear on the Treasury to raise Williams' salary. Such mutual back-scratching – a norm of organisational life – helped the wheels go round and got the job done. But there was never any suggestion of corruption or of nepotism.

Williams was unquestionably an ambitious man. He pursued both personal and organisational power – not for its own sake but to bring about beneficial change. In early manhood, he developed a clear vision of a more equal and less privileged society and worked tirelessly throughout his life to push people and policies in the direction he favoured.

Morpurgo claims that Williams soon abandoned the socialist values of his youth and progressively embraced a bourgeois lifestyle in company with the sybaritic Allen Lane.[25] Both men were certainly fond of their food and drink. They regularly conducted business meetings over an expense account lunch or dinner in Soho; and Williams makes frequent reference to his enjoyment of wine in his letters home to Lane.

Richard Witts has similar uncomplimentary remarks about Williams:

> Fervently socialist in the thirties, he drifted languidly to the centre and by degrees a certain snobbery pervaded his outlook. He had married Gertrude Rosenblum, who became professor of social economics at London University, and they lived a full, elevated, society-parading life together.[26]

That criticism lacks credibility and is backed up by no substantive evidence. Williams certainly mellowed politically in his later years, but he was never more 'fervently socialist' or radical in his politics than the average Hampstead Fabian. He was never a member of a political party. As he pointed out in October 1970: 'I had no political affiliations whatsoever, a form of virginity which remains unsullied'.[27]

Unlike his friend Kenneth Clark, there was no class snobbery in Williams' make-up. Gertrude Williams was eventually awarded a professorial title, but only on the eve of her retirement. If Bill Williams enjoyed the pleasures of London life at Covent Garden and the Café Royal, if he was something of an epicurean in his tastes, he was a puritanical epicurean. He certainly seems to have enjoyed his mature success, but his lifestyle was never vulgar or ostentatious. He always dressed well but he lived modestly, with an ever-present sense of financial insecurity. He never altogether abandoned the austere tastes and puritan work habits of his youth. Williams was a man who was constantly seeking opportunities to do good – and who often did well in the process.

By exploiting his many contacts and social connections, Bill Williams came to occupy some of the most prestigious positions in British cultural life. By the middle years of the 20th century, as Morpurgo notes, Williams had become 'Britain's arch-dispenser of patronage, much courted by artists, and consulted day in and day out by civil servants and ministers on issues connected with government support for the arts'.[28] Professor Robert Hewison describes him as 'one of the most powerful cultural mandarins in the country'.[29]

Above all else, Williams was a brilliant journalist and publicist, who did much of his best work to tight deadlines. But he was also a cultural strategist who refused to look for or judge results prematurely, in the short run. The parable of the grain of mustard-seed permeated his thinking precisely because it stressed the need to take the long view when judging any significant undertaking. The reason Williams reverted to that parable so frequently when reviewing cultural projects was his absolute conviction that the product of steady, incremental growth was always better than accelerated, hothouse growth, which often produced spectacular but artificial results, followed by early collapse:

> Among the few things in this world which cannot be created by mass production is an educated community or a dependable political electorate. Nor is a short superficial educational clean-up in adult years going to put right the mischief already wrought by the imperfect and misdirected ideals which still prevail in our primary school system.[30]

If we judge Williams' life's work by his own criterion of slow and dependable growth as the ultimate test of enduring value, what do we find? For over thirty years, from 1919, when he became a London schoolmaster, until 1951, when he resigned as Director of the Bureau of Current Affairs, including his war years at the Army Bureau of Current Affairs, Williams committed his life to adult education, in the broadest terms. How successful were his efforts? What remains of enduring value?

If we compare the priority given, and the resources devoted, to adult education in 1920 and 1950, there were highly significant changes, brought about by four principal factors: *first*, the changed attitude towards adult education following the First World War; *second*, the influence of the British Institute of Adult Education in the inter-war period; *third*, the experience of ABCA during the Second World War; and *fourth*, the impact of the 1944 Education Act and its pervasive influence in giving access to higher education to a much wider social mix. At least two of those four factors were strongly influenced by Williams' work and personality. If we then compare 1950 with 2000, there is no question that Williams' early vision of universal access to high quality, lifelong learning has become the conventional wisdom. Education for the privileged few is being slowly and belatedly transformed into lifelong learning for all. Politicians of every stripe and hue now endorse lifelong learning – even though governments continue to give precedence to the vocational needs of younger professionals over the cultural pursuits of a rapidly ageing population.

The current rhetoric of social inclusion and diversity resonates with Williams' insistence on the need to make lifelong learning accessible to the widest possible range of people. The part played by Williams in advancing that project has been largely overlooked. Yet there is a direct organic link between his work at the British Institute in the 1930s and that of its successor body, the National Institute of Adult Continuing Education (NIACE), Britain's leading national campaigning organisation for lifelong learning.

Williams was largely responsible for – and was himself a prominent member of – the influential committee of enquiry into 'Adult Education After The War', commissioned by the BIAE and chaired by Viscount Sankey, President of the Institute. Its Report, published in 1945, included amongst its conclusions this short paragraph, which bears all the hallmarks of having been drafted by Williams:

> The Committee noted that the most important contribution of the [adult education] movement has been to insist that education is not a discipline for youth only. It does not close at any particular age but is a process which should continue to the last moment of our lives. There is no 'finishing' school. It is as important to exercise the mind as to exercise the body.[31]

Bill Williams always insisted that education was 'not a discipline for youth only'. What's more, he clearly understood the distinction between education and learning – namely, that *education* is essentially formal, top-down, academic and authoritarian. It is largely what others require of us, provide for us, or thrust upon us. By contrast, *learning* is essentially informal, bottom-up, heuristic and democratic – what we do for ourselves, when we take charge and transform our own lives. Whatever its current deficiencies and distortions, lifelong learning now figures largely in very many people's lives. It has evolved from the efforts of Williams and others who worked alongside him in the 1920s, '30s and '40s to transform what was once called 'compensatory education' into 'adult education' or 'continuing education' and thence into lifelong learning for all. For that reason alone, Williams' life's work in pursuit of cultural democracy through lifelong learning should be remembered, saluted and celebrated.

Closely linked to that crusade for inclusive lifelong learning, and running parallel to it, was Williams' sustained campaign over many decades to make the arts more accessible to ordinary people. In 1934, when he launched *Art for the People*, British governments disdained any involvement in the arts, other than providing modest grants to a small group of national galleries and museums. Patronage of the arts was largely in the hands of the rich and the powerful, with a few charitable institutions, like the National Art-Collections Fund, playing a minor, useful role. By contrast, in the Soviet Union, Nazi Germany, Fascist Italy and Falangist Spain, the State exploited official art in support of political ideology. In the United States, in the depths of the depression of the mid-1930s, the Federal Government put thousands of artists, actors and musicians on the federal payroll, as part of President Franklin Roosevelt's New Deal for national economic recovery.

At the outbreak of the Second World War in 1939, there was still massive indifference to State support for the arts in Britain. The war enabled Williams and others to change all that. The urgent need to sustain civilian morale in the first gloomy winter of the war prompted Dr Thomas Jones and others to secure the first State financial support for the arts in Britain. Despite some vociferous protests and much sniping criticism from the philistine Left and Right, there has been no turning back. The Arts Council emerged at the end of the Second World War, and continues to provide the substantial basis for public arts funding in Britain.

Williams played a crucial personal role in that remarkable story. Dr Thomas Jones openly acknowledged that the original inspiration for CEMA came from Bill Williams' pioneering *Art for the People* exhibitions of 1935.[32] John Maynard Keynes, Chairman of CEMA, and later of the Arts Council, expressed his warm gratitude to Williams 'for the indispensable pioneer work which he had performed for them'.[33] The continuing role of the Arts Council in British cultural life – albeit in significantly modified form – is perhaps the single most important and visible monument to Williams' work to promote popular access to the arts.

Penguin Books was founded by Allen Lane on a tiny budget in 1935. Within one year, Bill Williams was deeply involved in nurturing its first tender growths. His special responsibility was the creation and development of the Pelican list, which was immensely influential in the years immediately before, during, and after the Second World War. His major contribution to Penguin Books, however, came in the 1950s and '60s when, as Editor-in-Chief, he profoundly influenced the whole range of Penguin publications. Today, a score of paperback publishing houses pay silent tribute to Williams' collaboration with Allen Lane in the critical and commercial success of Penguin Books over the past seventy years.

Bill Williams was a skilful exponent of the English language, in both speech and writing. To advance his causes, to promote his projects, and to achieve his aims in broadcasting and radio reviews, at education conferences, in editing and administration, in cultural committees, at editorial conferences, in adult education classes and in ABCA and BCA discussion groups, Williams never lost his appetite for advocacy, for rhetoric, or the art of persuasion through free and open discussion. Wyn Griffith praised him for his exceptional 'gift of speech – and, rare in a Welshman, the gift of silence'.[34]

Williams fervently advocated free and open discussion as the essential nutrient for cultural democracy. In everything he tackled, Williams was an unashamed pluralist. He understood that no single individual or group had a monopoly on truth – in religion, in politics, or in the arts. He was implacably opposed to fanaticism and extremism: hence his pursuit of gradualism, of slow, evolutionary change, of piecemeal social engineering rather than sudden, revolutionary change, of discussion and compromise rather than imposed solutions – in education, in the arts and in the wider society.

In his wartime work for the War Office, Williams insisted that company commanders must lead their men in the informed discussion of current affairs – because they would be better soldiers if they understood the values they were fighting to defend. In the words of the philosopher A C Grayling, the purpose of discussion is

> ...to help people recognise and appreciate alternative points of view, to show why it is important to approach others in a spirit of respect, to demonstrate how essential it is to think about the consequences of one's choices and actions, and to give an insight into the great possibilities that arise for people when their lives are lived in a setting of sympathy and tolerance.[35]

Those were exactly the visionary aims which Bill Williams embraced early in life and which he spent the rest of his life helping to realise. If British public life today is characterised by free and vigorous open debate over a wide range of social and political issues, it is thanks in significant part to Williams' pioneering work in promoting and practising open discussion. In adult education classes, in the pages of serious daily newspapers and weekly magazines, in radio phone-ins, and in television discussion and debating programmes, we see the realisation of Williams' dream: the right to free speech, the crucial exchange of ideas through peaceful discussion, and the toleration of many different points of view.

The final and most important question to be asked when assessing the life of any public figure must be this: What significant and long-lasting difference did that person make to the life of the nation? Some individuals make a highly significant *immediate* difference but its effects are short-lived; others make a *longer-lasting* difference, but of small significance. By contrast, William Emrys Williams' many contributions to the life of the nation were both highly significant and long-lasting. For it is not too much to claim that, by his own, direct, hands-on interventions, Williams transformed British culture in the 20th century and beyond. Of course, he could not – and did not – do it alone; but without him it almost certainly would not have been done at all.

Williams began work as an enthusiastic schoolteacher and WEA lecturer who gave his students their first taste of good literature. He put adult education on the map and virtually invented lifelong learning – though he seems never to have used that precise term – through his pre-war work at the British Institute of Adult Education. During the war, he created and directed ABCA (the Army Bureau of Current Affairs) for the War Office, so ensuring that British servicemen and women understood what they were fighting and dying for. He shaped the reading habits and filled the bookshelves of a generation through his thirty-year editorship at Penguin Books. He wrote or edited more than twenty books, including five anthologies of English poetry. A pioneering broadcaster in the 1920s and radio critic in the '40s, he was also an accomplished magazine editor and journalist. He took art to the people, a decade before it became fashionable to do so. As a result, he inspired wartime CEMA (the Council for the Encouragement of Music and the Arts) and its post-war successor, the Arts Council of Great Britain, where he served with distinction as Secretary-General for longer than any of his successors. In his seventies he resumed his earlier work of promoting the love of art through his dual role as Secretary of the National Art-Collections Fund (NACF) and as Art Adviser to the Institute of Directors (IoD).

Above and beyond those achievements, Bill Williams' most distinctive and long-lasting contribution to British history is probably best reflected in the much higher levels of democratic participation throughout the cultural life of Britain, as compared with the elitist society in which he grew up. His singular vision and the aim he most consistently pursued was to make Britain a cultural democracy – a participative democracy in which every citizen had access to more than material goods and services, important as he knew them to be. In the words of the anonymous author of his *Times'* obituary:

> The diversity of his interests was matched by the singleness of his aim: that the people should be given the facilities to learn, to know, to appreciate, and to enjoy.[36]

Williams never lost faith in the innate capacity of ordinary people to transform their own lives, given a helping hand. That insistence is the key to understanding Bill Williams' life, his character and his lifetime achievements.

Williams' own life – a story of slow personal growth, of sustained maturity and development, followed by brilliant fulfilment and achievement – provides a luminous example of that capacity amongst ordinary people 'to learn, to know, to appreciate, and to enjoy'. Bill Williams' consistent missionary purpose throughout his adult life was to provide ever-wider opportunities for others to follow his example. We who are his successors and beneficiaries owe an immense and belated debt of gratitude to William Emrys Williams – a man who deserves to be better remembered and to whom full justice remains to be done.

Notes

In editing the late Sander Meredeen's text we have been able to provide completed references in most cases. We would, however, welcome any suggestions, additions or corrections for inclusion in later printings.
p.* = Page reference unknown.

Preface

1. Robert Hewison: *Culture and Consensus: England, art and politics since 1940*, London: Methuen, 1997, p.79
2. Obituary of Sir William Emrys Williams, *The Times*, London, 1 April 1977
3. Nicholas Ridley MP, House of Commons debate on Government Support for the Arts, 27 April 1965, Hansard Column 283.

Prologue: Brandy in paradise

1. W E Williams to Allen Lane, 10 September 1968
2. Robin Huws Jones, interview with the author, February 1998
3. Obituary of Sir William Emrys Williams, *The Times*, London, 1 April 1977
4. Gertrude Williams: *W E Williams: Educator Extraordinary*, London: Penguin Collectors' Society, 2002, p.15

One: A youth in Wales

1. W E Williams: 'The Art of Biography', *The Listener*, 14 August 1935
2. John Worthen: 'The Necessary Ignorance of a Biographer' in John Batchelor (ed): *The Art of Literary Biography*, Oxford: Clarendon Press, 1995, p.227-444, p.241
3. Obituary of Sir William Emrys Williams, *The Times*, London, 1 April 1977
4. Gertrude Williams: op cit, p.16
5. Professor Gwyn Jones, presenting Sir William Emrys Williams for admission to the degree of Doctor of Letters, *honoris causa*, Congregation of the University of Wales, Aberystwyth, 11 July 1963
6. Humphrey Carpenter: *The Art of Literary Biography*, Oxford: Clarendon Press, 1995, p.268
7. Sylvia Bradford in conversation with the author, 22 November 1997
8. Obituary of Sir William Emrys Williams, *The Times*, London 1 April 1977
9. J E Morpurgo: *Allen Lane: King Penguin*, Harmondsworth: Penguin, 1979, p.120
10. W E Williams, letter to Dr Thomas Jones, 4 November 1940
11. W E Williams: *The Craft of Literature*, London: Methuen, 1925, p.3
12. Kenneth O Morgan: *Modern Wales: Politics, Places and People*, University of Wales Press, 1995
13. Gertrude Williams: op cit, p.16
14. ibid
15. ibid
16. Wyn Griffith: *The Welsh*, Harmondsworth: Penguin, 1950, p.36
17. ibid, p.155-6
18. Peter Stead: *Coleg Harlech: The First Fifty Years*, University of Wales Press, 1977, p.44
19. Peter Stead, in conversation with the author, November 1998
20. Wyn Griffith: op cit, p.157-8
21. W E Williams: 'D H Lawrence', *Highway*, June-September 1950
22. Kenneth O Morgan: op cit, p.474
23. ibid

Two: Manchester – the intellectual seedbed

1. W E Williams: 'An Open-Air Geography Lesson', *Manchester Central High School Magazine*, 1912
2. W E Williams: 'Legends of the Welsh', ibid, 1913
3. George Henry Borrow: *Wild Wales*, London: John Murray, 1862
4. Percy Simpson: Entry for Charles Harold Herford, *Oxford Dictionary of National Biography*, Oxford: Oxford University Press, 1949, p.423-4
5. Gertrude Williams: op cit, p.17
6. W E Williams: 'For G' in *The Serpent*, Manchester University Union, 1918
7. W E Williams: *Introduction to D H Lawrence: Selected Poems*, Harmondsworth: Penguin Poets, 1950

Three: Billy and Gertrude

1. John Crammer, in a letter to the author, 16 July 1998
2. Robin Huws Jones, in conversation with the author, February 1998
3. Lancashire Independent College, Annual Report, 1918
4. ibid, 1919
5. Gertrude Williams: op cit, p.18
6. Graham Adams, in a letter to the author, 17 February 1998
7. W E Williams: *Allen Lane: A Personal Portrait*, London: The Bodley Head, 1973, p.48
8. Clyde Binfield, in a letter to the author, 31 October 1998
9. Elaine Kaye, in a letter to the author, 10 November 1998

Four: London – 20 years of adult education

1. Gertrude Williams: op cit, p.19
2. ibid
3. ibid
4. W E Williams: *The Craft of Literature*, London: Methuen, 1925, p.3
5. ibid
6. W E Williams: *First Steps to Parnassus*, London: Methuen, 1926, p.*
7. W E Williams: *A Progressive Course of Precis and Paraphrase*, London: Methuen, 1927, p.*
8. W E Williams: *Plain Prose: The elements of a serviceable style*, London: Methuen, 1928, p.*

9. W E Williams: *George Henry Borrow: Selections chosen and edited by W E Williams*, London: Methuen, 1927, p.*
10. George Henry Borrow: *Lavengro*, London: John Murray, 1851, p.*
11. John Crammer, in a letter to the author, 16 July 1998
12. Robin Huws Jones, in conversation with the author, February 1998
13. Enid Huws Jones, in conversation with the author
14. Gertrude Williams, op cit, p.20
15. Edward Hutchinson, entry for Sir William Emrys Williams in J E Thomas and Barry Elsey (eds): *International Biography of Adult Education*, University of Nottingham Department of Adult Education, 1985
16. Gertrude Williams: op cit, p.21-22
17. ibid, p.22
18. Editorial, *Highway*, December 1929
19. Editorial, *Highway*, January 1930
20. Among those who had promised to write for *Highway* were: Professor Lascelles Abercrombie, T S Ashton, Dr Ernest Barker, H L Beales, Ivor Brown, J R M Butler, M. Carré, Professor Carr Saunders, Professor Charlton, Professor Henry Clay, G D H Cole, Professor G W Daniels, J A Hobson, F L Lucas, Professor L C Martin, Susan Miles, Allan Monkhouse, Professor Leonard J Russell, Sir Arthur Salter, W Olaf Stapleton, R H Tawney, Hugh Walpole, Professor Dover Wilson, Virginia Woolf and Barbara Wootton.
21. W E Williams to Thomas Jones, 12 September 1943
22. E L Ellis: Preface to *TJ: A Life of Dr Thomas Jones*, Cardiff: University of Wales Press, 1992, p.viii
23. Eden and Cedar Paul in *Highway*, May 1922
24. Barbara Wootton: Editorial: 'Education versus Proletcult', *Highway*, May 1922
25. Barbara Wootton: Editorial: 'Ourselves and Others', *Highway*, December 1923
26. R S Lambert: *Highway*, December 1929
27. Gertrude Williams: op cit, p.22
28. ibid, p.23
29. W E Williams: Editorial, *Highway*, October 1934
30. W E Williams: Editorial, *Adult Education*, September 1936
31. W E Williams: 'Guide for the General Reader', *Highway*, December 1936
32. W E Williams: 'A Wonderful Bird is the Pelican', *Adult Education*, June 1937
33. W E Williams: 'The Changing Map of Adult Education' in *Adult Education in Great Britain and the United States*, London: BIAE, 1938
34. ibid
35. ibid
36. ibid
37. W E Williams, in W E Williams and F E Hills: *Radio's Listening Groups: The United States and Great Britain*, New York: Columbia University Press, 1941
38. ibid
39. Levering Tyson: Introduction to W E Williams and F E Hills: *Radio's Listening Groups: The United States and Great Britain*
40. Board of Education Papers, Public Record Office, 1939

Five: Art for the People

1. W G Constable: 'Art and Adult Education', *Adult Education*, Vol. VII, 1934-35, p.8-17
2. British Institute of Adult Education, *Adult Education*, Vol. II, July 1934-35, p.153-4
3. W E Williams: 'Art for the People', *The Listener*, 19 May 1937
4. The full Steering Committee comprised John Rothenstein, Director of the Tate Gallery; Kenneth Clark, Director of the National Gallery; Philip Hendy, Slade Professor at Oxford; Sir Robert Birley, Headmaster of Charterhouse; James Laver, Victoria & Albert Museum; Eric Newton, Art Critic, *Sunday Times* and *Manchester Guardian*; R S Lambert, Chairman of the BIAE's Executive Committee, and W E Williams, Secretary, BIAE.
5. W E Williams: *The Auxiliaries of Adult Education*, British Institute of Adult Education, 1934, p.6-7
6. W E Williams: 'Art for the People' Exhibitions Pamphlet, BIAE, 1943
7. D H Lawrence: 'Pictures on the Wall', *Vanity Fair*, April 1930
8. Meryle Secrest: *Kenneth Clark: A Biography*, London: Weidenfeld & Nicolson, 1984
9. Kenneth Clark: *The Other Half*, London: John Murray, 1977, p.55-56
10. Dartington Hall Trust Arts Enquiry Report: 'The Visual Arts', 1946, p.46
11. For more on this, see Chapter 8, Army Bureau of Current Affairs (ABCA)
12. W E Williams: 'Art for the People' Exhibitions Pamphlet, BIAE, 1943
13. Isabel Swarbrick, letter in *The Listener*, 27 April 1944

Six: Penguin Books

1. Allen Lane to W E Williams, 14 April 1965
2. Jeremy Lewis: *Penguin Special: The Life and Times of Allen Lane*, London: Penguin Viking, 2005, p.58
3. Entry for Allen Lane in *A Dictionary of 20th Century World Biography*, Oxford University Press, 1992
4. Allen Lane, quoted in C H Rolph: *The Lady Chatterley Trial: Regina v Penguin Books*, Harmondsworth: Penguin, 1961, p.141-2
5. Allen Lane to W E Williams, 27 April 1943, cited in W E Williams: *Allen Lane: A Personal Portrait*, London: The Bodley Head, 1973, p.58
6. Andre Carvely, Iqbal A Saddiqui and Ellen Schaengold, letter in *The Times Literary Supplement*, 10 July 1973, quoted by Emil Lengyel: *Krishna Menon*, 1962, cited by Steve Hare: *Penguin Portrait: Allen Lane and the Penguin Editors 1935-1970*, Harmondsworth: Penguin, 1995, p.51

7. W E Williams: *Allen Lane: A Personal Portrait*, London: The Bodley Head, 1973, p.48 et seq.
8. Geoffrey Grigson: 'Shakespeare for Sixpence', *Morning Post*, 20 April 1937
9. Tony Goodwin: 'Carry On Penguins', *Times Literary Supplement*, 22 April 1973
10. W E Williams: 'The Penguin King', *New Society*, Vol. 2, No.51, 19 September 1963
11. J E Morpurgo: op cit, p.116-19
12. Edmond Seagrave: *Ten Years of Penguin 1935-1945*, cited by Steve Hare: op cit, p.52
13. J E Morpurgo: cited by Steve Hare: op cit, p.15
14. J E Morpurgo: *Allen Lane: King Penguin*, p.125
15. Jeremy Lewis: op cit, p.121
16. Professor Richard Hoggart recorded his own memories of Beales: 'I met later two of the three Pelican-inspirers, W E Williams and H L Beales. Years later, visiting Penguin's offices, I remarked that Beales was still alive, at 99. They'd thought him long dead but at once said they'd organise a party for him for his hundredth birthday. He died a few weeks later, just short of his hundred'. Richard Hoggart, 'A Penguin Parade' in *Pelican Books: A Sixtieth Anniversary Celebration, Miscellany 12*, Penguin Collectors' Society, July 1997, p.41
17. H L Beales: 'W E Williams', *Miscellany 12*, London: Penguin Collectors' Society, July 1997, p.21
18. Cited by Linda Lloyd Jones, interview with H L Beales and Mrs Jane Beales, August 1984, Penguin Archive, University of Bristol
19. Helen Gardner, quoted in C H Rolph, op cit, p.6
20. W E Williams: 'Style and Purpose in Literature', *The Listener*, 24 July 1935, p.169-70
21. J E Morpurgo: op cit, p.12-14
22. Richard Hoggart in 'A Tribute to Allen Lane' at a Service of Thanksgiving for his Life and Work, at St Martin-in-the-Fields on 18 August 1970, reprinted by the Penguin Collectors' Society to mark the centenary of the birth of Sir Allen Lane, December 2002
23. W E Williams to Allen Lane, 14 July 1947
24. W E Williams to Allen Lane, 13 September 1954
25. W E Williams to Allen Lane, 10 September 1948
26. W E Williams: *Allen Lane: A Personal Portrait*, London: The Bodley Head, 1973, p.12-13
27. W E Williams to Eunice Frost, 15 February 1973
28. W E Williams to Allen Lane, 10 September 1948
29. A D Peters to W E Williams, 20 September 1939
30. W E Williams to A D Peters, 29 September 1939
31. W E Williams: *A Book of English Essays*, Harmondsworth, Penguin, 1948, cover
32. ibid, 1965 reprint, cover
33. Richard Hoggart: *Life and Times: an Imagined Life*, Oxford: Oxford University Press, 1993, p.89-90
34. W E Williams to Allen Lane, 1 February 1962
35. Allen Lane to W E Williams, 9 February 1962
36. W E Williams to Harry Paroissien, 22 November 1965
37. W E Williams to Allen Lane, 22 August 1960
38. W E Williams to Allen Lane, 23 January 1951
39. W E Williams to Allen Lane, 11 October 1957
40. Richard Hoggart: op cit, p.89-90
41. W E Williams to Allen Lane, 13 February 1950
42. J E Morpurgo: op cit, p.275
43. Allen Lane telegram to W E Williams, 9 July 1955
44. W E Williams to Allen Lane, 9 July 1955
45. W E Williams to Allen Lane, 9 April 1958
46. W E Williams to Eunice Frost, 1 October 1958
47. W E Williams to Allen Lane, 22 August 1960
48. Allen Lane to W E Williams, 26 September 1960
49. Allen Lane to W E Williams, 11 October 1961
50. Allen Lane to W E Williams, 14 April 1965
51. W E Williams to Allen Lane, 20 April 1965
52. W E Williams to Allen Lane, 15 September 1968
53. W E Williams to Allen Lane, 20 September 1966
54. Allen Lane to W E Williams, 4 October 1966
55. W E Williams to Allen Lane, 14 September 1967
56. W E Williams to Allen Lane, 22 June 1968
57. W E Williams to Allen Lane, 24 July 1968
58. W E Williams to Allen Lane, 28 August 1968
59. Allen Lane to W E Williams, 28 August 1968
60. W E Williams to Allen Lane, 3 September 1968
61. W E Williams: 'The Founding Father', *The Sunday Times*, 12 July 1970
62. W E Williams to Eunice Frost, 22 October 1970
63. W E Williams: op cit, p.31

Seven: Bill and Estrid

1. Estrid Bannister Good: *Smørrebrød and Cherry-Blossom*, privately published, 1992, p.74
2. Gertrude Williams: op cit, p.17
3. Estrid Bannister Good: op cit, p.74
4. Joergen-Frantz Jacobsen, in a letter to William Heinesen, 17 November 1935
5. Andro Linklater: 'The Naughtiest Girl of the Century', *Telegraph Magazine*, January 1993
6. Estrid Bannister Good: op cit, p.75
7. W E Williams, cited by Estrid Bannister Good, op cit, p.97
8. Enid and Robin Huws Jones, in conversation with the author, February 1998
9. John Crammer, in a letter to the author, 16 July 1998
10. Estrid Bannister Good: op cit, p.93
11. ibid, p.93-94
12. ibid, p.77
13. W E Williams, cited by Estrid Bannister Good, op cit, p.92
14. ibid, p.91. The letters have disappeared without trace. When challenged by the author about the letters, Estrid's son Geoffrey, denied any knowledge of them.
15. ibid, p.97
16. ibid, p.99
17. ibid, p.101-2

18. ibid, p.107-8
19. ibid, p.111
20. ibid, p.108
21. W E Williams to Sir Kenneth Clark, 15 September 1940
22. Estrid Bannister Good: op cit, p.117
23. Douglas Rust, in a letter to the author, 2 March 1999
24. Estrid Bannister Good: op cit, p.126
25. Tanya Schmoller, in discussion with the author, 22 October 1998
26. W E Williams to Allen Lane, n/d June 1947
27. W E Williams to Allen Lane, 31 August 1948
28. Estrid Bannister Good: op cit, p.130
29. ibid, p.133
30. ibid, p.136
31. ibid, p.137
32. ibid
33. ibid, p.138
34. ibid, p.143
35. W E Williams to Allen Lane, n/d December 1963

Eight: Army Bureau of Current Affairs

1. Lord Croft to Dr Thomas Jones, 3 August 1940, Croft and Grigg Papers, Churchill College Cambridge Archive
2. Lord Croft to Dr Thomas Jones, undated, 1940
3. W E Williams to Dr Thomas Jones, 8 August 1940
4. Lord Croft to Sir John Grigg, 8 January 1943, Croft and Grigg Papers, Churchill College Cambridge Archive
5. Haining Committee Report: *Education in the War Time Army*, September 1940, PRO
6. General Sir Ronald Adam, quoted by Colonel A C T White: *The Story of Army Education, 1643-1963*, London: Harrap, 1964, p.96
7. W E Williams: *The Official History of Army Education*, unpublished manuscript, 1941, p.89-90
8. ibid
9. General Sir J G Wills, Foreword to 'Current Affairs in the Army: The Outline of a New Plan', 'Army Bureau of Current Affairs', August 1941
10. W E Williams: *The Official History of Army Education*, p.27
11. ibid, p.32
12. Dr Basil Yeaxlee, Memorandum to Central Advisory Council for Adult Education in H M Forces, 5 November 1940, PRO
13. Minutes of Central Advisory Council, 4 September 1941, PRO
14. W E Williams to Dr Thomas Jones, 17 February 1941
15. W E Williams to Dr Thomas Jones, 12 February 1942
16. W E Williams to Dr Thomas Jones, 12 July 1943
17. General Sir Ronald Adam, War Office Memorandum: 'Army Education and ABCA', September 1943
18. Colonel A C T White: op cit, p.96 et seq
19. Lord Croft to Sir John Grigg, 31 July 1942, Croft and Grigg Papers, Churchill College Cambridge Archive
20. T H Hawkins and L J F Brimble: *Adult Education: The Record of the British Army*, London: Macmillan, 1947, p.176/7
21. Kingsley Martin: 'Blimps and Beveridge', *New Statesman and Nation*, 1943
22. N Scarlyn Wilson: *Education in the Forces 1939-1946: The Civilian Contribution*, London: Evans Brothers, 1947, p.46 et seq
23. Colonel A C T White, op cit, p.99-103
24. W E Williams to Dr Thomas Jones, 10 February 1944
25. Dr Thomas Jones to W E Williams, 14 February 1944
26. W O Lester Smith, Chairman's Report on the Bureau of Current Affairs, 1950/51
27. Professor Boris Ford: *The Bureau of Current Affairs 1946-1951*, London: BCA, p.3
28. George A Short, *Sunday Telegraph*, 27 September 1970
29. Colonel 'Archie' White, *Sunday Telegraph*, 4 October 1970
30. W E Williams, in the *Sunday Telegraph*, 11 October 1970
31. United States Army, General Orders No.227, 7 August 1946

Nine: Encouraging music and the arts

1. Lord Macmillan, Minutes of Conference, 18 December 1939, Board of Education Papers, PRO
2. ibid
3. ibid
4. ibid
5. Dr Thomas Jones: *A Diary with Letters, 1931-1950*, Oxford: Oxford University Press, 1954
6. E L Ellis: op cit, p.147
7. John Maynard Keynes: 'The Arts in War and Peace', *The Listener*, 11 January 1940
8. *The Times*, leading article, 25 January 1940
9. Board of Education Memorandum, 18 December 1939, PRO. The initial absence of any representation on Council from the world of literature is surprising. The gap was soon filled by the appointment of Professor B Ifor Evans, later editor of *The Penguin History of English Literature*, Pelican, 1958
10. CEMA, 'Guidance Notes to Council "Policy and Structure"', 10 April 1940, PRO
11. ibid
12. CEMA, Council Minutes, 23 April 1940, PRO
13. ibid
14. *Daily Express*, date unknown, 1940
15. Kenneth Clark in CEMA, Council Minutes, October 1940, PRO
16. CEMA, Council Minutes, July 1941, PRO
17. R A Butler to John Maynard Keynes, 17 December 1941, Keynes Archive, King's College Library, Cambridge
18. John Maynard Keynes to R A Butler, 14 January 1942, loc cit
19. R A Butler to John Maynard Keynes, 16 January 1942, loc cit

20. Dr Thomas Jones to John Maynard Keynes, 19 January 1942, loc cit
21. John Maynard Keynes to Dr Thomas Jones, 22 January 1942, loc cit
22. CEMA, Council Minutes, 17 February 1942
23. *The Times*, leading article, 22 February 1942
24. CEMA, Council Minutes, 14 April 1942, PRO
25. *The Listener*, leading article, 2 July 1942
26. R A Butler to John Maynard Keynes, 22 September 1942, Keynes Archive, King's College Library, Cambridge
27. CEMA, Council Minutes, October 1942
28. CEMA, Council Minutes, 8 December 1942, PRO
29. John Maynard Keynes, article in *The Times*, 11 May 1943
30. CEMA, Council Minutes, 20 July 1943, PRO
31. CEMA, Council Minutes, 19 October 1943, PRO
32. Jasper Ridley to Christopher Martin, 21 January 1943, Arts Inquiry Archive, Dartington
33. CEMA, Council Minutes, 26 September 1944, PRO
34. Kenneth Clark to R A Butler, 11 December 1944, Butler Papers, Trinity College, Cambridge
35. ibid
36. CEMA, Council Minutes, 30 January 1945, PRO
37. ibid
38. John Maynard Keynes to R A Butler, 3 February 1945
39. *The Listener*, leading article, 21 June 1945
40. Mary Glasgow to Dr Thomas Jones, 30 October 1945
41. Dr Thomas Jones to Mary Glasgow, 2 November 1945. The plan in which TJ was interested was Williams' idea of converting wartime ABCA into the post-war Bureau of Current Affairs.
42. Mary Glasgow to Dr Thomas Jones, 19 November 1945
43. CEMA, Council Minutes, 5 June 1946, PRO
44. Ivor Brown: 'The Arts Council: Promise or Failure', *The Observer*, May 1945
45. Professor B Ifor Evans: 'Night Life for the Arts', *The Observer*, 6 October 1946
46. Adrian Forty: 'Festival Politics' in Mary Banham and Bevis Hillier (eds): *A Tonic to the Nation*, 1976, p.37

Ten: The Arts Council of Great Britain

1. See Robert Hutchinson: *The Politics of the Arts Council*, London: Sinclair Browne, 1982; Andrew Sinclair: *Arts and Culture: The History of Fifty Years of the Arts Council of Great Britain*, London: Sinclair-Stevenson, 1995; Robert Hewison: *Culture and Consensus: England, art and politics since 1940*, London: Methuen, 1995; Richard Witts: *Artist Unknown: an Alternative History of the Arts Council*, London: Little, Brown, 1998
2. John Maynard Keynes: 'The Arts in War and Peace', *The Listener*, 11 January 1940
See also Virginia Button in Jeremy Lewison: *Ben Nicholson*, London: Tate Gallery, 1993:
'In the thirties the 'elite' practice of modern art was criticised for its failure to communicate with the general public. At the outbreak of war the split within the London-based avant-garde, particularly between Surrealists and abstract artists, seemed to contradict the general thrust of the war effort, which called for social cohesion on all levels. The cultural elite united to cajole a rather reluctant government into supporting the arts, arguing for their value in terms of spiritual nourishment, entertainment and escape. The argument for the arts stressed that they signified the continuation of democratic freedom, representing the highest form of individual expression, and this became a widely discussed assumption. There could, it was argued, be no greater reason for fighting fascism than the defence of culture.'
3. Arts Council Minutes, 9 August 1950
4. Richard Witts: op cit, caption to photograph of WEW following p.210
5. Norman Lebrecht: *Covent Garden: the untold story: dispatches from the English culture wars, 1945-2000*, London: Simon & Schuster, 2000
6. Mary Glasgow, Statement to Arts Council, 9 August 1950, Arts Council Archive
7. Arts Council Minutes, 10 January 1951
8. Arts Council Minutes, 28 February 1951
9. Annual Report of the Arts Council, 1950/51
10. Arts Council Minutes, 10 January 1951
11. Robert Hewison: op cit, p.79
12. Treasury Minute, 12 January 1951, PRO
13. Treasury Minute, 13 January 1951, PRO
14. Sir Edward Bridges, Treasury Minute, 15 January 1951, PRO
15. W E Williams: Annual Report of the Arts Council, 1950/51. In *The Politics of the Arts Council*, Robert Hutchinson argues that 'The policy choice posited as between consolidating priorities and dissipating resources upon an extensive provision of the second-rate' represents a false antithesis. 'It was never as simple as that. Expanding the categories of work supported, the development of new kinds of organisation and new kinds of partnership with other agencies, high quality educational work, improving the standards of, and facilities for, amateur performance, support for individual artists of ability, are among the range of policy options that are left out of account, and that fell then and fall now within the Council's obligations'. op cit. p.61
16. Ivor Brown: *The Observer*, May 1945
17. Ruth Shade: 'Welsh Arts Council Funding of Theatre in Wales', Theatr Wales website 1997
18. W E Williams: Annual Report of the Arts Council, 1955/56
19. ibid
20. ibid
21. Anthony Everitt: 'Queen of Quangos', *Independent Saturday Magazine*, 21 March 1998
22. Robert Hewison: op cit, p.79

23. Kenneth Clark: *The Other Half: A Self-Portrait*, London: John Murray, 1977, p.26
24. Robert Hewison: op cit
25. ibid, p.80
26. Kenneth Clark: ibid, p.129
27. ibid, p.26
28. Meryle Secrest: op cit, p.194
29. David Piper, entry for Sir Kenneth Clark, *Oxford Dictionary of National Biography*
30. Richard Hoggart: op cit, p.51-52
31. Richard Witts: op cit, p.464-6
32. Oliver Lyttleton to Kenneth Clark, undated (February 1955)
33. Sir Alexander Johnston to Sir Thomas Padmore, Treasury Minute, T218/181, PRO
34. Treasury Minute, undated, PRO
35. Sir Kenneth Clark to Sir Thomas Padmore, 11 February 1955, PRO
36. Treasury Minute, 23 July 1957, PRO
37. Richard Witts: op cit, p.467
38. W E Williams: Annual Report of the Arts Council, 1961/62, p.14
39. Arnold Wesker: *Fears of Fragmentation*, London: Jonathan Cape, 1970, p.45
40. W E Williams: Annual Report of the Arts Council, 1961/62, p.8-9
41. Richard Hoggart: op cit, p.*
42. Tony Field, in a letter to the author, 5 December 1997
43. Tony Field, in discussion with the author, 10 March 1998
44. Sir Hugh Willatt, unpublished memoir of W E Williams, c.1981
45. Gabriel White to Gertrude Williams, 6 September 1980
46. Sir Roy Shaw: *The Arts and the People*, London: Jonathan Cape, 1987, p.124
47. Wyn Griffith: Annual Report of the Arts Council, 1962/63
48. ibid
49. Cyril Connolly: *Horizon*, December 1942, p.165
50. Philip Hope-Wallace: *Time & Tide*, 11 March 1944
51. Sir Roy Strong: *The Spirit of Britain: A Narrative History of the Arts*, London: Thames & Hudson, 1999, p.641
52. ibid, p.642
53. W E Williams, cited by Robert Hewison, op cit, p.26

Eleven: Broadcaster and critic

1. Sir Ernest Barker: 'The Constitution and the BBC', *The Listener*, 21 February 1934
2. W E Williams to R A Rendall, 10 March 1934, BBC Written Archives, Caversham
3. R A Rendall, BBC Internal Memorandum, n/d, ibid
4. Dr Thomas Jones: *A Diary with Letters, 1931-1950*, Oxford: Oxford University Press, 1954, cited by Asa Briggs, op cit, Vol.2, 1985, p.118
5. W E Williams to Mary Adams, 12 January 1935, BBC Written Archives, Caversham
6. W E Williams to Mary Adams, 15 July 1935, BBC Written Archives, Caversham
7. W E Williams: 'Broadcasting to Schools, 1934-35', *The Listener*, 1 August 1934
8. W E Williams: 'Style and Purpose in Literature', *The Listener*, 24 July 1935
9. ibid
10. W E Williams: 'The Art of Biography', *The Listener*, 14 August 1935
11. W E Williams to Norman Luker, 9 November 1936, BBC Written Archives, Caversham
12. Norman Luker to Sir Richard Maconachie, 25 November 1938, BBC Written Archives, Caversham
13. Norman Luker to his Head of Department, November 1938, BBC Written Archives, Caversham
14. Asa Briggs: op cit, Vol.2, 1985, p.148
15. R S Lambert to W E Williams, 9 March 1939
16. Virginia Woolf: 'Reviewing', Sixpenny Pamphlet, 1940
17. Paul Fussell: *Wartime: Understanding and Behaviour in the Second World War*, New York: Oxford University Press, p.180-1
18. W E Williams to Alan Thomas, 4 May 1939
19. W E Williams: 'Why Call It A Debate?', *The Listener*, 11 May 1939
20. W E Williams: 'How Hilton Does It', *The Listener*, 18 May 1939
21. W E Williams to Alan Thomas, 18 May 1939, BBC Written Archives, Caversham
22. W E Williams: 'Desmond MacCarthy', *The Listener*, 25 May 1939
23. W E Williams: 'A Motto for Talks', *The Listener*, 16 March 1944
24. W E Williams: 'The Celtic Touch', *The Listener*, 17 October 1940
25. ibid
26. W E Williams: 'The Perfect Broadcaster', *The Listener*, 24 April 1941
27. Paddy Scannell and David Cardiff: *A Social History of British Broadcasting, Vol. 1, 1922-1939*, Oxford: Basil Blackwell, 1991, p.162
28. W E Williams: 'Full Marks for Set Piece', *The Listener*, 13 August 1942
29. W E Williams: 'The Voice of the Masses', *The Listener*, 6 July 1939
30. D G Bridson: *Prospero and Ariel* (1971:52), quoted in Peter M Lewis: 'Referable Words in Radio Drama', in Paddy Scannell (ed): *Broadcast Talk*, London: Sage, 1991, p.14
31. W E Williams: 'Go to It!', *The Listener*, 20 June 1940
32. W E Williams: 'The Right Tone', *The Listener*, 18 July 1940
33. W E Williams: 'No Colouring Matter', *The Listener*, 5 September 1940

34. W E Williams on Trenchard Cox, *The Listener*, 10 August 1939
35. W E Williams on Middleton Murray, *The Listener*, 23 February 1940
36. W E Williams on John Rothenstein, *The Listener*, 9 April 1942
37. W E Williams on Clive Liddell, *The Listener*, 16 April 1942
38. W E Williams on Stuart Hibbert, *The Listener*, 12 August 1943
39. W E Williams on Richard Dimbleby, *The Listener*, 26 October 1939
40. W E Williams on Brian Vesey-Fitzgerald, *The Listener*, 6 August 1942
41. W E Williams on Thomas Woodroofe, *The Listener*, 27 August 1942
42. W E Williams: 'Marching On', *The Listener*, 3 September 1942
43. W E Williams on J M Keynes, *The Listener*, 23 January 1941
44. W E Williams on Desmond MacCarthy, *The Listener*, 25 May 1939
45. W E Williams: 'A Couple of Winners', *The Listener*, 3 October 1940
46. W E Williams: 'The Celtic Touch', *The Listener*, 17 October 1940
47. Keidrych Rhys to W E Williams, 25 October 1940
48. W E Williams to Dr Thomas Jones, 4 November 1940
49. W E Williams: 'Aces of the Air', *The Listener*, 8 August 1940
50. W E Williams: 'Wheel-Tapping', *The Listener*, 1 February 1940
51. W E Williams to Frederick Ogilvie, 29 November 1939
52. W E Williams: 'Duff Cooper Reads a Poem', *The Listener*, 27 June 1940
53. W E Williams: *The Listener*, 4 July 1940
54. W E Williams: 'Reading Poetry', *The Listener*, 13 April 1944
55. W E Williams: 'Don't Say It With Music', *The Listener*, 13 January 1944
56. Alan Thomas to W E Williams, 28 April 1940, BBC Written Archives, Caversham
57. W E Williams: 'Wireless Bores', *The Listener*, 21 November 1940
58. Frederick Ogilvie, BBC Internal Memorandum, 3 November 1940, BBC Written Archives, Caversham
59. Asa Briggs: op cit, Vol.3, 1985, p.38-39
60. W E Williams to George Barnes, 25 March 1941, BBC Written Archives, Caversham
61. W E Williams: 'A Change of Bowling', *The Listener*, 10 April 1941
62. W E Williams to Frederick Ogilvie, 17 April 1941, BBC Written Archives, Caversham
63. W E Williams to Frederick Ogilvie, 3 May 1941, BBC Written Archives, Caversham
64. W E Williams: 'The Stuff to Give the Troops?', *The Listener*, 19 December 1940
65. W E Williams: 'Curtain', *The Listener*, 6 July 1944

Twelve: Art adviser

1. W E Williams: 'Kennedys do not equal culture', *New Statesman*, Vol.1, No.27, 4 April 1963, p.30-31
2. National Art-Collections Fund brochure, 1963
3. Lord Crawford, Report to 61st AGM of the NACF, 10 June 1964
4. W E Williams: 'Notes and Comments', *NACF Review*, 1 May 1965
5. ibid
6. Michael Foot, entry for Jennie Lee in *Oxford Dictionary of National Biography*
7. Lord Crawford, Report to 62nd AGM of the NACF, 9 June 1965
8. ibid
9. Jennie Lee, Minister for the Arts, address to the 63rd AGM of the NACF, 22 June 1966
10. Sir Trenchard Cox, comments at 63rd AGM of the NACF, 22 June 1966
11. W E Williams: 'Notes and Comments', *NACF Review*, 1 May 1967
12. Kenneth Clark, address to 64th AGM of the NACF, 14 June 1967
13. W E Williams: 'Notes and Comments', *NACF Review*, 1 May 1968
14. Sir Gilbert Inglefield, address to 65th AGM of the NACF, 14 June 1968
15. Lord Goodman, address to 66th AGM of the NACF, 11 June 1969
16. ibid
17. W E Williams: 'Notes and Comments', *NACF Review*, 1 May 1970
18. *NACF Review*, 1 May 1970
19. Lord Crawford to W E Williams, 16 November 1969
20. The full list reads as follows: General Adviser: Sir William Emrys Williams, CBE DLitt (former Secretary-General of the Arts Council, and Trustee of the National Gallery, a Director of Penguin Books); Painting and Drawing: Lord Clark of Saltwood (former Director of the National Gallery and Slade Professor of Fine Art in the University of Oxford); Sir William Coldstream, CBE RA, (Painter and Slade Professor of Fine Arts, University of London); Sir Robin Darwin, CBE RA, (Painter, and formerly Rector of the Royal College of Art); Sir John Rothenstein, CBE, (formerly Director of the Tate Gallery); Sculpture: Henry Moore, OM CH (Sculptor); Sir Charles Wheeler, KCVO CBE (Sculptor, and Past President of the Royal Academy); F E McWilliam, CBE (Sculptor); Historic Objects: Sir Frank Francis, KCB (formerly Director of the British Museum); Sir Trenchard Cox, CBE (formerly Director of the Victoria and Albert Museum); Music: Sir Arthur Bliss, CH KCVO (Composer, and Master of the Queen's Musick);

Sir Adrian Boult, CH (Conductor); Theatre: Lord Olivier (Actor, and Director of the National Theatre); Sir Bernard Miles, CBE (Actor, and founder of the Mermaid Theatre); Peter Hall, CBE (former Director of the Royal Shakespeare Company, Stratford-upon- Avon); Ballet: Dame Ninette de Valois (former Director of the Royal Ballet, and founder of the Royal Ballet School); Dame Marie Rambert (founder of the Ballet Rambert); Opera: The Earl of Drogheda, KG KBE (Chairman, Royal Opera House, and Chairman of *The Financial Times*).
21. W E Williams: *The Theatre Today in England and Wales*, London: Arts Council, 1970, p.1
22. Sir Harmar Nicholls: Memorandum of Dissent, ibid, p.77-9
23. Sir Richard Powell in *The Director*, Institute of Directors, April 1977

Epilogue: In perspective
1. W E Williams to Dr Thomas Jones, 12 July 1943
2. Obituary of Sir William Emrys Williams, *The Times*, London, 1 April 1977
3. Sir Richard Powell in *The Director*, Institute of Directors, April 1977
4. Robin Huws Jones, in conversation with the author, February 1998
5. ibid
6. Richard Witts: op cit, p.353
7. Peter Cox: 'Regional Connections: South West Arts Association' in Report on the Arts Inquiry, Dartington, p.127 (n/d)
8. Peter Cox to the author, 28 April 2001
9. Sir Hugh Willatt, in an unpublished memoir of W E Williams, 1978
10. Edward Hutchinson, op cit
11. Sir Richard Powell: *The Director*, Institute of Directors, April 1977
12. Boris Ford, quoted by Steve Hare: op cit, p.46
13. Claire Morpurgo in the 'Introduction' to Gertrude Williams: op cit, p.16
14. Carol Peaker: *The Penguin Modern Painters: A History*, London: Penguin Collectors' Society, 2001
15. Tony Field to the author, 15 September 1998
16. Wyn Griffith: *Annual Report 1962/63*, Arts Council of Great Britain, London, 1963
17. Allen Lane on W E Williams, April 1965
18. John Crammer to the author, 16 July 1998
19. W E Williams: *Allen Lane: A Personal Portrait*, London: The Bodley Head, 1973, p.23
20. Boris Ford to the author, September 1997
21. Jeremy Lewis: op cit, p.118
22. ibid
23. Beatrice Warde's Foreword to P G Burbridge and L A Gray: 'Penguin Panorama' in *Printing Review*, 72, Autumn 1956, p.4, cited by Tim Graham (ed): *Penguin in Print*, London: Penguin Collectors' Society, 2003
24. Carol Peaker: op cit
25. J E Morpurgo: op cit, p.116-19
26. Richard Witts: op cit, p.353
27. W E Williams: 'The Truth about ABCA', *Sunday Telegraph*, 11 October 1970
28. J E Morpurgo: op cit, p.*
29. Robert Hewison: op cit, p.79
30. W E Williams: 'The Changing Map of Adult Education' in *Adult Education in Great Britain and the United States*, a symposium arranged by W E Williams, BIAE 1938, p.*
31. BIAE: *Report on Adult Education After The War*, London: Oxford University Press, 1945, p.58
32. Dr Thomas Jones: op cit, p.*
33. John Maynard Keynes: CEMA Council Minutes, 14 April 1942
34. Wyn Griffith: *Annual Report 1962/63*, Arts Council of Great Britain. London, 1963
35. A C Grayling: 'The last word on values', *Guardian*, 21 July 2001
36. Obituary of Sir William Emrys Williams, *The Times*, London, 1 April 1977

Photographs Note:
The photographs included in this publication are from the collection of Sander Meredeen and were obtained from family collections of Gertrude Williams and Estrid Bannister Good during interviews with or in correspondence with the author. It is assumed that copyright permission was obtained by the author and the publisher has reproduced the photographs on this understanding. Any advised missing credits will be added to future printings.

Photo credits noted on the photographs are as follows:
Lotte Meitner-Graf, London – p.ii, p.vi, p.128, p.186 (WEW)
Ward, Manchester – p.22, p.32
Middlesex County Press – p.76
Mark Gerson, London – p.186 (GW)
BBC, London – p.188
Belgrave Press Bureau, London – p.215
John Heddon, London – p.216

Bibliography

BORROW, George Henry
(1851) *Lavengro*, London: John Murray
(1862) *Wild Wales*, London: John Murray
(1857) *Romany Rye*, Nelson

BRIGGS, Asa
(1985) *The BBC: The First Fifty Years*, Oxford: Oxford University Press

BUTTON, Virginia
(1993) in Jeremy Lewison: *Ben Nicholson*, London: Tate Gallery

CARPENTER, Humphrey
(1995) 'Learning about Ourselves' in John Batchelor (ed.): *The Art of literary Biography*, Oxford: Clarendon Press, p.267-79

CLARK, Kenneth
(1974) *Another Part of the Wood*, London: John Murray
(1977) *The Other Half*, London: John Murray

ELLIS, E L
(1992) *TJ: A Life of Dr Thomas Jones*, Cardiff: University of Wales Press

EVANS, B Ifor and GLASGOW, Mary
(1949) *The Arts in England*, Falcon Press

FIELDHOUSE, Roger and others
(1996) *A History of Modern British Adult Education*, Leicester: NIACE

FOLEY, Adrian
(1976) 'Festival Politics' in Balan, May and Bevis Hillier (eds) *A Tonic for the Nation*

FORD, Boris
(1952) *The Bureau of Current Affairs: 1946-1951* London: BCA

FORTY, Adrian
(1976) 'Festival Politics' in Mary Banham and Bevis Hillier (eds): *A Tonic to the Nation*

FUSSELL, Paul
(1989) *Wartime: Understanding and Behaviour in the Second World War*, New York: Oxford University Press

GLASGOW, Mary
(1975) 'The Concept of the Arts Council' in Milo Keynes
(1975): *Essays on John Maynard Keynes*, Cambridge: Cambridge University Press, p.*

GOOD, Estrid Bannister
(1992) *Smørrebrød and Cherry-Blossom – An autobiography*, privately published

GRIFFITHS, Wyn
(1950) *The Welsh*, Harmondsworth: Penguin

HARE, Steve (ed.)
(1995) *Penguin Portrait: Allen Lane and the Penguin Editors, 1935-70*, Harmondsworth: Penguin

HAWKINS, T H and BRIMBLE, L J F
(1947) *Adult Education: The Record of the British Army*, London: Macmillan,

HEWISON, Robert
(1978) *Under Siege: Literary Life in London 1939-45*, Newton Abbott: Readers Union
(1986) *Too much: art and society in the sixties*, London: Methuen
(1981) *In Anger: Culture in the Cold War, 1945-1960*, London: Weidenfeld and Nicolson
(1987) *The Heritage Industry: Britain in a climate of decline*, London: Methuen
(1995) *Culture and Consensus: England, art and politics since 1940*, London: Methuen

HOGGART, Richard
(1970) 'A Tribute to Allen Lane' at a Service of Thanksgiving for his Life and Work, reprinted Penguin Collectors' Society, December 2002
(1993) *An Imagined Life*, Oxford: Oxford University Press
(1997) 'A Penguin Parade' in *Pelican Books: A Sixtieth Anniversary Celebration, Miscellany 12*, London: Penguin Collectors' Society, July 1987

HUTCHINSON, Robert
(1982) *The Politics of the Arts Council*, London: Sinclair Browne

JONES, Thomas
(1954) *A Diary with Letters*, Oxford University Press

KEYNES, J M
(1946) 'The Arts Council: its policies and hopes', reproduced in ACGB 1st Annual Report

KEYNES, Milo (ed)
(1975) *Essays on John Maynard Keynes*, Cambridge: Cambridge University Press

LEBRECHT, Norman
(2000) *Covent Garden: The Untold Story: Dispatches from the English Culture Wars: 1945-2000*, London: Simon & Schuster

LEE, Jennie
(1965) *A Policy for the Arts: The First Steps*, Cmnd 2601, London: HMSO

LEVENTHAL, F M
(1990) 'The Best for the Most: CEMA and State Sponsorship of the Arts in Wartime, 1939-1945', *Twentieth Century British History*, 3, p.289-317

LEWIS, Jeremy
(2005) *Penguin Special: The Life and Times of Allen Lane*, London: Viking Penguin

MINIHAN, Janet
(1977) *The Nationalisation of Culture: the development of state subsidies to the arts in Great Britain*, London: Hamilton

MORGAN, K O
(1995): *Modern Wales: Politics, Places and People*, Cardiff: University of Wales Press

MORPURGO, J E
(1979) *Allen Lane: King Penguin*, Harmondsworth: Penguin

NEWTON, Eric
(1935) *An Approach to Art*, The Arts Enquiry, Dartington Hall Trustees (1945-1949), BBC

PEAKER, Carol
(2001) *The Penguin Modern Painters*, London: Penguin Collectors' Society

ROLPH, C H
(1961) *The Lady Chatterley Trial: Regina v. Penguin Books*, Harmondsworth: Penguin

SCANNELL, Paddy and CARDIFF, David
(1991) *A Social History of British Broadcasting, Vol. I: 1922-1939*, Oxford: Blackwell

SECREST, Meryle
(1984) *Kenneth Clark: A Biography*, London: Weidenfeld and Nicolson

SHADE, Ruth
(1997) 'Arts Council Funding of Theatre in Wales' Theatr in Wales website

SHAW, Sir Roy
(1987) *The Arts and the People*, London: Cape

SINCLAIR, Andrew
(1995) *Arts and Cultures: The History of Fifty Years of the Arts Council of Great Britain*, London: Sinclair-Stevenson

SINFIELD, Alan
(1989) *Literature, Politics and Culture in Postwar Britain*, University of California Press

SIMPSON, Percy
Entry for Charles Harold Herford, *Oxford Dictionary of National Biography*, Oxford: Oxford University Press

SKIDELSKY, Robert
(1992) *Life of John Maynard Keynes: A Biography, Vol. 2: The Economist as Saviour*, London: Macmillan

STEAD, Peter
(1977) *Coleg Harlech: The First Fifty Years*, Cardiff, University of Wales Press

STRONG, Sir Roy
(1999) *The Spirit of Britain: A Narrative History of the Arts*, London: Thames & Hudson

WESKER, Arnold
(1970) *Fears of Fragmentation*, London: Jonathan Cape

WHITE, A C T
(1964) *The Story of Army Education 1643-1963*, London: Harrap

WHITE, Eric W
(1975) *The Arts Council of Great Britain*, London: Davis-Poynter

WILSON, N Scarlyn
(1948) *Education in the Forces: The Civilian Contribution*, London: Evans Brothers

WILLIAMS, William Emrys
See Appendix A

WILLIAMS, Gertrude
(1947) (ed) *Voluntary Social Service Since 1918*, London: Kegan Paul
(1947) *Explaining Economics*, London: Bureau of Current Affairs
(1957) *Recruitment to the Skilled Trades*, London: Routledge and Kegan Paul
(1963) *Apprenticeship in Europe: the lessons for Britain*, London: Chapman and Hall
(1967) *The Economics of Everyday Life* Harmondsworth: Penguin
(1967) *The Coming of the Welfare State*
(2000) *W E Williams: Educator Extraordinary: A Memoir*, London: Penguin Collectors' Society

WITTS, Richard
(1998) *Artist Unknown: An Alternative History of the Arts Council*, London: Little, Brown

WORTHEN, John
(1995) 'The Necessary Ignorance of A Biographer' in John Batchelor (ed) *The Art of Literary Biography*, Oxford: Clarendon Press, p.227-45

Appendix A:

Publications – Books and pamphlets

1925 *The Craft of Literature*, London: Methuen
1926 *First Steps to Parnassus*, London: Methuen
1927 *George Henry Borrow: Selections, chosen and edited by William Emrys Williams*, London, Methuen
1927 *A Progressive Course of Precis and Paraphrase*, London: Methuen
1928 *Plain Prose: The elements of a serviceable style*, London: Methuen
1928 *A Critical Commentary on "Shakespeare to Hardy"* (by Sir Algernon Methuen), London: Methuen
1934 *The Auxiliaries of Adult Education*, BIAE pamphlet
1935 *The Dorsetshire Labourers*: A Play in Two Acts by Richard Stanton Lambert adapted from the wireless version by W E Williams
1936 *Learn and Live: The Consumer's View of Adult Education*, by A E Heath and W E Williams, BIAE pamphlet
1936 *Biology in the World Today by Andrew L Fen, The World Today Series*: General Editor: W E Williams, Methuen
1938 *Adult Education in Great Britain and the United States*: A Symposium arranged by W E Williams, reprinted from the *Year Book of Education*
1941 'Art for the People', BIAE pamphlet
1941 *Radio's Listening Groups: The United States and Great Britain*, by Frank Ernest Hill and W E Williams, New York: Columbia University Press
1941 *The Official History of Army Education* (unpublished)
1943 *William Wordsworth, selected by W E Williams*, Harmondsworth: Penguin
1943 'Art for the People', exhibitions pamphlet, BIAE
1943 *A Book of English Essays, selected by W E Williams*, Harmondsworth: Penguin (reprinted 1948, 1951 and 1965)
1947 'What about UNESCO?', BCA pamphlet
1947 'Woman's Place', BCA pamphlet
1948 'Across the frontiers: The story of UNESCO', BCA pamphlet
1948 *Tennyson, Alfred, selection and extracts*, selected by W E Williams, Harmondsworth: Penguin
1950 *David Herbert Lawrence: Selected Poems*, chosen with an introduction by W E Williams, Harmondsworth: Penguin
1954 *Robert Browning: A selection by W E Williams*, Harmondsworth: Penguin
1956 *The Penguin Story 1935-1956*, Harmondsworth: Penguin,
1960 *Thomas Hardy: A Selection of poems*, chosen and edited by W E Williams, Harmondsworth: Penguin
1960 *The Reader's Guide*, edited by Sir W E Williams, Harmondsworth: Penguin
1964 *How to Commission a Portrait*, London: Institute of Directors
1964 *Investing in Art*, London: Institute of Directors
1966 *Patron: Industry support the arts*, compiled and edited by Alan Osborne, Consultant editor: W E Williams
1970 *The Theatre Today in England and Wales*, London: Arts Council
1973 *Allen Lane: A Personal Portrait*, London: The Bodley Head

Publications – Articles and poems

1912 'An Open-Air Geography Lesson', *Manchester Central High School Magazine*
1913 'Legends of the Welsh', *Manchester Central High School Magazine*
1934 'Broadcasting to Schools', *The Listener*, 1 August
1918 'For G.', *The Serpent*, Manchester University Unions
1935 'Style and Purpose in Literature', *The Listener*, 24 July 1935
1935 'The Art of Biography', *The Listener*, 14 August 1935
1935 'Can Literature Survive? I – The Novel and the Cinema', *The Listener*, 21 August 1935
1935 'Can Literature Survive? II – Theatre, Cinema and Broadcasting', *The Listener*, 28 August 1935
1936 'Guide for the General Reader', *Highway*, December 1936
1937 'Art for the People', *The Listener*, 19 May 1937
1937 'A Wonderful Bird is the Pelican', *Adult Education*, June 1937
1938 'The Changing Map of Adult Education' in *Adult Education in Great Britain and the United States*, London, BIAE
1939-1944 Critic on The Hearth 'The Spoken Word', regular column of radio criticism in *The Listener*, May 1939 – June 1944:
'Why Call it a Debate?', 11 May 1939
'How Hilton Does It', 18 May 1939
'Desmond MacCarthy' 25 May 1939
'The Voice of the Masses', 6 July 1939
'On Trenchard Cox', 10 August 1939
'On Richard Dimbleby', 26 October 1939
'Wheel Tapping', 1 February 1940
'On Middleton Murray', 23 February 1940

'Go to It', 20 June 1940
'Duff Cooper reads a Poem', 27 June 1940
'The Right Tone', 18 July 1940
'Aces of the Air', 8 August 1940
'No Colouring Matter', 5 September 1940
'A Couple of Winners', 3 October 1940
'The Celtic Touch', 17 October 1940
'Wireless Bores', 21 November 1940
'The Stuff to Give the Troops', 19 December 1940
'On J M Keynes, 23 January 1941
'A Change of Bowling', 10 April 1941
'The Perfect Broadcaster', 24 April 1941
'On John Rothenstein', 9 April 1942
'On Clive Liddell', 16 April 1942
'On Bruce Vesey-Fitzgerald', 6 August 1942
'Full Marks for Set Piece', 13 August 1942
'On Thomas Woodroofe', 27 August 1942
'Marching On', 3 September 1942
'On Stuart Hibbert', 12 August 1943
'A Motto for Talks', 16 March 1944
'Reading Poetry', 13 April 1944
'Curtain' 6 July 1944

1944 'The Ice Cracked', *The Listener*, 7 September 1944
1944 'Radio criticism', *The Observer*, 1944-1950
1945 'Television criticism', *New Statesman*, 1945-1946
1947 'The Third Programme: the first year', *The Listener*, 20 October 1947
1950 'D H Lawrence', *Highway*, June-September 1950
1950-1962 *Annual Reports of the Arts Council*
1963 'Kennedys Do Not Equal Culture', *New Statesman*, 16 April 1963
1963 'The Arts and Public Patronage', *Three Banks Review*, July 1963
1963 'The Penguin King', *New Society*, 19 September
1965-1970 'Notes and Comments' *NACF Review*, 1 May 1965, 1967, 1968, 1970
1970 'The Founding Father', A Tribute to Allen Lane, *The Sunday Times*, 12 July 1970
1970 'The Truth about ABCA', *Sunday Telegraph*, 11 October 1970
1973 'Allen Lane: Father of the Paperback', *The Times*

Appendix B:

Chronology of key events

1896 WEW born (5 Oct) at 16 Raglan Street, Hulme, South Manchester
1897 Gertrude Rosenblum born (11 Jan) at 35 Seabank Road, Southport, Lancashire
1902 Allen Lane-Williams (later Allen Lane) born in Bristol (21 Sept)
1904 Williams family moves from North Wales to Manchester
1908 WEW attends Central High School for Boys, Manchester
1914 OUTBREAK OF FIRST WORLD WAR
1914 WEW begins undergraduate studies at Manchester University
1916 WEW celebrates his 20th birthday (5 October)
1917 WEW meets Gertrude Rosenblum
1918 WEW and Gertrude Rosenblum both graduate
1918 FIRST WORLD WAR ENDS
1919 WEW abandons theology studies and joins Gertrude in London
1919 WEW appointed YMCA Boys' Club Leader, King's Cross, London
1919 Gertrude Rosenblum appointed Tutor in Economics, Bedford College, University of London
1919 WEW marries Gertrude Rosenblum (29 Nov) at Hampstead Register Office
1920 WEW begins work as a schoolmaster at Leytonstone High School for Boys
1924 WEW and GW move to 93 Wentworth Road, Golders Green
1925 WEW: *The Craft of Literature*
1926 WEW: *First Steps to Parnassus*
1926 WEW celebrates his 30th birthday (5 October)
1927 WEW: *George Henry Borrow: Selections*
1927 WEW: *A Progressive Course of Précis and Paraphrase*
1928 WEW: *A Critical Commentary on 'Shakespeare to Hardy'*
1928 WEW: *Plain Prose: The elements of a serviceable style*
1928 WEW appointed Staff Tutor in English Literature, Extramural Department University of London
1929 WALL STREET CRASH
1930 WEW appointed Editor of *Highway*
1933 PRESIDENT ROOSEVELT LAUNCHES NEW DEAL
1934 WEW appointed Secretary of British Institute of Adult Education
1934 WEW: *The Auxiliaries of Adult Education*
1935 WEW: *The Dorsetshire Labourers* (from a radio play by R S Lambert)

1935 First *Art for the People* exhibition
1936 CIVIL WAR IN SPAIN
1936 WEW celebrates his 40th birthday (5 October)
1935 Allen Lane launches Penguin Books
1936 WEW: *Learn and Live* (with A E Heath)
1936 WEW introduced to Allen Lane and becomes his chief literary adviser
1937 Penguin Books publish first ten Pelicans (May)
1937 WEW and Gertrude Williams move to Westbourne Terrace, Paddington
1937 WEW meets Estrid Bannister in London
1938 WEW: *Adult Education in Britain and the United States*
1939 WEW: First column of radio talks criticism in *The Listener* (11 May)
1939 OUTBREAK OF SECOND WORLD WAR (3 Sept)
1939 WEW attends formation meeting of CEMA (14 Dec)
1940 WEW appointed a Trustee of the National Gallery
1941 WEW: *Radio's Listening Groups: The United States and Great Britain* (with Frank Ernest Hill)
1941 WEW appointed Director of the Army Bureau of Current Affairs (ABCA)
1941 WEW: *Tennyson, selected by W E Williams*
1942 John Maynard Keynes appointed Chairman of CEMA
1942 WEW: *A Book of English Essays*
1943 WEW: *Wordsworth, selected by W E Williams*
1945 END OF SECOND WORLD WAR
1945 LABOUR GOVERNMENT ELECTED: PM CLEMENT ATTLEE
1946 Death of John Maynard Keynes (Easter Sunday)
1946 WEW launches the Bureau of Current Affairs
1946 WEW: *The Official History of Army Education* (unpublished)
1946 WEW awarded CBE
1946 WEW awarded the American Medal of Freedom
1946 WEW: First column of broadcast criticism in *The Observer*
1946 Royal Charter incorporates CEMA as the Arts Council of Great Britain
1946 WEW celebrates his 50th birthday (5 October)
1947 WEW: 'What about UNESCO?'
1950 WEW: *D H Lawrence: Selected Poems, with an Introduction by W E W*
1951 WEW succeeds Mary Glasgow as Secretary-General of the Arts Council
1951 FESTIVAL OF BRITAIN
1951 CONSERVATIVE GOVERNMENT ELECTED: PM WINSTON CHURCHILL
1952 Knighthood awarded to Allen Lane
1953 WEW appointed a Trustee of the Shakespeare Birthday Trust
1953 Kenneth Clark succeeds Ernest Pooley as Chairman of the Arts Council
1954 WEW: *Robert Browning, a selection by W E Williams*
1955 Knighthood awarded to W E Williams (9 June)
1955 Death of Dr Thomas Jones
1956 WEW: *The Penguin Story*
1956 WEW celebrates his 60th birthday (5 October)
1958 Estrid Bannister marries Ernest Good
1958 WEW made a Director of Penguin Books
1960 Lord Cottesloe succeeds Kenneth Clark as Chairman of the Arts Council
1960 WEW: *The Reader's Guide, edited by W E Williams*
1960 WEW: *Thomas Hardy, a selection of poems, chosen and edited by W E Williams*
1960 WEW gives evidence at *'Lady Chatterley'* trial at the Old Bailey
1961 WEW celebrates his 65th birthday (5 October)
1963 WEW retires as Secretary-General of the Arts Council
1963 WEW receives Honorary D Litt from University of Wales
1963 Gertrude Williams awarded CBE
1963 Ernest Good dies; Estrid Bannister Good widowed
1964 LABOUR GOVERNMENT ELECTED: PM HAROLD WILSON
1964 WEW appointed Art Adviser to the Institute of Directors
1964 WEW appointed Secretary of the National Art-Collections Fund
1965 30th anniversary of Penguin Books
1965 WEW retires as Director and Editor-in-Chief of Penguin Books
1965 WEW suffers a mild coronary
1965 Jennie Lee appointed Britain's first 'Minister for the Arts'
1966 WEW celebrates his 70th birthday (5 October)
1967 WEW and Gertrude Williams move into Grenville Paddock, Haddenham, Bucks
1970 Allen Lane dies (7 July) aged 67
1970 CONSERVATIVE GOVERNMENT ELECTED: PM TED HEATH
1970 WEW retires as Art Adviser to the Institute of Directors

1970 WEW retires as Secretary of the National Art-Collections Fund
1970 WEW begins work on *In Perspective*
1971 WEW celebrates his 76th birthday (5 October)
1973 WEW: *Allen Lane: A Personal Portrait*
1974 LABOUR GOVERNMENT ELECTED: PM HAROLD WILSON
1976 WEW celebrates his 80th birthday (5 October)
1977 WEW dies (30 March) aged 80, in Stoke Mandeville Hospital
1977 Joy Maudie Lyon commits suicide (1 April) aged 48
1979 CONSERVATIVE GOVERNMENT ELECTED: PM MARGARET THATCHER
1979 J E Morpurgo publishes *Allen Lane: King Penguin*
1982 Gertrude Williams completes *W E Williams: Educator Extraordinary*, unpublished
1983 Gertrude Williams dies (21 Feb) aged 86
1986 CONSERVATIVE GOVERNMENT RE-ELECTED: PM MARGARET THATCHER
1992 CONSERVATIVE GOVERNMENT RE-ELECTED: PM JOHN MAJOR
1995 Steve Hare publishes *Penguin Portrait: Allen Lane and the Penguin Editors*
1997 LABOUR GOVERNMENT ELECTED: PM TONY BLAIR
1998 Estrid Bannister Good dies (31 Dec) aged 93
2000 Penguin Collectors' Society publishes Gertrude Williams' *W E Williams: Educator Extraordinary*
2001 LABOUR GOVERNMENT RE-ELECTED: PM TONY BLAIR
2005 LABOUR GOVERNMENT RE-ELECTED: PM TONY BLAIR
2005 Jeremy Lewis publishes *Penguin Special: The Life and Times of Allen Lane*
2005 70th Anniversary of Penguin Books

Appendix C:

W E Williams – Career profile

1914 - 1918 Undergraduate studies, Faculty of Arts, Manchester University
1918 Graduates BA Manchester University
1919 - 1920 Leader, YMCA Boys Club, King's Cross, London
1920 - 1926 Schoolmaster, Leytonstone High School for Boys, London
1925 - 1931 Workers' Education Association (WEA) Lecturer
1928 - 1934 Staff Tutor in English Literature, Extramural Dept, University of London
1930 - 1939 Editor, *Highway*
1934 - 1939 Secretary, British Institute of Adult Education (BIAE)
1935 - 1939 Organiser, *Art for the People*
1936 - 1965 Chief Literary Adviser, Penguin Books
1939 - 1945 Founder Member, Council for the Encouragement of Music & the Arts (CEMA)
1939 - 1945 Critic of the Spoken Word, *The Listener*
1941 - 1945 Director, Army Bureau of Current Affairs (ABCA)
1946 - 1951 Director, Bureau of Current Affairs (BCA)
1952 - 1964 Secretary-General, Arts Council of Great Britain (ACGB)
1960 - 1965 Director, Penguin Books
1964 - 1970 Secretary, National Art-Collections Fund (NACF)
1964 - 1970 Art Adviser, Institute of Directors (IoD)
1965 Retires as Director, Penguin Books
1970 Retires as Secretary, National Art-Collections Fund (NACF)
1970 Retires as Art Adviser, Institute of Directors (IoD)

Index